THE APRIL KING

Isolde Martyn

SAPERE
BOOKS

THE APRIL
KING

Published by Sapere Books.

24 Trafalgar Road, Ilkley, LS29 8HH

saperebooks.com

Copyright © Isolde Martyn, 2025

ISBN: 978-0-85495-794-1

For Australia's leading Shakespearean actor and director, John Bell, whose talk on Shakespeare's Richard III *inspired the concept for this novel, and for the late UK author Nicholas Evans.*

LIST OF CHARACTERS

Fictional characters are marked with an *.

IN LONDON

SIR ROBERT CECIL — privy councillor, son of William Cecil, Lord Burghley, chief minister

QUEEN ELIZABETH I — Protestant Queen of England

ROBERT, EARL OF ESSEX — privy councillor, rival to Sir Robert Cecil and Ferdinando, Lord Strange

GARRETT TOWNELEY — former military captain, served in Ireland

WILLIAM SHAKESPEARE and **RICHARD BURBAGE** — members of Lord Strange's theatre company

LADY MARGARET CLIFFORD — mother of Ferdinando, Lord Strange, and estranged wife of Henry, Earl of Derby; grandniece of Henry VIII and cousin to Queen Elizabeth

FERDINANDO STANLEY, LORD STRANGE — in line to the throne and about to inherit the earldom of Derby, courtier and poet with his own company of players

ELIZABETH 'ROSE' BYRD *née* **DAVISON** — widow of soldier Oliver Byrd

WALTER DAVISON — her brother

FRANCIS DAVISON — her brother

CATHERINE DAVISON *née* **SPELMAN** — her mother

WILLIAM DAVISON — Rose's father; former diplomat and disgraced chief secretary of the queen

WILLIAM WADE (also spelled Waad) — Clerk of the Privy Council, the queen's spymaster

MARTIN LORIMER* — Wade's agent, servant to Rose

LORD BURGHLEY — Sir Robert Cecil's father, Lord Treasurer and Chief Minister

IN THE SPANISH NETHERLANDS
RICHARD VERSTEGAN — Papist printer in Antwerp
COLONEL SIR WILLIAM STANLEY — Ferdinando's cousin, commander of dissident Catholic army, funded by Spanish gold
LIEUTENANT COLONEL JACQUES DE FRANCESCI — Sir William Stanley's deputy
MASTER DAMPORTE, CAPTAIN O'COLLUN and **AIDAN MARKHAM** — members of Sir William's company
FATHER HOLT — Jesuit priest and colleague of Sir William Stanley
RICHARD HESKETH — Papist agent and relative of the Hesketh family of Rufford Hall, Lancashire
FATHER OWEN GRIFFITH* — Jesuit priest
DANIEL ('SNOW') FLECKER* — assassin and former mercenary

IN LATHOM, LANCASHIRE
ELIZABETH ('LIZBETH'), LADY VERE — daughter to the Earl of Oxford, niece of Sir Robert Cecil and granddaughter of Lord Burghley
AMY* — her maid
ALICE, LADY DERBY — the Countess of Derby, Ferdinando's wife
LADY COMPTON — Alice's sister
ANNE, FRANCES and **BESS** — Ferdinando and Alice's young daughters
JOHN GOLBORNE, EDWARD SMYTHE, EDWARD HALSALL — Ferdinando's secretaries

RICHARD ('DICK') DOUGHTIE — Ferdinando's Master of Horse

CHAPLAIN LEIGH — Ferdinando's chaplain

WILLIAM FARINGTON (originally spelled as Ffarington) — Ferdinando's receiver-general

GILES CLOTHIER — Ferdinando's body servant

FINIAN O'NEILL* — kinsman of Hugh, Earl of Tyrone

ANDREW BUCHANAN* — Lord Bothwell's emissary

SIR PHILLIP FRAYN* (aka Ralph Hawkridge / Sir Ralph Weld) — an English Papist

CHIRURGEON BATE and **DR CANON** — Ferdinando's surgeon and physician

DR JOHN CASE — physician, academic and Ferdinando's former mentor

JANE OF AUGHTON — white witch and healer

BARTHOLOMEW HESKETH — Lancashire lawyer, older brother of traitor Richard Hesketh

GABRIEL HESKETH — his son

ALSO MENTIONED

SIR RICHARD BINGHAM — English Governor of Connacht, Ireland

MARY, QUEEN OF SCOTS — executed Roman Catholic claimant to the English throne

KING JAMES VI OF SCOTLAND — Mary's son, possible successor to the English throne

GEORGE BYNG MP — wealthy relative of Rose Byrd's mother

EDMUND YORKE and **RICHARD WILLIAMS** — Papist activists

ARBELLA STUART — great-granddaughter of Henry VIII's eldest sister, possible successor to the throne

MICHAEL DOUGHTIE — older brother of Richard Doughtie; MP for Liverpool and Clerk of the Kitchen to Ferdinando

FRANCIS, LORD BOTHWELL — rebel Scots lord, dabbler in witchcraft

WILLIAM STANLEY — Ferdinando's younger brother and heir

LADY ANNE VAUX — English Papist

DR RODERIGO LOPEZ — Queen Elizabeth's physician, convicted of treason

SIR GEORGE CAREY — brother-in-law to Alice, Lady Derby and second cousin to the queen

Claimants to the throne of England in 1593

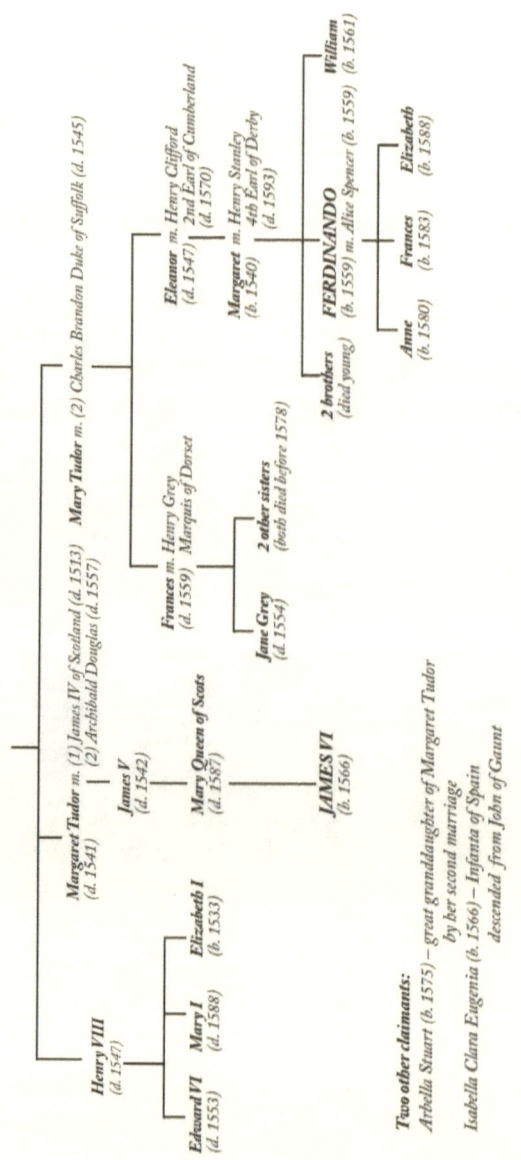

Henry VII

Margaret Tudor m. (1) James IV of Scotland (d. 1513)
(d. 1541) (2) Archibald Douglas (d. 1557)

Mary Tudor m. (2) Charles Brandon Duke of Suffolk (d. 1545)

Henry VIII
(d. 1547)

James V
(d. 1542)

Eleanor m. Henry Clifford
(d. 1547) 2nd Earl of Cumberland
(d. 1570)

Margaret m. Henry Stanley
(b. 1540) 4th Earl of Derby
(d. 1593)

Edward VI **Mary I** **Elizabeth I**
(d. 1553) (d. 1588) (b. 1533)

Frances m. Henry Grey
(d. 1559) Marquis of Dorset

Mary Queen of Scots
(d. 1587)

William
(b. 1561)

FERDINANDO
(b. 1559) m. Alice Spencer (b. 1559)

2 brothers
(died young)

Jane Grey
(d. 1554)

2 other sisters
(both died before 1578)

JAMES VI
(b. 1566)

Anne **Frances** **Elizabeth**
(b. 1580) (b. 1583) (b. 1588)

Two other claimants:

Arbella Stuart (b. 1575) – great granddaughter of Margaret Tudor
by her second marriage

Isabella Clara Eugenia (b. 1566) – Infanta of Spain
descended from John of Gaunt

PROLOGUE

'You must find a new agent, Sir Robert!'

'Yes, Your Majesty.' Sir Robert Cecil tried to keep pace with the queen, but being cursed with a humped back and uneven walk, it was sometimes a challenge.

This morning, she had ordered his attendance as she strolled in the garden of Greenwich Palace. Robert's father, Lord Burghley, reckoned he could estimate Her Majesty's anger by the rustle of her petticoats; today Elizabeth Tudor's were in loud voice and the lavender bushes either side the path were bruised by her progress. 'What possessed you to employ that wild Kit Marlowe as an intelligencer?' she exclaimed. 'A playwright! What foolishness is that?'

Robert disguised his annoyance. 'Madam, both Walsingham and my father found him useful.'

'But now *you* are his master, sirrah.' The royal feet acquired pace. 'He was supposed to be sending back reports not setting up a counterfeit money enterprise and, see, he's making more mischief! The man's a cursed atheist! Have you read this?' Her broad, embroidered skirts swung as she brandished a printed sheet. 'Lord Essex brought it to my attention.'

Ah, that explained matters.

'Why were you keeping it from me, changeling?'

Robert loathed it when she called him names. Imp, pygmy, changeling, little man. Hated that he was not tall and straight-boned like Essex.

'Madam, there were more urgent matters. Master Wade informs me that he has apprehended yet another Papist assassin sent over by Colonel Stanley. We are still watching to make sure Stanley doesn't entangle your cousin Ferdinando in his scheming.'

'And?'

'Nothing, as yet.'

'Nothing as yet,' she echoed scathingly. 'I told you watching Ferdy was a wasted effort.' Her lips thinned to a narrow seam.

As she resumed her walk, Robert was free to glare at the mesh of lace and wire which peacock-tailed her haughty old neck but, as always, his anger subsided. His existence depended on that fragile neck. Without her trust, an ambitious, misshapen creature like him would have fallen into despair. However, without the vigilance of his agents, she might have been murdered or deposed. It comforted him that for all her capriciousness, she accepted that danger was omnipresent; not just the second armada that King Philip of Spain was building but the covert invasion of Papist priests and zealots fired up to return England to the old faith if they could find a new leader.

While Elizabeth liked to delude herself that all the people loved her, Robert knew otherwise. Those who had survived the whirligig of religious change had long memories. He had not been born when King Henry VIII had ordered his soldiers to smash the faces of the stone angels that graced the ancient churches and turn the abbeys into ruins. Nor had he smelled the burning flesh of Protestant bishops in Queen Mary's reign, but he knew it could happen again when Elizabeth died. He and his father, Her Majesty's chief minister, would be the first to be tied to the stake if the wrong man seized the crown.

'*There must be no going back to Popish ways!*' His father maintained. '*Attrition will gradually settle matters, but it will take generations, centuries maybe. In the meantime, you and I must remove any threat to our own future. Any threat!*

'Imp, are you away with the fairies?'

'Your pardon, Your Majesty.' It would be easy to make some quip about being distracted in the presence of the Faerie Queen, but he left such taradiddle to idler men.

'Order Master Wade to find a replacement for Marlowe,' she commanded. 'We need a man who would die for his country and his queen.'

Pah, Robert had yet to meet an intelligencer who would. Most of them were venal lowlife.

'And tell Wade not to offer the new man any fulsome inducement.'

The royal fingers broke off a frond of honeysuckle to smell its fragrance. The breeze stirred the few hairs that lay against her cheek, silvery fugitives that had escaped her wig. All else was stitched down, the bows of golden ribbon, the knots of pearls, the diamonds, jewels that would fund an army for a week. Then she lifted her face, scenting the rain about to cross the river, and observed that Lord Essex was bowing to her from the steps, waiting to be beckoned. Essex, the golden lad who was everything that Sir Robert was not: fit and grandiose, except he was not a member of the Privy Council and there was gossip that Dr Lopez, Her Majesty's physician, was treating my lord for an infection of his manly appendages. Behind the queen's back, Sir Robert shot Essex a paper-thin smile.

The audience was at an end. Almost.

Aware of the rivalry between the two, the queen thrust Marlowe's broadsheet at Robert. 'Have the wretch arrested and brought before the Privy Council. Let his replacement be a soldier. I so like soldiers.' Beaming at Essex, she held out her wrist, a signal for the earl to come and cream her skin with charm. 'Dearest boy,' she trilled to him.

The fleet of her ladies waiting on the garden steps floated forward in his lordship's wake. Their farthingales sailed round the queen, and Robert found himself separated like some small ugly cog. No one noticed as he bowed his question-mark of a back and hobbled away.

1

In battle, decisions were made swiftly. Captain Garrett Towneley was not used to making slow ones. He sat hunched over his tankard, his usual optimism gone like a sold-off jacket. Almost at the dregs, this ale was the last drink he could afford and he put it down to three reasons.

Sir Richard Bingham, his former military commander in Connacht, had threatened to hang him if he ever set foot in Ireland again, his once heroic reputation was more threadbare than a beggar's smock and paying his soldiers out of his own coffers when their wages from the government were months in arrears had not been the wisest action. At least the men had something besides scars to take back to their families.

'More ale, your worship?' The tapster lad was courteous. Garrett's uniform still earned respect, but below the board his soles, like his prospects, had as much future as a leaky bucket.

There had been talk of a fresh campaign in Normandy under Lord Essex's command, but he had been told at Essex House that the noble lord would not be shifting himself until the spring. The last resort would be returning home to his stepfather's family in Warwickshire. Yes, he'd be welcomed with kindness but he didn't want the fatted calf. What he wanted was to earn his keep again, yet, to put it plainly, what use was a man with most of his fingers and honour sundered? For sure, he could still manage a rapier though his right grip was weaker, but an arquebus was not so easy with his trigger finger gone. Just clothing himself was a fumble with laces and fastenings.

At his elbow, the tapster coughed. 'Beggin' your pardon, your worship, but you bein' a soldier an' a visitor to London, you might enjoy Master Shakespeare's play at the Rose this afternoon. Or there's the Curtain an' the Theatre on the other side o' town.'

'Shakespeare?' There had been an older boy with that name at Garrett's grammar school in Stratford, the son of the town glove merchant, a suspected Papist. 'What's the play about?'

'Set in the reign of King Henry VI, sir, an' full of battles. We sometimes have plays in the yard here, too, when the weather is fine. I'd like to be a player one day,' the lad confided, adding so as not to offend, 'or a soldier.'

Garrett could see his younger self in the youth; that same relish of a ruddy good story enacted before his eyes. On stage, tyrants were brought down, evil punished, the just vindicated, and though love might be thwarted, it finally prevailed. He sighed inwardly. Watching those travelling companies had given him dreams to rise in the world, and ambition had made a good bedfellow until Life's mill wheel had sloshed him back into the common stream. He had to find a way back up, survive.

The landlord pointedly cleared away his empty tankard and Garrett was left staring at the ring of moisture on the scrubbed board. A fizz of hope surged in him. Well, if he could no longer make a living from soldiering, perhaps... Perhaps, he could become a player.

Using a tomb at St Mary Overy's in Southwark as a backrest, Garrett had little sleep that night and although he woke up feeling like one of the churchyard's permanent residents, he remembered his resolve. According to the tapster, there were three acting companies that attracted good audiences. He'd try the nearest first: The Rose Theatre in Southwark, and if the manager was not interested, then it would be a long walk across to the Curtain in Finsbury Fields or the Theatre in Shoreditch.

By nine o'clock, Mr Henslowe, owner of the Rose, had shown him the door but he had learned three things. Firstly, Shakespeare could be found at Burbage's theatre in Shoreditch; secondly, he needed a rehearsed speech to audition, and, thirdly, his chance of joining any company was as likely as Queen Elizabeth reopening England's monasteries. It did not deter him. He'd thought up a speech by the time he had crossed London Bridge.

It was noon when he reached the Theatre. Some sort of combat lesson was being held on stage and since there was no doorman to keep him out, he was free to watch from the lower stand. Mind, he heard heavy footsteps on the floor above, felt the sense of being noticed, but no one bothered to challenge him.

How glorious it would be to lose himself in this make-believe world where no one truly died. He followed the half-serious fight upon the stage, then it came again, that prickling on his neck as though someone was watching him from the gallery. Katherine?

He turned abruptly. The balconies were deserted. His gaze searched the empty benches for her spirit and his heart ached in remembrance, another burden to be endured — the guilt of the living. Now he was nine and twenty and Katherine, poor, sweet Katherine, was forever twenty-four. He flinched, his memory seeing her lean upon the wooden balcony and lift her hand in greeting, her smile as glorious as a summer's day.

He had been on leave from the army in Ireland and they had sat together in the second storey, he with a jingling purse and his arm about her. He had never proposed marriage and her parents, tired of waiting, had forced her to wed. Now she lay in death beside the husband whom she had hated lying with in life — both dead from the plague.

The player's shout brought him back to the present. Once more, he began to follow the exchange of blows. Although their false broadswords had blunted tips, the several actors laid on fiercely, and the theatre echoed with the whack and thwack of wood upon wood.

'Alas, I die.' The youngest actor clutched his chest and fell to his knees, groaning hideously.

'Hold!' Garrett dashed up onto the stage. 'No true soldier would slay him that way.' Before any of them could curse, he had tugged his rapier free. 'Here is a lunge that really kills!'

Someone damned him for his interference; then the 'dying' youth giggled. 'Lovely calves, soldier.'

Garrett cursed himself for a prize fool. 'Your pardon, friends. This is your business not mine.'

'Wait!' The older player grabbed his elbow. Garrett caught the swift glance at his right glove. He was about to turn away, unable to stomach the inevitable pity, when the man said, 'Show us again, your worship, but slowly.'

First, they watched, then aped him until they had the footwork, balance and the angle of thrust perfected.

Shifting to the side, he watched like a combat master. It was good to feel valued. No longer a stinking, useless bastard. By the Lord! He could have floated to heaven on a smoke ring of euphoria. But he should have known better.

'Put up your swords!' roared a sudden voice. The fury, the power, almost rattled the daub and wattle walls.

Astonishingly, this was no Ajax but a skinny fellow with an ebbing hairline and an armful of papers. 'I don't doubt you are enjoying yourselves,' said the newcomer dryly, 'but Act One requires your attention. And someone should have sent Dick word we have a visitor.' Large brown eyes piniored Garrett.

'Good morrow, sir, I was seeking Master Burbage ... or Master Shakespeare,' Garrett added as an afterthought. 'Philip Henslowe at the Rose told me he was here. I am looking for work.'

'Or Shakespeare. *Or?*' echoed the other man with disdainful horror, and the combatants started laughing.

'So doth God exalt the humble and chide the proud,' chuckled the older player. 'Give him a chance, Will.'

Mercy, Jesu! This thin bag of air was Shakespeare? Yes, there was a resemblance to the boy he remembered from school. 'Act One,' the playwright repeated to the actors. 'Dick will join you later.'

Ignored, Garrett sprang down from the stage and headed for the street.

'You can do indignation, I see.' Shakespeare was beside him now. 'Changed your mind?'

A grunt. He had known worse curs than this.

'That way then.'

'Well ... lead on!' he growled. With his boot soles crunching on the discarded nutshells and hubris of successions of audiences, he followed Shakespeare upstairs into the gallery.

'What's your name and where are you from?'

'My name's Towneley.'

Shakespeare looked round. 'A Lancashire Towneley? I spent some time up at Rufford Hall. Old Sir John Towneley came to dine. Quite a fellow. I hear he had plenty of bastards.' The implication was obvious.

'I grew up outside Loxley, southeast of Stratford. I expect you know it.'

'A Loxley lad.' The arched eyebrows lifted a fraction. 'So the Warwickshire lasses have rough-hewn you and shaped your end. Amused them, did you?'

'I believe so,' Garrett answered coldly, with a squaring of shoulders that usually scared away knaves who bothered him.

'And I suppose they told you that you might one day make a player?'

The urge to grab this joker by his lace-edged collar was almost irresistible. 'I know I shall, Master Shakespeare.'

'Knowledge exceeding faith! Ah well, there is hope yet.'

Mollifying glover's brat! Pray God, Richard Burbage would be more amenable.

Shakespeare's thoughts must have also dwelt on gloves. 'I observe you've lost some of your touch already, Master Towneley.'

'Hacked by an Ulster rebel. This, on the other hand,' he added dryly, 'was an accident with an arquebus. Unfortunately, the universal dose of sack, liquorice and aniseed balls was to no avail. The army physician recommended severance.'

That bridled Shakespeare's breeziness. 'You are fortunate then that it was not your arm. Through here, if you please, Master Towneley.'

A doorway had been cut through into an adjoining house and after more stairs they arrived at a sunlit chamber that ran the length of the upper floor. The centre space was dominated by a long trestle table, spined with trays of inkpots, untidy with beer tankards and peppered with crumbs. In the room's far corner leaned a fingerpost announcing 'To Leicester XII miles', with a crown dangling absurdly at one end, and in the other corner stood an oak, spreading its painted branches towards the fire mantle. Along the inner wall, ladies' caps, crespinettes and veils frothed from hooks, and a tangle of painted roses, red and white, brightened a lattice.

A sewing-woman nodded to them from the window seat. She was forcing a needle of black thread through a band of pale fur with her fingerstall. Common rabbit transformed to royal ermine! Next to her sat a man binding a leather strap around a canvas scabbard. All illusion, thought Garrett, trying to convince his ravenous appetite that the loaf and cheese on the table were painted too.

'Lewis, be kind enough to find Dick. Tell him we have company.'

The man set aside his work. Passing by, he gave a wink as saucy as a stew girl's. Garrett nearly stowed it in, there and then. Why in hell was he, a soldier, wasting his time here, except...

'Richard Burbage does the hiring.' Shakespeare gestured him to a bench and retreated to the far end of the trestle, where he took up a quill and pulled a half-written sheet towards him. 'What rhymes with "relenteth"?'

'Tormenteth?'

'Oh, excellent, sirrah, and said with such feeling!

"*Art thou obdurate, flinty, hard as steel,*

Nay, more than flint, for stone at rain relenteth?

Art thou a woman's son, and canst not feel

What 'tis to love?

How-want-of-love-tormenteth!"'

Save for Shakespeare's quill making corrections, the room fell silent. Only when the bells of St Leonards, Shoreditch, rang the hour did they hear feet upon the stairs. As if on cue, the door crashed back, and a huge figure wearing a plumed, broad-brimmed hat and a gaudy doublet of crimson panelled with gilt popinjays, halted upon the threshold. When no one greeted him, he swaggered in with creaking boots and jingling spurs, exclaiming:

'Where is this presumptuous worm who craves to jiggle and jerk before the London mob like a cursed traitor?'

Garrett rose to his feet, his temper fraying further.

'His name is Towneley.' Shakespeare busied himself again. Forget Stratford Grammar School. No geographical support was forthcoming.

'I understand you want to be spat at,' Burbage said, swaggering up to face Garrett. They were of equal height, mayhap brewed in the same year, and both wide in the shoulder save that Burbage's were padded.

Garrett held his ground. 'It's not an experience I anticipate, Master Burbage.'

'Spat upon, jeered at, pelted with offal, told you're a mincing strumpet, that your cock hangs limp.'

'You speak from experience, Master Burbage?'

He heard Shakespeare's nib pause and watched as a tight smile edged Richard Burbage's mouth. Slowly his interrogator began to laugh, a laugh that shook his large frame. Garrett could imagine him one day playing Old King Harry, the queen's father. Then abruptly the merriment was sliced to silence. Now Burbage was pouting like a cheerful whore looking him over.

'Can you read and write? Have you a feel for verse, an eye for mannerisms? Can you ape your betters to perfection?'

'Try me, most gracious lord.' A shine of vowels with an exquisite flourish.

Burbage shrugged. 'I concede you have the bearing, Master Towneley. An excellent leg. The ladies will swoon as you swagger on, eh, Maria?' The woman was smiling. 'Mind, our voice needs a tad more strut but that's easily done.' He picked up a knife from the table and hacked himself some cheese. 'What I desire to know,' he said, pointing the blade at Garrett as he chewed, 'is why a man so capable of still besting England's enemies on the battlefield is wiring his sword above the mantle shelf and wanting to become a player?'

Garrett drew a deep breath. Now was his chance to prick these playing-card heroes. 'When you kill someone on stage, do you pierce a bag of fake blood?'

'And what's your point, man?' growled the actor.

'Well, I have pierced living men's lungs with my sword, Master Burbage. I have slid blades through to their hearts, watched blood spurt from their mouths. I've smelled blood warm from a man's veins, and seen my armour, my gloves, my face, spattered with gore as I've sliced off fingers, wrists, arms in the name of England.' Turning, he snared Shakespeare, stilled now, as a cat in a hedge, watching, listening. 'Your kings would understand in the cold hours of night how the dead return to haunt the living.' He paused, letting his thoughts dwell on Katherine, his face conversant with his inner pain. 'Call me a coward but I'm sated. There's a rot within me, a panic that makes me short of breath at the sound of a trumpet, shivers my limbs as though I have an ague. I had rather die than return to fight in Ireland.' He drew breath, wondering whether he should continue, but they were still listening. 'Behold, I am become a half-man, mocked and scourged by those who have never fought a battle in their lives.' His voice fell to husky bitterness. 'I despise this weakness, but it chains me to the stake like a captive bear.'

Enough. For an instant, the very air seemed frozen. Burbage was staring at him like a gasping fish.

Shakespeare cleared his throat. 'A half-man? No, I think not.'

'Very well done!' The sewing woman applauded.

Burbage ran a thumb and finger up and down his nose. 'I agree, excellently delivered. And did you write it as well as con it, Master Towneley?'

'I did, Master Burbage.' Damn it, surely he had proven his worth? However, some unspoken conversation played out between the two actors and it was Burbage who picked up the gauntlet. 'I'm impressed, but then…'

'Then…?' Garrett waited for an offer.

'It's your timing that's at issue.'

'*Timing?*'

'I mean your entrance, Master Towneley. You either come tardily or too soon upon the call. In other words, naught doing, lad. We can't help you.' Burbage's front teeth caressed his lower lip. 'Full up. Speak to Philip Henslowe at the Rose.'

'A piss on that! *He* directed me here.'

Again, Burbage exchanged a glance with Shakespeare. 'Where are you staying, Master Towneley?' Why were they bothering to ask?

'Nowhere anymore.' The admission hurt, and pride made him add, 'Perhaps I should speak directly with your patron, Lord Strange —'

Again, some unspoken communication that had him puzzled.

'It's pronounced "Strange" as in "blancmange",' corrected Burbage, 'and I do the hiring, Master Towneley.'

Garrett's belly rumbled. 'Then I beg pardon for wasting your blessed time.' Rot them! Blancmange indeed!

'Look, I'm truly sorry, friend.' Burbage finally shed his bombast. 'To be frank, the Burbage purse rattles in emptiness. And if the plague comes upon us again, they'll close all the theatres.' He reached out for one of the tankards, turned it upside down, stared gravely at the three drops that plopped upon the wooden board and then he looked up at Garrett with a sincerity that was no longer stubble deep. 'Oh, you may be as good as me one day, have the crowd roaring for you, but we just haven't the funds to test your mettle. No, friend, don't say you'll clean up our chamberpots just to hang around. Go be a soldier once more.'

The room was silent save for another hunger rumble as Garrett picked up his hat. 'What rhymes with "Pluck it", Master Shakespeare?'

Shakespeare smiled. 'I used to know a girl from Loxley. "Know" as in the Biblical sense and very alluring she was, too. Perhaps you could tell us over supper if you knew her. The cost is on me. Shall we say The Mermaid Inn?'

The invitation was generous even if proffered with such damn diffidence. As though he had a score of other offers, Garrett gave the appearance of weighing the proposal before he nodded. At least he would eat tonight and for all their stabbing wit, he grudgingly liked them.

'An excellent decision on your part, Towneley,' chuckled Richard Burbage, slapping him on the back like a drinking crony. 'I just hope the Loxley wench, whose physical attributes we are about to remember with glorious metaphors, wasn't your sister!'

Garrett woke on the theatre bench with a dagger sticking out of his chest. Once he had yelled in panic and tumbled off, he discovered a message attached to the faux blade.

Be at the corner of St John's Street and Cow Cross Lane in Clerkenwell at 10 o'clock.
WS

WS? His groggy mind recalled that last evening Shakespeare had left the inn early for another appointment. Had he mentioned Garrett's need for work to someone? Picking up the dagger, Garrett smiled, and then in panic checked the angle of the sun. Clerkenwell? Maybe if he cut across Finsbury Fields...

Freshly sluiced with clean water from the old Charterhouse conduit, he managed to arrive at the appointed place with his hair sleeked down and his face scrubbed to a glow, and now he waited, trying not to eye each passer-by like some eager whore. As the bells of St James's and St John's struck the hour, he felt a tug on his slops and turned to find a girl of about seven. 'Captain Towneley? This way.'

The house he was led to might have belonged to a miser for it did not take a builder's eye to notice the faded paint on the carved timbers or the rot eating into the window frames. Rented, for sure. His small hope of a good fire in the hall was disappointed, too, as he followed the child through the depressing interior. Even the tapestries had seen better days. His little guide pointed him down stone stairs. Hand on his rapier hilt, he descended warily. A rat streaked across his bootcaps and then a deafening explosion had him stagger. Hail rattled the inside of the door in front of him and before he could retreat, a ripe male curse rang out, the door crashed open and a finely clad fellow emerged in a confusion of smoke, cursing and coughing.

'Are you hurt?' Garrett exclaimed.

The man grabbed his arm and leaned upon it for a moment. 'Captain Towneley?' he wheezed, before straightening up.

'Yes, if my ruddy wits haven't been blown to kingdom come.'

'Oh, the fumes won't hurt you.' A woman in her fifties materialised at the threshold. Her red hair was suppressed beneath a cap, edged with pearls and scarlet enamels, and an unbleached apron covered her dark skirt and stomacher. Removing a glove that would have better served a workman, she held out a ringed hand.

'Margaret Clifford,' she asserted airily. 'I live here, and this is my son, Ferdinando, Lord Strange, who is visiting. Do come in.'

Rhymes with blancmange. Garrett's mind sprang into genealogical leapfrog. He was probably staring at them froglike, too. If this coughing nobleman was Shakespeare's patron, then the woman must be Lady Derby, cousin to the queen. He delivered his best bow.

'Oh, fie, none of that!' Her ladyship drew him into the smoky cellar. 'Your pardon for the stink, Captain Towneley.'

Pieces of hot, broken pottery dotted the flagstones and broken glass vessels lay like a wrecked citadel across the trestle table. It was a wonder the shelves of phials and jars had survived unscathed.

'Alchemy,' the countess explained. 'I do not see why it should be only a man's prerogative.'

'Quite,' Garrett agreed dryly, taking care not to tread on one of the exploded fragments. 'Do you consider yourself close, my lady?'

'Hardly,' her son snapped, 'but she can manage a good poison.' He toed a deceased rodent into a corner. 'Maybe you can manage some refreshment, too, Mother. Sit, sir!'

The countess left them, and Garrett obediently swept the residue from a stool and sat down, pleased at the lack of ceremony. Lord Strange ran a long, thin finger beneath the neck of a generous lace collar, grunted, and shook his head despairingly at the disarray. 'She would have been happier as an apothecary,' he muttered, 'but then we are not given much choice, are we? Will Shakespeare tells me you need employment.'

'Yes, my lord.' Even though the miasma was making his eyes water and catching in his throat, Garrett could hardly believe his good fortune. He knew from Shakespeare and Burbage that their patron had an honourable reputation unsplashed by scandal or corruption, as well as being heir to an earldom, a poet in his own right, and one of the planets that orbited the queen. Garrett had never been this close to such a paragon and he tried not to gape like a peasant at the nobleman's finery. An emerald brooch with its pendant pearl ornamented Lord Strange's black velvet hat; a green brocade cloak jutted at his thigh, elegant chevron patterning enhanced the cream satin doublet and canions of his matching breeches and weighty gems adorned his manicured fingers. Unlike Lady Margaret, it seemed his lordship did not depend on his father for income.

The nobleman's amused cough made Garrett's gaze gallop back up past the cupid-bow mouth and small, neat beard to find himself observed just as thoroughly. He was used to calculated, gruff assessment by his military commanders so it was refreshing to find himself assessed by a young, direct and thoughtful gaze, although it was blessed hard not to be transfixed by the wart above his lordship's left eyebrow.

'Very well, tell me why you are out of work, man, but make it brief, I have to leave for Greenwich shortly.'

Garrett spoke of his service in Ireland, how he'd risen from ensign to garrison commander and discovered his predecessor had been claiming for men who didn't exist, selling the decent victuals instead of feeding his force, not to mention pocketing half their wages.

'It was nothing new, my lord. Many of the garrison captains were doing the same. But when I brought this to the attention of the Comptroller of Victuals in Dublin, seeing it was his job to report quarterly to the queen's Privy Council, nothing came of the matter and the officer I reported was given preferment. Then in January, my commander, Sir Richard Bingham, accused me of supporting Hugh O'Neill, the Earl of Tyrone. Two of my officers were bribed to bear witness against me and I was put under arrest.'

'They flogged you?'

'No, thank God. Fortunately, my corporal and the castle chaplain had actually seen the officers accepting the money, so the case was eventually dismissed, but Bingham told me to quit Ireland and never return.'

'Hmm.' A nod and then more digging. 'Master Shakespeare tells me you are Sir John Towneley's saddlepack son.'

'So my mother informed me, but I was raised by my stepfather, a man I esteem greatly, a worthy gentleman and a true Protestant.'

'And *your* faith?' His interrogator took another glance at his pocket watch.

Garrett shrugged. 'Let's say I do not care for any man who professes he has a bell rope to swing messages from God.'

Lord Strange gave a bark of laughter.

'Will he do?' asked the countess, sweeping back in, followed by the child carrying a tray of sugar-sprinkled pastries and three modest ale cups. She waved the girl out and served Garrett herself. 'Liftleg,' she informed him. It was one of the cheaper ales. Maybe she considered he did not deserve quality but he could see that although the stuff of her sleeve was fine, the turn at her wrist was worn and shiny. 'He requires a spy, Master Towneley.'

Stunned, Garrett lowered his cup.

'Mother!'

'Oh, fie, Ferdy, stop beating about the bushes and tell him what you need. Do have something to eat, Captain Towneley.'

Her son drew an exasperated breath. 'Master Shakespeare tells me you desire to act, Towneley. Well, the work I am proposing certainly requires a player. What I am about to say stays in this room. Is that understood?'

'Yes, my lord.'

'Have you heard of my cousin, Sir William Stanley?'

'Captain Stanley, my lord?' Garrett hastily swallowed a mouthful of pastry.

At one time, it was wagered that such a hero would be made the Viceroy of Ireland, but the queen had never rewarded him because he was a Papist. Perhaps that was why, when serving with the English army in the Low Countries, Sir William had turned an entire town over to the Spanish. That had been a disaster that made any honest Englishman turn puce at the mention and Garrett could remember the anger of his fellow soldiers.

'Stanley calls himself "colonel" now,' his lordship said sourly, and Garrett realised how much it must have shamed the Stanley family. 'Have you ever met him?'

'Not face to face, my lord,' Garrett confessed, adding diplomatically, 'I know he was much praised for his service in Ireland.'

'And now he's a pensioner of the King of Spain and commands an army of Papists in the Spanish Netherlands.'

'So I believe, my lord. A pity that.'

'See, Towneley,' the countess flounced between them, 'would you be prepared to go across and enlist with him, if my son pays you enough?'

'Madam, will you leave this to me! Towneley, I need an intelligencer.'

Garrett's shiny new optimism instantly dulled. Clothe the work with a fancy term, it still stank. Informers were unprincipled, venal peddlers who sold to the highest bidder. They betrayed their fellows, their commanders, their country.

Ferdinando, Lord Strange, read his disappointment. 'Do not dismiss it so lightly,' he commanded. 'You would be highly acceptable to my cousin. You're an experienced soldier but you appear to have no resources and plenty of reason to be discontent. What's more, your father is quite notorious, a stubborn old Lancashire recusant. You have the perfect history.'

Garrett felt his face redden. 'All news to me, my lord. I only met the old man once when I was just an infant, I've never set foot in Lancashire, and your pardon if I sound an utter greenhorn, but it isn't clear to me why you need an informer in your cousin's camp.'

'Isn't it obvious, man? He has dishonoured my family and ferments rebellion.'

'And you fear the infection he spreads will contaminate you, my lord?'

'It already has. Others watch me now as they never did before. I find myself obliged to convince people of my loyalty. That's why I've had Master Shakespeare write a play about King Richard III to remind the queen that she owes her crown to my great-great-grandfather. If he and his brother had not changed sides at the Battle of Bosworth, we would still be ruled by the Plantagenets and obedient to the Church of Rome.'

'Tell him I should be the next Queen of England,' Lady Derby interrupted again.

'Mother, hush! That is not the point.'

'Do not silence me, Ferdy! Now that the Queen of Scots is dead, I am the heir to the crown when Elizabeth dies. That's no lie, Captain Towneley. It's written in old King Harry's will that my blood has precedence. I am granddaughter to his sister, who was Queen of France. But will that creature name me as her successor? Oh no, I am shunned, see?'

Garrett saw that Ferdinando Stanley bore a dangerous blood legacy, not to mention an uncontrollable mother with her loose tongue and thwarted ambition! By Heaven, he was almost feeling sorry for this nobleman. Getting born to the wrong parents was something you could not blessed well change, and the capricious old queen could lop off this man's head just for existing, for having some Tudor blood. She might still. Her father had already killed off the last of the Plantagenets.

To be honest, Garrett didn't care much whose royal arse dented the cushions of the throne once Her Majesty expired, so long as the new monarch upheld justice, but there was a decency about Ferdinando, Lord Strange, that earned his sympathy.

'Well, Towneley?'

He drew a deep breath, anxious not to offend. 'To do as you ask, my lord, would be extremely perilous. If Her Majesty's ministers add me to their list of traitors, I shall never be able to return to England without fear of arrest and punishment. And if Sir William Stanley were to discover my duplicity, I'd likely be stabbed to death in some dark backstreet.'

'As I might order, were you to prove false. But you're really talking about your fee, aren't you? There's the subtext.'

'No, that's not the issue,' Garrett corrected hotly. 'Yes, I'm penniless, my lord, but what you require of me would hammer my reputation, rotten as it is now, further into the mire and it's all I have left.'

The nobleman stared at him with a strained expression and then, as if forced, named a figure that had Lady Derby wrinkle her regal nose. 'For heaven's sake, Ferdinando, that's half of what your father pays to support me!'

Garrett swallowed his astonishment but stuck to his principles. 'No, my lord. I am flattered that you believe me trustworthy and would offer such a sum, however, I am sure you can find plenty of men out on the streets with a similar story to mine.'

Only the restlessness of fingers against his belt betrayed the noble lord's dislike of being thwarted. 'Listen, my cousin wants the queen murdered and the old faith restored. He is dangerous, don't you grasp that? You would be serving your country.'

'Even so, my —'

'Enough! Take a few days to think about my offer and, on your honour, neither mention this to anyone nor seek me at my house. Attend me at the Theatre on Wednesday.'

It was flattering that his lordship shook hands in farewell.

'You could be looking at your future king, Captain Towneley,' said the countess.

With her words ringing in his brain and the smell of alchemy in his clothes, Garrett was dismissed up into the daylight feeling he had just been cudgelled.

It would have been gilding matters further if Ferdinando had offered a ride back to the city, but that was the nobility for you. His lordship's coach passed him west of Aldersgate. However, the walk back offered time to weigh matters. While it was pleasing that an earl's son deemed him trustworthy; the other side of the coin was Ferdinando must be as barking mad as

Lady Derby in being so frank to a stranger, even on Shakespeare's recommendation. Last night, Garrett could have spun the playwright a web of lies.

As for cozening up to the traitor Colonel Stanley? No! Garrett had had a bellyful of overseas soldiering, let alone throwing dissembling and dishonour into the brew, and yet by the time he turned into Cheapside, hungry again, his resistance was at low ebb. He'd counted the beggars along the roadside rattling their bowls, many of them veterans of the wars. There was talk of a pension for the wounded but those poor wretches certainly hadn't had a whiff of it. Hands, legs, eyesight missing. Seemed he was blessed to have only lost half his fingers.

At least Ferdinando had tossed him a decent coin as he left the cellar. With his feet arguing he needed new soles more than food, he arrived at the alley off Bow Lane, glad to find that the cobbler, who he had used last time he was in London, was still in business. While his boots were being given new life on the last, he waited on the bench outside the shop.

Soon another customer, equally shoeless, joined him and they fell into conversation. This fellow, Hal Peckham, was a man-at-arms working for a clerk to the Privy Council named Wade, and after they had chewed the cud about insufficient wages and lack of pensions, Garrett inquired if Wade was likely to take on more soldiers.

'I dunno, you being an officer already, your worship,' replied his new acquaintance, eyeing the lace edging of Garrett's collar.

Was an officer.

'If you hear of anything in the next few days, friend,' he told Peckham, as the cobbler's apprentice arrived with his boots, 'leave a message in Shoreditch at the Theatre. Name's Towneley.'

A shake of hands and he set off back to Shoreditch. As he reached Bishopsgate, the street was blocked by a swarm of citizens, buzzing with anger. Taller than most, he could see a soldier come out from a house laden with a fine monstrance, brass pyx and several books. After him came an officer, followed by several soldiers hauling an old couple and a younger man to a dray.

'What's going on?' Garrett asked the nearest bystander.

'Where you been, away with the fairies?' came the rude answer. 'They was hidin' a soddin' Jesuit, of course.'

The spitting, the lobbing of stones and the snarls of ugly hatred confirmed Garrett's resolve to refuse Ferdinando's offer. The hard part would be explaining to Shakespeare about turning down employment that couldn't be mentioned.

'You lucky bugger,' exclaimed Burbage, ambushing him the instant he arrived back. 'One of my players has gone to bury his father so I'm a man short for a few days. You can play Second Murderer. No wages, but I'll give you the loan of King Richard III's camp bed.'

'And after all your soldiering,' Shakespeare added with a grin, as he joined them, 'you know the bed will be hard, but the murder should come easy.'

2

Being on stage was like going into battle. The groundlings in the cockpit were bawdy but the young rich swaggerers, who had purchased stools on the actual stage, were the worst. Flourishing their pomanders and kerchiefs, they vied to insult and distract the actors, and it took mental strength to withstand their ugly comments.

It was on Garrett's third day playing in *King Richard III* in the scene when he was helping to drown the Duke of Clarence in a barrel that he felt a youth's boot on his backside for a second time. He loosened hold of the duke and turning, deliberately stared over the gallant's head. His gaze found a slender young woman, standing with two youths, and he made play of gesturing would she go out with him? The young fellow standing next to her looked displeased but the crowd loved it. Even Lewis, the First Murderer, went along with the by-play and the duke briefly roused himself from the barrel much to everyone's amusement. The pretty object of attention blushed mightily, but then something changed in her face and she slid her fingers up to her forehead masking her face. He'd embarrassed her.

'Heigh!' he yelled as Lewis gave him a clip about the ear. With a loud sigh, the duke obligingly lowered his head back into the barrel, and they finished drowning him. The applause was exhilarating and so was the opportunity to *accidentally* kick the rude gallant's ankle hard as they hefted my lord of Clarence's corpse from the stage.

Backstage, the young woman's fine-featured face stayed in Garrett's mind. Better quality than most of the other groundlings.

'Ah, such a puff of comic descant, Captain,' Lewis observed dryly. 'Just as well for you that we have our regular man back tomorrow.'

'You mean it was stupid to flirt?'

'No, I mean kicking that spoilt coxcomb. He'll be looking for revenge, see.'

'I can deal with that.' The young loudmouth was barely out of the schoolroom.

'Aye, maybe *you* can, a big fellow like you, but I don't want to have my ribs broken on the way home, so behave.'

Garrett saluted with a grin, and for the rest of the play he was kept clear of the rich sprig. It was tempting to catch the young woman's glance, too, but he did not want to embarrass her again and she had a beau to see her home.

Didn't she?

'You don't mind walking back to the city without us, do you?' Rose Byrd's oldest brother, Francis, asked as they left the pit of the Theatre.

'There's a cockfight in Spitalfields,' explained Walter, her younger brother, 'and we've promised to meet friends there.'

Rose appreciated their concern. There had been times when each of them had been spat upon or rudely jostled because of their father, William Davison — the man who had acquired Her Majesty's signature on the death warrant of Mary Stuart, Queen of Scots. Even though there had been no incidents for a while, being singled out this afternoon by the Second Murderer had been unfortunate.

'I'll be safe,' she replied, though a sense of unease was tugging at her. Still, it was bright daylight, she would have her maidservant at her heel and there were plenty of respectable playgoers strolling back towards Bishopsgate. Besides, she was no green virgin, easily cozened, but twenty-three years old, a soldier's widow. 'Just mind you come back with winnings this time!'

'And you keep your purse to the front, Rose.'

'I will,' she promised.

Her mind was preoccupied with the play, especially the actor who had flirted with her. Of course, he'd only done it to annoy the youth who had been sitting on stage insulting the players. Even if she'd loathed the public attention, he had rekindled her yearning for affection, reminding her that life was swiftly passing her by.

'Mistress!' Her maidservant came level with her as they neared Bedlam. 'Ain't that your mother's kinsman ridin' this way an' his nephew with 'im?'

That whacked the reverie out of Rose's head. 'Mercy, they mustn't see us!'

An ardent reformer and Member of Parliament, this distant cousin, Sir George Byng, had offered to clear some of her father's massive debts. However, he deeply disapproved of the theatre. 'Ferments mischief, gives the rabble ideas,' he had exclaimed at their table. There had been discussion, too, of Rose marrying the nephew. Not that she cared for the fellow, an opinionated Puritan, but one who had plenty of influence with his uncle.

She tugged open the ribbons of her outer robe. 'Quickly, Tabby, swap your cloak for this. We'll separate until they've passed us! If need be, I'll see you back at our lodgings.'

Grabbing the shabbier garment around her kirtle, she hastened to the opposite side of the street. Once her kinsmen had passed, a cart divided the crowd and the press was so great that she was forced to keep moving. Distracted with seeking Tabby, she saw nothing sinister in the two gentlewomen who drew level either side of her.

'Greetings, my dear,' exclaimed the taller one.

They looked to be in their forties. The heftier of the two wore a modest ruff above her high-buttoned stomacher and a French hood that matched her gown. The second, stockier woman had her hair tucked into a simple white lawn cap and her bolstered skirt was of Abram damask. Before Rose could answer that she did not know them, each jovially linked arms with her and she was whisked around the corner into Half Moon Alley.

Were they Papists? Oh God, what a fool she had been to stand in the theatre pit for all to see. If only the Second Murderer had not locked eyes with her.

'Pox take you!' she cursed, struggling fiercely to break free, but one of her assailants wrenched her right hand up behind her back and she found herself thrust face first against the nearest wall. With an arm almost breaking and jagged mortar biting into her cheek, Rose prayed desperately for a rescuer.

'Take a message to your accursed father, you filth,' hissed the taller woman. 'Tell William Davison that those who follow the True Faith are going to hack out his belly and set his head on London Bridge for the crows to peck.'

'I'll bear your message. *Now let me go!*'

Her forearm was released but before she could escape, the larger woman's arm came around her throat and she was hauled from the wall. Her purse was cut free, her cap, veil and Tabby's cloak were wrenched away. Blinded with tears of pain, she lashed out. Far fiercer fingers — she heard the second shrew's laboured breath — grabbed the centre of her bodice neckline and hacked a small dagger blade down through the laces of her stomacher, her best stomacher, then her chemisette and the tags of the borrowed cloak. Horrified, she felt her bodice thrust aside and the air chill upon her exposed breasts.

'God's mercy,' she exclaimed, freezing as the knife touched her skin.

'I'll mark her!' hissed the shorter woman.

'No, save that for next time!' Her companion gave one of Rose's teats a painful tweak. 'Next time, we'll slice these off and make you swallow them along with your father's bollo—' At the warning jingle of harness, they abruptly let go.

Rose staggered back against the wall, snatching up her cap and trying to draw her ruined bodice together.

'What's this to-do, mesdames?' demanded a young man's voice. Her blood ran cold. The rider was the ill-mouthed, swaggering blade who had sat upon the stage.

'See this strumpet, sir? She tried to grab my purse,' exclaimed Rose's shorter assailant.

'Well, well, the wench from the pit,' he drawled with a leer. 'Go, good gentles, I'll deal with her.'

'No, you won't!' Rose snarled. 'I am neither bawd nor strumpet. They attacked me. That's my purse in her hand.' She needed to run before worse happened, but the steely eyes of the women offered no chance.

'I pray you, sir, give the creature a good thrashing,' exclaimed the taller, all eyelashes and genteel distress. Putting an arm about her companion, she said, 'Come, dear, let's go home.' Heads held high, offended virtue masking their glee, they strutted off.

'Just us, then, player's whore.' The braggart kneed his horse towards Rose. He was tonguing his cheek, his stare lascivious and cruel. 'Firm duckies, I see.' He lewdly fingered the air. 'Now show me what else you offer, goosy! Raise your petticoat!'

Rose risked his riding crop. Darting forward, she slapped the horse's rump. It reared and before its startled master could mouth a profanity, she grabbed up her skirts and ran. Not out into Bishopsgate Street, where the two women might set a hue and cry on her, but west along the lane, glancing left and right as she fled, avoiding courtyards where this man might corner her, and desperately seeking somewhere he could not ride.

She hurtled through an unlatched open gate, slammed it shut behind her, raced round a chicken run, and struggled through a thick hedgerow of nettles, ivy and blackthorn. The briars snatched her hair and snared her clothing, but she wrenched herself free. Scratched, lungs almost bursting, she crouched in the ditch below the hedge, foul that it was, and heard the rattle of harness as her pursuer stood up in the stirrups seeking her. God grant he could not hear her tortured breathing! At least there was insufficient space for him to take the hedge, then came the rattle of bridle as he turned the beast's head. Cursing her loudly, he spurred back towards the lane.

With dismay, Rose realised she was in the Moorfields. Open common land stretched out before her. In the distance, she could see archers practising at the butts; nearby, washer women had lain out their laundry, some dozen lots of sheets, all spread like sails of caravels across the tussocks.

Except for a gate further down that linked to the laneway, the hedgerow, her only shelter, ran unbroken towards Cripplegate. In the other direction, it joined the high wall that skirted Petty France and Bedlam Hospital. No chance of climbing that. To reach Moor Gate and the city would mean crossing the open field where there was not one decent sized tree or bush to hide her. If the horseman found the lane gate, he could ride her down for sport. Would the washer women beat him off her? Not in a thousand years! Who would face a horsewhip to rescue some bedraggled vagabond? And Rose knew she looked a sight with her brown hair capless and tangled, her breasts bursting from her bodice and her kirtle soiled and putrid.

She stared towards the laundered sheets once more. Then, snatching up her skirts, she sped towards the nearest. Falling on her knees, she wriggled beneath it. Thistle spikes pricked her; a bramble frond caught at her kirtle. Edging in until her heels were fully covered by the damp fabric, she pressed her face into the coarse grass and flattened her body as best she could, thankful her skirt was unbolstered and not a farthingale.

Count, she ordered herself and with each frantic heartbeat, mouthed the numbers, praying that no one would haul her forth. Fingers to the ground, she heard the drum of hooves and the rider shouting. A hundred heartbeats she counted and many more before she felt a poke to her shoulder. The tip of the whip? It came again, harder, demanding. Discovered, what choice had she but to face her enemy? Crawling forward, she stuck her head out.

Inches away from her nose stood a pair of small feet clothed in sacking. Above them were two grubby knees, a loose shirt of coarse linen and at a higher altitude, the amazed but curious eyes of a child about six years old.

'Do not yell,' she suggested firmly to their owner.

'I wasn't gonna,' he said proudly. 'Why are you under my ma's sheet? You playin' hide and seek?'

'Yes,' muttered Rose, feeling like a worm in peril from a Robin redbreast. 'There's a bad man on a horse looking for me. Can you see him?'

There was a pause. 'Nah.'

Clutching the sheet to her front, she wriggled out and with a shiver looked around. The only four-legged beast was a laden mule being led towards Moor Gate.

'Is that your ma over there?' she asked. Two women, baskets on hips, stood talking on the path. Mercifully, their backs were turned.

'Nah, thems not 'er. I always guard the sheets against thieves while she takes supper to my Da. Was you goin' to steal somefink?'

'Have you anything you'd recommend?'

'Nah.' He laughed, showing the gap where his front milk teeth had been. 'Ma'll have to wash that sheet again. You're putting muck all over it. She'll blame me. She won't believe a woman wus playin' hide and seek.'

'Nor will my ma,' Rose agreed, and watched him roll his eyes in sympathy.

'She'll want payment, Ma will. Thruppence to wash that sheet again.'

Rose's hand went instinctively to find her purse but, of course, it had gone. She felt for her pearl earrings. Only one had survived the scramble and she unhooked it with a sigh. 'This will pay for the sheet to be done a hundredfold, and I'd like to buy that.' She pointed to an overgown of hare-coloured saye cloth spread out nearby. Its folds would cover her bosom.

'It ain't ours to sell.'

'I'm sure your ma can think up a good tale. This earring is worth far more.'

'I s'pose. Deal!' The child spat on his palm and waited for her to do the same. They shook hands solemnly on the bargain.

'Please fetch it over for me.'

'It's still damp. I didn't tell yer that.'

'No matter.'

'Know what?' he puffed, dragging it across to her. 'I reckon you're one of them lunatics from there.' He jutted his chin towards the roofs and spire of Bedlam, then he weighed the earring in his fist, his expression growing mean. 'Maybe I should call a sergeant.'

'Maybe you should,' Rose said with a breeziness that was only smile-deep, 'but since I'm not from there, he'll give you a beating for wasting his time.'

She put her arms through the sleeveless overgown and wrapped the chilly cloth across her before she clambered to her feet. Looking down on the little boy made her feel more secure but the child could still draw unwelcome attention. 'I've given you generous payment and you've spat on the deal so there's no going back or God will punish you,' she reminded him severely as she tried to tidy her hair. 'So, fare you well and see that you give the pearl to your ma!'

Trying not to shiver, she walked away as stately as she could. On her lips was a prayer that the boy would not yell out; and to her surprise, for the first time in a very long while, someone in Heaven took notice.

'The mud has flaked off but the fabric is quite ruined.' Rose's mother, Catherine, inspected the bodice in the window light. 'It was never a good dye anyway. I daresay a tailor could narrow the side seams and insert some eyelets down the front, but these days lacing is not fashionable unless you're a milkmaid and know no better.' She flicked the broad white collar over. 'Now this is redeemable, see, if you reverse it so that the dirt stains are hidden.'

'Am I'm reversible too?' The bruises to Rose's confidence were clearly unimportant.

Her mother thrust the bodice aside. 'Your poor husband, God rest his soul, would turn in his grave to hear you speak so. Those earrings were his last gift to you. What is your next fantasy, pray, losing your wedding ring?'

'The earrings were won at dice, and my fantasy, Mama, would be wearing a rapier so I could defend myself.' *Or a decent man coming to my rescue*, she added silently.

'Well, you'd better go take combat lessons, then,' scoffed her parent. 'At least God be thanked that Cousin Byng did not see you. He is so close to helping us, so close.' A further shake of the head.

Rose stoppered her anger and took a draught from the beaker of mulled ale warming her palms. Around her, the parlour was quiet save for her father's snoring. His mouth and the book on his knees were both open. He looked hanged already.

'And you will say nothing of this to your father. *Nothing*! His health won't take it.'

Expecting sympathy from either of her parents was like trying to buy meat on a Friday, not on offer! Why had she come here, then? To borrow a clean stomacher? To be made guilty by the inevitable verdict that she had been too foolhardy, thoughtless, extravagant and the rest? Oh, all of that. But the thought of returning straight away to her sunless rooms above the apothecary's shop in St Swithin's Lane had been less appealing. Only her servant's cheerful company made it bearable. God willing, the maid was safely back there.

With a shiver, she drew the blanket closer round her. It must be the shock still making her goosefleshed but, as her mother had pointed out, there had been no harm done. Her body had not been ravished nor her bones rearranged; she carried no welts and the bruises on her face would fade. But her nerves? Who would mend those? Her brothers? Not them. Returning full of babble about beaks and spurs, their bellies sloshing with Flemish beer, their purses inside out, they would laugh at her adventure and huzzah her escape. Tomorrow, they would waken with fraternal bristling, demanding vengeance, but by ten o'clock the talk of family honour would falter into nothingness and Francis would be off to Gray's Inn, his tousled head more occupied with rhyming couplets rather than Chancery procedures.

Yes, she would leave before their return. Her petticoat was already dry although the *Parfum de Shoreditch* might attract an army of stray dogs to sniff at her hems on the way home.

'I hate playing the almswoman, Mama,' she murmured, 'but do you think I might have next week's allowance in advance, please?'

Despite giving one of her Puritan snorts, her mother disappeared upstairs to wrestle the small strongbox from its timber nest.

Rose winced as the floorboards creaked above her head. Independence eluded her, much to her annoyance. She wanted to be useful, feel needed, but work was hard to find in London unless you were an enthusiastic strumpet or a skilful seamstress. Besides, her parents expected her to be reliant on them; it gave them mastery. When her father eventually died (and providing she evaded the unpleasant kinsman), she would be willed like a second-best bed to her brothers for keeping.

After all, unsupervised, the 'Roses' of this world might fall into sin and other mischiefs. How very pleasant!

'I'll not have any daughter of mine labouring for a living,' her father had decreed, slamming a fist on the table when the family had discussed her circumstances following her husband Oliver's death. 'You're a privy councillor's daughter, a Davison, and not some skinner's get.'

Sometimes Rose reckoned it would be easier if she was 'some skinner's get'. To have worn satin and the finest of lace round her throat and now make do with mourning doole seemed like failure. Was it sinful to yearn for her blissful childhood, when her father had supped with the greatest in the realm and she had played hide and seek with future earls and rich men's daughters?

'Here you are.' Her mother returned with a makeshift purse. 'This is all I can let you have. If you'd have stayed home like a virtuous widow, you wouldn't need to ask.'

'Mama, it was a history play about King Richard III and how he lost his throne.' She looked about her. 'Where do you keep the clothes brush now?'

'Theatres are naught but markets for bawds to find their customers,' her mother sermonised, still in the pulpit as she fetched the brush. Instead of handing it over, she grabbed Rose's skirt and delivered her anger in downward swipes. 'And if your King Richard was such a lackwit, I don't know why you bothered.' She shook out the folds then gathered the fabric to her face. 'Faugh! It still stinks. I doubt they'll let you into church in it. Fine for the theatre, though, it won't be noticed there, I warrant. How many hours was this history play? I've heard that the lazy knaves piss in the pits rather than go out to the jakes.'

'Yes, and pots for the gallery are 6d each for hire.'

'Ha, now you are gulling me, you wretched girl. Turn around! Let me do your ties.'

'Mama, you are being old-fangled. Why even Her Majesty likes the theatre.'

Catherine tugged the skirt down over Rose's bosom so hard that the stitches cried for mercy. 'Don't you rile me, you wicked girl! You know I'll not have her name spoken.' Checking that Rose's father was still slumbering, she continued in a fierce whisper, 'Sent to the Tower, his health ruined, his good name a byword for treachery, and us here on a pittance in Bartholomew Lane. But you don't think of how I still suffer. No, you go seeking trouble.'

'Mama, that's —'

'Well, I just pray that those foul Papists who attacked you haven't followed you here, my girl. Oh, we have paid a great price, a great price.' Then her jaw slackened. 'What, are you going so soon?'

'Yes. Plenty to do.' Rose bundled up her damaged clothes. 'I need to make sure my maid has returned safely.'

'You'll not wait for your father to wake up?'

'No, Mama. You said yourself that you don't want him to be concerned.'

'You know he gets upset about these things.'

'Yes, I know.'

Her mother followed her down the stairs. 'Leave by the back door, won't you?'

A swift check of the lane then she let herself out the wicker gate, startling two red kites gorging on a dead rat. No neighbours were in sight, so she leaned back against the fence and sleeved away her tears. Would she find turds smeared on the door of her lodging? She was so weary of it all. It was over five years now since her father had 'tricked' the queen about the death warrant.

Tricked? Yes, according to Her Majesty, Queen Mary's beheading had been a '*miserable* accident'. Not only had Elizabeth blamed the whole Privy Council, but she had also required a whipping boy for her royal conscience. Because Lord Burghley and Sir Francis Walsingham had been too craven to stand up to her and defend their gentle colleague, Rose's much respected father had been interrogated by the Star Chamber, fined outrageously and then sentenced to two years in the Tower of London at Her Majesty's Pleasure. Mercifully, that was what had kept him unscathed since his release: most of England's Papists believed he was still there.

Rose had been baptised Elizabeth to honour the queen, but after her father had been arrested, she refused to use it anymore, renaming herself 'Rose'. After marrying, she had dispensed with her family name too, becoming Mistress Rose Byrd. It had given her some protection. Except in February this year on the anniversary of Mary's execution, there had been another Papist pamphlet cursing her father, and people started remembering. So, after this afternoon's attack, Rose took care to meet no one's gaze as she walked back to her lodgings, especially as she passed the line of housewives queuing for water at Aldermanbury Conduit.

'Find a new husband to protect you,' her brothers had advised. Pah! Apart from Cousin Byng's nephew, her only other suitor had disappeared like pipe smoke the instant he learned who her father was.

'Hey, young mistress, good day to you.'

She looked up fiercely then hastily made the rider a curtsey. It was William Wade, clerk to the Privy Council, and one of her father's fair-weather friends.

The gentleman dismounted and, nodding to his groom to walk his horse, he drew her to the side of the street. 'This isn't like you, my dear, scurrying along with your face... Oh, is your father taken ill again? I was on my way from Wood Street to visit him.'

Really? She hid her scepticism. 'No, sir, he is well enough. It's me who is shaken. I was attacked again this afternoon.'

'Oh, my dear child.' Above the thick beard and moustache, Master Wade's eyes offered the kindness of a father, and she so needed kindness. 'By recusants?' he was asking. It was the government's polite name for Papists who refused to attend Protestant church — people who kept to the old Roman faith.

She nodded. 'I went to a play in Shoreditch with my brothers, you see, and maybe that was wrong but —'

'I'm not judging you,' he interrupted. 'But I'd like to hear what happened if you've time.' He led her into the nearby churchyard of St Mary's, shooed away a pair of almswomen and seated her on the steps of the preacher's cross. 'I don't want to get piles,' he explained, excusing the tidy cushion he made of his amber velvet cloak before he sat down beside her. 'Well, cough up, young woman. Better out than in!'

Sharing the story uncorked some of the anger and when he chuckled heartily about her hiding beneath the sheet, she smiled, too.

'Now a man wouldn't have had your quick wit to do that,' he applauded.

'A man wouldn't have needed to,' she answered, rueful that she was only pint-sized and female. Gazing up at the soaring flock of jackdaws making a thumbprint against the sky, she added, 'If only this business with my father were over, forgotten.'

Her companion managed an appropriately solicitous expression. If he still felt any share of guilt for her family's circumstances, she knew it would never be admitted.

Staring levelly at him, she said, 'I mean no treason but sometimes I wish that Queen Mary was still alive.'

The starched points of William Wade's moustache wobbled as he shook his head. 'No, never think that, my child. What your father achieved was something that neither Lord Burghley, Sir Robert Cecil nor any on the Privy Council could manage. Mind, how your dear father prevailed upon Her Majesty to sign I do not know, but, believe me, Mary Stuart's death was necessary for the security of the realm.

'But let's return to this day's matter, shall we? I'll have a look through my papers and see if any on our lists of recusants meet your description.'

'Sir, no, I want no one imprisoned on my behalf. People like them are … misguided.'

'Misguided, eh?' His eyebrows arched. 'Well, that's charitable of you but compassion doesn't safeguard us against traitors.'

She must not forget this man's authority, she thought warily.

'Compassion doesn't win wars, child,' he was saying, 'and this is a war! There is an enemy among us. An insidious enemy, like the harridans who threatened you — traitors who put their obedience to the Pope before their love for England.' The lines in his face seemed to harden with the intensity of his thoughts. 'Every week I receive reports of Jesuit priests being smuggled into this country, not to mention all manner of books and pamphlets calling for Englishmen — Englishmen, mark you! — to create terror among our people and rebellion against the queen.' His gaunt body heaved now with the fervour of his loyalty. 'You'd be amazed to read the daily reports from our intelligencers. Conspiracies funded by Spain to destroy our ships and plots to take Her Majesty's life. And this misguided — this *misguided* flock, as you call them — are looking for a new leader now Mary Stuart is beheaded, and sooner or later, someone will emerge. We have to be vigilant.'

It would have been treason not to agree. At her sad nod, the vehemence left him and he subsided back into a friendlier presence. 'Oh, child,' he exclaimed, patting her hand. 'Be proud of your father. The queen has never appointed another man to fill his office and he still has a pension. Lord Burghley and I saw to that. We stood by him.'

She bit back her true opinion. 'Well, I wish you might console my mother, sir. She never ceases to lament her former state.'

Wade drew in a deep, sad breath. 'No, I do not think that Catherine will ever forgive us.'

'Or forgive my father, sir.'

'You need a new husband to safeguard you. I can raise this with your father, perhaps.'

'I manage, sir.' Her marriage had been far from the Garden of Eden, more like a wasteland. Yes, she had known some affection from Oliver even though he had disliked being crossed, but the other side of the coin had been loneliness; the long months when he was on campaign and the pain of not knowing whether he would come home maimed or in a coffin.

'And you have sufficient income?'

The hint of a smile was necessary. 'I make do. Father gives me a token allowance.'

'Might it not be simpler for you to move back home?'

Her sparkle surfaced. 'Come, sir, would you have wished to live with your parents for the rest of your life?'

He winced good-humouredly. 'Indeed not, but to be male requires independence.'

'And to be female?' She rose to her feet. 'Another day, I'll dispute that with you, but to be honest, my mother and I do not trot easily side by side.'

'Yes, well, nothing to do about that, I daresay.' He lifted his palms in acceptance. 'I must bustle on and see your father.' Accepting her hand to help him up, he kept hold of her fingers longer than he should. 'What if I could put some money your way?' Then, he swiftly corrected, 'I do mean *honest* work.'

'Oh.' She smiled with relief and added eagerly, 'Father says I write a fair hand. I could do some copying if you are short of clerks.'

'No, we've plenty of those but...' A stare at her slender fingers. 'You've given me an idea. How would you like to see your family restored to Her Majesty's favour?'

Wade worked for Lord Burghley and Sir Robert Cecil, men with great influence over the queen. It would be folly to refuse.

'I think my family would be very grateful,' she said.

3

Every Englishman was expected to attend church on Sundays. Those who didn't could be fined and endure stern questioning; those who did hoped for a rattling good sermon, and because the parson of Bishopsgate was known for sulphurous language and some brilliant parables, St Helen's was already packed when Garrett arrived. He managed to squeeze into a pew on the old convent side where the nuns used to sit screened off from the laity. Shifting onto his knees, he suggested humbly to the Almighty that he could do with some divine help in decision-making.

It was Ferdinando Stanley's entitlement to the throne that whispered like Satan at Garrett's back. Two women and the Scots king had better claims, but his lordship was Protestant, English, male and mature. If the queen decided to choose him as her successor, Garrett would be performing valuable service for a future king. What better patron could he find? Should he risk his life for that possibility? On the other hand, becoming an informer was mucky, perilous, yet better than starving, and hadn't he been risking death every time he'd put on his boots in Ireland?

The Papists reckon we have a choice what happens to our souls, while the Protestants say it's already decided. So, tell me, Lord God, am I going up to Heaven or down to Hell?

He sat back on the wooden seat, resisted conversing with the gentleman next to him, thought a bit about the young woman at the theatre and looked around for her. No, she must be from a different parish. He did, however, recognise some of the citizens who had jeered when the Papists had been arrested.

The subtle exchanges in the congregation were coy, civil or superior depending on age and rank. Idly observing these, he suddenly froze. *He* was being watched and it wasn't just by the well-bosomed widow with wandering eyes. Although the gentleman a few rows forward made pretence of looking over his shoulder as though seeking friends, his gaze found Garrett, who let it be known with a lift of his chin that he'd noticed. Perhaps the man recognised him from the stage. That was all there was to it, except...

Except, the next day in Cheapside as he worked his way through a theatre shopping list for Burbage, Garrett realised he was being trailed along the slop stalls. This time it was a skinny jackstraw, unremarkable but stealthy, though not quick-witted enough to evade eventual capture. After leading the fellow through backstreets and alleys to test if he was following, Garrett waited behind a corner and grabbed him. 'You'd starve if you were a cutpurse. What the devil are you at in following me?'

'Wood Street,' replied the man doffing his cap with a grin. 'One o'clock today, outside the Compter.' Then as Garrett loosened his grip in amazement, the man bowed and scampered.

Curiosity, worse than a touting apprentice, tugged at his sleeve all morning and with his errands in Cheapside complete, Garrett leaned for a few minutes on the churchyard wall of St Mary-le-Bow and then decided to investigate Wood Street.

London was one of those cities where you could think yourself safe, but then cross an alley and find the neighbourhood had suddenly soured. Garrett found Wood

Street like that, full of splendid houses with carved timber until the Compter. Not a counting house but a prison! He stooped, making pretence of rearranging his load, and observed the building. Broad and of brick, it had three storeys and plentiful diamond-paned windows. Beyond the central arch, guarded by two pikemen in blue uniforms, he glimpsed an inner courtyard.

'Visiting a prisoner?' inquired a voice at his shoulder. An unpretentious ruff, long spade-cut beard and neat high-crowned hat embellished a shrewd face.

Garrett straightened, hiding his annoyance that he had been so acutely read. 'No, your worship, just curious.'

'It mainly holds harlots and debtors but being central, it has other uses. Towneley, is it? Come along, then.'

Garrett held his ground. Being a head taller helped. 'My mother always warned me not to wander off with strangers. Who might you be?'

'William Wade, Clerk to Her Majesty's Privy Council. Shall we?' A gloved hand indicated they should cross.

Wade? It took a moment to remember the conversation outside the cobbler's but any eagerness for employment was instantly doused as he realised they were heading into the prison. The interior of the hall — the stink of pisspails and cheap tallow — brought back memories of the few, foul days he had spent in the military gaol in Dublin.

His hand instinctively went to his scabbard as two guards stepped towards him.

'Is this man to be questioned, your worship?'

'Only by me,' replied his companion. 'Any messages this morning?'

'Yes, from Master Topcliffe at Bridewell, sir.'

Topcliffe! Garrett's blood ran cold. Even in Ireland, he had heard of the notorious torturer who racked men's limbs until they screamed for death. Had Bingham, his vindictive former commander, written to the government denouncing him as a troublemaker? Christ have mercy! Mouth dry, he tried not to show his shock as he followed Topcliffe's superior up the stairs to a door off the first landing.

With whitewashed walls and two windows overlooking the street, the large office was hardly a torture chamber, however, the parcels of documents tied with red cords stacked in piles upon the long trestle table might be confessions. A man in a dark gown, who Garrett recognised as the stranger who had stared at him in St Helen's Church, set down his quill and rose to his feet.

'Topcliffe said to tell you he has some new names, sir. The woman who was brought in yesterday for hiding the Jesuit has confessed there have been others this month.'

'I'll read the report later. Sit down, Towneley.' Dismissing the secretary from the chamber, Wade took the carved chair at the head of the table, leaving Garrett to place himself on his right, and drew a silver tray towards him. 'You'll partake of some small ale.'

'Thank you, no.'

'Actually, it wasn't a question. Here.'

Garrett managed the proffered tankard with one hand and no spillage despite it being almost full. He set it down without drinking and pulled off his leather gloves. 'Is this what you want to see?' he demanded, splaying his ruined hands upon the board.

A long stare before Wade's gaze rose back to his face. 'You can still manage a sword?'

'Yes.'

'Thank you,' spoken courteously. 'You may re-cover them now.'

With a grind of teeth, Garrett slid his palms out of sight, leaving his gloves on the table. 'Master Wade, if you'd like to step level with me now, I'd appreciate it. You are clearly a very busy man.'

For a moment, as his host took a slow draught from his ale cup, only a fly struggling to find a way through the window glass had anything to say. Garrett felt the sweat dampening his back. Then Wade leaned forward.

'I see your honour is as damaged as your fingers, Captain. Tell me about your disgrace.'

Garrett sat back and made a guess. 'Wouldn't that be a waste of time when *your honour* has already read Governor Bingham's account by now?'

'Perhaps. Tell me yours.'

If this was an interrogation, there would be some scrivener noting down the answers, but Wade still expected compliance. Garrett relented. Here was an opportunity to convince at least one member of Her Majesty's government that he was still employable. Telling his side would leech the poison of bitterness that had been slowly destroying him.

His host listened, rarely interrupting, save to clarify a point or two, and when Garrett was finished, gave his catlike smile. 'Exactly what I hoped,' he said.

Beneath the board, Garrett's remaining fingers made dents in his palms.

'You did well each time noting you were being observed. We need a new intelligencer in the Spanish Netherlands. You have, no doubt, heard of Colonel Sir William Stanley?'

Garrett stared at Wade like a mouse surprised in a pantry. Was this man privy to Ferdinando's proposal or was it an entirely separate offer or even some sort of test of his allegiance? Uncertain how to respond, the actor in him decided on bluster.

'That's… Are you likening me to Stanley?'

'No, but he would, I'm sure. Another disgraced, disgruntled officer. You would, of course, pretend to be a devout Papist, but after a week or two of rosary training, that would be easy. I'm sure you can convince Stanley you've been turned.'

Yes, he possibly could. Frankly, he didn't give a fig *how* men worshipped so long as they were tolerant, honest, compassionate and, well, Christian. However, such religious indifference expressed out loud in Elizabeth Tudor's England could burn him. Wade could burn him.

'Who do *you* answer to, your worship?' he probed. 'I mean, apart from God.'

Wade looked taken aback. 'For a start, I do not have to answer to the likes of you, sirrah. Nevertheless, it is a reasonable question. While I report to the Privy Council, I especially communicate with Sir Robert Cecil and his father, Lord Burghley, who has, of course, been Her Majesty's chief minister since she came to the throne. There will be no change of guard, Captain, though *some* might wish it.'

Some? Garrett managed a grave nod, wondering in panic how the Cecils — Burghley and son — regarded Ferdinando? Was he in their camp?

'Of course, there are established groups of Papist English traitors throughout Europe,' Wade continued, 'Rome, Prague, Madrid, but with your military training we feel that if you can inveigle yourself into Colonel Sir William's confidence, you will be able to provide a great deal of useful information. Who knows what bigger fish we may catch? We realise it won't happen overnight and building trust takes time, but getting you there as soon as possible is important.'

Bigger fish! This was some mighty dangerous maelstrom blowing up around him. If he turned down this offer, would they see him as disloyal? And how would Ferdinando react?

Garrett cleared his throat. 'I … well … we're not talking weeks here, are we, your worship? This could take me away for months, years even.'

'Come now, Garrett, you wanted to be a player. Isn't this a form of acting? Better than starvation. You could restore your reputation.'

'Yes, your worship, and there are crocks of gold at the ends of rainbows. All the world would see me as even more of a traitor.'

'It's not how the world sees Christopher Marlowe.'

'Marlowe? What, *Tamburlaine* and *The Jew of Malta* Marlowe? The playwright?'

'You would be replacing him, you see.'

Garrett whistled. Wade wanted *him* to replace Marlowe. Preposterous. The man must be bamming him.

'Marlowe is a like a gemstone,' observed Wade, lifting his hand into the sunlight for Garrett to observe the large sapphire adorning his forefinger. 'A clever, many-faceted creature. We feel a soldier like you would be much more dependable.'

'We?'

'The Privy Council. Her Majesty.'

Garrett blanched inwardly. Jesu! The previous day he'd asked for Divine help — but this! Heaven had him up against a wall. Seems he wasn't being given a choice, after all.

'But how would I report to you?' Something he had been going to ask Ferdinando.

'We intend to set you up with a false "betrothed". My instructions will be in your beloved's letters. You will write back to her. You can still write, can't you?'

'Yes.' Sullenly spoken.

'There could be a tap on the shoulder for you.'

Arise, Sir Garrett? About as likely as going to Paradise!

'How so? I mean no disrespect, your worship, but I observe that performing this service for Her Majesty has not earned you a knighthood.'

Wade blew out his cheeks. 'Hoist with my own petard. However, with the queen taking an interest and you being prettier than I am, let's consider it as a possibility. What say you? Captain's pay. Three shillings a day, paid into an account with one of the Lombards here. More than you'd get on stage.'

'Yes, but you only get pretend-killed on stage. An advance?'

'Definitely.' Wade rose, offering his hand. 'So, are we agreed?'

What to do? Garrett was over the proverbial barrel. How to explain his change of heart to an irate and powerful nobleman?

'Well, not quite agreed, begging your pardon,' he argued, picking up his gloves. 'I'd be a fool not to take time to consider. Will you have me killed if I refuse the work?'

'I could have you hauled in as a suspected heretic, man. After all, Ireland is a damnable nest of Popery. I want your answer by Thursday. Why are you smiling?'

Thursday! The day after he was to meet Ferdinando at the Theatre. Garrett nearly burst out laughing. The irony would have been comic if it wasn't so cursed gut-chilling. 'I'm smiling,' he began, trying to think what answer would content this man. 'Soldiering, acting, spying, they all quicken the blood, don't they? What quickens yours, Master Wade?'

Fortunately, the older man did not take it as impertinence. 'Outwitting Her Majesty's enemies, Captain Towneley. You'd be wise to see it that way, too.'

True to his word, Ferdinando came to the theatre; not to the gallery, where he left his entourage, but alone to the tiring room. Garrett expected to be swiftly drawn aside to give his answer but the nobleman seemed in no haste. In fact, his lordship was inclined to sit down and had to be moved several times as the props were needed. There was no doubt he was enjoying himself. Perhaps there was envy beneath the lordly façade. In fact, Garrett wondered if the earl's son had ever trod the boards in disguise.

Now he had played in *Richard III*, Garrett recognised the order within the chaos as the players rushed to change their costumes. He even felt envious at being out of the frenzy, no longer the Second Murderer or the First Citizen. 'Lady Anne' was wriggling out of his kirtle to become the oldest prince; Lewis had the barrel ready in which they would soon drown the Duke of Clarence, and — required for the next scene — Burbage, who was playing Richard, exited the stage, collapsed on Henry VI's coffin and mopped the sweat from his brow. 'My blessed back is agony. No wonder Crookback Dick died at Bosworth.'

'But very bravely,' corrected his lordship. 'Stayed on his horse and rode straight at Richmond. Almost killed him before my ancestor's men closed in so Richard can't have been that crippled.'

'Ah, but it's not just Richard I'm playing, is it, my lord? Did you hear our audience's mirth, note the elbowing? They knew.' Seeing Garrett's confused expression, Burbage hunched his shoulder and mouthed, 'Sir Robert Cecil.'

'Christ!' Garrett turned, expecting to find disapproval in Ferdinando's face, but his lordship's subtle smirk implied encouragement. 'But this could put you all in the Tower,' he gasped.

'Just coincidence, Towneley, of course,' Ferdinando answered smoothly. 'I mean, would a man so important as Sir Robert Cecil openly acknowledge a likeness to himself? No, I don't think so. It would not benefit his reputation one iota. I'll be upstairs.'

Unhappily, Garrett watched him go through to the staircase. Expected to follow, he waited a moment or two then slipped away. He'd just seen a different side to his lordship. Tweaking Sir Robert Cecil's tail showed courage but whether his lordship was motivated by amusement, rebelliousness or downright recklessness...?

His mouth was dry at the thought of refusing. Caught like a hapless flea between two thumbnails, he was, and he'd be making his will if he had anything to leave anyone.

He found Ferdinando alone in the familiar long room in the adjoining building, and as he entered, the nobleman set a small leather bag upon the table. 'There's a ship sailing from Queenhithe on Friday. Shall you be on it?'

Curious as to what he would be missing, Garrett stepped forward and shook out the contents. A gold ring. With a wry face, he replaced it and pushed the bag back towards its owner. 'The answer would have been yes, my lord, except this week everything's become more complicated.'

Only the slight rise of the slashed blue velvet doublet across his lordship's breast indicated astonishment and possibly anger. 'Complicated?'

'That's the word, my lord.'

Ferdinando leaned back against the table and folded his arms. 'Go on.'

'I've been approached by William Wade, Clerk to the Privy Council, to serve Her Majesty's government with the self-same work — I mean, as an informer in your cousin's army. It seems a remarkable coincidence. Did your lordship suggest that?'

If Ferdinando wanted to seem unmoved, he was performing well. 'No, I have no dealings with William Wade. How do *you* explain it?'

'Me, my lord? Why, only that I had been asking around for work, my lord.' He did not say when. 'I met this man-at-arms and he must have put a word in.'

'And you informed Wade of my offer?'

'No, a plague on that, my lord! Unless some knave overheard us or —' He did not like to imply that Lady Derby was untrustworthy. Jesu! Was someone listening in now? He slid a suspicious gaze along the oak panelling. 'If need be, I can find the soldier and ask him.'

'I'm prepared to believe you.' His lordship pensively rubbed a finger along a crack in the table board. 'Wade is Sir Robert Cecil's creature. Damn! It could be that they see you as Christopher Marlowe's replacement. Kit, stupid wretch, was counterfeiting money in the Low Countries and is likely to face charges in the Star Chamber.'

A scream came from below the open window; on stage Queen Margaret was cursing Gloucester.

'Did Marlowe work for you, my lord?'

'As an agent? No, only as a playwright at the Rose.' His lordship sighed. 'Kit's a brilliant writer but such a complex man. Yes, I was once proud to be his patron, but there are some lines that you do not cross.' He walked over to the casement and stood staring down with a grave expression. 'I admit that his absence has let Will Shakespeare's star shine brighter but I would not wish Kit's creativity snuffed out. I know Archbishop Whitgift wants him nailed for atheism. I rather fear he will be sent to the Tower or, if he isn't...' He drew the window closed and then made sure Garrett clearly understood. 'It doesn't take much to hire assassins, Captain Towneley, so don't ever let Wade find out that your first loyalty is to me or you will end up … *punished*.' He faced him across the board. 'It *is* to me, isn't it? Your loyalty?'

'Wait on, my lord,' Garrett protested. 'I have not yet agreed to *any* of this.'

'Then let me help you decide, Towneley. I think you should warm to Wade's proposal.'

'You do, my lord?' This was a surprise.

'Yes. Two fees, eh?' The ring bag was slid his way like a chess pawn.

Garrett stared at its leather drawstring. 'You mean I should *still* work for you?'

'Why not? Wade doesn't need to know of our arrangement. Listen, Towneley, all I want is an untroubled life, however, my birthright means that ambitious men like Sir Robert Cecil and Lord Essex — *particularly Lord Essex* — would love to discover me tangled up in some conspiracy to make myself king. That's one of the reasons I used my mother's house for our meeting and why I now speak with you here. So, what say you?'

Garrett needed to weigh his answer with a goldsmith's care, especially if this nobleman had a royal future and decades of life ahead.

'Is it that hard?' his lordship persisted. 'There's no treason in this. I only require word if you hear anything that might endanger my life or members of my family. You can manage that, surely?'

Could he? Fly into such a web, with three hungry spiders to please: Ferdinando, Wade *and* Colonel Sir William. It was already enough to addle his own poor brain and he hadn't even set foot across the Channel. Next thing, some lackey of the King of Spain would be jingling a bag of ducats at him.

'Your pardon, but why are you willing to trust me on such brief acquaintance, my lord?'

'Ah, I never mentioned this last week but your name is not unknown to me. I know more than you told me. Excellent military service in Connacht in '86, risking your captaincy by accusing your commander's brother of slaughtering Dutch mariners without a fair trial. No, don't interrupt! Having the courage to speak up against corruption and malpractice. And I've another reason as well. Do you recall being at a performance of Marlowe's *Tamburlaine* with a young woman and some others?'

Garrett dredged his memory. Ah yes, with Katherine and her friends. 'Yes, yes, I do, and on the way home we came across a man being set upon.'

'I was told you went to his rescue with your fists.'

The others had watched but courageous Katherine had whacked the puniest of the two cutpurses in the belly with someone's broom. 'The thieves got away, though.'

'That man you helped was one of my most valued servants — God rest his soul, he died of plague last year — but he told me of the incident and how you had given him your name but refused any reward. He made inquiries about you, that's how I found out about your military reputation. Anyway, by the time he'd discovered where you were staying, you'd left the city.'

'That was several years back. You have a long memory, my lord.'

'For those who have done me favours, yes — and for those who have done me harm. You can judge a man by the decisions he makes in the heat of the moment.'

'The young woman I took to the play was another man's wife, my lord. Doesn't that argue dishonesty and immorality on my part?'

Lord Strange shook his head. 'Not in my ledger, it doesn't. I told you we made inquiries. The wife's neighbours were quick to divulge that her husband cruelly beat her when he was in his cups. She probably only knew happiness when she was with you. Do you still see her?'

'No, my lord, both she and her husband died of the plague.'

His lordship nodded in sympathy. 'I'm sorry.' Ringed, tapered fingers flexed. 'However,' he said with a sigh, 'let's deal with the present matter, shall we? I was hoping you could leave in two days' time but now Wade has moved into the game, we mustn't be hasty. He will need to instruct you so let him make all the arrangements and pay for your crossing. What's your answer, Towneley?'

A fork in the crossroads of his life. Good money, no hostage to fortune and if he survived, maybe he could return and join one of the acting troupes. Better still, join the household of a future king. Spying still stank, but he didn't want to sleep in the ruddy open again with rats using him as a highway. If this Colonel Stanley was amassing an army to invade England and ferment a civil war that would see innocent people slaughtered just because they celebrated Mass differently, then he needed to be stopped.

A violent knocking crashed through his reasoning. His hand went straight to his rapier hilt, but it was only the sewing woman, Maria, who hurtled in. 'We can't find "Sir James Tyrell" for the next scene, my lord,' she panted.

'Well, don't look at me,' muttered his lordship dryly.

The woman was already thrusting a shabby cloak into Garrett's astonished arms. 'It'll have to be you, soldier. Will says make haste!'

'What? But I haven't —'

'Will says you know the play by heart and Burbage will help you.' She tugged hard at his arm.

'Make a decision, Towneley,' Ferdinando commanded, and it was not about acting.

'Very well, I'll do it, my lord.'

He had taught himself to juggle knives as a boy. Serving three masters was a similar matter of skill and mindfulness.

Or so he hoped.

Thinking up a believable excuse for disappearing from their company taxed Garrett's powers of creativity as he sat drinking with Burbage and Shakespeare at The Swan alehouse in Bishopsgate. Next day he would be swallowed into the gullet of Whitehall Palace and crammed with ciphers and codes.

'You've found employment, then?' boomed Burbage. Shakespeare, more discerning, nudged him to lower his voice. 'If we ask no questions, Dick, then we are told no lies.'

'I can see he's squirming, Will. You've not taken the work at the stew by the bearpits, have you, Garrett? They've been looking for someone to bang heads together.'

'Dick!'

'Pax vobiscum,' intoned Burbage, drawing a benediction in the air. 'Then, since you are now in the money, friend Towneley, you can buy the next round.'

Apart from several lessons improving his rapier skill at Saviolo's Fencing School on Ludgate Hill, Garrett spent the following week with Arthur Gregory, Wade's chief codebreaker. He was schooled until he was ripe to be spat out like Jonah from the whale and able to ask for ale and pickled herring in Flemish, repeat prayers in Latin, plus memorise loving phrases that translated into enemy troop movements and other informative morsels. Once verbally equipped, he was to be shipped from Gravesend and unloaded at the bustling port of Antwerp, except he had not yet received his final instructions from Wade.

He was summoned to Whitehall the day before he was due to sail.

'Colonel Stanley and his troop are frequently on the move so when you reach Antwerp, you need to find out his whereabouts. I suggest you go to the house of Richard Verstegan and see if he will help you. Present yourself as exactly what you are, a discontent, aggrieved soldier. Name the bastards who wronged you — Bingham, Fitzwilliam. If you play your cards right, Verstegan should give you a Letter of Introduction to present to Colonel Sir William. Make things much easier.'

'And who exactly is this Verstegan?'

'He's a Papist printer and a cunning smuggler,' replied Wade. 'And don't be taken in by his nice manners, he's as dangerous as a prodded viper.'

'That's reassuring,' muttered Garrett dryly. 'Do you have an address?'

'Yes, but you shall not have it. Play the stranger. You're "on the turn", remember, willing to kiss the Pope's arse if it will bring you work.'

'Sounds a tad unsubtle.'

'Don't play clever with me, Towneley. You know exactly what is required.'

'Your pardon. You haven't mentioned where in London I'm supposed to direct my "love letters".' Arthur Gregory, care of Whitehall, doesn't quite take the mustard.'

'I was coming to that. St Albans.' He read the surprise in Garrett's eyes. 'We are moving some of our clerks out of London before the plague season hits again. We lost some very bright people last year. The name you will write to is Rose Byrd.' He spelled it out. 'BYRD.'

Better than Rose Bud or Mistress Black Bird, but he bit down on that quip.

'One last thing. Someone else desires to meet you.'

Wade led the way through several sets of doors, each manned. It had to be Lord Burghley, Garrett surmised, glad he had put on a clean shirt beneath his doublet. The old man must be in his seventies.

Lute music and chatter. It was the queen who sat in a chair before the fire, her aged face away from the sunlight flooding through the diamond windowpanes.

'Hat!' hissed Wade.

Garrett snatched it off and had to be led forward.

'Ah, the soldier.' She held out a hand to be kissed. Garrett fell to one knee and lowered his face to the white creped skin, a vein beneath his lips. Then he dared to smile. Wouldn't his old commander be livid with rage if he knew that Garrett was being given an audience with Queen Elizabeth Tudor.

'You are much better looking than Kit Marlowe,' she purred. Her ladies laughed politely. Garrett shook a little. So it was true. He was a replacement for Christopher Marlowe. But wasn't Marlowe imprisoned in the Tower? 'We didn't want another playwright,' she was saying. 'We are informed you are a friend of Master Shakespeare's. When you see him again, tell him we would like another comedy.'

Garrett nodded.

'Towneley is to sail for Antwerp tomorrow, ma'am.' Sir Robert Cecil stood to one side. Oh God, he was hunched, so like Burbage's version of Richard III.

'Don't let our enemies turn you, Master Towneley.' The queen's eyes were brown, her skin daubed with white cosmetic, her lips thin. She must have been extraordinarily attractive once, but now…

'My loyalty is to Your Majesty, I assure you.' He wanted to say he had been in her service since he was fourteen.

'You are not an atheist like Marlowe, I trust?'

'No, nor a wordsmith, Your Majesty.' A nod and the long royal fingers dismissed him. Not a wordsmith, he repeated to himself, as he rose. The cold chill of panic remained as he bowed and shuffled backwards to the doors; if he got the love letters wrong, it might be a very slow and ugly death.

4

Tucked down the mouth of the Scheldt River on the east bank, the bustling Dutch port of Antwerp made London's weekday quays seem quiet as a Sunday. The variety of flags blowing about on the carrack masts spoke of vessels from all points of the compass and the workmen busy at the derricks ranged from winter-pale Baltics to tall, sinewy Nubians.

It was raining as the longboat set Garrett ashore and at every step along the quay, he was pestered by either officials wanting to see his travel papers or peddlers trying to gull him into buying counterfeit diamonds. Yes, he had clear instructions from Wade: to present himself as a discontent at the house of a printer named Richard Verstegan, but he was far from comfortable. Antwerp belonged to England's greatest enemy.

Spain had held the Low Countries for over a hundred years. As a boy, Garrett remembered the jubilation in England when the Dutch Protestants had rebelled against King Philip. They now had a free republic in the north so only the southern provinces remained under Spanish governance — Catholic governance — that could send heretics like him to the Inquisition. He was glad of the cross about his neck and the rosary on his belt but these trinkets were no armour should he arouse suspicion of the authorities. Think like a soldier, he told himself. Memorise the streets as you go, observe, learn.

He left the quay and discovered that behind its gaudy port, Antwerp was showing its ribs. It needed fattening. The city walls and many of the warehouses carried scars of the siege and ransacking by the Spanish seven years earlier, and some of the doors he passed were pitted with artillery shots. Many of the shops were boarded up. Rotting signs, English, Dutch, Jewish, spoke of flight, investments shifted. However, restoration was more in evidence as he reached the city's heart. The cathedral had half a tower missing (had they run out of money?), but the finished spire was a masterpiece. Lace in stone, it soared, delicate and slender. The city hall also looked recent but Garrett considered it lacked grace. For him, it was in the Grand Place that the riches of Antwerp shone. Golden adornments glinted on the stepped gables and costly glass panes brooched the merchants' houses. Here was the splendour! How many jewels had slid across the green baize tables of trade behind those illustrious walls?

He did not want to ask directions. After Protestant London, it felt odd to see men of holy orders in the street, or niches bearing gaudy new statues of the Virgin Mary with her face unsmashed. Patrols of the Spanish governor's red-breeched soldiers were everywhere, well equipped with helmets and armour. Twice he was halted in the main square and asked to provide an explanation for his presence. The second time, because of the language dilemma, he truly thought he would end up in a Spanish gaol, yet a passer-by — an Irishman not a Fleming — not only intervened but cheerfully directed him to Verstegan's house. It wasn't by chance.

Wade had forewarned him: 'Have a shave in Antwerp and within the hour Verstegan will know what you said to the barber. The moment your soles touch the land, someone will report your arrival to him.' That seemed right. He recalled seeing the same Irishman loitering down on the quay.

'Remember when you deal with Verstegan,' advised Wade, 'keep your story as close to the truth as possible. If you fail, expect to be bagged and exported to the Spanish Inquisition.'

Not surprisingly, he was ratcheted tense as a primed crossbow as he arrived at Verstegan's, a four-storeyed house with carved wooden shutters and crow-steps gable. He was shown into a library walled with dark oak panels and floored with black and white tiles. Religious tracts occupied the shelves along two walls but there were treatises on soldiering, too, ones he almost knew by heart, like William Garrard's *The Arte of Warre*. Above the fireplace hung an engraving of a man being burned at the stake and curiosities crowded a sideboard: bizarre shells, a scatter of injured coins, ancient pilgrim badges, a little casket reliquary and a delicate miniature diptych.

'*Es mundus excrementi!*' The ugly voice came from a cage by the window. A flap of testy feathers and the African grey parrot repeated its insult.

'Forgive him his foul language, sir. His chickhood was in one of Rome's bordellos.' A gentleman in his early forties stood in the doorway behind Garrett. With his flaxen hair and brown eyes, he looked Flemish, but his dialect was homegrown English. 'You know the rules, Pius,' he scolded, crossing the room.

'*Futue te ipsil,*' shrieked the bird as its cage was covered.

'Your bird speaks Latin?'

Its owner turned, his shrewd gaze growing more temperate. 'Oh, Pius can swear in many tongues.' He held out an ink-tipped hand. 'I'm Richard Verstegan.'

Apart from the bird dropping on one of the round-toed shoes and a downy feather clinging to the sleeve of his black overgown, the man looked scholarly. According to Wade, he was also a skilled goldsmith, engraver, writer, printer and the spider at the heart of the Papist web, a correspondent of cardinals, kings and commoners.

'Garrett Towneley.'

Immediately realising that only half of his guest's glove was occupied, Verstegan made the inevitable enquiry, exclaimed his sympathy and waved Garrett to a cushioned chair by the hearth.

'You keep pigeons, Master Verstegan?'

'Indeed, I do. I appreciate their intelligence — in all meanings of the word.' His gold-ringed middle finger stroked the polished arm of his chair. 'So, satisfy my curiosity, young man. Who was it in London recommended that you call on me?'

'No one, your worship.' Garrett had been made to spend an afternoon reading Verstegan's banned books (Wade had a complete set). 'I found your account of the blessed Edmund Campion's execution very moving, sir, and *Theatrum Crudelitatum Haereticorum Nostri Temporis* as well.' Gruesome illustrations of cruel deaths. Exaggerated, too. Or so Garrett hoped.

Verstegan snorted. 'Really? How did you manage to get hold of those? I thought most of the copies in England had been bonfired.'

'Not in Ireland, sir. They were passed around the army.'

Verstegan's doublet swelled. 'Were they, indeed? Excellent, excellent.' Then he slapped his hands down on his black breeched knees. 'I expect you are hungry. Let's have some refreshment, eh?' He rang a little brass handbell.

Garrett inwardly crossed himself. So far, all to the good, but since he had arranged no lodging yet in the city, he'd need to keep this visit to the purpose, say as little as possible.

'So why are you here, young man?'

'I was wondering, your worship, if you happen to know the whereabouts of Colonel Sir William Stanley?'

'Do you carry letters to him?'

'No. I should like to join his army.'

Verstegan rose, consulted his bookshelves and withdrew a folded map. 'At this very hour, his regiment is outside Nijmegen. Know where that is? About a hundred miles north-east from here, just across the border from the United Provinces. Here!' He let Garrett spread the map upon the tiled floor. 'See, they're there. Bit too far for the morrow, eh?'

Garrett got down on his knees for a closer look. Wade's clerks had made him study a map of the Low Countries; this one was better. His groan was not feigned as he sat back. 'I thought … ah well, no matter. Seems like I'll have to buy a horse.'

While Verstegan's servant served them with crisp sweet griddlecakes, he studied the map further, estimating how long it would take to reach the regiment.

'The roads are good.' His host traced the way between Antwerp and the Waal River, south of Nijmegen. 'The camp will come south eventually. Has to move around else it gets high on the nose with the local people. You'd know that coming from the military.'

'Yes, I do,' Garrett agreed with feeling. 'Why there, though? Do they suspect the Dutch Republic is planning an attack?'

Clearly wary of the direct question, his host hesitated before he answered. 'No, the colonel is just familiarising his men with the borderland region, should that occurrence ever happen. Now you said you want to enlist?'

'That's the plan, your worship.'

'Know much about Colonel Stanley, do you?'

'I know he changed sides in '87. Turned a town over to the Spanish, isn't that what happened?'

Verstegan nodded and jabbed the river Ijssel, some thirty miles north-east of Nijmegen. 'It was here. Deventer. The

Dutch Protestants were trying to take over the Netherlands and Elizabeth Tudor, God rot her, sent over an army under her lover, foolish old Leicester, to help the bastards. *Qualem blennum*, eh Pius?

'Anyway, Leicester's force captured the towns of Zutphen and Deventer, and Sir William was put in charge of Deventer's garrison with a force of six hundred men. Fortunately, he decided at that point to change sides and surrender the town to the Spanish. Half his force, a lot of them Irish, stayed with him. His fellow captain, Rowland Yorke, did the same with Zutphen.' Verstegan didn't add that both towns had been retaken and were now part of the Dutch United Republic.

'Must have made Leicester look a right turnip,' commented Garrett. 'And how many men does Sir William have now?'

'Oh, easily double. Good Catholics like yourself joining every day. Doesn't suffer ditherers. Valuable man, Stanley. His military muscle will be crucial, but staying informed counts as well, Master Towneley. Knowing the grain from the chaff, where the chess pieces are. We all do our humble bit.'

'Humble' was debateable. Over goblets of jenever, with the bird muttering sulky obscenities, Garrett learned how his host had become the connection, the glue, 'the hub' of all the English exiles. A veritable Papist Walsingham!

As if written evidence was needed, Verstegan showed him a letter of commendation bearing King Philip's signature and then took him down to his printing press. It was indeed a business. Subversive tracts and engravings; scurrilous sketches — one of Elizabeth with withered breasts in bed with humpbacked Sir Robert Cecil and a large cod-pieced Lord Essex; bread and butter books in Dutch and Flemish; and multiple copies of tomes that would earn a prison sentence if owned in England.

'These would not be easy to smuggle over, your worship,' Garrett probed hopefully.

'Ways and means, young man.' A tight smile.

Returning upstairs, Garrett clinked glasses with him yet again, careful not to overindulge. Wisely so, for Verstegan finally drew rein on his own merits and whipped the conversation around to his guest's soldiering experience and faith. Garrett thought himself answering well until Mistress Verstegan joined them. Demure and delicate was his first impression for she was tiny and narrow-waisted, but he was wrong in assuming her meek; the cart of conversation took a dangerous bend.

'Do you have a wife, Captain Towneley?' It seemed an innocent inquiry, softly asked as she sat down with a small sewing frame.

He managed a sheepish look. 'I have a betrothed, a widowed gentlewoman.' Yes, with whiskers and a clerk's salary.

'Is she well to do? No, Richard, do not frown so. Women like to know these things. You don't mind me asking, do you, Captain?'

He *did* mind. Clearing his throat, he said, 'She has been left comfortable, sufficient to rent a small house.'

'How fortunate, let us hope you have no rivals for her affection.' The lady's needle glinted. 'May I ask where she lives?'

There was no way he could be vague without arousing their suspicion. 'St Albans, mistress.'

The needle stilled. 'Ah, it is a most agreeable town, is it not? And not too far from London. Is her house in one of the streets near the clocktower? We know the place well, don't we, Richard?'

Hell! Garrett squirmed inwardly. 'That I cannot tell you, mistress. She was moving there after I sailed — they are predicting a bad plague summer in London.'

'Probably wise. The rooks are building high this year.' Watching his hostess threading a new silk, he thought himself off the rack until she asked, 'Is she is of the true faith?'

'Yes, of course.'

Verstegan filled the small glasses again. 'Older than you if she's a widow?'

'No.' Garrett feigned a laugh. 'Not unless she has lied about her age.'

'Comely?'

He quickly needed to picture a woman. Remembering the girl in the pit, he gave a sigh. 'She's as sweet as violets. Forgive me, Mistress Verstegan, but this conversation reminds me how I shall sorely miss her.'

'Oh, that is charming, Captain. What is she called?'

'Rose.'

'Not a Mistress Bud?' she teased.

'No.' Thank God Wade had invented a woman for him. 'Byrd, Mistress Rose Byrd.'

'And she will be waiting anxiously for your letters, I'm sure.'

'Ah, yes,' said Verstegan, rising to poke some more life out of the fire. 'You must let me handle your letters home, Towneley. I flatter myself that I have a very reliable system.'

'You are kind, sir, but, of course, I shall not be in Antwerp.' The last thing he needed was his reports going through this couple's hands. They would be sure to have ways of opening seals without detection. He got to his feet. 'The hour grows late, and I have taken too much of your time. Thank you for your kindness and your assistance.'

'But you must sup with us — a carbonade stew tonight, eh, my dear?'

'Of course. He is most welcome.' Mistress Verstegan set her work aside. 'We would appreciate your company and we always keep a chamber for guests of the true faith.' The play of glances between the couple told Garrett that little was undisclosed between them, especially when the lady added, 'Why do you not write a letter to your widow and assure her that you have not been swallowed by a whale or taken captive by pirates.'

'I think I have imposed long enough, good mistress.'

'Nonsense, you shall stay. I'll show you to your room and you'll have time to write before supper. Bring it down when you've finished, and you can use Richard's sealing wax.'

On his own at last, Garrett discovered that while Verstegan had been showing him the printing press, Mistress Verstegan or one of their servants had been checking through his bag. His small writing board was now facing a different way.

With a sigh, he put pen to paper and not daring to use any of the double-meaning terms that the cipher clerks had given him, he wrote a simple love letter.

Try making anything of that, Master Verstegan!

Outside he heard the beat of wings in the courtyard as a pigeon was tossed heavenward; Sir William Stanley was about to be advised that another recruit was on the way. Or so he thought.

On the morrow Verstegan conducted him to a respected horse dealer and by mid-morning he was out of Antwerp. With the Low Countries being — well — low, his dun gelding managed over twenty miles a day. Although there had been times in Ireland when he had ridden hard, he took care not to overwork the beast. The journey took four days. Four days for his tiresome mind to juggle with ifs and maybes and whys? Deception still bothered him, though he was beginning to acknowledge that Master Wade had not underestimated the threat to Protestant England. The beerhouses he had supped at each evening were full of rumours that the King of France, Henri IV, was about to turn Catholic and that was troubling. Elizabeth's England would be left without allies save for a few Lutheran states. The time was ripe for another armada. Maybe playing the spy was worthy after all.

Fear rode with him; concern about the welcome he'd receive from Colonel Stanley. What if the pigeon message from Verstegan had been '*Clap him in irons on his arrival*'?

Panic was ruddy unheroic he told himself as he finally saw the forest of pennons and knew he had found the colonel and must cross the Tiber. Garrett hid his misgivings as he convinced the regiment's outer sentries to let him through. Then, as he rode past the tethered horses and unhitched wagons, and smelt the smoky air, his misgivings fell away like broken fetters; the old familiar feel of an army camp revived his courage.

He could do this.

Estimating the number of tents that he could see from horseback, he realised that Verstegan had been right about the numbers. If they were swashbuckling and thumbing their noses at the Dutch Republic, it wasn't today. Today was at half-cock: a dozen butts had been set up but only a few archers were practising; clusters of men sat playing at dice, several were making repairs to their equipment and plenty were just sitting around the campfires. Too slack, too idle. Already Garrett itched to impose some changes. Yet as he was led up the camp's street and across the 'market square' to the colonel's pavilion, he needed to remind himself that this army might be used against his own countrymen.

Ferdinando's traitor cousin, Colonel Sir William Stanley, was an imposing man of King Henry VIII-like proportions, even down to the cut of his bristly whiskers above the generous ruff. Had Garrett been a young recruit, he'd have been overawed; instead, he noticed the stick beside the chair, the back cushion and the wince of pain as the older man rose to greet him.

'Well, well, one of old John Towneley's impoverished by-blows. Last time I heard of you, lad, you were clobbering the hell out of the wretched Irish. What's changed? That bugger Bingham had it in for you?'

'Change of heart, Commander. If you can do it, by God's will, I can, too.' Briefly, he felt a flush of pride that Colonel Stanley had heard of him. Or had his military service been reduced to concise phrases around the pigeon's leg?

It seemed not when he asked. No feathery arrivals from Antwerp. It made him uneasy that Verstegan had given no recommendation. However, talk slid easily to the various campaigns in Ireland and 'whatever happened to so-and-so?' and by the time the colonel hedged round to where Garrett's religious loyalties lay, the relationship wheels were turning sweetly, greased with mutual respect. Of course, the phrase 'try you out' was sensibly aired before Sir William sent for his second-in-command.

A rapier of a man on the cusp of forty, Jacques de Francesci of Antwerp was swarthy as an Italian with his crow beard and olive skin. No soldierly garb for him. He was clothed in black, relieved only by the pectoral cross gleaming against his silken doublet. Like two stranger dogs, there was a twitch of tilted noses as Garrett and he assessed each other with instinctive dislike. It was no surprise that de Francesci's questions were serrated with suspicion, but the colonel had made his mind up.

Ferdinando had proved right in his prediction that Garrett's vast military experience would be welcome; the formidable soldier had already taken to him like a famished raven seizing a meat gobbet. Mind, to his disgust, Garrett emerged from Stanley's quarters with only the rank of sergeant, but then he had anticipated it would be a snail climb up the gritty path to the colonel's intimate circle.

By that afternoon, he was set to training Irish new recruits how to use Spanish artillery. It felt good. Despite his damaged hands, despite his blighted reputation, he was no longer on the dung heap of Tudor England.

While Garrett could admire Sir William for persuading the King of Spain into funding this raggle-taggle force, he soon realised the difficulties that the tenacious old battle horse confronted. Keeping the dissidents' morale vertical, their bellies full and their campfires stoked, especially on this windy plain, where they had hacked down most of the trees for firewood, were daily challenges. To make matters worse, while they might be within glaring distance of the walls of republican Nijmegen, that city was tantalisingly beyond the pale for the discontented — rather like coming down with leprosy on sighting Holy Jerusalem after a year's walk in uncomfortable sandals. The men grumbled how weary they were of stockfish and Dutch herrings, so poaching was rife and anything with prickles, scales, fur or whiskers had been hunted, fished, trapped and eaten, much to the fury of the local villagers. However, unlike Her Majesty's soldiers, Stanley's force was paid regularly, and their pensions of Spanish ducats were discreetly conveyed into the camp in firkins.

As a sergeant, Garrett missed out on the better fare served at the colonel's table; he also missed out on useful information. His instructions were to inform Wade about any visitors who held close conference with Colonel Stanley in his chambers; any undesirables being dispatched imminently to British shores (such as Spanish armadas, Jesuits and assassins); and somehow send the information back without arousing suspicion. Ha!

At Whitehall, the cipher clerk had given him a code list to memorise. Verstegan was 'books', Colonel Stanley was 'love', de Francesci 'desire', Philip II was 'fortune'; and there were codes for other Spaniards and place names in the Low Countries. Burn, fire, hunger, embrace, lips, kisses, bosom, duckies, heart, arms, fingers, breath: all had a meaning.

That first Sunday, concocting his first coded letter had him cursing, especially as he had little to report save that he'd enlisted. Would Wade be able to work out that the army was at the eastern border?

No words can yet express what I truly wish to say.

Books have I found, but now I am already acquainted with love and dark desire, it is as though standing on the edge of this known world I behold the sun in the east for the first time in my life.

Then he added:

I long to hold your fragrant body in my arms, breath in the sweet smell of you. Can you believe, my darling, how lusty such imagining makes me feel.

Half of it was twaddle; the other half could get him killed. Now he had to send it.

There were couriers. Myntar, a former tailor, served as one of the colonel's carriers to associates in Brussels or across the French border. The common soldiers relied on Laurence, a crony of Verstegan's, who regularly travelled up from Antwerp.

'You can't give it to me,' protested the fellow in a broad Yorkshire accent, when Garrett waylaid him. 'Letters have to go through Master Damporte, Sir William's lawyer.'

'God's teeth, I'm not buying a plot of land,' protested Garrett. 'This is to my betrothed and it's private. Take it!'

Laurence kept his hands on his flanks. 'That's what they all say. Rules is you give in the letters first thing at sparrow fart and I carry 'em out after noon, so if you want your wagtail to hear from you before Judgement Day, Sergeant, you'd better take it over to Damporte *tout de suite*.' He fished out his pocket dial and angled it. 'Aye, I'm leavin' in next quarter hour so you best be quick. There lies your way.' He jabbed a finger at one of the more expensive tents.

Well, at least it might earn him acquaintance with one of Sir William's inner circle. Inside the tent were two scriveners with writing boards and a knife-nosed, spectacled wight in a lawyer's gown sitting at a small desk.

'You left it late.' Disinterested, the latter held out a hand without looking up. 'Thank you, that will be all. No, wait! You've sealed it,' he complained in disgust, seizing a penknife.

'A murrain on that,' exclaimed Garrett with fake outrage, returning to snatch it back. 'It's a love letter.'

For the first time, the lawyer deigned to regard him. 'You do want it sent?'

'Yes.'

A disdainful hand was held out. 'Then it will have to be read and checked, won't it? Some of our letters fall into the wrong hands. Come!'

With blatant sheepishness, Garrett surrendered it for the lawyer's perusal then hid his amusement as Damporte's ears pinkened against his cap. 'Hmm. You must be quite a lad in bed.' Bringing the paper close to his face, the man sniffed it thoroughly.

'Does the paper smell do something for you, Master Damporte?'

A pompous glare and a rabbit twitch of nose. 'Of course not. But *you* might use lemon or onion juice between the lines.'

'Why should I do that?' Garrett blustered, enjoying himself.

The lawyer glanced down again at the juiciest phrases with a tight smile. 'I see your point. It's fragrant enough in ink. However, what if you were an enemy intelligencer? Hmm?'

'Ah. Plenty of lemons round here, are there?'

A roll of eyes as the lawyer passed it to one of his assistants who resealed it, added a small cross beside the seal and dropped it into the box beside him.

'Anything else, Sergeant Towneley?'

'Yes, I have a little daughter outside of Burnley.' This had been Ferdinando's suggestion. 'From time to time I write to the woman who is fostering her. Surely you won't want to read that as well?'

'Same procedure. "Many things fall between the cup and lip" as the saying goes.'

'So, everything I write…'

'I read,' finished Damporte. He offered a superior smile. 'I shall look forward to your other letters, Sergeant.' His assistants smirked.

You can do indignation. Garrett fiercely slapped aside the tent flap as he left. Success! Damporte had been so busy reading the more titillating parts that he had not attended to any of the phrases that mattered.

Now Garrett had to desperately hope that 'Rose Byrd's' letters back to him passed scrutiny.

5

St Albans, 1593

Rose laughed aloud at the row of little hearts impudently framing her address. It was another letter from the queen's secret intelligencer — a report masquerading as a love letter.

For *Hart Lane, off St Peter's Street, St Albans, Hertfordshire*, he always used ordinary quill strokes but she liked the teasing way he wrote *Mistress Rose Byrd*, especially the caressing flamboyance of the 'M', 'R' and 'B', and this time he had playfully added a circle above the 'i' of 'Mistress' and set tiny eyes and a smiling arc of mouth within it. Whoever he was, he had a sense of humour.

Her fingers itched to break the seal but the contents were not for her. Instead, Martin Lorimer, her manservant, another of Wade's people, would ride with it to London, where it would be passed to the chief cipher clerk at Whitehall. There, the seal would be examined for tampering and the handwriting of the address compared to the writer's previous letters. If decreed acceptable, the contents would be copied and interpreted. A few days later Rose would write an affectionate reply in her own hand, but the words were Wade's not hers — coded instructions for his spy to follow. The address was always: *G. T., care of Master Laurence, Bookbinder, Antwerp, Flanders*. She was informed G. T. called himself Garrett Towneley, though Wade never used the name, preferring to begin '*My dearest love*'.

Clearly, this intelligencer was important; Rose's furnished house, Martin and the maidservant, who came alternate days, even the betrothal ring on her finger were paid for by Her Majesty's government.

She turned the ring now, wondering as usual where Towneley was and what dangers he faced. Did he work on his own, pretending to be a merchant or a travelling scholar? Perhaps he was a mercenary in the payroll of the King of Spain? She ran a finger across the love hearts. Whatever disguise he used, he was no celibate.

With the letter in her hand, she walked across to the parlour window, opened the latch and stood gazing towards St Peter's Street. Market day, another week gone by. She could hear the shouts of the stallholders and the rumble of carts. St Albans was bustling despite the drizzle. Everyone with a purpose. Except her. She was drifting nowhere, rusting on the inside.

It had seemed like the answer when Master Wade had offered her employment, but how long must she do this to earn Her Majesty's forgiveness for her family?

'It is predicted the pestilence will ravage London cruelly this summer,' he had told her, 'and if you are to work for us, my dear, we must safeguard your health. St Albans is less than a day's ride from the city and there are other advantages, too. No one there will know your history. You shall no longer be Secretary Davison's daughter but a soldier's widow and newly betrothed.'

To a shadow!

Despite Martin's reassuring and unthreatening company as her aged servant, a role he played to perfection in sleeping in the attic and keeping to the kitchen (save when he accompanied her to market or to Divine service), he was busy inveigling himself into the Papist community, and he and Rose neither ate together nor conversed much. She felt increasingly isolated though she conceded that Wade had been right in moving her here. Many London citizens including the Lord Mayor had died of the plague. Certainly, she was grateful to be alive and have an income, yet this false correspondence could not endure much longer. And what then? Back to the city and a meagre allowance from her father?

The sound of a fist on the front door below vanquished her thoughts and when, after the third knocking, Martin did not answer the door, she went down herself, believing it was her neighbour returned from a morning's coursing. No skinned hare was held out to her. Instead, two unfamiliar men stood outside. Because their hat brims were tugged low and the tails of their cloaks were flung over their shoulders against the weather, she could not gauge their rank. One hefted a plump satchel.

Beholding her small ruff and black silk gown, they instantly doffed their hats. At least they had manners.

'I do not give alms to strangers,' she exclaimed firmly. They could be carrying the pestilence if they had come through London. 'Good day to you!'

A swiftly placed boot stopped her shutting them out. 'Mistress Byrd?' asked its owner.

No longer hidden, his well-trimmed brown hair and double cambric collar proclaimed him a gentleman. Intense, assessing eyes gleamed down at her.

Where was Martin? With relief, she heard him come up behind her, brushing his palms. 'Who wants to know?' he demanded.

'Our mutual friend in Flanders has asked us to call,' the second, older man answered quietly. 'Mistress, may I assume you know of whom we speak?'

Within her skirts, her fingers clenched. Who were they? Was Wade testing her or were these Papist agents come to discover if she was truly the intelligencer's betrothed?

'It's all right, Martin,' she said, managing a smile.

'No, mistress, this pair could be the Devil and Mephistopheles for all I know so please state your business, sirs.'

The younger man laughed. 'Of course, let me show you some evidence of my identity.' He slid a hand inside a respectable fig-brown doublet and handed her a folded letter. It was from an Italian bank in London asserting that Ralph Hawkridge was in funds and that any debts would be honoured. Seemingly genuine. She handed it back.

'But this is for you, good mistress.'

With its fabric petals still warm from his body, he held out a creased nosegay of cloth violets. With a reserved face, she took it and unwound the twist of vellum from its bound stems. 'I miss you, my darling,' said the flowing script and there was a circle with a smile above the 'i'. She had the wit to run a finger lovingly along it and part her lips in feigned delight. These visitors were no friends. Her intelligencer always rounded the tail of a 'y' and added a tiny impertinent tilt. This 'y' certainly looked like a snake inspecting its tail tip, but dipping the quill again, the writer had forgotten that extra flick. Nor was there the regular infinitesimally tiny dot of ink somewhere close to the first line.

These men were here about the intelligencer. God help her to be convincing!

'You had better come in, gentlemen,' she said. Bidding Martin take their cloaks to dry before the kitchen fire and then bring refreshment to the parlour, she led the way upstairs with a straight back. 'Pray be seated, sirs.'

They waited politely until she was comfortable in her chair. The older man's pack clanged slightly as he set it down by the hearth and the noise provoked a twitch of disapproval from his companion. With an embarrassed smile, he sat down stiffly, veined hands favouring his damp, brown-hosed knees. Behind his trim, greying beard, his expression was stoic, his blue eyes weary.

'My name is Fa— Farmer, James Farmer.'

'Have you come far today?' Rose asked.

'From friends.' He rubbed a finger across his thin moustache, looking to his companion for elaboration.

There was none. Master Hawkridge made show of warming his hands behind his back while his observation took in the neighbour's gable beyond the tiny windowpanes, the pile of books at Rose's elbow and the jar of quills. It was an effort for Rose to keep her fingers from tensing as the sharp gaze slewed sideways to assess her, moving over her eyes and lips, and downwards to the heart pendant about her throat and the pledge ring on her left hand. Heaven help her, she would trust this man no more than she'd welcome a viper between her bedsheets.

'I expect you miss him, Mistress Byrd.' He sat down, his eyes never leaving her face.

'Oh, we write to each other regularly. One day, I trust,' she twisted the ring, 'we shall be wed. But, yes, I do miss him. Is he well?'

'Yes, in good health,' Master Farmer answered. 'There has been plague in Flanders as well as here, however, with the season cooling, every man is feeling safer to go about his business and God has spared us.' His fingers lifted and then, as if his hand changed its mind, they curled and took refuge on his lap again. 'Yes, indeed.' Then he added, 'It cannot be easy for you being promised to a soldier, mistress.'

Ah! So, her 'lover' was a fighting man.

'I thank you for your concern, sir, but my late husband also served with the military, so I am already used to solitude.'

'You have no children, mistress?'

She shook her head.

'Clearly, your first husband, God rest him, has left you well provided.' Hawkridge's gesture took in the furnishings but beneath his question lurked another: all this on a soldier's pay? And he must know that under the law, a widow convicted as a Papist might have two-thirds of her property seized by the Crown.

This was edging into the dark without a lantern. Would he ask if she had suffered a fine or been taken in for questioning? 'My family are not without influence,' she muttered tersely and was relieved to be rescued by Martin coming in with a modest flagon of canary and some raisin pastries. 'Ah, thank you, put it there.' She rose and shifted a book off the small table.

Hawkridge accepted a cup but he was not distracted from asking, 'You have your family's consent to wed our friend, Mistress Byrd?'

'Why would I not, sir?' She caught a *be careful* glance from Martin before he bowed at the door and left.

'Forgive me, mistress, I mean no offence. Just that in these uncertain times some fathers would not approve of a suitor who must earn his bread beyond these shores.'

'Do you have any family nearby?' asked the older man.

'Not as nearby as I should wish, Master Farmer. I do see my first husband's sister from time to time.' Then adding some eagerness, Rose asked, 'But tell me, please, do you have close acquaintance with my betrothed, sir?'

'We dine together often, Mistress Byrd.'

'Are you staying long in England, sir? If you do return to Flanders, please tell him you find me impatient to see him soon.'

'Of course.'

This conversation, evasive on both sides, was like picking a way through a marsh on a moonless night. Although the older man declared himself a merchant, she guessed otherwise. It was the way he broke the pastry, the slight pause before he raised it to his lips as though he were saying a secret grace.

'And how do you find living in St Albans, my dear?' he asked.

'Healthier than London, but, as I mentioned earlier, rather solitary. I keep myself to myself.'

There were no questions about whether she was on the list of the town's recusants and not allowed to travel outside of five miles from her dwelling. They must assume so.

Evidently, all her answers so far passed muster because Master Farmer risked taking her hands in his and offering to perform a Mass. He carried the necessaries with him, he told her. The final test! Wade had prepared her for just this circumstance. She agreed — how could she not? — pretending much enthusiasm and inviting Martin to be present.

Lighting candles, they adjourned to the cellar. Murmuring the correct Latin responses and accepting the wafer, she hoped for the sake of Wade's intelligencer that she and Martin had been convincing. 'You will receive good news soon,' the priest told her afterwards as she helped him pack away his makeshift altar.

'Truly? He is coming home?'

'No, mistress, I speak of a change in England's fortune. A phoenix from the ashes. A new leader. Meantime, I ask you to pray that our cause will prosper.'

They clearly expected a donation before they took their leave. She obliged. She'd send the bill to Wade.

'You didn't have to give them that much!' Martin huffed later after he had let their visitors out into the back lane.

'But I was supposed to be loyal to the cause.'

'Not with Her Majesty's money, you weren't,' he chuckled. 'Ah well, no matter. Did you learn anything useful?'

'They spoke of a new leader.'

He looked impressed. 'You know, Rose, I had my doubts about using a woman, but this arrangement has proved worthwhile after all. You certainly gulled them. Master Wade will be most satisfied, and our intelligencer may safely continue his work.'

'He may, but I shall not! That is, I do not want to continue, Martin. I found that younger man extremely menacing.'

'Easy, easy. I doubt they will come again if they went away satisfied.'

'But if they think me a good Papist, they may send others desiring funds or requesting me to hide them.'

'Perhaps,' he shrugged. 'I'll pass on your complaint, although I warn you, good mistress, there are fine ladies in the service of Her Majesty's government paid to do far more than you.'

'On their knees the entire time, I suppose?'

'Oh yes.' A grin as he turned away. 'On their knees or their backs.'

How brilliantly peevish! The latest missive from the cipher clerk in St Albans had Garrett smiling. Not only was it written in such a good imitation of a woman's handwriting but also with such convincing female sentiments that it slid easily through Damporte's inky paws.

Swear to me you are not giving your allegiance to some foreign Jezebel. I miss you so much. Write to me more of your love. Only that sustains me.

More mundanely, 'she' added that she was pleased with her decision to move to St Albans because plague was cruelly ravaging London, as well as another contagion that left its victims wrung out like ageing rag clothes. Then she reverted to the business in hand:

You rouse me to such passion when you write words of love.

And, finally, a demand that her lover write more often.

He would, fumed Garrett, if he had anything to write about! The Towneley morale needed a stout splint: his chances of sending worthwhile information to Wade were as likely as informing God what the Devil was up to. What's more, he had to accept orders from an inept superior officer; he found the pancake horizon dispiriting after the misty hills of Ireland; and the entertainment was equally flat — apart from the one decent beerhouse.

When Colonel Stanley announced at Sunday Mass that the camp would be moving south closer to Antwerp, Garrett muttered a *Deo gratias*. At least he could report that morsel. Back from the church service, he sat down on his trundle roll and drew out his writing board, only to shove it away swiftly as the shadow of de Francesci fell across him.

'You, Sergeant! Sir William's chambers *now!*'

Garrett was sweating as he stood before the colonel's desk. Had some two-faced informer back in Whitehall seen his name on a paylist? Or had they discovered there was no genuine 'betrothed'? Blessed Christ protect him! He'd diligently attended every Catholic Mass, but perhaps he'd not dabbed on the holy water properly or said the beads right. Some poxy little error that only a —

'I've been watching you, lad.'

Oh, it could have been bloody Bingham sitting there.

'Then about time someone has been watching me, Colonel!' he retorted vehemently. 'I've been working my bollocks off trying to put some spine into your rag-tag whiners.'

Like the slow flicker of an angry cat's tail, only Sir William's thumb moved upon the table.

Garrett waited.

'You have a cool head,' the colonel grunted, as though the admission had been wrenched out with pincers, 'but you do have wandering eyes during the Mass.'

'Just like you have, Sir William,' Garrett answered fiercely, though inside every nerve was ringing alarms. 'And perhaps you'd like to know the reason.' *Keep your shoulders easy*, he warned himself. 'As a child, I was told the story of the di Medici brothers. Maybe you know it — how Giuliano de' Medici was stabbed to death at High Mass in the cathedral? The lesson stayed with me.'

Did that sound plausible?

The colonel languidly lit his pipe from a spill. 'But you are among friends here.'

'Am I? I begin to wonder to what damn purpose. If you lead this green bunch of malcontents across the Channel in their present state of mind, Sir William, they'll go off like tossed firecrackers, just bang and smoke. All this heated talk of a rebellion in England! Pah, those loudmouths couldn't capture a laundry basket. As for the rest...'

'The rest?' Stanley drew on his pipe then raised his gaze to pinion Garrett. 'Go on!'

'The older men are homesick, rejected, resentful. They should be kept busy. It's not because of what blessed church they go to that most of 'em are here, it's because some son of a whore has taken their livelihood — kicked them out of their regiment or off their land. I don't know how soon you are hoping they'll see any action but —'

'Whoa, rein in there! I do grasp that, and I know what game you are playing, you knave.'

Garrett swallowed. All that was missing was the black kerchief.

'Best form of defence is attack, eh?' chuckled the colonel, rising to his feet. 'Well, you misjudge me. I called you in to thank you, you blessed varmint, not haul you over the coals, and to tell you that His Majesty of Spain has agreed to put you on the same pension as our other captains.' Rounding the desk, he took him by the shoulders, his face so close that Garrett could smell the stink of tobacco on his breath. 'You were a captain in Bingham's regiment, weren't you?'

A stiff nod.

'Then be so again, *Captain* Towneley.'

It twisted his gut. Stanley was the sort of commander he had once dreamed of working for. But not like this.

'Thank you, Colonel,' he said huskily.

Shame that Stanley was a bloody traitor.

Establishing the new camp at Aarschot, within a day's ride from Antwerp or Brussels, was like supping a hearty pottage; it revitalised everyone. Because the colonel was provided with an entire house as his headquarters, courtesy of the provincial governor, and the officers were given lodgings in the town, Garrett's promotion meant he didn't have to listen to rain dripping down the canvas inches from his nose. He now dined at the butt end of Stanley's table, yet although this offered the chance of getting closer to the major players, they proved a tight-knit bunch and he felt hobbled in grasping everything said there because the colonel, de Francesci and the army secretary, Anthony Thomas, were all excellent linguists. Conversation might prance between Dutch, Flemish, French or Spanish (depending on who they were entertaining). Besides, with the loud hubbub of some twenty men it was hard to eavesdrop.

The least affable of the company was Father Holt, the sulphur-tongued zealot who always sat at Sir William's right hand and whose ruddy features seemed trapped in a rooster glare. The several captains included Morgan, who had lost an eye serving Her Majesty and turned traitor for lack of recompense; White, an old messmate of the colonel's; and O'Collun — all beak and spurs. One of the younger lieutenants, Aidan Markham, a former retainer of the Earl of Shrewsbury, seemed more open, though not part of the inner circle. He and his cousin had fled England the year before, and because the latter had joined the English dissident group in Prague, Garrett decided that friendship with Markham might reap some grains of interest to Wade.

Occasionally supping were the army chaplains and visiting hotheads. Some of these young zealots had been turned while doing university degrees or indoctrinated at the English seminaries of Douai or Valladolid. They were intense, uncomfortable company, fired white-hot with the old faith. Their language was vehement; their talk was of returning to sink the English fleet and slaughter all the Protestants. Just listening to them debating whether the old lady, Queen Elizabeth, should be murdered with a small pistol or a poison-tipped rapier made Garrett's blood run cold.

He avoided getting into arguments with them. For his part, he did not care whether Christ was in the Mass bread or not. Did the Almighty really bother with what you believed about wine and wafers so long as you said your prayers with a true heart? Nor did he believe the Apocalypse was imminent. But these youths, willing to risk excruciating torture, saw death for their faith as glorious martyrdom! Promising them sainthood, it was young men like these that Sir William and Father Holt had been lobbing into England, not merely to evangelise but to ferment fear and division — human powder kegs with their fuses lit. That was why Garrett was here; to forewarn Wade if any were being readied.

Now that the dissidents' camp was closer to Antwerp, Verstegan rode in and spent an hour closeted with Stanley and de Francesci before he joined everyone else at the dining board and announced he had brought astounding news from London: Christopher Marlowe had been stabbed to death in a riverside tavern brawl!

'Not one of ours,' commented the colonel from the head of the table, taking a puff of his pipe. 'Marlowe was an atheist. Must have been the queen's pygmy getting rid of an irritating flea.'

Garrett almost choked on his beer. Marlowe murdered on Sir Robert Cecil's orders? Could that allegation have legs? A popular playwright slapped out of existence like a squashed fly? Where did that leave Garrett Towneley — about as welcome as the Spanish pox if Wade found out he was also reporting to Ferdinando?

'Heigh, I hear you are a captain again,' Verstegan called down the board to him, lifting his wineglass in congratulations. 'And how is your young widow?' It wasn't a caring question. While it produced hoots from the others, Verstegan's eyes had a cunning mien.

'Oh, *I* can tell you he is missing her,' remarked Damporte dryly, evoking laughter. Ribald jests pelted Garrett. Somehow, he had become more accepted, except … that ugly sense that Verstegan had acquired some hold over him? Quitting the smoky chamber, he hastened downstairs, out into the courtyard, glad of the moonless sky, sick to his stomach. Oh, for a featherbed in England and that pretty woman from the Theatre in his arms.

The creak of door and then the sound of piss against the wall. 'Are you angry about something?' asked a familiar voice.

'I've had a gutful, Markham.'

'You're leaving?'

'Maybe. What's the point of all this?' It helped to slap the rainwater barrel. 'A toast to the invasion?' he sneered. 'Bollocks! This lot haven't even a leader to put on the throne. Sir William can't make himself the ruddy king. You can't maintain an army of this size for years on ifs and maybes.'

A rustle of clothing pulled straight. 'I can think of a leader.'

'Who? The canny King of Scots?'

'*He's* not canny,' corrected Markham. 'Has enough trouble controlling the clans let alone acquiring another kingdom. No, I was thinking of a true Eng— *Merde!*' A shadow clapped fierce hands down on both their shoulders.

'And who would you be thinking of, Aidan, lad?' It was de Francesci, the catfooted bastard!

'N-no one, Lieutenant Colonel, just conjecture.'

'*Conjecture!* Conjecture has the habit of escaping like piss from an old man's bladder.' A grunt of pain from Aidan. 'See, Aidan, before you know it, the ignorant will start to believe it. No idle talk, eh!'

'What in blazes was that about?' muttered Garrett, thumbing his nose at de Francesci's departing shadow. 'You were saying…'

The light from the upper window showed the disquiet narrowing Markham's eyes. 'No, he's right.' The young man's lower lip was a sulky jut as he stared up at the casement. 'Who knows the truth about anyone here? Good night to you.'

He codenamed Aidan Markham 'lack of sleep'. It brought a swift answer from Wade.

Even though this must sound heartless, my dearest, it pleases me to hear about your lack of sleep, for I am as afflicted as you.

Maybe a few rounds of drinks at the *De Tevreden Ezel* might help but before he found the opportunity to soften Markham's resistance with the local beer, he received a summons to the colonel's inner sanctum.

'Ah, you've made it to the Holy of Holies.' Damporte's side-squish of mouth betrayed interest at Garrett's presence. 'Well, if there are no more to come?' He closed the door and leaned against it.

'We have a problem,' de Francesci informed the room, his dark eyes glinting. 'A traitor in our midst!'

Caught raising the winecup to his lips, Garrett froze. It took all his control to set it down with a steady hand. He could feel the flames of suspicion. They all could, judging by the uneasy faces.

'How shall we punish him?' de Francesci pursued.

Jesus! thought Garrett. *This is like the White Tower meeting from Will Shakespeare's* Richard III. The silence was frightening. He waited, inwardly terrified, for the indictment to fall on him. The colonel slammed his hand down on the board. 'By death!'

'Then we need an executioner,' smiled his deputy.

Was it to be done now? A trio of dagger thrusts? Or would they make it public, in the camp square before the entire force? God's mercy!

De Francesci's gaze was moving across their faces like a salivating mastiff. 'It will require a superior swordsman. Myself! You!' He pointed to O'Collun. 'You!' he looked across at Morgan. 'And *you*, Towneley!'

Garrett swallowed. 'But who the hell are we talking about?'

'Your friend, Aidan Markham.' That came from Damporte.

'Mayhap you can tell a *feallttóir* by the company he keeps,' sneered O'Collun. 'Share his ruddy sympathies, do you, Towneley?'

'What ruddy sympathies?'

'Essex for king?' sneered de Francesci.

'Essex? What, Lord Essex?' Garrett's surprise was genuine. 'Well, that explains plenty.' Then like a plain-speaking soldier, he remarked disobligingly, 'Heigh now, is that such a bad thing? Wouldn't you wager his lordship could be our man if he changes his faith? What's wrong with that?'

'Essex is no more likely to become Catholic than the Ottoman Sultan's cock,' scoffed O'Collun. 'Are you that green?'

'Yes, probably.' Garrett swung round to face Stanley. 'Why does that make Markham a traitor?'

'His loyalty is not to our cause, Captain. We reckon that he may have been feeding information back to his lordship for the last year. Several of our priests and two of our agents have been arrested by Lord Essex.'

Damporte nodded. 'And last month, we tested him out. We fed him something juicy and, would you believe, Essex raises it in the royal council. Can't resist showing the old queen that he's the best at protecting her. Proof, eh?'

'I see,' Garrett looked away, unhappy that Markham's fate was sealed.

'Prepare the straws,' ordered de Francesci.

It was Damporte who went to the cupboard and let down the board. The room was silent save for the sound of his knife before he turned and held out a fist of four short wax tapers.

'Let God decide,' intoned Father Holt.

'Draw!' Three of them obeyed, drawing spills of equal length. The lawyer uncurled his palm. 'This then is yours, Towneley. The short straw.'

'Go shit on nettles, the lot of you!' Garrett kept his hands at his sides. It wasn't only Markham being judged. 'The man should be given a fair trial.'

'Read for yourself!' snarled de Francesci, seizing up the letter that lay before the colonel. 'God's chosen you as his executioner. Markham shall fight you for his life.'

'What is this,' sneered Garrett, chin high, 'a school yard? No, I'll have no part of it. Hang him yourselves!' And he walked out.

In the darkness he leaned back against the outside wall, his heart racing. Maybe everything was over now. Would it be a swift slicing across his throat, a taut wire, a rope next to Markham's?

A creak of hinge around the corner. He smelled the tobacco on the older man's clothes, watched the small glow of the pipe blossom. 'Can your hands no longer defend you, Garrett?'

'Is that what they are thinking, sir?'

'Perhaps.' A weary sigh. 'It's a sad business. Essex would be the last man I'd trust if I was Markham. Vain, pampered sod. Who'd want to crown that one? Lord Leicester spoiled him.'

Was this a reprieve for him and Markham? Had playing the naive soldier saved his friend? Garrett bit his lip, wondering.

Above their heads the moon was veiled like a pagan houri in a great temple of stars. 'Who would *you* crown then?' he asked and heard a rat scamper across the roof before the colonel answered.

'Give it a month and we'll know.'

Markham had disappeared by next morning and it was a toss of the coin whether he had fled or been disposed of. Garrett did not ask; he busied himself with arquebus training and avoided his fellow officers. However, that night at the *De Tevreden Ezel*, he was shocked to see Markham, resurrected and sufficiently brimful with liquor to be dangerous, elbowing towards him through the drinkers.

'I've heard you've been saying I'm a traitor, Towneley.'

Garrett shook his head. 'Then your hearing must have been awry, my friend.'

'*Friend?*' Markham's abscess of resentment had been drawn to bursting point. 'You call me friend when I'm told from all sides about your mouthin' behind my back. Well, you're the pissin' turncoat, you filthy whoreson.'

It happened in an instant. The drawing of a dagger. An empty platter seized in time.

'Sober up!' he warned. 'Make this later.' But about them the space was emptying, trestles and benches scraped back; here was sport, the evening's entertainment.

With an oath, he jerked out of the way of a second lunge, but Markham was like a bull with its horns lowered to gouge him open.

The colonel intervened. 'Draw your tuckes, both of you!' he snarled. 'I'll wager ten ducats on Captain Towneley.' The rest began laying odds. That riled Markham further though it gave Garrett time to bind his fingers to the hilt.

The two men circled, each armed with a rapier and a dagger. 'We've been set up, you fool!' Garrett hissed as steel slid upon steel and their faces almost met.

Markham spat. Momentarily blinded in one eye, Garrett failed to parry, felt flesh rip open down his forearm. His opponent had tasted blood, had the right number of fingers, was agile, competent, angry.

I don't want to kill him. This is stupid, futile.

He needed to hold him off until the *kasseistampers* arrive. Surely someone had sent for the watch?

'Stop arsing around, Captain! Give us a decent fight!' shouted O'Collun.

The restraint broke. Sparks flew as blade rasped blade. The cheers ceased. The air grew tense, dry-tongued, as though the whole company held their breath. Garrett was hot, sweat running down his brow. He should have stripped to his shirt. He managed a hit on Markham's shoulder, but the younger man had stamina. They circled again, watching each other's eyes, lethal points teasing the air.

How in hell was he going to end this foolishness?

Around him, voices began a chant: 'Fight, fight, fight.' Tankards slammed, boots stamped. Beneath the rushes, the floor vibrated.

That lethal blade came at him again and again, breath meeting breath as they faced each other across the close rasping kiss of steel. The rapier was almost spun from his hand as Markham exploited his weakness, laying blow upon blow, preventing him from strengthening his grip. Garrett cast aside his dagger, needing both hands as he was driven back on a trestle, belaboured until he felt a tankard shift behind him. He grasped it and hurled. For a heartbeat, Markham staggered, then as he lurched an attack again, Garrett doubled his hold and thrust. Then it was over. Almost in disbelief, he saw the thin deadly point pierce through the soft leather — slide so easily into Markham's breast.

Sycophantic slaps shook his shoulders; he did not heed them. Yanking the blade out, he set it aside and knelt, cradling the dying man. 'Aidan, I was ever your friend.'

There was no sad understanding, only blood a-bubbling and a final gasp.

Behind his heels, de Francesci was giving orders to carry the body back to camp. Several men in his troop offered to buy Garrett a drink, but grabbing up his weapons, he rose and walked through them iron-faced.

De Francesci caught up with him in the street. 'You'll face a court-martial tomorrow. Just a procedure, of course.'

Garrett halted, squared his shoulders. Not looking round, he said, 'I can think of any number of words to describe you, de Francesci. Fair, just and honourable aren't among them, so fall away and leave me with my anger or by God, I'll run you though as well.'

He heard the heartless chuckle behind him as he walked away.

6

The fight increased Garrett's standing among the men, won him respect on the upper rungs of the colonel's chicken coop, but he missed Aidan, and the man's death was a warning. His luck might not hold out much longer; nor might Queen Elizabeth's. In July 1593 came the news that King Henri of France had abandoned his Protestant faith. England was now a lonely island in a sea of hostility.

After talks in Brussels and a flurry of pigeons and correspondence, the colonel announced that he had received word from Lancashire that Ferdinando, Lord Strange, was about to succeed his dying father as Earl of Derby.

'Why, now's our chance then,' exclaimed Damporte. 'Lancashire saw a good Catholic rising a few years back and the new earl has a strong claim to the throne.'

'But is he likely to support us?' Garrett challenged.

'Let's find out,' demanded Father Holt, stabbing a finger up into the air. 'If he would only turn Catholic, I'd go to the stake to make him king.'

'Ha, I've heard he's a dark horse as regards religion,' muttered de Francesci. 'Could even be an atheist. He's your cousin, Colonel, what do you say?'

'Well, his family have given board and lodging to my father and sons all these years despite that bloody William Wade trying to get hold of them. Yet, as for leading a rebellion —' he snorted — 'what Ferdy knows about soldiering could be writ on a pinhead. Courtier to the backbone, fancies himself as a love-sick poet, probably writes rustic verses to the queen's wigs.'

He's smoothing plaster over lathes, thought Garrett. In Colonel Sir William's eyes lurked the tiny, excited glow that promised to ignite a bonfire. 'However —' a theatrical pause as the soldier rose to his feet — 'it's been decided that we'll make him an offer. May God deliver him to us!'

'*Amen*!' It was the news that they had been waiting for. Goblets and tankards smacked heartily.

'Are you going over to England, Sir William?' Garrett asked, cornering the colonel and de Francesci later away from the rest. 'Or if you need a messenger…?'

A shrewd gaze. 'No, Captain, we already have the perfect ambassador, Richard Hesketh, a childhood friend of Ferdinando's. He will be on the road to the port of Hamburg by now. Been living in Prague.'

Hell, Garrett needed to get a warning to Ferdinando as soon as he could.

'Of course,' growled de Francesci, 'if word of this escapes this room, I'll slice the blabber's lips off and send them to his widow.' His stare swung like a lantern held to each man's face.

'What a lovely manner you have with people, Lieutenant Colonel,' Garrett growled as the scrutiny crossed him. 'Perhaps *you* should go across yourself and make sure the job gets done to your satisfaction.' He turned to the colonel with an expression that said: *At least I volunteered for something.*

Thank God it wasn't to kill the queen.

Hesketh was sentenced to be hanged. Ferdinando had handed him over to Wade.

Perhaps it was because Garrett had sent a doll from the Antwerp market to Ferdinando's little lovechild in Burnley — a prearranged warning. Whatever the truth of the matter, the news rattled the colonel's inner sanctum like an earthquake.

The shock of it truly hit Garrett when he was told that he would be escorting a Jesuit priest across to witness Hesketh's martyrdom on the scaffold.

It would be like riding into Hell with a snowflake!

'What good will it serve?' he demanded of de Francesci, thankful at least it was not a rescue mission.

'Because Hesketh — God give him strength — might appreciate his presence, you ruddy unfeeling dog! Father Griffiths was his confessor in Prague.'

'Your pardon, Lieutenant Colonel,' Garrett muttered contritely, crossing himself. He must be more careful. Besides, guilt was seeping beneath the bandage of detachment. 'Does this Father Griffith realise the risk he's taking?'

'Of course, he bloody well does. And you need to know the execution won't be at Tyburn because the plague is still whoring in London.'

'Where then?'

'St Albans.'

'*Christ!*' In London, they could have been swallowed up into the myriad of tenements. Places to hide. Did the colonel know he wrote to St Albans?

'So where is this priest now? Growing his tonsure?'

'Rode in this morning. Sir William suggests you travel as uncle and nephew since you are of like colouring. You leave at first light tomorrow.' De Francesci clanked a purse down upon the table. 'I'll say this, Towneley, I know that you and I don't run easily in harness, but if any bloody bastard can bring Griffith back in one piece, you can. Disappointed still? Next time we'll find you something really meaty, like putting a petard up Sir Robert Cecil's arse.'

'I am alight already.'

With a tight smile that hid his displeasure, Garrett fisted the air and because his third finger was missing, de Francesci fortunately missed the insult.

By the time he sighted the dark sliver of Essex coast after hours of seasickness trapped on a Dutch vessel that bucked and tossed like an unbroken colt, Garrett had pails of sympathy for regular smugglers. Father Griffith had kindly prayed over him during the voyage but that had not helped his nausea. Perhaps the Deity was busy comforting the doomed Hesketh.

At least Owen Griffith (now calling himself Dr Buckley of Monmouth) was a likeable character, who possessed a tankard-full optimism, devout faith in 'Gott' and 'Jeshu' and sufficient knowledge of medicine to pass for a Welsh apothecary. What concerned Garrett was firstly, that with his slight build, the priest could have been laid out with one blow, and secondly, the wavy-haired wig stitched to his scholarly cap to cover his tonsure went ill with the man's skin colour. However, when the wig blew off and headed towards the North Sea, Owen sensibly shaved the front of his head and let the elements buffet his newlybare scalp. It was an improvement and, together with his spectacles, scarlet dragon brooch and over-robe smelling like a herbal cupboard, he could have passed for Merlin in something written by Shakespeare. Whether his disguise could outwit Her Majesty's finest lay in the lap of 'Gott'.

Under the moonless sky, the *Witte Duifje* glided into the estuary of the River Blackwood on the high tide and weighed anchor in a safe depth off the northern bank. Aided by the current, two of the Dutch crew took their human cargo upriver in a longboat. Garrett, Griffith and a clumsy, newly ordained cleric, who was on his way to Cambridgeshire to evangelise any weak-livered Protestants, took turns with the oars. A couple of times they encountered sand spits and had to jump out and heave the boat off.

Eventually, a light waved a vague greeting from the distant bank.

Friend or foe? Garrett liked to see any potential assailants and know the lie of the land. Here, it was like wearing a blindfold.

His missing fingers were aching as he helped Owen Griffith from the longboat and, after the hours at sea, the mud lurched and rebelled beneath his soles. Holding his rapier at the ready, he led the way through the Essex reeds. It was as though the icy water was seeping into his very bone marrow. No payment covered this, being dumped like a crate of banned books in some ruddy estuary.

Blackwater, this godless water was named. Supposed to be safe, uninhabited and a mile downriver from the nearest town. God's mercy! 'How much of this stinking marsh is there?' he muttered to the uncaring darkness as he led and, slithering, swore.

'Don't blaspheme!' scolded the young cleric. The whey-faced, useless prick! At least Garrett didn't have to sheepdog him to Cambridgeshire or wherever the brat was going to cause a nuisance.

Where was this welcoming party? Tightening his grip on his sword handle, he halted, peering into the darkness for the lantern that had signalled earlier. The Hollanders had promised to linger but already he could hear the regular rattle of the oar grips. They had been abandoned.

'There, look you!' Owen whispered. Some twenty yards ahead, a reckless Papist traced a benediction in the frosty air. Young Wheyface crossed himself in relief but before he could step forward, Garrett grabbed his arm. 'Let them come to us!'

They tensed as the light slowly bobbed closer. Two pairs of heavy footsteps halted and the damn addlepate carrying the lantern once more blessed the darkness. Jaw clenched, Garrett hoped no others had glimpsed it. Gruffly, he offered a swift handclasp to their welcomers and urged they make haste onto firm ground.

Marsh surrendered to bog, endless it seemed, before they eventually came to a ploughed field, but even the path along its edge was squelchy from the recent rain. The honest earth of England should have felt more reassuring beneath Garrett's feet, damn it! What he wanted was a hearty inn breakfast and a warming fire in nearby Maldon but, no, it would be a hiding hole beneath some Papist's floorboards and he'd be as welcome as a plague bubo.

Think like a soldier, he upbraided himself. *It's a war. You've seen worse bogs in Ireland and plenty hanged.* But he did care about keeping Owen safe.

The Jesuit, Christ love him, knew there wasn't a chance in Hell of visiting Hesketh in his cell and giving him *viaticum*, the Papist last rites of confession, absolution and the Sacrament of Extreme Unction, but he wanted to be there in front of the scaffold saying the words in his mind. Whether Hesketh would even realise that Owen was risking his life to be present was unlikely. Picking out a friendly face in a crowd of baying mongrels would hardly be a priority in the condemned man's mind when he saw the noose. Mind, according to Owen, it was all about glorious martyrdom.

Martyrdom? Struggling through a hedgerow, Garrett was tempted to tell him where to stuff that notion. He just hoped the Welshman wasn't going to end up in William Wade's interrogation cellar. Illegal priests were vermin to be hunted and ripped to pieces by the salivating hounds of the royal authority. And St Albans would be like the blessed kennels.

'How much further?' Wheyface whined to the man carrying the lantern. *Not a happy pilgrimage, eh? Not enjoying yourself?*

'About another mile.' *Hell!*

Owen had said he had friends all along the way to St Albans who would take them in. What, to sleep in some blasted, freezing barn or behind the fancy scrollwork?

Well, heigh-ruddy-ho! Hiding holes and then a hanging.

Welcome to the ugly underbelly of Elizabeth's England!

7

Rose opened the parlour window. Someone was attacking the doorknocker but she could see no horse being walked. More Papists? God forbid! Not when one of their faith was being hanged tomorrow. She braced herself to confront strangers and then to her relief, Martin ushered in her eighteen-year-old brother.

Francis was clad *à la Gray's Inn* — a student's sleeveless black gown covering most of his grey fustian doublet. 'What ho, Rose! This is all very agreeable!' he exclaimed, looking about him. Dropping his pack behind the door, he pranced towards her, one hand doffing his black cap and the other clawing his curls into a semblance of respectability. 'The plague's abated in the city but best not to embrace me. Like my new scent?'

'Horse?'

'No!' He drew back offended. 'Cost me a fortune.' Plonking himself down on the settle, he stretched out long legs to the fire. 'So, where's the old lady who owns all this?' But before she drew breath, he espied the love-heart letter at her elbow. She thwarted his snatch for it. 'Ha!' he crowed. 'I thought there was something else going on. There's no old crow. You've been cozening us for months, you wretch. Where is he?'

'Away,' she conceded, quickly folding the unopened missive and stuffing it down her cleavage. 'I'm my own person, Francis.'

'Are you?' She did not appreciate the sudden steel in his eyes. Good God, he was already taking on the role of her father!

Swiftly unclasping her hands — she was not on trial! — Rose calmly took up the jug from the table and poured them each a glass. 'You will say nothing to our parents, you hear me!'

'I'm not sure I do hear you, sister.'

'Very well, Francis, if you must blab, tell them I pose without my clothes for an artist.'

A glimmer of fraternal humour mercifully resurfaced. 'Doesn't look like it,' he commented, eyeing the furnishings. 'So, who is this beau, sister mine? One of Oliver's old cronies?'

'I am not telling you.'

'Spoil my sport, will you?' He took a swig and winced. 'Urgh, perry! Haven't you any decent canary?'

'No, and what are you really doing here? Aren't you supposed to be studying?'

The grin she knew so well serifed his lips once more. 'Changing the subject, are we? All right, I've been pestering Lord Derby to read my latest play, see if his company would put it on. The new earl, I mean. You do know the old man died a month since and Ferdinando, Lord Strange, is now earl? He was in the gallery at the end of *Richard III*. I pointed him out to you, remember?'

Ah yes, Ferdy, she could remember a glimpse of scarlet cap with a white plume and below it, a small, well-trimmed beard. He had leaned a nonchalant arm, expensively gloved and richly sleeved in the French fashion, along the wooden rail. Had her father been the queen's secretary still, she might have tried to renew her acquaintance.

'Surely my Lord Derby either dwells in Her Majesty's presence or, well, in Derby?'

'Lancashire,' he corrected. 'But he's coming here tomorrow for the hanging of that Papist traitor, Richard Hesketh. See, I thought I'd follow him here, the earl, I mean, watch the entertainment and call on you at the same time. I can stay the night, can't I?'

'Of course you may, but must you speak so blithely about a hanging?'

'Women! Anyway, I brought this for you.' Tugging open his doublet, he extracted a letter bearing a chunky red seal. 'It's from Elizabeth de Vere, my Lord of Oxford's daughter. Thought I'd better deliver it in person. As cheap as sending it by carter.'

Rose expected him to make her jump for it but he handed it over in sober fashion. 'Lady Vere! How very curious,' she murmured, breaking the seal and carrying the parchment to the casement. 'Why would Lizbeth write to me? I haven't seen her for years. She's now one of the queen's maids-of-honour.' Scanning it swiftly, she gave a cry of pure delight.

'You've been offered the hand of the next Earl of Oxford?' her brother prompted, rising to saunter over and read it over her shoulder. He gave a marvelling whistle. 'Oh, by God, she's offering you a position. Rose, you have to —'

They both looked round as the door opened, but the man standing on the threshold froze as his gaze fell upon Francis. He unpeeled the riding scarf that half-concealed his face.

Rose recovered first and held out her hand. 'Master Wade, of all people! This is a surprise.' An unwelcome one. Beside her, Francis had gone rigid with disgust. Surely... Oh God forbid! He must be thinking she was old Wade's mistress!

Her visitor cleared his throat. 'I give you good day.' No fool, the man had quickly assessed the situation, aware that he needed to stamp out the fire of suspicion. 'Your pardon for this unexpected visit, my young friends. I'm here as an officer of Her Majesty's Government. No, what I mean is I'm here for the hanging.' His voice gathered strength. 'As a family friend, I thought I would come and pay my respects to you, Mistress Byrd. Young Master Davison, your servant!' A slight bow.

Francis's reciprocal flourish was grudging, his mouth a seam of disbelief and he stiffly broke the awkward silence that followed. 'If you will forgive me, sir, I have some business to transact.'

'Let me guess. A play to sell to our new earl?' Wade was taking care to block his way. 'Perhaps I can help. Would you like me to introduce you to his lordship on the morrow?'

Rose watched greedy excitement swiftly replace the disapproval in her brother's face. 'Thank you, Master Wade, I certainly would.'

'Then come to the hanging. His lordship will be there. May I sit down?' At Rose's nod, Wade took the seat by the fire.

Having declared he must leave, Francis gave a cool nod to Rose. Before he reached the door, Wade made certain of him. 'Perhaps you would perform a small task in return for me, young man. I am staying at the Fleur-de-Lis. Could you inform the landlord I shall be there to dine in half an hour?'

'Yes, your servant, sir.' A bob of deference.

Alone with Rose, Wade sat back with a smile. 'The last time I had to do that was when I was sixteen and wanted to kiss my mother's chambermaid. It cost me a whole penny to send my sister from the room.'

'Francis is no fool, sir.' Her brother's suspicion still lingered like a foul aroma.

'But he has ambitions.' *And, therefore, is easily manipulated,* Wade's smirk told her as he placed his hat and gloves beside the chair.

'My "betrothed" is not dead, is he?' she asked, uneasy at his continued presence.

'Why, have you not heard from him these last few days?'

'True, I have.' Turning away, she retrieved the letter from her bodice and held it out to him.

'Ha, the rogue was alive and frisky when he wrote this,' her visitor snorted, wrinkling his nose in disgust at the effusion of hearts.

'It is supposed to be a love letter, Master Wade.'

'Yes, but it draws the eye unnecessarily. There is no need for him to be excessive, and since he wrote very hotly last time about "the perfection of your breasts", in your next letter you will chide him.'

'But doesn't "the perfection of my breasts" have a meaning in the cipher? Like "the Spanish are preparing to invade next Tuesday"?'

'No, it does not,' he replied testily, 'and I have to reprimand you, too, young woman, for your reply last week.'

'Oh.' She felt the warmth rise in her cheeks. During the dictation, there had been an interruption and she had mischievously taken advantage of the clerk's distraction to add a few words of her own: *Ah, my love, I remember your caresses as we listened to the nightingale.*

'Nightingale, indeed!' scolded Wade. He had sent his clerk all the way back to St Albans next day to collect a corrected copy from her. 'Towneley would have been racking his brain wondering what the devil we meant by it. It must not happen again. Our purpose is to discover Her Majesty's enemies, not run a matchmaking enterprise.'

Rose managed not to laugh. 'I'm sorry, sir,' she offered contritely. 'I did spend a sleepless night wondering if *you* were going to jilt me.'

'Enough!' he had said sternly. 'May I remind you once more that your "betrothed's" letters are providing us with crucial information and he is only safe so long as you play your part. I came to warn you to be careful. I have no doubt this town is crawling with Popish lice come to watch Hesketh become their latest martyr.'

Rose did not believe any Papist would be that reckless, but for Wade, just one flowerpot might hide a score of Jesuits.

'A ripe time for you to catch Her Majesty's enemies then, sir,' she observed, as she saw him to the door. She needed this to cease. It wasn't just tomorrow's gruesome hanging unsettling her, but the future. Lizbeth de Vere's letter was timely; it offered an end to her discontent even if it meant losing the house, but she would broach that with Wade on the morrow.

The intelligencer of Antwerp was going to be jilted.

'Isn't Elizabeth de Vere younger than you?' Francis asked as he poulticed his supper bread with a thick helping of butter.

'Yes, about five years.'

'Five? Younger than me then. What does she want with an old tabby like you?'

'Old tabby!' Rose hurled her crust at him. 'Beast! I was like an older sister to her and her friends. I used to make up all sorts of games for them, hide and seek, pirate ships...' She observed his gaze roll heavenwards. 'Oh, really!' she growled. 'You saw her letter! She has been invited to visit the new Countess of Derby in Lancashire, and her grandfather, Lord Burghley, desires her to have a respectable companion for the journey. I'm older, widowed, Protestant and available.'

'Ah, maybe he wants to help you to a northern husband out of charity. Favour to Father and all that.' Francis' voice took on a northern brogue: 'Eee, ah'll warrant there must be a whole crop of Lancashire gentleman ravenous for southern brides, lass.'

'Stop baiting me!'

'No, it's good sport. By the way, Wade set me right that you are not his mistress. Still like to know who the fortunate man is, though.'

'I'll say when I'm ready.'

'Well, I hope you're being careful.'

'Thanks, *Father*!'

He grinned and added with his mouth full. 'How come you so are so peevish? Squeamish about tomorrow's hanging?'

'I'm not going to the hanging.'

Wade had told her that he wished to dictate his reply to the intelligencer early next morning. At least he would not have time to stay and argue when she informed him about Lizbeth's invitation to accompany her to Lancashire. The proposal had her curious. Was it to avoid the plague or a scandal? Lizbeth had been betrothed to the young Earl of Southampton since childhood but the instant he had come into his majority he had broken the arrangement and, although threatened with a fine of £5,000, he had refused to change his mind. All very humiliating, but that wasn't recent, and Rose knew the queen hated her maids-of-honour falling in love. Was this to save Lizbeth from an affair or its 'aftermath'?

Being an experienced diplomat and clerk to the Privy Council, Wade's face showed no immediate displeasure as he read Lady Vere's letter the following day.

'Very flattering but you will ignore it, won't you.' It was not a question.

'No, Master Wade, I intend to accept,' replied Rose. 'Please understand that I'm grateful to you for all you've done to help me, sir, but there is no reason for me to refuse Lady Vere's offer. Indeed, the world would consider it great folly were I to do so.' A position in a noble lady's house would secure her future.

She slid off her betrothal ring and held it out to him. 'I hereby quit myself of this arrangement.'

'Nonsense, you cannot do this!'

'Really?' Rose placed the ring on the table between them. 'One of your skilled clerks could easily forge my handwriting.'

'Out of the question. Come now, do you not want your family to be restored to Her Majesty's favour?' Receiving no answer, he added sternly, 'I have been at great expense to set you up here. You cannot suddenly spurn your betrothed.'

'Spurn him, sir?' A wry laugh escaped her. 'My brother is asking why "my betrothed" has not asked Father for my hand. My family are becoming suspicious.' The tiny veins on her employer's nose and cheeks were growing red and angry. She felt ashamed to displease him but Lizbeth's invitation glowed before her like the Holy Grail. 'And supposing I have another sweetheart, Master Wade? A flesh and blood suitor here in St Albans? Are you telling me I cannot marry him?'

'Have you a real suitor, Rose?'

'Well, no,' she admitted, 'but I would not turn down a good man's offer because of my work for you.' She picked up Lizbeth's letter. 'You once said yourself I must always act as the world thinks fit. This is fit.'

'I understand, my dear.' His tone had changed to condescending. 'The hour bells are tolling and you are not getting any younger.' He fished out a dial from his pocket. 'Speaking of which, I have an execution to attend forthwith. I shall see you there shortly.'

See her at the execution?

'Indeed not, sir,' she exclaimed. 'I have no intention of attending.'

Wade turned, his smile counterfeit. 'But, my dear, if you want young Francis to meet our new earl and present his manuscript, I suggest you be there. After all, this hanging is a lesson in loyalty for all of us. I've given your brother passes for the pair of you to enter the mayor's stand.'

'But, sir, I'm supposed to be a Papist and if there are any hidden in the crowd like that man Hawkridge, won't that be remarked upon?'

'Not if you veil yourself. You won't be the only Papist in the stands, I'm sure.'

They stared at one another. Like icy water hurled at her face, Rose at last felt the ugly power that this man could enforce. 'Make haste now and be sure to dress yourself warmly,' he added smoothly as he eased his hands into his fur gloves. 'After all —' and now there was no mistaking the irony — 'it is very cold out there.'

Her brother's enthusiasm for executions matched the excitement of the town, Rose observed with sad disgust as she and Francis came out of the laneway onto Holywell Hill. Despite the numbing air, more stall keepers than usual had set up outside the Moot Hall and a lot of cursing was coming from French Row where several newcomers were brazenly determined to squeeze their barrows in among the regulars. Everyone knew there was profit to be made at hangings. Pedlars and piemen were bawling their wares, pushing their trays heedlessly into other men's backs to get through the growing press of people. Church Street, which sloped down to Romeland, the common ground at the west end of the abbey where the traitor would breathe his last, was crammed with a slow-moving river of humanity.

'Most of the blasted countryside has traipsed in to gape. We should have set out earlier,' grumbled Francis as the bells in the great flint tower that presided over the marketplace sounded an urgent summons. 'Is there a back way behind the shops?'

'We can try.' They struggled across the street into the lane behind the Eleanor Cross but plenty of others had the same notion and it was a shuffle through the muddy yard of St Peter's Abbey before they joined the throng funnelling through the dark archway of the Bell Gate. In some cell above their heads, the condemned man was being given his last meal. But she forgot about Hesketh as rotten breath rimed with ale assailed her cheeks. Lascivious fingers goosed her. 'In God's name, get behind me, Francis!' she ordered, grabbing at her brother's sleeve.

'I thought that's what your bolster was for,' he laughed, but he pulled her in front and kept his hands upon her waist as they edged forward into the multitude.

For once she was glad she was not taller. Only by standing on tiptoes and craning, could she glimpse the gibbet and the black-hooded head of the hangman. 'Here will do.'

'Not when we can be in the stands and have the perfect view,' Francis growled, hauling her now towards the soldiery protecting the places reserved for people of rank. 'We have passes!' he exclaimed, brandishing papers as he thrust her past the halberds. Scowls and a score of upturned noses were directed their way from the cluster of local gentlemen with their crisp-ruffed wives waiting to welcome the dignitaries. However, before anyone could challenge their presence, the crowd gave a roar as the pikemen ruthlessly forced the common people back to make way for the horses of Her Majesty's officers.

Rose recognised the leading horsemen — Sir Nicholas Bacon, Lord Keeper of the Great Seal, and Sir Thomas Egerton, the Attorney-General. Behind them rode two finely clad men, the first with a great fur collar drawn up about his ears so his face was almost hidden. Ferdinando, Earl of Derby. Ferdy. It was years since she'd last seen him. At his stirrup, the hunched rider in a tall-crowned hat also looked familiar though she could not name him. Following were William Wade and Francis Babbe, the Mayor of St Albans, and then a tail of lesser worthies.

'Rose,' Francis whispered, as they stood back to let the aldermen welcome the noble lords, 'do you see the crookback fellow riding next to Wade? Isn't that Lord Burghley's son, Sir Robert Cecil?'

'You're right,' she said slowly. 'It is him.' Not since her father's disgrace had she spoken with Sir Robert. Like Ferdinando, he belonged to the world of her childhood. Yes, it must be Robert. His back betrayed him. Five years older than her yet he looked more like forty in his black mantle. The thick beard, the colour of dark ale, which lapped his breastbone, added years as well. Maybe that was what he wanted. The world knew he was trying to step into his powerful father's shoes and become the queen's favourite adviser. In fact, Rose had always suspected that Lord Burghley had been glad to see her father removed from office since it left an opening for his son.

'To think our families were once friends,' she murmured cynically. 'We used to get invited to stay at Theobalds House. You didn't, of course, because you were still in the nursery.'

'Was I? Pity!' Lifting his glove to shield his words, Francis muttered, 'Well, have a care what you say in his presence if he recognises you. Rumour has it that he's taken over

Walsingham's work ferreting out Her Majesty's enemies. I've heard he's the one who decides which recusants are to be rounded up, and old Wade oversees the interrogations.'

'Well, we have nothing to fear,' she replied assertively, as if, like the Lord's Prayer, the spoken thought could stifle the rising panic in her. The two men were riding side by side now, the vapour of their breath intermingling as they shared some jest.

Most of the crowd were in similar spirits. Most. Scanning the faces through her dark veil, she noticed a tallish man observing the stand. A broad-brimmed hat shaded his features but for an instant, she glimpsed his face. He had his hand on the shoulder of a shorter companion, an older man, who wore the earflaps of his cap drawn down. Something about him reminded her of the Second Murderer, the player from the Theatre who had singled her out. Just imagination, she chided herself, glad her face was hidden. Why would he be in St Albans? Although, there were plenty of strangers here. Hard-faced ones, too, women as well as men, hungry for the spectacle. Glad that she might shut her eyes behind her veil, Rose shivered in the cold wind, praying it would soon be over.

This hanging is a lesson in loyalty for us all.

Wade and Cecil were surveying the field of faces from their saddles, like perched buzzards watching for prey. Oh merciful God! Yes, there could be Papists here, come with foolhardy courage to support the condemned man with their silent prayers.

'Francis,' she murmured. 'Do you think there could be Popish priests in this crowd?'

'Sure to be. We are a divided people, Rose.'

The irrational fear that he or their younger brothers could have been secretly converted to the old faith suddenly gripped at her heart. They were the perfect age for recruitment. 'You haven't —'

'Lord, no, silly! I want to end up a successful playwright not a pile of ashes. Ah, tally ho! Wade's seen us.'

'I'll stay here,' she protested but already they were being beckoned.

'Good morrow, Mistress Byrd,' beamed Wade, doffing his cap to her. 'See, Sir Robert, here are Master Davison's son and daughter come to join us.'

Sir Robert Cecil inspected her from the saddle as she curtseyed. 'You were the little maid who used to watch me play chess with my father at Theobalds.'

'Yes,' she said, knowing he now moved human pieces. 'You used your queen very well, I recall.'

For an instant, he looked taken aback and then to her relief, he laughed. 'I hope I still can, Mistress Byrd, but I find some of the other pieces deserve my attention.' He exchanged an amused glance with Wade that hinted he knew of her employment. 'I hear you are still friends with my niece, Lady Vere.'

'Yes, she has asked me to join her when she goes north to stay with Alice, Lady Derby.'

The queen's privy councillors looked again at one another. Sir Robert showed surprise. 'When did you last hear from Lizbeth?' he asked, and Rose sensed the ground shifting beneath her feet.

'Yester—' she began but her brother cut in. 'No, Rose, actually the letter arrived a week ago. I didn't deliver it to my sister until yesterday, your honour.'

'Oh dear, Mistress Byrd, then you won't know that Lizbeth's little sister, Susan, is taken ill. Not the pestilence, I'm happy to say, but a winter sickness of coughing that has been spreading through the city like an ill wind. My niece has been caring for her.'

Instinct told her Sir Robert was being sparing with the truth because there was a subtle challenge in his eyes as he added smoothly, 'I'll ascertain how matters are when I return to London but until Susan is quite recovered, Lizbeth will not be travelling anywhere.'

Rose picked up the gauntlet. 'Then I shall write to her offering her my good wishes for her sister's return to health and expressing my disappointment.' She kept her smile ingenuous. *Let's see what Lizbeth writes back.*

'Do that, mistress,' murmured Master Wade. 'Either Sir Robert or I shall be happy to convey your letter.'

Checkmate.

'Oh no, I can do that,' offered Francis. His eager face blazoned his ambition to stick his toe in the de Veres' hallway. Lizbeth's father, the Earl of Oxford, was said to be a closet poet.

'Perhaps I should call on them —' Rose began, but both Wade and Sir Robert had lost interest. They were watching Ferdinando Stanley. The new earl had been shaking hands with members of St Albans' Corporation. Now he was back in the saddle, and the other distinguished guests reined their mounts aside to make room for him. At first, she could not see him properly for he was flanked by two henchmen, a sandy-haired young man in Puritan garb and an older man with similar curly dark hair to the earl, perhaps a kinsman. As the drums began to roll, they reined their horses back, leaving her a clear view of Ferdy.

Like Sir Robert, Ferdinando had been one of the older boys in her childhood world. His mother's family were descended from King Henry VIII's sister, Mary. No wonder the Papists had wanted him to lead a rebellion.

That's what today was about, she thought sadly. Hesketh, the condemned man, had tried to intimidate the new earl to treason. They had known each other as children, so the gossip ran. What was Ferdy feeling? Regret? Contrition? The profile half-hidden within his lordship's bearskin collar looked haggard. Could he have secret leanings towards Popery that he dare not reveal? Was he cursing his cousin in Antwerp for sending Hesketh across?

Antwerp! A breath held. Had her intelligencer in Antwerp forewarned Wade? Could this mean she was part of this unfolding horror? Christ forgive her! She stared across at the brazier and knives on the table before the scaffold. Every instinct screamed at her to plead some female malady, run away, but glancing round, she was utterly hemmed in. Well, she would not look, would not condone this.

Her brother's voice crashed through her thoughts. 'Your pardon, Master Wade, but you won't forget to introduce me to his lordship, will you?'

Oh, no, Francis, not here! Not now! Yet there was William Wade leaning across to tap Ferdy on the shoulder and then her brother was at the earl's stirrup, pulling out his precious manuscript from the breast of his doublet. Of all the times...

'I presume you have read your brother's work, Mistress Byrd?' Damnation! Sir Robert had deigned to notice her again.

'Not this one, no,' she answered carefully, dragging her gaze from her brother's happy face. 'I fear he will never be on the same rung as poor Master Marlowe or —'

'Have you seen Master Shakespeare's latest play?' he cut in.

'*Richard III*, you mean? Why there's a witty, clever villain.' But as she spoke, it suddenly dawned on her that the bustling hunchback in the play might be a mirror of the man before her now. 'Have you seen it?'

'I cannot say I cared for it much. It was written for one reason only.'

'To show King Richard as a tyrant and Henry Tudor as a hero?' she answered.

His face tightened. 'It was about tyranny, certainly, although I cannot believe that one man was guilty of all those murders. No, Mistress Byrd, the play was commissioned by our latest earl —' he glanced sideways meaningfully — 'to remind Her Majesty that she owes her crown to his ancestor, Lord Stanley.'

'But, meaning no disrespect,' Rose replied, remembering that the play ended with a beaming Thomas Stanley offering Richmond the crown, 'that is true, isn't it?'

Sir Robert leaned down towards her. 'Meaning no disrespect to your understanding, either, Mistress Rose, any play that shows the overthrow of an anointed king can plant the seed of rebellion in gullible people's minds.'

'I ... I never thought of it that way.'

'Seeds grow unless...' A slow clench of fist. Was that a warning shot of words across her bow? No, it was Ferdy that Sir Robert was observing with the intent expression of a cat in the undergrowth as a blare of trumpets tore the air and they heard the whoops of the crowd across the hanging ground; the sheriff was ordering that Hesketh be brought out. 'That's what today is about, Mistress Byrd,' Sir Robert told her, lifting his chin towards the gatehouse. 'You betray your country, you die a traitor's death.'

Hesketh's thinning fair hair was ragged and greasy. Clothed only in a meagre white shirt and stained breeches, he was hunched against the cold and visibly shivering. As the sheriff's soldiers hauled him towards the scaffold, he looked back to the earl, his eyes pleading.

As the lordly hands holding the reins answered with a dismissive gesture, Hesketh began to struggle, bawling his innocence, his desperate face still directed at the earl, but when his knees slammed against the wooden steps, he suddenly calmed as if he realised that it would be better to die with dignity.

The Church of England priest in attendance leaned forward to offer solace and a helping hand but Hesketh, being a Papist, ignored him. He mounted the scaffold and his guards compelled him to face the earl. Now the poor wretch looked as though his mind had truly numbed. The crowd hushed and in the silence before the drum roll, the hangman's assistant at the table below the scaffold deliberately drew his hacking blade along the steel sharpener.

Hesketh trembled at the sound, the crowd cackled and then the drummers obeyed the sheriff's nod. Sweet blessed Christ! Rose stared at the vicious hook and knives set out upon the board, the waiting cauldron of tar. This wasn't just a hanging. Please, God, let Hesketh die on the rope!

The traitor's crime was proclaimed, and the crowd waited for the inevitable speech that was the prisoner's right. At first, he could not find his voice. 'Ah...' Despite the cruel laughter, he tried again, his northern vowels ringing out across the space. 'I have been misled by those who should know better and I curse the time I listened to their counsel.' People jeered but the man found extra strength. His voice grew louder with every word. 'I commend my soul to Almighty God and I die in the true faith.' Then his bound wrists rose slowly as though on a string and, as he pointed at Ferdinando, the crowd drew a unison breath of horror. 'I curse Sir William Stanley who sent me but above all I curse you, Ferdinando Stanley, Earl of Derby! *May the Devil take you to an early grave!*

The ancient abbey might have offered solace to Rose after the gruesome execution except it was impossible to reach the west door without going past Hesketh's dismembered body. Appalled and shaken, she hastily left Francis kissing his potential patron's hand, though Ferdy, ashen-faced, had hardly been listening.

Passing the crowd cramming the door of the Tabard Inn, she fled into Spicer's Row towards the muddy alleyway that led to the field behind the inn yard. There, she swiftly pulled back her veil as her breakfast left her. Leaning against one of the fenceposts, she silently cursed Wade as she mopped her eyes with a kerchief and then wiped her mouth. That was when she saw the man's body lying in the grass. Except he wasn't dead. He was shuddering as though he had a fever and he was not some poor beggar but well shod.

'Sir, are you ill?' she called out, keeping a distance that respected him and safeguarded her in case he had the plague. 'Sir?'

Slowly he pushed himself back onto his knees and, holding a cuff to his lips, turned to look at her. His eyes showed unbelievable anguish, his cheeks were wet with tears, and bruises discoloured most of his face.

'I'm s-sorry, sir,' she stammered, embarrassed that she had barged in on his grief.

'Leave me, lass.' A northerner by his dialect and educated, too; the long, dark overgown over his clodie-hued garb suggested lawyer or scholar.

Compassion overwhelmed her, though she sensed he might be a Papist. Crouching, she set a hand on his shoulder. 'Shall I fetch you some ale from one of the sellers, sir, or see you to your lodging?'

He shook his head but, wincing, he held out an arm for her to help him to his feet.

'You are ill, sir.'

'Gout, little mistress, and two busted ribs as yet unhealed.'

'You've been attacked? Do you need a physician?'

He straightened somewhat, taking stock of where they stood before he looked down at her and let go his clutch upon her arm. 'I thank you, finding my hat will suffice.'

The same dialect as Hesketh's, she realised, as she returned, brushing the grass from the cap's soft brim, and there was something familiar in his features.

'You knew him.' The statement escaped her before she could muster a discreet question.

'The man they've just hanged and ripped to pieces? Aye, I knew him very well. Now I expect you will run away and summon the soldiers.'

She understood his bitterness. 'I think you've already been in custody, sir.'

He nodded. 'Questioned in the Marshalsea like a common criminal. They let me out in time for…' Tears oozed from the corners of his eyes again. 'I have not blubbed like this since a boy,' he muttered.

Had William Wade interrogated this man? Dear God, she did not want to know.

'Was there injustice here today?' she dared to ask. 'Was Hesketh innocent?'

The gentleman gulped back his tears to snort angrily. 'Innocent in his head! No, more like a numbskull, thinking he could change history.'

She thought of her father. 'Sometimes it is possible, sir, but there is always a price to pay.'

A familiar voice hallooed her.

'There's your young man seeking you.'

'My brother,' she explained.

'Be glad of him,' the man replied with feeling. 'The hanged man was mine.' He reached out and took her hand in both of his. 'My name is Bartholomew Hesketh and I thank you for your charity, good mistress. God's blessing on you,' and he turned and limped away.

William Wade called on Rose on the pretence of offering an invitation to Francis to ride back to London with his entourage.

'I shall be brief in what I have to say, Rose,' he began softly, taking up a stance before the fire while Francis went upstairs to collect his pack. 'You will only leave Her Majesty's employment when you are dismissed and not before.'

'I'll be brief, too, sir.' Rose had her arguments mustered. The morning had taught her she wanted nothing more to do with the government and its agents, and she certainly was not going to mention her meeting with the hanged man's brother. 'I am very grateful for all your generosity in providing me with this living, but I need a future, sir, and your niece is offering me a chance to step up again in the world. A permanent position in a noble lady's household would suit me very well.'

His nose wrinkled angrily; the diplomat had taken leave. 'Then perhaps I need to point out to you, William Davison's daughter, that for several months you have been corresponding rather affectionately with a Papist soldier in the pay of Colonel Sir William Stanley. An English jury might consider that a hanging offence.'

Rose stared at him in astonishment. 'But your man is in the queen's service. The Privy Council know that.'

He leaned across the table. 'But the world knows him for an assassin, Rose. We can produce evidence he purposed to kill the queen.'

'I don't believe you.'

'My dear, why do you think I advised you to keep his name secret from your family and friends?'

'You never told me that...' She broke off, confused, suspicious that he was bluffing.

'There are witnesses,' he said, but she refused to be gulled.

'What of it, sir? I assume your man had to tell Colonel Stanley such a story otherwise, well, they would not trust him.'

Wade gave her a pitying look. 'My dear, most agents are like whores. They take money from anyone. Sometimes it is hard to know who is working for whom.' He made his way to the door. 'Now can we consider this discussion over? May I assure Her Majesty you are her loyal servant, despite your father's great misdemeanour?'

Pah, he thought her trapped on a treadmill of obedience, did he? True, the government could haul her into prison at any time on false charges, but if she did not stand up for herself, no one else would.

'I want this,' she said bravely, brandishing Lizbeth Vere's letter once more. 'If she asks again, I shall say yes, and you do well to remind me how much my family have suffered for their service to Her Majesty. It is comforting to know that I, too, am to be rewarded for my loyalty with the threat of death.'

'Have you anything else to say?'

'Yes. Yes, I thought you were my friend and patron. How can you deny me my chance to —'

'Find yourself a new husband so you can be wealthy and secure?' he interrupted. 'If that is all what you really want, my dear, we can arrange it eventually. A rich dotard with few wits left who won't ask questions.'

Just so she could continue writing to this intelligencer?

'Is he that necessary?' Gall edged her voice.

'The dull-witted husband?'

'Your mockery is unkind, Master Wade. You know very well who I mean. Tell me, must my path be forever hedged with briars because of this agent?'

'My dear girl, you know I cannot tell you more. What I am trying to say is that none of our other agents have managed to get such close access to our enemies' plans. If our intelligencer's story is suddenly thrown into suspicion — and it will be if he starts writing the same words to some other woman, then all this —' his palms acknowledged their surroundings — 'has been a waste. Ah, I hear your brother's feet upon the stairs.' With a cold smile, he turned and opened the door to let Francis in. 'Ready, lad?' he asked heartily. 'Excellent! Kiss your sister farewell.' With a bow, he left her to fume. Biting back a curse, she closed the door behind them and leaned against it.

I'll manage this somehow! she vowed. *And be damned to you!*

8

By the time what was left of Richard Hesketh had been tarred and removed from the place of execution, Garrett observed that detachments of Her Majesty's soldiers were cobwebbing every street and laneway out of St Albans, at the ready to snare any Jesuit flies that had been foolhardy enough to be present for the Papist martyr's death. If he had not been safeguarding 'Uncle Owen', he would have tried to get through Ferdinando's retinue and snatch a private word. Maybe later.

Owen had been stalwart, his gaze upon Hesketh had never wavered as though willing the suffering man to know that he was anointing him with holy oil, forgiving him his sins and praying that God would raise him up. Yet now it was all over, the poor priest's complexion was the colour of an ageing parsnip, and the wobble of his Adam's apple betrayed he was spiritually exhausted.

Unbuckling the hipflask from his belt, Garrett passed it over. 'Here, take this, it might help.'

Had Hesketh even realised Owen was present for him? In such agony when your innards were being yanked out, did one face in the crowd give you heart? Well, Garrett hoped so. By God, it had been sordid. He had known his reports might mean arrests, but to see the outcome and know he might bear some responsibility was like an icy hand gripping his heart. On the other hand, if Ferdinando had said yes to Hesketh, his lordship could have ended up in the Tower beheaded for high treason with his family disinherited. Well, Garrett was grabbing tight to that mental driftwood while the rest of him struggled not to perish in a sea of guilt.

Receiving the flask back, he took a draught, glad of the liquor's powerful warmth as he observed the passing faces. He was supposed to entrust Owen to the care of a local Papist but the fine gentleman was late and that made Garrett increasingly on edge. Damn it, they were in the right place, at the corner of French Row and Church Street, not far from the Bell Tower. Where was the man? Had something gone wrong? Owen would be facing torture and death if Wade sniffed his presence. The priest-catcher had been at the hanging, hobnobbing with Ferdinando and Sir Robert Cecil as though it was some pageant.

How much longer? Rain was spattering his cloak and although they had a jut of building above their heads, there was a limit as to how long they could linger, pretending to make conversation when neither of them felt like talking. Someone would notice and, well, imagination perhaps, but the stench of Hesketh's disembowelment still clogged the air. Garrett didn't want Owen's Welsh insides to end up as rarebit.

A group of Her Majesty's military were sauntering up the hill towards them now. Human wolves sniffing the air for prey, the stink of fear.

'Start walking!' Like a drinking crony, Garrett flung his arm about Owen. 'Maybe we should take our ease at an alehouse for an hour like honest men,' he muttered brazenly, eyeing the string of taverns edging Holywell Hill.

Owen shook his arm away. 'I haven't the stomach for food, Garrett.' But then he glanced back and saw the soldiers. He almost crossed himself. Almost.

And Garrett *almost* thanked God as he saw two of the military grab a chapman who had been trying to get past. Now the poor wretch was spreadeagled against the nearest shopfront while they searched him.

'Well, let's hope that wasn't your host for tonight,' he muttered, hastening the Welshman along the greasy cobbles. 'Mingle, shall we?' They plunged in among the market stalls cluttering Chequer Street. 'Eye the women! Admire the goods!'

The soldiers were behind them again.

Owen stuffed his hands into his sleeves only to receive a growl and Garrett's fierce hand on his elbow. 'God's death, don't do that!'

'I... I...' The unfinished apology came from lips pale with shock. The horror of what the priest had witnessed was biting now. Shock made a man vulnerable. They needed shelter. Trouble was, if the poor wretch fell into a fever in some lodging, God knows what he'd blab out. And it was a good wager the soldiers would search the inns. They'd search every bloody rabbit burrow before morning.

'What if C-Coningsby doesn't f-find us?' Owen stammered.

Shops edged the road ahead, but they'd reached the end of the stalls. They could plunge back in among the barrows or —

'Keep walking!' The reports he'd sent to Wade had a St Alban's address, but where in hell was it? Asking for directions might be — 'Sweet Jesu!'

Riding towards them was none other than Wade, with a young man riding at his elbow and half a dozen horsemen in breastplates and helmets behind him. The man was scanning the street ahead like a cruel-eyed hawk out for the kill.

Garrett touched his hat brim as in salute but made sure it came further down to hide his face. 'Into the next shop!' he ordered his companion. 'Now, but easy. Slowly.'

Owen had the wit to comply; however, the mercer's was hardly the perfect refuge as the priest found himself nose to bale with a selection of linens for female undergarments. He immediately shifted to a stack of kerseys, canvas and frisado.

An apprentice was instantly at their side. 'May I help you, masters?'

'No, Gabriel, I'll attend these gentlemen.' A barrel-shaped man past forty strutted from behind the counter. Behind the well-oiled smirk of greeting was a mental calculus assessing their rank.

'Hmm.' Garrett cast a second look around the shop, slow and considered this time, before he ran his fingers across the bales. 'This one.' A cream silk.

'Filozel, sir. Is it for a lady's chemise?'

'Well, it's not for mine, friend.'

'I can see that, sir.' The smile was fraying. 'How much would your worship be requiring?'

Garrett made show of glancing from his elbow to his fingertips. 'Four ells, I think she said.' Then, leaving the fellow to extricate the bale with the help of the apprentice, he sauntered to the counter where Owen was waiting. Raising his eyebrows, he pulled a what-was-I-suppose-to-do grimace.

At least it had given them time to get upwind of Wade's company.

'Does the lady live in St Albans?' asked the mercer, nosey bastard, as he measured the quantity.

Garrett ignored the fellow. Instead, he extricated a frothy garter of scarlet lace and tiny rosebuds from a basket on the counter and playfully whirled it on his finger. 'What do you think, uncle? Will these take her fancy?'

To anyone discerning, Owen's shrug was edged with tension and he stupidly had his gloved hands tucked up his sleeves again. With a laugh — not too forced he hoped — Garrett picked out the garter's mate and tossed the pair on the counter. 'That's sufficient, I think.'

'Seven shillings, sir.' The price was outrageous. Clearly, the shopkeeper's arithmetic was at fault or else he had overestimated this customer's stupidity.

Garrett leaned across the counter. 'Is my hearing amiss?' he asked menacingly. The mercer's well-clad spine could have sought the security of the shelves behind the counter; instead, he smoothly revised the sum. 'Your pardon, my error. Five shillings and eightpence, if you please.'

It didn't please but Garrett was not disposed to argue further. He counted the exact amount out of his purse and then stuffed the purchases into the breast of his doublet.

'Anything else I may help you with, gentlemen? I can recommend the meat pies at the Peacock, and the Fleur-de-Lis boasts no bedbugs if you be a-wanting lodging for the night, though I daresay it will be full of visitors who came for the Papist's execution.' A probing stare at the older gentleman before the mercer dropped his gaze to the basket of garters. 'Ah, but…'

'Indeed,' agreed Garrett. 'Good morrow to you and a very good night to me.'

Outside, they glimpsed Wade's retinue had halted ahead of them. A pincushion of pikemen was standing to attention, and an officer looked to be making a report as he stood at the master investigator's stirrup.

Owen swallowed. 'Gott have mercy!'

'Pah, bread-and-butter stuff. Once the old man leaves the town, they'll slacken like old bed ropes.'

In fact, old man Wade spurred his horse into a trot and the officer, beckoning his small troop to follow, strode across the street to a wealthy-looking house and hammered on the door with his fist, demanding admittance. Two of his men were doing the same at the next house.

'Ha, Owen! That'll keep 'em busy.'

'I'm done with this, Garrett. We have to get off the street.'

'Weren't we just doing that? Very well, back to Church Street, then, and let us hope one of your flock has arrived to say he's tidied up a hiding hole for you.' He led the shortest way back through French Row.

Ah, three chilly recusants waiting at the corner. Woollen cloths scarfed the lower half of their faces against the cold. Not unexpected on a November day with the east wind whipping down Church Street. One of the men was stocky, perhaps grey-haired beneath his plumed hat; the other had the stoop of the very tall.

'Whoa!' Garrett cautioned, slowing his stride.

The woman with them uncovered a bread loaf in her basket. 'There's the signal.' Owen's shoulders lost their tension. 'It means "Gott is with us".'

'I'm glad you think so. Just be careful.' Garrett had expected some cryptic greeting like 'The speckled hen is laying again', but there was no such nonsense. The shorter of the two men held out a hand. 'Well met! I'm Sir Thomas Coningsby, and may I present my wife, Jane, and Master Henry Gill.'

The latter eyed the priest's complexion with concern: 'How fare you?'

Chin angled sadly, Owen spread his hands. 'I grieve deeply for our departed brother, Master Gill.'

'As do we all, Father,' asserted Lady Coningsby, 'but we do hope you will feel hale enough to hold a service tonight.' Her haughty tone implied disappointment was not acceptable.

'Willingly, my daughter.' Anticipation of celebrating Mass and the guarantee of a hearty meal looked to be chivvying the colour back into Owen's bearded cheeks.

Reassured that their spiritual needs would be satisfied, the Coningsbys' attention turned to Garrett. 'Are you coming with us as well, friend?'

'No, I thank you.' Garrett had had enough of makeshift Masses and being hidden in cramped holes. He had said nothing to Owen of his supposed betrothed and he certainly did not want these people asking questions. 'And the arrangements for the morrow, Sir Thomas?' he asked briskly.

'Be here at five o' the clock tomorrow morning. Gill, here, will bring you to a safe house where there's a cellar passageway that comes out on the other side of one of the southern barriers. There you'll find horses and he will guide you back to the London road by way of the causeway. We've arranged for a cooper's cart to be waiting in a side lane. There'll be clothing for you to disguise yourselves and then you'll drive the cart to London.'

'Excellent,' Garrett muttered dryly. He touched his hat brim in thanks and headed back to Holywell Street. He would call on Wade's cipher clerk just before curfew but what he desired now was a strong ale. Now that he had no urgent need to safeguard Owen, he felt exhausted. Unbidden, his mind replayed the terror of the morning and he felt humbled by the priest's courage, awed that a man who had already suffered imprisonment in the Marshalsea could risk being caught and tortured again. Such faith!

Suddenly his soldier's gut was yelling a warning.

'Hey there!'

He froze, took a deep breath, relaxed his face and turned to discover he was being hallooed by a handful of pikemen, clad in the scarlet tunics of Wade's military. Had they seen him earlier with Owen?

One of them stepped towards him. 'Ah, it *is* you, Captain. Well met, eh? Remember me, sir? Hal Pekham? You have found employment, then?'

It was the soldier who'd recommended him to Wade. Relief flooded through him. He was not to be asked for his papers though he'd need to dredge up a story if the conversation continued. 'Yes, I thank you, Hal.'

'Deployed for the hanging, then, sir?'

'No, passing through.'

'Then you might not have time for a drink with me — with us — but we'd be honoured if you would.'

'You are not on duty, lads?'

'A short respite, Captain. Sort of mingle and watch.'

His intelligencer character firmly back in place, Garrett grinned. 'Then it would be a pleasure to join you.'

They headed for the Peacock Inn and it proved a half-hour well spent. His companions commented on the talk in London that Hesketh had threatened the new Earl of Derby, telling him he would be assassinated if he refused to lead a rebellion, so it was little wonder his lordship had handed him over. However, Garrett found the snippet curious. Was it true? Or had it been given out by Her Majesty's government to make Hesketh seem more dangerous?

He also learned that Ferdinando was in trouble with the queen for not turning Hesketh over immediately. The royal sulk meant that his lordship was neither welcome in her presence nor had she reconfirmed the posts he had been holding as Lord Strange, offices which would have brought a lucrative income. Pekham, who knew one of the royal jakes cleaners, even reckoned that Lord Essex had been poisoning the royal ear against the earl. Aye, and it was said anyone wanting favours from Her Majesty had either to grovel to Lord Burghley and his hunchback son or charm Lord Essex.

'So is the new Lord Derby grovelling?'

'Not yet,' chuckled Pekham, 'but it won't take long.'

A disappointing observation. Garrett was hoping his patron had grown more powerful. He wanted the earl to be a future king, not a lily-livered toe-licker.

'His lordship can chew Sir Robert Cecil's ear on the way back to London, I suppose.'

'Missed opportunity, Captain. The earl's already hotfooted it out of town. Going back to Lancashire to sulk, I daresay.'

Damn! Garrett had lost his chance to see if Ferdinando still wanted his service. Though with Wade, his other employer, in town, that would have required a great deal of stealth. Still, this conversation with these Londoners had been useful, and it might have been possible to glean more gossip but the clocktower bell had the men back on their feet, leaving Garrett sitting a while longer. He'd mingled; now he'd watch.

The taproom was filled with young braggarts already half-mast with ale. With a good memory for faces, he was recognising plenty from this morning's crowd. St Albans would be ugly tonight. Guilt, that's what he smelled along with the ale fumes and the meat turning on the spits. The good men of Hertfordshire would be quaffing so as not to feel, not to remember how they'd jeered as a fellow Englishman had died in agony for his faith. Oh, there would be earnest toasts a-plenty to Good Queen Bess and loud cursing of 'farkin' Jesuits' and fingers lifted meaningfully — for jabbing up the Roman Pontiff's arse. At curfew they'd spew out of the taverns to vomit on the cobbles and yell to each other as they made water against the walls. God protect any tapster wench running to home this night.

He could feel the bag with the garters and silk against his shirt and hardened at the thought of enjoying a woman. He'd been celibate too long but for good reason; Spanish pox wasted more soldiers than any war and he wasn't going to take the risk. A pity he was corresponding with a clerk and not a real woman.

He'd insist Wade's clerk let him sleep by the hearth. And if the fellow was away in Westminster and he had the house to himself, all the better.

'I'm going to the secret Mass tonight, lass,' Martin informed Rose after he'd heaved in the scuttle of wood to keep the parlour fire alight until bedtime. 'They'll wonder else, seein' I'm supposed to be a dyed-in-the-wool Papist. Should be a squeeze unless some of 'em are too lily-livered to come out from under their stones. There's a Welsh priest to do the business. Knows the Pope.'

'Does he? Impressive.'

At least Martin wasn't implying she should attend as well. So far, she had managed to avoid any acquaintance with the local Papists, though clearly they knew of her through Martin. She was dressed for comfort. The farthingale and hood she had worn to the hanging had been replaced with a simple house gown. Her hair, uncovered, unpinned and not yet plaited for bedtime, was loosely gathered into a ribbon over her shoulder.

'Rather you than me tonight,' she added, shaking her head at her companion's recklessness. St Albans was still too full of clanking pursuivants to be safe. Soldiers would be keeping watch on any religious suspects. She should not wonder if there was some informer watching her door. Although she attended Sunday church and played the sorrowful widow who valued solitude, people may have wondered about her reclusiveness. 'Where's the Mass to be held, Martin?'

'Coningsby Hall, lass. They've a hiding hole if anything goes wrong.'

'Well, promise me you'll be careful.' He might be agile for his age but he was no young rooster. 'If the soldiers break in and put you all under arrest, they're not to know you are one of theirs. You could be badly beaten before I can get word to Master Wade. Do you have some token you can show to prove whose side you're on?' Because she was a gentlewoman Wade had never suggested such a thing for her, but Martin in his servant's homespun might be far more vulnerable.

'Don't worry, lass.' He glanced across at the raindrops streaking down the window. 'Dusk will come early an' Her Majesty's finest don't like the wet an' cold any more than I do. I'll leave before curfew and come home in the mornin' when plenty of folks are about.' Stooping, he took a spill from the pot on the hearth and poked it in the flames before he carried it across to light the candles. The smell of wax wafted into the warm air. 'Anyhow,' he muttered, flinging it into the fire. 'Wade has ordered me to go. He wants a list of all those who attend.'

'So they can be fined?'

He chuckled. 'Or suffer free lodging courtesy of Her Majesty's government. I'll leave your supper out for when your appetite comes back.' Seeing her wince, he added, 'Wade should not have insisted on you attending this morning.'

She came to stand beside him at the hearth and stretched out her fingers to the heat. 'I can still hear the poor wretch's screams. Why was he so cruelly punished, Martin? He never murdered anybody.'

'Aye, but he might have been quite happy to put a noose round Lord Burghley's neck an' his son's' He gave her shoulders a fatherly hug. 'Try and put it out of your mind, eh?'

Easier advised than done. 'Sir Robert was there. Did you see him?'

'Aye, so he can report to the queen. Fellow's as opportunist as Beelzebub. And if truth be told — though never quote me on this — I reckon your da' got shoved aside to make room for the young 'un.'

'You are probably right.' Rose fought down the bitterness. 'Lord Essex was the only one who begged the queen to free my father from the Tower.'

'Ah, we're just pawns on the chessboard, Rose.' Martin dropped his arm away and moved towards the door. 'Tell you this, I'll warrant Sir Robert and his da' must be quaking in their boots lest Her Majesty drop dead tomorrow. It ain't for England you and I are working, see, it's to keep them Cecils in fancy cushions and bed hangings.' Rose could not help smiling as she caught the cushion he tossed from the settle. 'I'll be off then, an' listen, it's not just me who needs to take care,' he warned, knowing how weary she was of St Albans. 'You, too, must watch the shadows at your back!'

The sound from the kitchen made her set her book aside. It was only an ordinary sound, a plate being shifted, perhaps the clink of a spoon, but it was a relief to know that Martin was back, that something had made him turn for home. With a shiver, she rose from the window seat. Outside was darkness, and her reflection, fractured in tiny panes, looked bleakly back at her. She could hear that the wind had changed direction, blown aside the rain. Now it was rattling the casement like a lonely ghost yearning to be human once more. It made her wonder what had become of Hesketh's soul but at the same time, contrarily, mundanely, she realised she was hungry and then she heard the stairs creak. Bless him, Martin was bringing up the supper tray as usual. No reason to think anything amiss about the gentle thump of his elbow on the door before the handle turned.

In an instant she grabbed the iron poker because the aproned man who stood in the doorway holding her supper tray between gloved hands was a stranger, tall and wide-chested. For a heartbeat he looked as shocked as she felt, but he recovered first. 'Good, don't scream,' he said, eyeing her with the calculation of a boy about to smash a spider.

'And why not?' she said through her teeth, brandishing her weapon like a broadsword.

'Because your father said you'd be hungry by now. He should have introduced us. May I put this down for you? Do you usually eat this late?'

'My *father*?'

'Yes, before he went out.'

What? This intruder had met Martin, and Martin had gone away *until tomorrow*. She gulped, considered strangling Martin on his return, but meantime...

The stranger was no longer watching the poker but eyeing her with a degree of amazement rather than impudent speculation. 'You know I reckon I've met you before, mistress.' His gaze, sliding down her hair as it lay upon her shoulder, and then across her breasts, alarmed her further. 'So why not put that down,' he coaxed, ignoring her tightened grip upon the poker. 'I could disarm you easily.'

'My ... my father will be back at any moment.'

'Don't think so.' Stepping forward, he set the plate on the floor while he shifted her jar of quill pens and the dish of comfits from the table beside her chair with familial diligence. 'He said you might appreciate my company.'

The candlelight showed her a strong face as he lifted the tray back up and tidied the napkin, but it was the sudden dazzling, impudent smile that dimpled his cheeks which made her catch her breath. God's mercy! The last time she'd seen this man he'd been bare-chested and murdering a duke. Feeling she was snared in some bizarre nightmare, she tried a grab at sanity. 'Why...' she began. The large man's smile widened, waiting. 'Why is a second-rate London player bringing in my supper?'

His cheerful dog expression changed to peeved cat. 'Second Murderer, maybe, but second-rate?' Then understanding gleamed in his hazel eyes. 'Ha! That's where I saw you. By heaven, you're the wench from the pit.' The toss of words was not flattering and before she could give him a cutting answer, he gestured to the supper. 'Don't let me hinder you.'

Rose offered her sweetest smile. 'Would you like to fetch yourself something and join me?'

'Well, if you wish.' Gratitude lit his face. 'It's pleasing warm in here.'

The instant Rose heard his feet heading downstairs, she grabbed the other small table, wedged it against the door and picked up the poker once more. Absurdly, she heard the actor humming and the clatter of dishes. Then the stairs creaked once more beneath his boots, the tray tinged as it met the door timber. She heard him put it down, then try the ring handle.

'Go away! Leave this instant!'

'Mistress?' The handle shook.

'*Get out of my house!* I don't care if you played Richard III or you are the Archangel Gabriel with a message, leave now!'

'Mistress, I swear I mean you no harm. I only want to eat supper with you.'

Absurdly, Rose thought of Adam and Eve. Food was mischievous, seductive. It could change the whole course of history. Well, an apple had, and women were still being blamed for it.

Oh, God help her, the door was edging open, bullying the table. With the poker stowed beneath her arm, she shoved the table back with all her strength. 'I *will* scream.' A deep breath.

'My name is Garrett Towneley,' he said quickly, 'and your father said... He said it was all right.'

'I don't give a d—' She swallowed the blasphemy as the possibility hit her. GT? Garrett ... Towneley? *The intelligencer?* 'Is your name supposed to mean something?' she replied contrarily and stopped pushing.

A mutter before he answered. 'Only that I was once ducked in a font. I never asked.' The table began scraping towards her again. 'Has your father ever mentioned Wade, clerk to the Privy Council? I work for him.'

Rose's shoulders sank. 'Yes,' she managed with a growl. 'And you are scratching the floorboards doing that. Just wait.' Without losing her weapon, she heaved her wooden battlement aside but kept it between her and her unbidden visitor. He toed the door open, picked up his tray and, looking very put out, squeezed past.

'What I'd like to know,' she declared assertively, 'is why my *father* did not introduce us? He's not gagged and bound, is he?'

'Not unless Her Majesty's lads are having some sport.' Her visitor gestured downstairs. 'Do you want to see for yourself?' Ignoring her indignant glare, he moved a plate of cold mutton onto a footstool and took a seat behind it on the settle. Only then did he remove his gloves. Swiftly, courteously, she lifted her gaze from his damaged hands. The same could have happened to Oliver, her late husband. He, too, had been an artillery man. Peeking beneath her lashes as her guest leaned forward to serve himself, she observed he was quite dexterous in his own way. Necessity, she supposed. A man's way of eating could demonstrate the depth of his civility.

'Anyway, what did you think of *Richard III*?' her visitor asked, with a mouth full. 'Burbage evil enough for you?'

Engaged, she could not resist answering. 'Enough to make Sir Robert Cecil displeased.'

A lift of eyebrow and a nod. He took a second helping.

Still wary, Rose sat down, set her weapon on the floor at hand and then, trying to look very worldly and in control, she nonchalantly slid a slither of cheese on her bread.

'You're betrothed, I see,' he observed pleasantly. 'A fellow here in St Albans, is it?'

'Oh yes,' she said coolly. '*You.*'

Garrett choked. His coughing fit endured until, hot-faced, he gratefully accepted a cup of ale and took an easing swig. His reluctant hostess waited before him. Her concern was not forced but only a fool would miss the smugness in her eyes that it was she who had done the disarming.

Finding his voice, he asked huskily, 'Are you sure?'

Slender fingers slid the betrothal ring free and held it out to him. The metal was warm from her skin and though the fleeting touch of her fingertips against his might be indifferent for her, it was sensual for him. He was glad to turn away and raise the ring to the candlelight.

It was no light trinket and etched into the silver were his intertwined initials. 'God be merciful,' he said softly and twisted round to face her. 'They never told me. And there was I thinking my loving widow was a gorbellied Whitehall clerk with bad breath. I presume it's your father, then, who handles the ciphers?'

'No, your letters are carried to Westminster,' she corrected archly. 'The man you met downstairs is my manservant.'

Digesting his error, he made pretence of staring at the ring a moment longer before he offered it back. 'Then I did the right thing.' It was spoken more to himself than her. No wonder the Coningsbys had not shown offence when he had refused their invitation to the Mass. They knew about shapely Rose Byrd; he had been expected to visit here. To have not visited 'his betrothed' would have aroused surprise, even suspicion. *Or worse.* He was an absolute dolt not to have realised there had to be a real woman involved. Thank God he'd come here.

He thought back to the Theatre. How looking up from murdering the duke in the barrel, he'd seen this woman, her violet gaze enthralled, her pretty lips a 'o' of horror. And now to find himself alone with her — and her sitting there with her hair gathered into a luscious love-knot and no stiff stomacher to conceal her attributes — was more than luck. Yet none of this made sense and coincidences made him wary. Although her manner and circumstances proclaimed her a gentlewoman, true gentlewomen didn't frequent theatre pits. What hold did Wade have over her? How long had 'Rose Byrd' — was that even her real name? — been working for the Cecils before she took on this 'betrothed' role? Maybe she was nothing more than some quick-witted harlot who could play a part and use her looks.

'The man you met downstairs is Martin Lorimer, he's Master Wade's man,' she was explaining. 'The letters to you, however, are in my hand. And all this,' she gestured with a pretty unfurl of palms, 'is for Master GT.'

'Captain.'

'Your pardon, *Captain*.'

It was flattering to know that Wade had gone to such costly lengths on his behalf. Garrett made show of inspecting the furnishings with greater appreciation, but his gaze quickly returned to his hostess. And was *she* for him as well?

It had been a while since he had enjoyed making love, but to engender pleasure required two willing parties and adequate trust. He could not expect a real gentlewoman to indulge him. Whatever her history, Rose Byrd was showing more ease now, the napkin and plate comfortable upon her lap. Had her indignation been genuine? What else had Wade required her to do for the sake of England? She was in her twenties, presumably experienced. Maybe he was the greener of the two of them.

'Has all this been worthwhile?' he asked.

'For you, yes, Captain.' As if shielding herself from his direct scrutiny, she served herself from the flagon, and before he could question further, she enlightened him. 'We had visitors during the spring, you see. Two men, outsiders. One claimed his name was Ralph Hawkridge. The other called himself James Farmer and he was definitely a priest.'

'The names mean nothing to me.' *Jesu*, he thought, *what would they have done to her, had they realised?*

Setting her plate aside, she fetched a purple posy from the sill, unwrapped a scrap of paper from its stems and held both out to him. 'They claimed to have brought this from you.'

He shook his head in wonderment at the forgery, then he examined the artifice, grimacing at the whiff of heavy dousing that still clung to the flowerheads. Wait! He remembered now describing his mistress being as sweet as violets. But to whom? Verstegan! God's mercy!

Straightening the petals, his mouth grim, he realised how close he had come to sharing Aidan Markham's fate.

'Not from me,' he informed her gravely, handing the flowers back.

Holding the posy against her breasts, she fondled the tiny mauve petals. 'Hawkridge scared me,' she admitted. 'But he must have gone away satisfied or you would not be here now.'

'Mistress, I think I owe you my life.' He could admit that and be grateful.

She smiled and replied with a worldly shrug. 'I'm glad I was convincing. Time passes slowly in this town if you avoid making friends.' Resuming her seat, she took another helping from the platter. That gave him leave to sit back. He watched her over the rim of the pewter ale cup. How long would they use her to safeguard him?

'Tell me, mistress, were you sent to the Theatre by Master Wade?'

'To recruit you, sir? No, that was mere chance, save I paid dearly for it. The gallant you incited on stage tried to assault me on my way home.'

That rattled him. Such a consequence had never passed his mind. He would have thrashed the knave. 'Your pardon, mistress, had I been on hand...' Then he added, eyeing the poker, 'I'm sure you dealt with him.' However, if he expected complacency, he was wrong; pain flashed in her eyes.

'Yes, I managed.' The ambiguity again. How close had the bastard come?

'I'm truly sorry.'

Why was she so hard to fathom? There was a strength in her, but from what? He wanted to know more but common sense bridled his tongue. Better not ask. Meeting her had made him more vulnerable. His masters in the Spanish Netherlands could manipulate him by threatening her.

'Tell me, when those two men came to verify my story, did they mention anyone called Verstegan?'

'They gave no names. They copied your hand exactly, didn't they? It was almost convincing.' She shook her head, delicately wiped the crumbs from her lips. 'Would you believe it was partaking in the Mass that worried me most. Master Farmer thought he was doing me great service.'

Garrett nodded wholeheartedly. 'I'm glad we did not have to attend the service tonight, which brings me to ask another favour. I've been travelling for days. May I stay until morning, use your servant's room? He said I was welcome.'

He watched her consider. Slowly a pale rose suffused her cheeks. 'I understand.'

'Your pardon, mistress, what do you understand?'

'That you must come here. Had it been another town, you would have gone to the Mass.'

'Yes,' he admitted, with a sheepish smile.

'I wish Martin had warned me.'

'He didn't know.'

If their theatre encounter had led them to meet straightaway, he would now be taking her to bed, making love, then falling asleep with his arms around her in a desperate joyful night that would make up for the loneliness, the months of missing each other; instead, they were strangers. 'Believe me, I'm no threat,' he assured her. 'I'll sleep downstairs beside the kitchen fire if you prefer.'

'No, be comfortable.' She rose, shaking out her skirts, gesturing him to stay seated. 'I'll find you fresh sheets.'

He was gratified she thought him trustworthy; disappointed yet pleased she was not wanton. A woman as attractive as her could take her pick. Perhaps it was her confidence in who she was that made him feel uncomfortable. Not to mention her intelligence. Was she, like him, weighing the consequences of this encounter? Gazing down at him, her brow puzzled, she asked, 'How much of what you write is code, Captain?'

'Most of it, mistress. Sometimes I put something in to … well, annoy Wade.'

Once more, a pleasing blush. 'I was wondering whether it is possible for you to add something that tells *me* all is well.'

Again, she had surprised him. He smiled. 'What about a cheerful sun on the address?'

Her lips parted, laughter lighting her gaze. 'Yes, I should like that. Master Wade tells me nothing.'

A log crumbled in the silence between them. He rose, set the *couvre-feu* across the embers, then he stayed standing with his back to the hearth, even though the sleeplessness of the last few nights was weighing on him like ankle fetters. Both his mind and body craved a restful night and yet he was lingering in the moment. A house like this; a pretty wife; babe in a cradle. Instead: a soldiers' camp.

Just an arm's length away, she had another question. 'Are you able to tell me any… I mean, are you returning to the Spanish Netherlands and do you know for how long?'

She was not tall. Kissing her would be easier with her on his lap. Clearing his throat, he answered, 'I start back tomorrow. As to how long, I'm not sure.' It would depend when and how the colonel intended to deploy him.

A nod, resigned, unsurprised, then she said awkwardly, 'Well, if you would like to wait here, I'll fetch that bed linen.'

'Thank you.' The evening was at an end. 'May I?' he gestured to the flagon.

'Of course, I won't be long.' He liked that she had not commented on his hands. Most women would ask but she was different.

When she returned, flushed from exertion, he fixed her gravely. 'Listen, I don't know anything about your circumstances or why a woman of your quality would take on this employment, but I suggest you free yourself if you can. The men I associate with are killers, Mistress Byrd. Not all, but some. Plenty want to kill the queen.'

'I don't believe Hesketh did.'

He stared down at her in surprise. 'Then I think you are wrong. It's a war. There's nothing honourable on either side.'

'I'm trying to extricate myself, sir. It's … it's not easy.' Remembering she had brought a candlestick for him, she took it across to the candelabra. 'I'll show you to your room.'

'I'll find it.' He wanted to leave the town knowing she'd be safe, yet how? And if she did quit Wade's service and was no longer his alibi, what then? 'Thank you,' he said, receiving the lit candle. 'Don't stay up for me. I'd like to write my report for Wade if you can kindly provide some writing paper.'

Opening the window seat, she took some out. He had already handled the jar of quills on the table next to her chair, seen the glass-stoppered inkwell and the small pot of pine dust.

'Then I'll bid you goodnight, sir.'

'Mistress.' A soldier's bow, and despite the risk of repulsing her, he reached out his disfigured hand and carried her wrist to his lips. 'Your servant, mistress.'

For an instant, she gazed up at him and he was so tempted to draw her close. Instead, he offered a formal smile and, walking to the door, opened it for her. 'Farewell and thank you, I'll be gone before morning. Take heed and quit St Albans,' he warned one last time.

'But if I do, what about you?'

'I'm a soldier, mistress. Goodnight to you. Sleep well.'

She didn't.

Even after her mind had finished boning the evening's conversation, the Devil (or was it her imagination) began to whisper all manner of suspicions. Was her visitor truly the Antwerp agent or another Papist sent to test her? Which might mean she had put the real intelligencer at risk. And if this visitor was a Papist, would he end up like Hesketh? Torn, quartered?

He'd been gentlemanly, not tried to seduce her, and yet...

She listened for his foot on the stairs. Sensations that were rusty tempted her to recklessly invite him to her bed. But another soldier? *No, resist such a sin*, her common sense argued, hadn't she been bruised enough by Oliver, neglected, used? *Yes*, whispered the Devil, *but you are more assured now. Very soon you will be at the back of the pantry shelf, a wrinkled old apple with too many regrets.*

No, Rose decided, her future lay in becoming Lizbeth, Lady Vere's companion.

The unseduced Rose was in the grumps as she attired herself the next morning. It would have been sensible to shake her feelings into the air with the briskness of a dusting housemaid but, like motes in the sunlight, her emotions were inexplicable, beyond her grasp. Her anger with Martin, however, was straightforward and needed to be made clear.

She found him on his knees at the kitchen hearth, clearing the ashpan. The set of her mouth told him immediately that he deserved the kennel but like any sharp-witted man, he forestalled her. 'Present for you, wench,' he said, jerking his chin up at the table. 'It were there when I let myself in. Must be the Hobgoblin Puck come down the chimney.'

Something lifted in her heart. She ignored the cheerful whistling as he bent again to his task, and foolishly unwrapped the parcel. 'Aught useful?' he queried.

Rose stared speechless at the outrageous scarlet garters and the expensive creamy silk spilling out from the wrapping. It made matters worse to have Martin climb to his feet and look over her shoulder. Had he asked if the gift was a thank you, she'd have punched him.

'It seems Puck's picked the wrong house,' she said with a chill voice. 'Possibly a gratuity to the stew in the next lane, I daresay.'

'Look, summat more slipped out.' Sucking in his cheeks, Martin stooped and handed her a paper.

Thank you for your hospitality!

It was signed with a love heart and the initials *GT.*

'Seems your Puck had a good go at the cheese in the pantry, an' did some report writing.' Martin was grinning. 'Taken with the garters, are you, Rose?'

Hands on her hips, she turned on him with all the heat of an angry fishwife. 'This isn't amusing, sirrah! Last night, knowing I'd be alone, you let a stranger — a man — into this house. Why?'

Beneath his beard, Martin's weathered skin reddened. 'I didn't think any—' Seeing her flinch, he set kind hands upon her shoulders. 'No harm done, eh?'

'That's not the point, Martin. You allowed this because you were gullible enough to believe his story.'

'But it was expected he'd come to see you.' The anxious look was back. 'But it were him, weren't it? See, same writing!' He pointed to a crisp, sealed letter propped like a reminder against his satchel.

'Well,' she said coldly, 'you'd better see it is delivered.' With unbidden, foolish tears threatening, she turned away.

'Why are you so angry?' Martin asked gently. 'Wasn't he good company? Fellow seemed manly, decent. I thought —'

'Yes, yes, I know he had to visit.'

'Then...?'

She couldn't explain. Going into the parlour, she'd seen the shavings in the hearth where he'd sharpened a quill, the cushion discarded from the seat because he'd used her chair; a book left open, the others rearranged; the scatter of fine pine dust beside the used cup and the writing board left for her to tidy away. The man had asked her permission and yet...

There was more. Over her shoulder, she said huskily, 'He didn't use your bed though I put fresh sheets on.' In his role of servant, Martin always slept in the attic. 'He slept in the other bedchamber across the landing. He didn't use any sheets.'

'That'll save on the washing.'

She turned. 'My bedroom door was ajar when I woke up.' The garters flew from her hand. 'Damn it!' she exclaimed.

Martin toed the fallen gift. 'You are throwing a tantrum yet for the life of me I've no idea why.' That was a lie. 'Won't it become easier now you've met?'

'No.' A shrug to match the sulky can't-you-see-I'm-confused sniff. 'It's just that —' They both hushed as the daily maidservant came into the outside yard.

'So shall I throw these on the fire or donate them to the strumpets round the corner?' he chuckled.

'Enough!' Adding a scorching oath, she swiftly snatched them from him and ran to the stairs. 'Enough!'

'You've not brought Father Griffith back,' Father Holt accused, mopping his streaming nose.

'I am not his keeper,' Garrett answered stonily, staring the priest down. If this blethering zealot had, like him, endured hiding holes, a discreet beating up in London's Thames Street just to help him to continue to look genuine (courtesy of William Wade), a tempest on a smelly herring boat and then a ride over half the Netherlands trying to find the colonel's latest headquarters, he might be as touchy as a wounded bear as well.

With a cheekbone still showing bruises and a temper hardly stoppered, Garrett was facing the triumvirate of Colonel Stanley, de Francesci and old Holt in the smoky upstairs chamber of their new headquarters. They were in a row on the long side of the table. Like smug, bloody magistrates. And Garrett was not pleased to be criticised before he had even sat down. Striding across to the window, he opened it to let in fresh air and stood fuming. Below on the Antwerp-Brussels *rijweg*, a dog lifted its leg against the barrow selling cheeses.

'What was I supposed to do with Father Griffith?' he asked over his shoulder. 'Rope him to the mast? Block his ears against Protestant sirens? Witnessing Hesketh's death changed his mind about teaching at Saint-Omer. He's put himself under Father Parson's orders in London.' *God help him!*

'This man's insolence is unacceptable.' Holt rose angrily to his feet.

Garrett swung round. 'What, Father? Will you not stay to hear how sweetly Hesketh met his end?'

'Sit down,' growled the colonel, from the head of the table. '*Both of you!*'

Holt lowered his bony arse with a glare that threatened a vicious amount of penance as Garrett took a place opposite, shoulders stiff with defiance. While these three had been playing chess with their army, moving even closer to Brussels, their hapless pawn had been punished with all the brutality that the English government could wield.

Garrett made his report, sparing no details, but if he expected pale, squirming guilt across the table, he was wrong.

Colonel Stanley's thumb beat the table. 'Are you saying Hesketh threatened that *we* would kill my cousin unless he consented to lead a rebellion?'

'Such was the gossip, Sir William.' *That's how Ferdinando understood it.*

The colonel was staring at his deputy. 'He wasn't supposed to do that, Jacques. Hesketh was to put forward our proposals and if my cousin wasn't interested, he was to get out of there immediately.'

De Francesci shrugged. 'I warned you Hesketh could gallop off the track.'

'No, he must have —' Appalled, the colonel pressed his fingers to his temples. 'Hesketh was supposed to warn my cousin that he could be killed within the next six months and therefore he should support us. Killed not by *us* but on Sir Robert Cecil's orders. Oh God,' he crossed himself, 'either the poor fool told it wrong or Ferdy misunderstood.'

'Why would the Cecils want your cousin dead, sir?' Garrett asked, contrition chilling his spine.

Stanley jabbed the air. 'For a start, Lancashire, our family's shire, never abandoned the true faith and would gladly rebel against the south. Secondly, the lad has an honest claim to the throne and, thirdly, because of his kinship to me he is already damned. But he's a decent fellow. Her Majesty's arse-wipers in Whitehall have been clamouring for him to give up my old father and sons to be sent south as hostages so they can be held against me, but he has them hidden away.'

Garrett was persistent. 'But do you know *for certain* that the Cecils want him dead?'

'Yes, Towneley, we've informers in Burghley's household.'

Run by Wade? How far would the Cecils go? Christ's snowy-coated Protestant sheep in Whitehall might be nothing more than brindled goats on the bridlepath to Hell.

'Either way, this sets us back no end,' muttered Holt. 'We need to review matters.'

Hallelujah! Maybe they'd unleash Ferdinando from their plans as well. Of course, if the curmudgeon of a queen would name the earl as her successor — both he and Ferdy-lad could relish a promising future.

Colonel Stanley chewed his bottom lip. 'But at least my cousin did not hand Hesketh over straightaway. He listened. That's a good portent. We'll give him more time to settle in as earl then we'll approach him again. Allows us a chance to have all our allies primed.' He looked across at Garrett. 'And next time we'll send a delegation, which can include you, Towneley. You can make sure everyone sticks to their instructions. No fancy footwork.' Sitting back with a smile, he added, 'We'll approach him at the *exquisite* moment, this time make it impossible for him to refuse.'

'How *exquisite*?'

'A multiplicity of ways, Captain,' said de Francesci. He stood up and strode round the trestle to look down at Garrett. 'We play with him. Here and here.' He touched his fingers to forehead and heart, then seating himself beside Garrett, he grabbed his belt purse. 'Here and finally … *here*!' Before he could defend himself, de Francesci's right hand grabbed him by the codpiece. 'Any further questions?'

A swipe of fist knocked the offending arm away. 'F—k you!'

Laughing, the colonel's deputy swung back onto his feet and returned to his bench.

Stanley grinned. 'What Jacques means is that we will be able to offer my cousin two things: Spanish gold to pay his many debts and an alliance to put him on an empty throne.'

Empty throne?

Garrett winced inwardly. 'And how is this *exquisite* set of circumstances to be achieved?' He leaned forward. 'Let me speak plainly, Sir William. You thought that being an old acquaintance, Hesketh could steal under Ferdinando's netting without being remarked upon. It didn't work. Besides, even if your cousin wanted to listen — and I say *if* — he had no choice but to turn poor Hesketh in since I imagine Burghley and his hunchbacked son have informers everywhere, so how will —'

'You're right,' interrupted the colonel. 'Doughtie warned us there was at least one of Burghley's agents in Ferdy's household.'

'Doughtie?'

'Dick Doughtie, my cousin's Master of Horse. There's an older brother, too, but he's not of the faith, more's the pity.'

Garrett tensed inwardly. *More doll's clothes needed to convey a warning.*

Across the board, de Francesci flung the quill he was fondling aside and leaned back. 'Anything else, Towneley, since you are so pessimistic about the future?'

'I think you're wagering on a rocking horse. As Sir William said months ago, the earl's more a poet than a soldier. I advise we look elsewhere for our rebel leader.'

'No, it must be him,' snarled Holt, slapping the table. 'We have more of the faith in the north than anywhere else in

England and we've hundreds of followers in Ireland and across the Scots border.' The other men nodded.

Garrett despaired. If word reached the queen, the new earl would be sent to the Tower, even beheaded. That was how King Henry VIII had served his cousin, Buckingham. 'Sirs, I say again you are wagering on the wrong horse.'

Stanley shook his head. 'No, he's bridled now. All he needs is to be spurred.'

9

Mistletoe had a lot to answer for, fumed Rose, returning along the frosty North Road to St Albans after spending Christmastide at her parents' new residence (rented courtesy of Cousin Byng) in Stepney.

While her mother had accepted the lie of her living as a companion to a wealthy gentlewoman, a limited truth might have been better since Mistress Davison persisted in declaring to the world that her widowed daughter was available. Consequently, Rose found it nauseating to be fumbled and kissed by Sir George Byng's nephew. Convincing her parents that she was not going to have any Byng marital fetters clamped upon her had worn her patience and yesterday she had stormed out of Stepney.

If returning to St Albans meant foregoing snowballs, skating and tobogganing with her brothers and a return to dismal solitude, her consolation was helping to ensure Captain Towneley's continued safety even though he had unselfishly told her to break free.

Pah, easy for a man to say.

Then in early February, when St Albans was shrugging off its latest mantle of snow, Life toed open the door to a different future. Martin brought her two letters from London.

Grandfather and Uncle Robert have changed their minds and I may go to Lancashire, wrote Lizbeth. *Shall you accompany me?*

Indeed, she would!

The second missive was from Wade's clerk: *Mistress Byrd is instructed to accompany Lady Vere and ingratiate herself into Lord Derby's household.*

Spy on Ferdy? That was asking too much. What's more, she felt some loyalty towards the intelligencer.

And so the game of wits with Wade had begun anew: threats from him, refusal from her, more threats, more resistance, then manipulation by him and consent by her. Precarious consent. What tipped the balance was unexpected — an invitation from Lord Burghley to Theobalds — an opportunity to ask the most powerful man in England to speak with the queen on her father's behalf. A public forgiveness would restore her poor father's spirits.

Lord Burghley's Hertfordshire house was a reminder to Rose of how his lordship and the grovelling Privy Council had let down her father, yet the estate also held precious childhood memories for her: boating on the pleasure lake, hide and seek through the great mansion and access to the wonderful library. Now, on the afternoon of her arrival, it was in that library that Sir Robert Cecil not only reacquainted her with his illustrious and arthritic father, but also brought her face to face with the queen!

Or to be accurate, nose to the royal knee as Rose sank into a nervous curtsey. The astonishment was not just on her part; Elizabeth Tudor seemed taken aback as well.

'Davison's girl!' she exclaimed in disgust. Any recall that she had once taken her secretary's little daughter onto her lap and fed her comfits was clearly not for an airing. 'Why the devil have you brought her to me, Imp? Take her away at once!'

Rose, miserably pinioned to the carpet by Sir Robert's hand on her shoulder, stared at the bunion half-buried in the queen's right slipper and hoped desperately for release.

'Mistress Byrd has consented to be Your Majesty's eyes and ears in Lord Derby's household,' explained Lord Burghley, leaning upon his stick behind the royal shoulder.

'No, with respect, I haven't yet, Your Majesty.'

Jesu, have I said that? It was the child in her, the child that recalled the queen had once respected honesty. *But now?*

'Look up, girl!' The royal right foot poked her knee.

Rose's gaze crawled up the broad farthingale stitched with jewels, found the nadir of the royal bodice and stumbled over the gold-stitched brocade through the vines of pearls. White cosmetic to obscure the creases and blemishes, which sixty years or more had etched, covered the queen's bosom, throat and face. A king might have claimed veneration for his silvering age and worn the scars of power with pride, but Her Majesty evidently yearned for the elixir of youth. Her hair, if it was hers, had some red dye rubbed through it.

The inspection was mutual. Tudor eyes, enhanced by the unnatural whiteness of the royal complexion, glared down at Rose with the piercing glare of a gull.

Sir Robert had removed his hand from Rose's shoulder, as though distancing himself from such an embarrassing protégé. Now he stood to one side of the queen's chair, hunched like a tethered hawk.

'How fares your father?' demanded the queen.

'He's not well, madam. The years … in the Tower have affected his health.'

Her Majesty snorted. 'If that unfortunate incident had not occurred, he would be standing by us now.'

Silence could be a weapon. Rose used it, disgusted that the queen was still not accepting responsibility for Mary of Scot's beheading.

The royal foot twitched. For an instant, Rose thought she might be kicked, but the queen instead asked, 'Why don't you want to go to Lancashire, girl? Too rural for you?'

'I do not like being coerced, Your Majesty.'

'Neither do I. Your father should have known that.'

Rose closed her eyes in pain. 'I believe he did it for England, Your Majesty.'

The queen huffed. 'And what does your mother do these days? Is she still alive?'

'Yes, Your Majesty. She makes an occupation of grumbling.'

Lord Burghley coughed. 'Your Majesty might be interested in knowing that Mistress Byrd has been good enough to correspond with Marlowe's replacement.'

'Might I?' asked the queen. 'Bullied you into that, too, did they, girl?'

Rose nodded with reluctance. 'It was not that brutal, Your Majesty. I wanted to restore my family's honour and I needed the income. My husband died from wounds fighting in Ireland.'

'Not asking for money now, are you?'

'No, Your Majesty.'

'Or favours?'

'No, Your Majesty.'

'Good! It is our wish you go to Lancashire. The de Vere girl has asked you politely, hasn't she?'

'Yes, Your Majesty.'

'And you would go to please her?'

'Yes, since it also pleases you, Your Majesty.'

'"Pleases" is not the term I choose.' The royal tone was withering. 'I don't usually let my maids-of-honour out of my sight, but Sir Robert and his father have been persuasive.' A scorching glare sparked out at Lord Burghley; a royal shoe twitched. 'So, girl, can you keep that young hoyden from losing her heart to some undeserving rascal?'

'Madam, I believe Elizabeth de Vere has the same good sense as her more illustrious namesake.'

'Faith, this one's a diplomat like her father, Imp,' the queen observed and then her sharp gaze once more fixed on Rose. 'Any mischief and you and she will go to the Tower, believe that! And don't let her come back a Papist either. Why I'm letting her go to that godforsaken corner...'

'Madam.' It was as though Lord Burghley was reminding her of arguments already settled.

With a sharp breath, the queen flung up her hands with a shrug. 'Very well, and she shall carry my letter to Alice. It will save on messengers. I shall not write to Ferdy yet. He is not in favour. Well, that's all, young woman! Shuffle away now, shuffle away!'

Crammed like a blasted question mark in a hole behind the window seat in his Papist host's manor house outside Kingston upon Hull, Garrett was back in England and his temper was a keg of gunpowder with the fuse lit. His feet were numb with cold, he was sitting on a pile of mouse turds, and cupboarded with an ash-haired fellow agent from Prague, one Daniel Flecker, known as 'Snow'. What's more, judging by the approaching thumps and bangs, the queen's pursuivants would shortly be inches from where his bootcaps were kissing the back of the panelling.

He should be used to this game. Like the hiding places he and Father Griffith had used last November, this one had been contrived by a Jesuit called Nicholas Owen. The latter's most ingenious secret rooms were behind other secret rooms; less popular were the ones that involved crouching inside a staircase or flattening oneself in the wall behind a smelly close stool. The ploy worked best if you had the physique of a shrivelled peapod. He didn't.

His stomach uttered a gurgle and he jabbed his elbow in to silence it. This was the trouble with playing at spies for a livelihood; he didn't get the featherbed and the good dinner. If only he was headed for St Albans. However, indulging in a fantasy about Rose Byrd wasn't useful in these cramped conditions.

'Don't you *dare* break that!'

The shriek of their hostess penetrated the woodwork. She was the Papist. Her husband, whose religious fervour burned with less heat, must be wetting himself with fear. Probably standing with his fingers stashed between his armpits and his buttocks clamped. Garrett had sympathy for him. It wasn't just the worry of the soldiers ripping the tapestries or pinching the silver; if the hiding place was discovered, the gentleman knew they would all be carted to Topcliffe's torture chamber in Bridewell. For sure, Wade would have Garrett beaten before he 'managed' to escape, but mine host and his dame might suffer the same fate as Hesketh.

The butt of a pike hit the panel. It was hard not to flinch; hard not to curse the colonel, curse Wade, curse himself, but some evil enterprise was brewing and, God willing, he'd thwart it if he could.

Garrett had been told only that his mission was to ride north and persuade Ferdinando, Lord Derby, to meet a delegation of Papists during Easter week. At least his lordship knew that trouble was looming. Several weeks before they sailed, Garrett had dispatched the rest of the doll's clothes, the warning — another messenger was on his way.

Ironic that it turned out to be him.

'What if your noble cousin doesn't agree to a meeting?' he had asked the colonel.

'Oh, he will this time. The circumstances will be different.'

'Circumstances, Sir William? How so?' Garrett knew two others were about to leave for Gravesend. Alas, any temptation for Stanley to divulge more was brushed aside by de Francesci. 'No more information, Captain,' the deputy had declared smoothly, clunking down a purse for Garrett's expenses. 'Follow orders. That's what you are paid for.'

'Aye.' The colonel tapped a tobacco-stained finger against his nose. 'Just be a persuasive cog in the wheel of this enterprise.'

What perturbed Garrett as he shivered in the hiding hole was that this time it might be a very bloody enterprise. Two of the colonel's agents in Brussels, Yorke and Williams, had been sent over a few months earlier to seek employment with Lord Essex, spinning a story that they had been ill-treated by the dissidents. A third man, Captain O'Collun, had left at the same time. All this he had already reported to Wade. Hopefully, all three were under surveillance.

He kept thinking about the sinister phrase that the colonel had used back in November: *An empty throne?* Was that going to be the 'changed circumstance'? He needed to warn Wade to doubly guard the queen, and the instant he freed himself from Snow's company, he'd pen an urgent message to St Albans.

Snow's presence bothered him. Reputedly a skilled swordsman, he had arrived at the camp from Prague a few days earlier. Lean, well-spoken, unremarkable if you didn't know otherwise, he had the openness of a nailed coffin and the cold calm of an executioner. What Garrett did know was that wound inside the brass buttons that fastened Snow's doublet were messages to some of England's Papists and that when those were delivered, Snow would be joining him to press Ferdinando into treason.

Another thud shook the panel. Christ! The bastards really meant business and he was holed up here for how long? His left leg screamed to straighten and his missing fingers throbbed. It was going to be a long night.

He and Snow spent almost two days in the wall's dark womb before crawling forth to wish each other farewell, not to mention a much-relieved host! Snow, enigmatic as ever, melted away into the dawn to pursue his own urgent role in the treasonous agendum, leaving Garrett as euphoric as a beggar healed by Christ to be on his own again — even if Her Majesty's highroads were pot-holed with danger. Twice he was stopped and questioned, the first time in Yorkshire by local pursuivants just after he had sent the report to Wade, and the second time by a patrol of soldiers outside Halifax. Then he struck out for Burnley where his 'bastard daughter' lived.

Before leaving Antwerp, he'd received a missive from the child's mother thanking him for the doll and saying that she still had his clothes and a few other belongings, and 'if ever he should visit, they would be returned to him'. Well, a change of guise might make him less visible, although he would be disappointed if it proved to be the ragged clothes of a vagrant. However, on reaching Burnley, he was grateful that Ferdinando had been as thorough as William Wade.

'There are plenty of Lancashire Towneleys tucked in around those parts, so you having a child there is quite plausible,' Ferdinando had explained.

The 'lovechild' was real and although the little girl resembled the earl with her dark curls, any suspicious stranger could well believe that her hazel eyes had come from a Towneley father.

The child's foster-mother ran a large alehouse. She offered Garrett free lodging and, unlocking a clothes chest, handed over a buckram bag that had been delivered for him. It contained a well-dyed blue mantle with black wool lining, a gentleman's slate-blue doublet with stylishly plumped-out sleeves, a darker velvet jerkin with ivy embroidery on its guards, two linen shirts, several detachable lace collars, trunk hose with blue stitching on the cannions, a purse with sufficient coin to purchase a better ambler from the hostess's cousin, who was a horse-dealer, and a token, which she said was for him to send to the earl when he arrived in Ormskirk.

Not surprisingly, he slept like a well-fed mouser, and best of all, there was no news from the south, no explosions, risings or regicide — so God willing, he should be able to reach the earl before Snow arrived.

The budge-lined coat was a blessing for the rest of his journey. Although blackthorn blossoms were dappling the hedgerows, a chill wind was still fisting the air on the morning he rode into Ormskirk, two miles west of Ferdinando's palace at Lathom.

Since it was not past breakfast time, the gabled roofs were rimed with last night's frost and black ice veneered the municipal cobbles. The heart of the town lay on a rise where two great roads met and today was market day. Officialdom was lurking so although an outsider would be less obvious among the clutter of loaded barrows and the melee of farmers and shire folk venturing in from behind their rural hedges, being a large fellow, Garrett tugged his hat brim down and his purse to the front before he dismounted. It seemed wiser to lead his horse straight through the crowd rather than cut through a backstreet where he'd be more obvious.

With his belly in need of sustenance, he strode past the leather and linen sellers. Plenty of stalls were flaunting local cheeses and sweetmeats but it was the warm spicy smell of the town's gingerbread that finally made him unbuckle his purse.

The stall's plump, young goodwife assessed him saucily. 'You be here for the quarter sessions then, sir?'

'No, mistress, visiting friends.'

'Ah.' It was a very knowing sort of 'Ah' as though he had accidentally given a password. A more respectful gaze gleamed now but no less interested. She leaned forward, her fleshly assets well displayed, and out of courtesy he was forced to lean down to catch her whisper. 'I won't say nowt, but maybe you could lay the table the way we like it round these parts afore you go further.'

For an instant he thought himself in Bedlam and then he remembered it was a covert way of talking about the Mass. Naïve woman, he could have her hauled before a magistrate. She needed a rebuke to teach her caution.

'I don't lay tables, mistress.' Seeing the panic flash across her face, he quickly added with a rueful grin, 'Nor eggs.' He could have hinted roguishly that he was open to other 'laying'. He wasn't. Not this time. 'Excellent gingerbread,' he declared, savouring a mouthful.

Apprehension still tensed her lips. 'I'm sorry, sir, you bein' a stranger, I —'

'Rest easy. No harm done. Now tell me the way to Lathom.' He was testing the gossip about the new earl's religious leanings but the young woman showed no misgivings as she cheerfully directed him to turn onto Burscough Street and then right into Lydgate Lane. So, if this buxom Papist had no fear of him reporting her at Lathom, did that argue that Ferdinando was sympathetic to the old faith, or merely lax?

*

Before leaving Ormskirk for Lathom House, Garrett arranged lodgings near the town cross and while his horse enjoyed a feed, he sought out a barber. Clean shaven and freshly clad, he found his way out of town to the porter's lodge at the south gate of the earl's demesne, delivered the token, a metal disk with the Stanley eagle claw, and waited.

Within half an hour of the porter's boy hastening up to the hall, Giles Clothier, Lord Derby's body servant, rode down to tell him that his lordship would meet him at Burscough Priory ruins, a mile or so to the east across the fields if he did not want to go the longer way by road.

The deserted priory was easy to find. *Agent stuff indeed*, Garrett thought wryly, as he tethered his horse out of sight in a clump of trees behind the ruin. He might be here for a while, depending on how skilfully Ferdinando could shrug off his attendants. Shooing some Protestant sheep out of the nave, he made himself comfortable on the remains of someone's tomb-slab, ate the rest of the gingerbread and waited.

The priory was one of the countless religious buildings ripped apart by Henry VIII's ruffians. After half a century without a roof, plenty of weeds had found niches in the remnant walls. Here and there, spatters of droppings revealed where the summer swallows nested, grasses thrived between the broken tiles and most of the building stones had vanished, pilfered for a renaissance in splendid manor houses. Only part of the tower pier remained, like a warning finger, and time would knock down the few jagged arches that were left.

Peppered with sheep turds, the useless debris lay scattered — shattered angels, dismembered columns and monuments, chevrons and crockets, all broken. The craftsmanship, the holiness of centuries, smashed to pieces in hatred. No wonder the Papists still seethed with bitterness.

And it was blessed draughty.

A weak sun was bursting through the clouds by the time he heard the jingle of harness. He slid off the stone, tugged his doublet straight, and edged to the ruined south door, taking care to stay out of sight.

Ferdinando, Lord Derby, looked fitter. Gone were the huge London sleeves. Beneath his long cloak, he was clad in dark green leather and carried a hooded hawk. He shifted the bird to Clothier's gauntlet, dismounted, and handed up his horse's leading rein. Then, tugging the floppy brim of his hat forward, he strode into the ruins, leaving his servant to keep watch.

A swift check that Garrett was unaccompanied; then a flick of finger bade him rise from his knees. 'I haven't much time,' the earl informed him. 'You are well, Towneley?'

'Yes, my lord.' Hat in hand, he followed his lordship's meander round the tumbled stones, and politely shifted his pack so his superior might occupy the sunniest slab.

'Made yourself comfortable on my ancestor, I see.'

'My lord, I —'

'I'm jesting, man. They moved most of ours to Ormskirk. Couldn't save this though.' A sorrowful curl of fingers that took in the devastation.

Garrett nodded, waited while the earl sat down. Again, the gesture of command — to perch himself on the hiccough of stone pillar opposite — then he was under the earl's inspection, his garb noted and (judging by his lordship's lift of eyebrow) approved.

'Thank you for your warnings, Towneley. You have done well. I see you stopped off in Burnley.'

'Yes, my lord, I am very grateful for the better clothing and a decent horse. Your little daughter was thriving and —'

'Good, good, but let's to business, eh? Am I still to expect an emissary from my cousin or are you the man?'

Relieved to be treated with the same trusting directness that had been shown in Shoreditch, Garrett was happy to reply in kind. 'No, I was sent as support, my lord, and to arrange a meeting. Your cousin's ambassador is Daniel Flecker, known as "Snow", and he plans to arrive in Ormskirk on Easter Monday. I suspect he will be presenting a far greater offer from your cousin than Hesketh did. You understand me, my lord?'

'Rot his balls! I'm to be threatened again, am I?'

'Actually, my lord, Sir William asked me to set you straight on that. Hesketh's mission was also to warn you rather than threaten you.'

'Warn me?'

'So your cousin alleges.'

'Be hanged to that, Towneley. Hesketh said I'd be killed within the next half year if I didn't agree to lead a Papist rebellion.' Then the sharp gaze slid. 'Besides, man, who the devil else would...'

...want to kill an heir to the throne? Who, indeed?

'No!' Denying that his greatest enemies lay at the court, his lordship rose, slapping his riding crop against his high boot. 'Christ! It's why I handed Hesketh over — that bloody threat. If I was wrong...'

'I don't know, my lord.' Was the image of Hesketh writhing beneath the noose still fresh in his lordship's memory?

Ferdinando's mouth became a sneer of fury. 'Oh, come on, man! My wily cousin will say anything to have me dance to his tune.'

Garrett could offer no absolution. 'You know Sir William better than I, my lord.'

'I did, once.' Spoken with bitterness; a childhood hero smashed.

'Clearly, my lord, you are of more value to him alive than dead.'

The possibility — realisation — that Ferdinando had misunderstood Hesketh's warning lay like a hefty branch across the path, needing time to be assessed and dealt with. Both men fell silent. Only the March wind stirred, sending a scurry of old leaves down the torn-up nave.

Garrett waited, watched the earl's jaw clench as he looked towards the missing altar. 'After years at court, Towneley, I know the hunger for power can corrupt even the tenderest souls. Once it is in their grasp, they cannot let it go. They cling to the mountaintops with their fingernails and kick rocks down onto the rest of us. I am referred to as 'the baker' in their cyphers. God help me, Towneley, there are agents under my very roof who inform their masters in London about everyone I deal with.'

'As I must, eventually.'

'As, of course, you must.' A cynical snort.

'I swear my loyalty is foremost to you, my lord,' Garrett said earnestly, keeping his expression hopeful. Perhaps another gem might be forthcoming for his wages, but only a flask was passed across for him to take a swig. Flattered at the kindness, though, Garrett took a draught before he passed it back.

Ambition uncurled and stretched once more within him as the liquor warmed his stomach. A great deal could happen in a week, couldn't it? If England was suddenly without the queen, then ... then maybe the man before him would accept the crown. It might even be offered lawfully. And Captain Garrett

Towneley might rise high in the service of King Ferdinando I! His breast swelled. Ah, but should he now mention Colonel Stanley's talk of an empty throne? Had his warning reached Wade?

So many ifs and maybes.

'Towneley?'

His sense of right reasserted itself: he mustn't let Ferdinando be contaminated by Colonel Stanley's scheming. Surely the earl would refuse a meeting with Snow.

Fingers snapped in his face. 'I asked a question. How does this man Snow plan to approach me?'

'Your pardon. Oh, er...' Garrett ran a hand across his brow. 'He will claim he brings a letter from your brother in Italy.'

'Ha, that's rich! My brother is as likely to write to me as kiss my arse. No, that won't do. In God's name, keep the knave from Lathom!'

'He won't be easily shovelled away.' A wince as he realised the play of words.

'Oh, I see that,' Ferdinando replied dryly. 'Listen, if I consent to hear him — *if* — it must be managed secretly.' He drew a gloved finger pensively across the ancient stone lettering by his thigh. 'Tell him I'll meet him during a hunt. Leave the arrangements with me for now.'

Jesu! Here's a turnabout. What was spurring this? Garrett regarded him with astonishment. Had banishment from court through a long winter corroded Ferdinando's allegiance to Her Majesty? Or was it curiosity to hear Colonel Stanley's offer — the kingdom of England after this sojourn in the northern wilderness? This would be far too dangerous.

'Are you sure you want to take the risk, my lord? Such an encounter could imperil you like it did with Hesketh.'

You must say no to your cousin's offer, my lord. Tell Snow to go and be hanged! Even if he tries to punish me for failure.

The earl was not angered by his forwardness. 'I'm sure I want to *hunt*, Towneley, preferably for a week. That's all you need to report to William Wade. Understood?'

'Understood and thank you.'

Ferdinando offered the flask again. 'Not easy, is it? You must feel like a bloody weathercock serving three masters.'

'It requires concentration, that's for sure, my lord.' There were questions he must ask. 'The spies in your household, do you know who they are?'

'Could be the whole blasted lot.' Ferdinando sighed. 'Perhaps my cousin is right. There are plenty who'd like to see me tidied away into the Tower. Burghley for one. Ever since he started to get his hose knotted over who will succeed Elizabeth, I've been under his wretched magnifying glass. Christ!'

Garrett did not comment. He could tell when a man needed to vent.

'As for Essex, that bastard's been fanning the queen's suspicion of me whenever he damn well can, asking why I took so long to hand Hesketh over for questioning, and the stupid old woman is listening. After all my loyalty down the years!' Bitterness oiled every word and that troubled Garrett further. Was he hearing a great lord ripe for treason?

'See, Towneley, when Father died, I should have been granted the Earldom of Chester and Lordship of Lancaster, as was my right, but it's nearly six months now and the queen is still withholding them.'

And that would be shrinking his income, Garrett thought to himself. Not good when you owed six thousand pounds to London tradesmen — mostly your tailors (according to the colonel).

'Lord Essex has tried to pick quarrels. He seeks to make me discontent, do you see, to prick me into rebellion. By proving me a mighty traitor, he can show the queen that Burghley and Cecil are inept at safeguarding her.'

Garrett shook his head in sympathy. 'Well, my lord, I thank God I am not at court.'

'Faith! I just want an untroubled life — hunt, fornicate and write poetry — but no, others must use me for their own purposes. You know what, my friend, I would wager Essex lusts to make himself the queen's successor — when the time is right.'

That gave Garrett pause, especially remembering Aidan Markham. 'I was acquainted with one of his agents in Flanders, my lord.'

'Were you, indeed? See, that proves my point. He has eyes and ears all over the damn place. Fellow still over there?'

'No, I … I killed him. In a beerhouse.'

How very *à la Marlowe*,' Ferdinando commented dryly. 'Did Wade order that?'

Garrett lowered his gaze to the hat brim still in his fingers. 'No. Your cousin discovered Markham was a spy and made me his executioner to test my loyalty.'

'Hell!' The earl's face stiffened for a moment but as he thought about it, his features softened again. 'Well, I won't think the less of you for that. Don't do it to me, eh?'

'No, God be my witness!' Garrett crossed his heart. 'It was a duel, though,' he added, to dispel any black-hooded image in his employer's mind, and noticed Ferdinando's stare move to his gloves. However, no comment was made. His companion fell silent as though digesting what decisions might lie ahead. Eventually he stirred. 'So how many men are there under my cousin's command and how truly influential is he at present?'

'It varies. Nigh on a hundred most times, my lord. The bulk of them are the Irish soldiers who defected with him at Deventer. As for his power, he corresponds with princes and with prelates. What they think of his bravado, I cannot say, I have only Sir William's word that the Pope and Philip of Spain believe him a hero and a kingmaker. What may interest you, though, is that there has been much traffic of messengers betwixt Scotland and Ireland in the last two months, though I do not know to what purpose. Your cousin keeps his cards close to his chest.'

'I see, and —' The earl broke off, aware of distant bells tolling out the hour, and there came a whistle from his servant. 'I have to go,' he muttered, rising. 'I will question you further in a few days' time when you come to Lathom.'

'To Lathom, my lord? That would be excellent, but on what excuse? How should I approach you?'

'Well, you'll need to have freedom to come and go. Tell you what, arrive at Lathom as my former brother-in-arms. I served under Leicester's command when I was in my twenties.'

'Your pardon, my lord, Wade might check the veracity of that if it's reported back to him so why not stick to the truth? You once rewarded me for saving a friend's life and we became well acquainted.'

'Oh, very well, and, if any of my household question you further, plead a hero's modesty. Can you manage that, Friend Garrett?'

'Assuredly. A former courtesan married to a baron could not be more reticent.'

That produced a laugh of sorts. 'And on occasion, you may call me Ferdy.'

'Only when the purpose serves.' Garrett escorted him to the threshold of the south door.

The earl halted. 'Another thing — Colonel Stanley's father and sons are under my protection. You don't need to know where. Burghley and Cecil would like me to surrender them, but they are not Papists, they give me no trouble and I would not cause them ill. Perhaps you'd like to report to Wade that they are not present in my household.'

Garrett bowed. 'As you command.'

'That's all then.' An offered handshake.

'Just one last question with your permission, my lord. If your major enemy is Essex, what does that make Sir Robert Cecil in the long term?'

'Friend, so my wife, Alice, believes. She thinks of him as her kinsman.'

'But what do you think?'

'I don't know, Garrett. I suspect he is more than happy to see Her Majesty withhold favour from me. Yet what mightily puzzles me — and I should have mentioned this sooner — is why his young niece, Lady Vere, is coming on a visit to my wife. Imagine our Virgin Queen allowing that! A maid of honour let off the leash, her maidenhead at risk in Lancashire! Tsk!' The whistle came again and he clapped Garrett's shoulder. 'My duties call. I will see you for Eastertide at Lathom, my friend. How will you amuse yourself until then?'

Garrett bowed. 'A good soldier should always know the lie of the land.'

'And a bad one knows only the taverns. Stay out of trouble! I don't like the smell of this one bit.'

10

'Ahm hoping we are not going to be bored coming oop here,' exclaimed Lizbeth, Lady Vere, sounding as though she had been brought up in the port of Leverpole. 'But ah've heard that Lard Derby is expectin' oos.'

'Brat,' scolded Rose affectionately. The eighteen-year-old was a brilliant mimic. Yesterday, after crossing the Mersey River at Warrington, they had dutifully attended the local Good Friday service and the minister's lengthy sermon and long vowels had already given Lizbeth's sharp ears the chance to pick up the region's dialect. The young woman's wit needed bridling, though. Such mockery would offend.

'There's so much of England that we southerners don't know, Lizbeth,' she remarked tactfully. 'Has Her Majesty ever travelled north of Kenilworth?'

But her companion wasn't listening. 'Oh, Rose, you should have seen the stable lad's expression this morning when our coachman asked if the horses were saddled.' She lifted the travelling mask protecting her chin and mouth from the cold and screwed up her face to demonstrate. 'He could have been talking Dutch for all the lad knew. Do you think we'll need an interpreter?'

'You'll soon find out.'

One of Lizbeth's grooms had already galloped ahead to forewarn Alice, Lady Derby, and the huge gates of the demesne stood open in welcome. A round-bellied porter whistled his dog away from their horse's heels and saluted them through.

Riding ahead of their coach and escort, the two young women followed the road through pasture. Sheep not yet shorn of their winter mantles halted their munching and with the grass still sticking out their mouths watched indifferently. Only the lambs showed curiosity, frisking over to see the horses and ignoring come-back-here bleats from their wary mothers.

Rose had heard Londoners speak of Lancashire as some untamed wilderness, a foreign country almost. True, some of the villages she had travelled through seemed dowdy, and the furrows of the highway north of the Mersey had not been filled in since the winter, however, most of the shire's fields were well stocked and this estate looked to be as well-managed as any in the south, even if it didn't boast a lake and labyrinths like Theobalds House.

'Gramercy!' Lizbeth drew rein and pointed with her riding crop at the sight of a formidable gatehouse. 'Oh, Lordy, a deep moat *and* a drawbridge. Do not say it will be one of these old castles where the chimneys smoke and the towels are speckled with mould.'

In the moist morning drizzle, the massive curtain walls with their crenelated watchtowers loomed dank and uninviting and, rising from within its inner bailey, Lathom House seemed undecided whether to be a palace or a fortress. The ancient, square keep meant narrow spiral stairs that could play murder with the young women's wide farthingales, but there was some hope of warmth and decent passageways: cuddling onto the old building from either side were far younger edifices, and a more recent owner had dabbled thoughtfully with chimneys.

'At least they've put pennons on the gatehouse to welcome you.'

'To welcome *both of us*.' The young woman straightened haughtily and tidied a dark curl back under her cap. 'Believe me, I feel like turning tail.'

'Too late, you are being waved at.' Three young girls, steps in height, were gesticulating from the ramparts above the gatehouse and inside the walls, a horn boomed dolefully.

'And they may be still in mourning,' groaned Lizbeth, removing her mask and waving graciously back.

However, despite the rusting jaw of the portcullis, Rose was agreeably impressed by the spacious, clean courtyard and the diligence of the half-dozen grooms waiting to lead the horses round to the stables. She slid from the side-saddle and accepted help onto the cobbles. Leaning against the stone rail which edged the front steps of the house, she let feeling return to her feet. Leaving Martin and Lady Vere's maid Amy to oversee the unloading of the two leather travelling chests (more of Lizbeth's gowns were in a cart a day behind them on the road), she gazed up at Lathom's walls.

At least there were windows. That's what she always looked for. These were not arrow slits or poky embrasures but diamond-paned, extravagant windows that brought in sunlight to dapple the rushes and warm the heart. And, yes, there were windows everywhere. She stood there smiling. The sense of adventure that had stayed with her since leaving St Albans was even stronger now and just being in young Lizbeth's company this last week had been like sloughing off the last five years. Be damned to Wade.

'You are looking unreasonably happy,' remarked her friend, shaking her skirts as she joined her. 'Just because it might make an excellent place for hide-and-seek or murder.'

'Not mine, I trust. Ah, here's our welcome.'

Expensively ruffed with black lace, a dark-haired lady in her mid-thirties was intent on greeting them. Her fashionable black skirts were dogged by the three children from the gate tower and an assortment of attendants, mostly gentlemen, who swiftly sorted themselves into a deferential line of welcome behind her. Only a handful of women servants, Rose noted.

'Lady Vere! Mistress Byrd!'

The arrivals curtseyed formally and then in turn were gathered into the arms-length embrace of Alice Spenser, the new Countess of Derby. Following introductions to her widowed sister, Lady Compton, her daughters, her chaplain, and the courteous bows from the rest of the household, my lady led her guests inside.

After they had been offered use of the house of ease, they were conducted into the gabled hall nestled against the keep and led through to a candlelit, wood-panelled parlour warmed by a blazing fire. Jugs of mulled wine and honey cakes were brought to them and gentle music was plucked out by a cittern player.

Once Lady Derby had discreetly established that there had been no recent cases of pestilence among her guests' acquaintances, she visibly relaxed. 'We truly are so glad to welcome you both. My husband's parents did not live together so this has been rather a male demesne for many years, but Lord Derby and I wish to change that and, apart from my sister and our neighbours, the Ruffords, you are our first household guests since the late earl's funeral, God rest his soul.'

'Then we are very honoured,' answered Rose, feeling somewhat shy because she had not seen Alice since her father's shameful dismissal, and she was conscious of their difference in rank and years.

Although the conversation limped like a wounded soldier through obligatory formalities, it eased gradually with the trading of news into a more relaxed exchange. Lizbeth slid into the role of cheerful raconteur, exaggerating the muddy furrows, the number of lost horseshoes and gruffest of the innkeepers. Lady Derby and her family listened in delight, so entranced with their London guest that their distraction gave Rose the chance to silently sigh with relief. No more worrying about the state of the road, the tedium of waiting at the post-stages for the coach horses to be changed, whether there were fleas and bedbugs in the blankets or thieves and vagrants in the wild woods.

As the servants lit more candles, Rose felt pleasingly drowsy in the warmth. Beyond Lathom's diamond-paned windows, rain clouds that were no longer her concern further dulled the daylight. As if there was any treason here, she thought contrarily. Her missives to Whitehall were going to be very humdrum. Reports, nevertheless, were expected: ones of an avian nature. A humourless cipher clerk had visited St Albans and tutored her in a fresh vocabulary. Henceforth, 'house martin' signified a local recusant; 'willow warbler' stood for Jesuit priest; 'chaffinch' was any man come recently from the Spanish Netherlands; 'robin's nest' was a conspiracy; Lord Derby was 'a sparrowhawk' and his bedchamber 'the meadows'. 'Hearing a tawny owl' indicated that the earl had had private speech alone there with a visitor after nightfall. Perhaps, like her Antwerp intelligencer, she should create some phrases just to be mischievous. 'Ate peacock for dinner' might send the Privy Council into apoplexy.

She was not sure how long they would stay at Lathom, but Whitehall Palace expected a weekly report. Each letter was to be addressed to Rose's brother Francis and sent to the care of

Lady Susan, Lizbeth's sister. Wade had arranged for a servant to call for them. As for GT of Antwerp, she assumed he had been informed that she would be absent from St Albans. Perhaps he would write to her here. If not, it broke the only bond between them and that was a pity, for she had been thinking about him a great deal.

'...maidservant to the field for a call of nature and...'

Jolted from her reverie, she straightened. What mischief was Lizbeth at?

'And I suddenly heard this scream from behind the blackthorn hedge and there was Mistress Byrd protecting the girl and remonstrating with a monster of a billy goat.'

'Oh come now, my lady!' Rose protested, glad that her face was already ruddy from the fire's blaze. 'He was no monster.'

'Mightily horned, though,' Lizbeth insisted.

'So what did you do, Mistress Byrd?' asked ten-year-old Lady Frances, the second of the earl's daughters, her mouth a small rosette of awe.

Rose shrugged modestly. 'I took off my mantle, shook it at him and shouted "*Whoosh!*" and...' She broke off as everyone's attention streaked from her. Accompanied by his officers, Ferdinando, Lord Derby, was making his entrance. Rose curtseyed with the rest but her attention was snared by one of the earl's retinue, a tall man who stood for an instant in the doorway then melted into the shadows. Towneley? Excitement rose in her only to be staunched. No, impossible! He was still in the Spanish Netherlands. His most recent letter had been from Antwerp.

'And this is Mistress Byrd, my lord.'

Not surprisingly, Ferdinando appeared at ease, so different from the stern lord at Hesketh's hanging. He was thirty-seven now to Rose's reckoning, very fit, and while he might be greeting his visitors with his countess by his side, she recognised a speculative male gleam as he halted, looking down upon her. A gesture bade her rise. It was deflating that he did not recognise her from their younger days. Worse still, while lineage and virginity put Lord Oxford's daughter, Lizbeth, in the *Noli me tangere* out-of-bounds stall, Rose Byrd, widow, was in open pasture. His lordship's sense of entitlement might need to be handled carefully.

'Mistress, you were in mid-whoosh, I believe.'

'Fending off goats, my lord,' she replied brightly and then hearing the rumble of humour from his attendants, she realised she might have offended him.

'Very wise,' he agreed dryly, much to her relief, and turning, ruffled his youngest daughter's hair. Importuned for a pick-o'back, he refused the child, announced he would join his guests later for midday dinner, and left.

Shortly after that, Lizbeth, stuck with making chit-chat to Master William Farington, the earl's hoary-headed receiver-general, began sending out rescue-me glances. Rose edged in and retrieved her, suggesting they might need to refresh themselves before the main repast and requested a servant might guide them to their bedchamber.

'That was hardly a welcome from Ferdy,' Lizbeth muttered, taking Rose's arm after they had left the company, 'but there was one good-looking gallant attending him. Lordy, the weather is looking even more disgusting,' she added, wrinkling her nose at the heavy raindrops running down the windowpanes as they followed the servant through the Long Gallery. 'That means we shall have to stay indoors all afternoon and procession past these boring family portraits or, worse still, endure some dreary Calvinist tract. Grandfather says Alice Derby is godly about everything — except extravagance.'

'At least tomorrow is Easter, a banquet is promised, and we can eat meat again.' Rose halted. 'Lizbeth, I'm very grateful to be your companion. But during the journey, you never said why.'

'Why what?'

'Why you invited me? I'm not of noble blood.'

'Oh, lots of reasons. Because I am fond of you and we have always kept in touch, haven't we, despite your father's disgrace? Besides, you're older than me, a gentlewoman, a widow. You were Grandfather's suggestion and then Uncle Robert said, yes, use her. Those were his exact words.'

Not *choose* her, but *use* her.

With a different agendum and because he was not expected to dog Lord Derby's noble heels like the household officers, Garrett took care to melt away from the welcome for Lord Oxford's daughter. Why had Lord Burghley set loose his Protestant grandchild into the wilds of Papist Lancashire? Not his concern, except… Except the voice of Lady Vere's attendant had sounded so like Mistress Byrd's. How likely was that? In the fading light it had been hard to see her face and she'd been wearing a cap and hood which covered her hair. He had not stayed to stare. The last person he needed to think of on his way to meet Snow in Ormskirk was Rose Byrd. She'd disturbed his peace of mind ever since he'd left St Albans.

The memory of her sweetly asleep with an ancient cloth toy tucked up beside her had stayed with him like a saint's medallion. He had knocked on her door in the early morning to say farewell. Although she was too deep asleep to bid him enter, he had done so, nevertheless. For a long moment, he had lingered in the doorway like a creature tethered by enchantment. Sadness that he would never, *should* never, see her again overwhelmed him. Desire, too. As a king might sight a distant, beautiful land and yearn to add that to his dominions.

He had left the garters and linen for her. To have lain such a provocative gift on the coverlet without a by-your-leave would have been crude discourtesy. Instead, he put the package on the kitchen table, then he pilfered a few items from the pantry for the day's journey and let himself softly out of the back door. If Verstegan ever questioned him again about his betrothed, at least he'd manage a truthful answer, but today she was an unwanted distraction.

'Never think of a woman when you are riding into battle, lad.' That had been an old sergeant's advice to him when he had first entered the army. 'Keep her memory for when you are being hanged.'

Wise counsel in meeting with Snow — assuming the agent had survived hiding holes, frosty barns and suspicious officers of the Crown. Hand on heart, Garrett could declare that all was going well.

During the few days before arriving at Lathom, he had reconnoitred: from Knowsley up to Rufford, the mosses and the meres, and west to the coast. Then, as Ferdinando had promised, he had been received like an old friend and consequently the earl's servants were treating him with respect. So far, he had not been able to fathom which of them was Wade's spy nor had he received any instructions from St Albans, but Richard Doughtie, Colonel Stanley's supporter, had been forewarned of his arrival. Although an overt Papist, young Doughtie had just been made Master of Horse. Ferdinando's trust and tolerance amazed Garrett. It argued that his lordship might prove a very compassionate king.

The other surprise was to hear that Shakespeare was in residence, a refugee from the plague. 'Don't worry about explaining things to Will,' Ferdinando had said, drawing him aside. 'He knows you are working for me. He won't ask questions.'

Just as well! He'd been told they'd be sharing a bedchamber in the Eagle Tower, below the library and muniment rooms. 'Being in the old keep will give you more liberty to come and go, Garrett,' his lordship explained. 'Most of my lads can't abide the place. Too many stairs!' He had handed Garrett a cup of spiced wine. 'To the Queen, God keep her!' They clinked goblets.

Well, God was doing His best. There had been no dire news from London, yet Garrett still had a sense of foreboding as he rode into the town to meet Snow.

Since it was the eve of Easter Sunday, Ormskirk was predictably quiet as he rode towards the town cross. Snow was punctual, leading his horse out from the yard of The Brewer's Arms as the parish church bells clanged three. He looked to have arrived without chilblains afflicting his feet or musket balls up his breeches. At a covert nod from Garrett, he mounted and, wisely, did not spur forward to ride heel by heel until they turned into Lydgate Lane. Beyond the sight of any dwellings, at an entrance to a fallow field, where there was space to draw their horses off the road, Garrett dismounted and waited.

No longer appended with rodent turds dagging his garments, the Papist agent could have passed for a down-at-heel merchant. Beneath his woollen cloak, he was garbed in a tightfitting doublet of sad tawny with matching slops and netherstocks. Only the keen-eyed would have noted his sleeves were an inch short and it was wise not to remark upon the thin isthmus of bloodstain behind the buttons.

'Any encounters?'

A curl of lip. 'None that I couldn't deal with. You?' At Garrett's shrug, he prompted, 'So…?'

'All bridled up for a meet on Thursday. But, mark me, not up here at Lathom.'

'Why in hell not? There's surely woods around the place.'

'It's because Lord Burghley's granddaughter is visiting and there may well be an agent in her entourage, not to mention the other treacherous weevils already in his lordship's pantry.' Ignoring his companion's disgusted look, he added, 'And don't ask me why the wench is come. Maybe some noble sprig has kindled a babe in her.'

'So where, then?'

'Lord Derby has land at Knowsley, a couple of hours' ride south.' Noting Snow's scowl, he seized a stick and went down on his haunches to draw a map and fill in the main landmarks. 'I've been down there to take a look. Besides a fine house, there's a modest hunting lodge in the woods. His lordship purposes to stay there for a full week with just a few of his household. And here, about half a mile away,' he jabbed the map, 'is a flat glade with the remains of a charcoal burners' kiln — not used for years. That's where he'll meet you, so I suggest you get to know the lie of the land in case aught goes wrong.'

Snow nodded. 'Thursday, eh? What time?'

Garrett scuffed out the map with his heel. 'Two hours after noon. Lord Derby and his Master of Horse, Doughtie, who is one of ours, will lose themselves from the rest.'

His companion raised a mocking eyebrow. 'Intimate, are they?' The approach of a wagon staunched any comment from Garrett; he swiftly turned his back to the road and they both leaned upon the gate like a pair of grumpy farmers discussing cattle murrain until the vehicle had rattled round the next bend.

'And you are sure his high-and-mightiness won't hand us over to the sheriff?' Snow asked, straightening. 'I hear that's what he does with old friends?'

Garrett smiled tightly. 'Not this time. Thanks to Lord Essex, he's still out of favour with the queen, ostracised from court and much aggrieved.' Then he aired the question that had been burning within him. 'When is the assassination of the queen to take place?'

Come on, man, that's the plan, isn't it?

Snow was staring at him as though he was unhinged. '*What?*'

Now he had no resort but to brazen it out. 'Once the news of her death reaches here, it will be easy to convince the earl to seize the throne, so when shall we know of her murder, or is this meeting with the earl just a sweetening?'

'I have no answer for you, Captain.'

Garrett hid his frustration. 'Ah well, we'll carry on regardless,' he muttered with a shrug, but then the other man surprised him. 'Murder doesn't always go to plan, Towneley. Sometimes it requires patience and then —' With a cruel smile and frightening swiftness, Snow drove an imaginary poignard into Garrett's chest. The violence was unexpected; his grimace of pain masked the shock that his suspicion was true.

'Now I have a question for you, Captain.'

'Really?' He made an effort to meet Snow's stare and hide the loathing that this man evoked in him.

Irritation flashed across Snow's face. 'Am I welcome at Lathom tomorrow, as we arranged? I intend to present a letter from the earl's brother.'

'No!' Spoken too hastily. 'Won't wash,' Garrett added more graciously, taking care to lean back in relaxed fashion against the gate. 'His lordship and I have spun a tale that I saved a friend of his a few years ago, but he reckons another stranger turning up will arouse suspicion.'

'Then what if I appear as an actor seeking work? I'm told his lordship has his own players.'

'It won't work, my friend, all the theatres are closed and his company is either touring or disbanded for the present. There's already a player here tutoring my lord's daughters, hardly sets foot outside the library.'

An angry grunt from Snow. 'Colonel Sir William told me to get close.'

'Lord Derby said not.' Garrett raised a hand to stifle argument. 'Now, tell me, who's the delegate you are bringing to this meeting or is it just us now?'

'Just us? Holy Mary, man, no, there's going to be three others. We need to convince his lordship that we have powerful allies.'

That caught Garrett by surprise. '*Three*? Bollocks! Who the devil else?'

'One is Andrew Buchanan, Lord Bothwell's emissary.'

Bothwell, first cousin to King James of Scotland, was a notorious adventurer — convicted of witchcraft, let alone attainted for insurrection. 'Bothwell! Isn't he a Presbyterian when he's not practising the Black Arts?'

'Once, perhaps, but he's now joined with the Scots Catholic lords.'

How convenient! Garrett hoped that this Andrew Buchanan was more reputable than his master. 'Who else, then?'

'Finnian O'Neill, here on the behest of his cousin, Hugh O'Neill, Earl of Tyrone. You'll know of Hugh from your service in Ireland.'

Garrett nodded. 'I've even met him. Several times. A large thorn in Her Majesty's flesh.'

'And the third is Ralph Weld, an English Catholic. He may arrive under another name.'

'Wonderful,' Garrett applauded sourly. 'All we need is Pope Clement dressed as a washerwoman. You realise Lord Derby is not expecting a blessed regiment to turn up. He may refuse now.'

'Then you'll change his mind.' It was not a request.

Taking his horse's rein, Garrett asked grimly, 'Are we finished then?'

'No. Finnian O'Neill wants assurance that there'll be no betrayal.'

'Jumpy with fleas, is he?' Garrett muttered, thinking swiftly. 'If he has surety from Master Doughtie, will that suffice? Tell him to come to the stables at Lathom House an hour past noon tomorrow. I'll make sure Doughtie's there.' He set his foot in the stirrup and swung his leg across. 'Take matters slowly is my advice, Snow. Advise the others it would be best not to be hasty or harangue his lordship. I reckon our disgruntled earl will remain in Lancashire a good while unless the queen changes her mind.'

'Oh, she may.' Snow looked up at him. 'Yes, indeed, Towneley, or it will be changed for her.'

Garrett hoped Wade had received his warning about increasing the safeguards round the queen. He stared down at the other man. 'Why not by you, Daniel Snow? I'm sure *you'd* have done the deed by now.'

'That's very true, Towneley, but I've been given other orders.' He grabbed Garrett's wrist, leaning upward, his breath for sharing. 'You're to make sure his lordship agrees this time or...'

'Or what?'

'I'll cut your throat.'

Easter Sunday began with Divine Service in Lathom Chapel attended by friends of the earl and countess. Rose would have wagered that most of them were salivating about the day's feast rather than the message of the sermon and it was a very cheerful congregation that proceeded to the Great Hall. Waiting behind the carved wooden screen that separated the old buttery and the stairs to the kitchen were a line of servants with platters piled generously, and King Arthur himself would not have disdained the blazing fire, the great wheels of candles lighting the high table with its crisp linens and glistening *cristallo*.

With Lent over, every course of meat — seethed, stewed, coffined, baked, drenched in sauces or dressed in feathers — was utter pleasure, and after her lonely time in St Albans, Rose was glad to be back in company again. Lizbeth, on the other hand, was missing a daily dose of flattery.

'I'd have thought they would have invited some *younger* nobility, Rose,' she grumbled behind her feather fan after the repast as they followed Lord and Lady Derby up to the Long Gallery to be entertained by Ferdinando's viol players.

Rose sighed. 'We weren't expected until next week, remember. I'm sure the young men of Lancashire will be queuing to kiss your slippers once word gets around.' She received a covert poke of tongue for her sarcasm. 'How can you possibly be discontent?' she continued. 'There's the Pace-Egging after supper tonight — you know, a mummers' play.'

'Presented by the Ormskirk mechanicals?' Lizbeth rolled her eyes. 'Master Much the Miller with a sooty face and wooden sword?'

'But they will be so well rehearsed,' Rose teased. 'Lady Derby says they've performed at each of the local villages today.'

Lizbeth winced. 'My heart is on fire with anticipation!'

Rose sympathised. Oh dear, Pace-Egging! A far cry from the splendid entertainments she remembered — the extravagant, gorgeous masques of her childhood at Richmond Palace, Greenwich and Theobalds when all the court, including a much younger queen, had donned glittering masks and shimmering draperies.

'At least Ferdy has promised to take us hawking tomorrow if the rain clears,' Lizbeth consoled herself.

God willing! thought Rose. Keeping this maid of honour sweet was going to be a challenge.

As the gloom outside deepened, more candles were lit along the gallery. One of the lady guests drew Lizbeth aside to ask about the latest fashions at court, and seeing Rose momentarily on her own, two of the earl's officers joined her. Secretary Edward Halsall, Ferdinando's bastard half-brother, and Richard Doughtie, the handsome Master of Horse. The latter was not talkative. Perhaps he had been drawn from discussion of a more pertinent nature like ordering new saddles, the price of horse oats — or religious differences! Hanging below his ruff was not just a cross but a saint's medallion that proclaimed him a Papist. Astonishing! She had heard that Lancashire had never been fully cleared of Popery but this was blatant. Nor was he the only one. She had already espied a rosary hanging from a gentleman-usher's belt and several of the visiting gentry were clearly of the old faith.

Protestants *and* Papists! This was so different from London where neighbour could suspect neighbour of hiding priests up their chimneys. On the other hand, if the lords and gentry of Lancashire were lax in prosecuting recusants, then the ignorant were vulnerable to glib-tongued Jesuits inciting them to rebellion. Or perhaps the ignorant had never changed their faith? How on earth was she to make report of all this to Wade without endangering Ferdinando and Alice?

'Mistress Byrd, your servant.' John Golborne, the youngest of the earl's four secretaries, reintroduced himself with a cool smile.

He looked to be of a Puritan persuasion because his black and white doublet was austere, surmounted by a stiff white ruff, scarce broader than a hangman's rope, and although he was comely with fine sandy hair combed back from his brow and well-lashed blue eyes, there was an altitude to his chin as well as his stature that implied the world could never meet his standards. Banter was probably not acceptable, but before Rose could test that, he added, 'Lady Vere enlivens this sombre time.'

It was an observation not a compliment. Rose followed his gaze to where one of the other secretaries, Edward Smythe, was explaining a portrait to Lizbeth. Oh dear, the girl was like a playful mermaid, all splash and wriggle now there was no ageing Queen Elizabeth here to glare at her behaviour. If Master Golborne had not been so sneery, Rose would have gently reined in Lizbeth's high spirits.

'And I would have expected her companion to be of more mature years,' Golborne added. Was this provocation a northern method of flirting? No chance of that, Rose decided.

This man could find employment with the Spanish Inquisition if he ever changed his faith.

'I have been known to Lady Vere's family for many years, sir.'

'You are most fortunate then. I take it your husband is related to that Papist composer, William Byrd?'

'*Was* rather than *is* and definitely distant, Master Golborne. My husband, God rest his soul, died of wounds in Her Majesty's service, and I have never met Master Byrd. A pity, for I should like to compliment him on writing such glorious music.'

'However, you are of noble blood, I take it?' He obviously presumed she wasn't.

She offered a tight smile. 'Suffice it to say that my family were high in favour at court until my father was retired.'

'And who was he, then?'

Happily, before she could answer, Lizbeth and Smythe came between them. 'Have you any coin on you, sweet friend? The gentlemen are having a wager and I should like to join them.'

'It's whether the menials from Ormskirk will disgrace themselves, Mistress Byrd,' Secretary Smythe explained with a grin. 'Highly likely.'

'Then I'll lay money against that,' Rose countered. 'Just because they are tradesmen, it does not make them inept. Isn't fine acting a matter of observing others' mannerisms and pretending to be someone else?' Her smile coincided with Golborne's stare of disapproval.

'Have you…?' Lizbeth drew her aside, looking hopefully at the slit in Rose's skirt which hid her pocket.

'Oh, here.' Burrowing into the seam, Rose drew out her small drawstring purse and Lizbeth seized it jubilantly, tapped out the contents onto her palm.

'Here's mine!' She held up an angel and then everyone started joining in. Even Golborne was unbuckling his belt purse. 'You must pardon my impertinence, Mistress Byrd,' he murmured, as Lizbeth danced away, 'but perhaps your charge needs a firmer hand than yours, except —' an elegant gesture — 'here you are.'

'Are you implying I am an interloper?' Rose feigned amusement as his cold blue eyes blinked down at her with an owl-like study.

'I'm not sure yet. Enjoy the evening, Mistress Byrd. I hope your faith in our Ormskirk artisans will be justified but I, too, rather doubt it.'

Ouch! Had they not been surrounded by respectable company, she might have poked her tongue out at his back.

'*Voilà!*' Her purse was pressed back into her hand. 'Would Master Golborne be eligible as a second husband?' whispered Lizbeth.

'I am *not* in hunting vein!' Rose said firmly. Thirsty, she beckoned the page serving refreshment to attend them.

'Whatever you say, but you have certainly gained an admirer. Ah, wine for you, and something disgustingly cordial for me. Yes, Golborne's looking round again.'

'Maybe that's because you keep turning your head. Eyes to the front, if you please.'

Lizbeth laughed, lifting her fingers as blinders. 'By the way, I told Lady Compton we were both very good at reciting. She is wondering if we would like to perform something with the children. One of my lord's players from London is here and can help us. Oh, and she assures me they have a very good library in the Eagle Tower. Poor sweethearts, it's such an intellectual wilderness here, not like London where you can go along to Paternoster Row when you wish to buy a book. Rose, you are looking at me very oddly.'

'One of the London players is here at Lathom?'

'Yes, the rest left shortly before we arrived, off to East Anglia. How wretched that we missed them, but apparently one has stayed on. Ferdy is allowing him board in return for tutoring the girls. I cannot blame the fellow for wanting to avoid the winter pestilences.'

Rose seized Lizbeth's hand. 'Let's excuse ourselves and go in search.'

Out of breath from ascending the stairs to the keep's upmost storey and unsettled at the thought of encountering Towneley once again, Rose unlatched the heavy wooden door and preceded Lizbeth into a shadowy, cold chamber that smelled of leather and beeswax. It must have once looked spacious. Now the remnants of a chained library, that would have been the pride of some nearby abbey, furnished half the room and the rest of the space was stacked, cluttered and packed with books, manuscripts and rolls. Tall unlit candelabra presided either side of a large oaken writing table. Clearly not territory for a tutor — the carved chair of noble proportions set behind it bore the Stanleys' eagle talon.

However, the library did contain human form and she caught her breath in hope. Across by the window, a man was seated at an ancient sloping desk. Huddled into a scholarly robe against the chill, he had his back to them and was leaning on his elbow. Alas, she was so disappointed — the dark hair that danced along his white lace collar and thinned in altitude did not belong to Wade's agent — how disappointing — and yet the man looked familiar.

'Don't say a word!' he commanded, not bothering to look round, and carried on writing.

The tide of winter daylight was ebbing fast and the neglected fire was too far gone to light a spill. Best to return in the morning, yet just as they turned to leave, the tutor sat back with a squawk.

'Ivory globes!' he exclaimed as his palms rose to cup the air before his chest. *"Ivory globes, rivered with...*' His hands gesticulated. 'Ah, *with blue.*' He dashed his quill nib into the inkpot and resumed writing with furious pace.

Rose glanced down at the cleavage of her breasts and raised an eyebrow. 'Blue?' she mouthed at Lizbeth.

'He thinks he's Shakespeare.'

'Or your father,' Rose whispered back.

'A pair of...' murmured the man, staring up at the panelled ceiling for inspiration. Cursing, he crushed the paper and flung it to the ground. 'Where are you, plague take you, you cursed muse?' he exclaimed. 'I've been waiting since noon for an audience *and getting hungry.* Have you brought the meat pie you prom—' The question expired as he turned to face them. 'Oh! Your pardon!' Rallying his manners, he unwound his legs from the screw of the stool. 'Two muses, yet not the one I was expecting.' A touch of forehead in polite salute. 'Forgive me if I am tardy to rise. My feet are no longer in parlance with my legs.'

'I assume you are the new tutor?' Lizbeth stated.

He clutched the desk with pale fingers to steady himself. 'With all respect, young mistress, I shall not take you.'

'*Take me,* sir?'

Rose tried hard not to laugh. Yes, Lizbeth looked younger than her years.

The schoolmaster's right palm rose emphatically. 'The agreement was two little maids and no more. Half the day for tutoring and half for entertaining my muse — when the fickle wench bothers to call,' he muttered to the empty air.

'Quickly, Rose, which shall I choose?' Lizbeth whispered behind her hand. 'Indignation or hysteria?'

'Try disappointment.' Raising her voice, Rose called across to the tutor, 'We quite understand, sir. May I ask if you are writing a work of verse?'

'A poor thing but my own. Are you familiar with Ovid's *Fasti*, mistress?'

She nodded and was further amused to see him hesitate and bestow a cautious glance on Lizbeth. 'I am writing about Sextus Tarquinius' uninvited assault on a Roman lady's virtue.'

Oh, very tactfully couched but Lizbeth's ears had heard much worse.

'I believe, sir, the term eluding you is "rape",' Lord Oxford's daughter retorted. 'I trust you will treat Lucrece with sympathy.' With that shot over his bow, she turned away to inspect the shelves. To his credit, the tutor made no trite response.

'Alas, sir, maybe your muse thinks you've rejected her,' Rose exclaimed. She swept across to a free-standing wooden lectern by the window. 'It must be very convenient to have one.'

'Damnably *inconvenient*,' corrected the tutor, brushing a finger across his moustache and as though sensing a challenge, he stepped across to face her from the other side of the lectern. 'What's your argument, *madonna*?' he asked.

Pleased to be indulged, she stroked her fingers down the gilded edges of the open book.

'Why, sir, I have two younger brothers in London who profess to write dramatic verse — unfortunately, they spend most of their time flicking cobnut shells at any player who forgets his lines. My point is that whenever their woolly heads are empty of inspiration, they blame their muse for not arriving when they call for her. I don't believe in muses, sir. Surely inspiration comes from within?'

She would have welcomed a friendly argument but before the man could answer, Lizbeth flounced up beside her, haughty with entitlement. 'Maybe the muses are all down in London attending on my Lord of Oxford.'

'Perhaps we should introduce ourselves,' Rose intervened gently, touching her friend's arm. 'This is Lady Vere, Lord Oxford's eldest daughter, and I am my lady's companion, Rose Byrd.'

'*Mea culpa.*' Although the schoolmaster's eyes widened with appropriate respect, there was a smile on his lips as he acknowledged Lizbeth with a deep bow. 'William Shakespeare, my lady.'

Rose gave an involuntary gasp. She had been hoping for the actor who resembled Wade's agent, but to meet Shakespeare… Of course, it made sense that Ferdinando would give lodging to his most competent writer while the theatres were closed. 'Why, how excellent that you are here, sir,' she exclaimed. 'Isn't that so, Lady Vere?'

However, being the daughter of a noble lord much praised for his verse, Lizbeth displayed indifference to the poet's fame. 'We will leave you to your difficult labour, sirrah. Come, Rose.'

'A tragedy that you do so, my lady,' the poet retorted roguishly, 'methinks you would make an inspiring midwife.'

Lizbeth refused to flirt. 'You are impertinent, sir!' she snapped and with a disdainful jerk of chin, she left the room.

Rose lingered. 'We were looking for inspiration for an interlude that can involve the children, Master Shakespeare.

We should be grateful for your help and participation. Maybe we can return when the room is warmer?'

'Of course, mistress.'

She halted as her fingers touched the door ring, remembering he had expected someone else. 'Master Shakespeare, you wouldn't have the Second Murderer from *Richard III* here with you by any chance?' Seeing his expression become guarded, she regretted her question. 'No?' A weak smile. 'My imagination, then. Good day to you — what is left of it — sir, but if you do see him, tell him he needs to make an entrance.' Then seeing the poet's amused lift of eyebrows, she realised how salacious that sounded. 'Make himself known,' she corrected and fled.

Safe on the other side of the door, she halted, furious with herself. Furious about the scarlet garters, furious that she did not know what to report to Wade, furious at Master Golborne's condescension and Shakespeare's amusement and well, like any sensible woman in these times when she had to be so dependent on others' good will, just *furious*.

'*Rose!*' The imperious tone came from the stairwell and the swift slither of descending train told her that Lizbeth was chilled and hungry. There had been plenty such occasions on the journey. With a sigh, she followed, taking care on the narrow tapering steps.

By the time she reached the first floor and the passage to the newer building, she could see that Lizbeth had company. The meagre light showed her a well-clad gentleman, cap in hand, straightening from a bow. Despite his civil garb, a fearsome rapier hung from his belt. Her agent! Younger-looking, shinier than he'd been in St Albans — a presence that accelerated her heartbeat and her breath. The shaggy locks had been cut away and his beard was short and well-trimmed. She supposed he must have come up the outside stairs because the fringe curling along his forehead was sodden with rain and great patches of damp darkened his mantle across his shoulders.

Yet the pleasure of seeing him again was straightaway ruined; the instant he recognised Rose the gallant smile he was displaying to Lizbeth slid from his face, replaced by the cold expression of a stranger.

'Ah, here is my companion, Mistress Byrd,' exclaimed Lizbeth. 'Rose, this is Captain Towneley, one of Lord Derby's friends.' Swift work, indeed, ingratiating himself already onto the blue ink side of Lizbeth's ledger.

Rose did not curtsey.

'Mistress.' He gave her a very reserved nod.

'Your face looks familiar, Captain. Have we met before?'

'If we had, mistress, I'm sure I would have remembered.' A warning, stern and clear — *noli me tangere*!

Rose inwardly flinched. Taking a humbler position at Lizbeth's elbow, she was able to send him a stare that would have looked well on a Bridewell interrogator's face. *What in hell are you at?* For an instant, his gaze softened. It might have been an apology.

'The scholar in the library upstairs is complaining he lacks a muse. Do soldiers need muses, too?' Lizbeth purred, with a flutter of eyelashes.

'England is my muse, my lady. When she calls, I answer.'

'And is she calling you now?' Rose interrupted sweetly. 'Because I certainly hear nothing.'

That was ignored. 'I trust you left Her Majesty in good health, Lady Vere?'

The nobility had the habit of stamping on the flow of conversation when commoners overstepped themselves. 'Last time I saw Her Majesty,' Lizbeth replied loftily, 'two weeks ago, I think it was, she was nowhere near demise, rather frisky in fact.'

It might not have been the answer he was wanting and before he could reply, an equally condescending voice hailed him.

'You, sirrah!' It was Golborne. 'Towneley, Lord Derby requires your presence. I am required to escort you thither. Ah, Lady Vere, your pardon. *Now, if you please, sirrah!*'

The captain turned to face him. He topped the other man by a finger width. 'I am not quite done here, Master Golborne,' he said courteously. Dislike fizzed the air between them. 'However, if Ferdy commands…' With a bow to the women, he contrarily stepped out into the rain.

'No, it's this way,' protested Golborne, pointing to the passageway, but he was forced to follow.

'I hope they both get soaked,' muttered Lizbeth, as she hastened ahead, then dispensing with pomposity, she giggled and grabbed Rose's hand. 'So marvellous that we have a captive Shakespeare to do our will. Father says his style still needs to mature but I declare the wretch shall write a masque for us to perform with Alice's girls. Yes, with fairies!'

'Fairies?' Rose halted in mock outrage. 'Gauze and spangles? *In April* We'll freeze.'

'I fancy playing an elfin queen in the greenwood.'

'As long as you stay a "virgin" queen!' Rose quipped. 'Only I'm the poor watchdog required to keep you unsullied for your bridegroom, whoever the poor madman is who eventually signs the papers for y—! Oh, your pardon!' Recalling Southampton had paid an immense fine to be free of Lizbeth, she reddened. Had she gone too far?

'Two things,' Oxford's daughter declared in a stern manner, though she kept hold of Rose's hand. 'Firstly, if we don't laugh about it, Southampton's insult will continue to haunt me forever, secondly, *you're too late.*'

'*What!*'

'You need not stay, John.' Ferdinando, standing at the hearth in his large bedchamber, waved Garrett in. Master Secretary John Golborne withdrew but the language of his body conveyed disapproval that this outsider should be so familiarly received.

'You had a successful meeting?' the earl asked after the door had closed.

'Yes, my lord.'

Frowning, Ferdinando strode across to a table to pour them both a drink. It gave Garrett a moment to marvel for never had he been in such a luxurious chamber, a room so vast that even the large bed with its weighty green and silver hangings did not predominate.

Being a dynastic bedchamber, reminders of a martial past competed with the tapestries: an ancestor's sword and breastplate; an Isle of Man coat of arms and a battered shield showing the Stanley eagle claws device with *Sans changer ma verrite* misspelt beneath it. More claws, painted in gold, enlivened the wooden ceiling, while above the fireplace, looking rather smoky, was an old battle standard with a gruesome glowering eagle. There were gentler furnishings: a virginal stood near the window and an expensive screen — dancing naiads — hid the earl's washstand. Beyond it, the recess with the close stool had been made into a separate room.

The earl's servants were diligent: no clothing was strewn upon the large oaken chests and his lordship's shoes and boots were neatly arranged on a wooden rack. With its groan of papers, the only untidy feature was Ferdinando's writing desk, lit beneath a generous bay window that carried another ancestral crest in coloured glass — golden medallions and stag heads upon azure bands.

On the left of the hearth were several shelves of books, presumably his lordship's personal collection: treatises on government, essays, religious tracts, poetry and plays. Garrett had frequented enough bookshops to know that the several of the taller books had been purchased discreetly — erotic art hiding behind respectable Latin titles.

'Good health!' The earl took a swig and set his cup aside. 'I want you to read this,' he said gravely, drawing a letter from the breast of his doublet. 'It's from Carey, my brother-in-law. There, the part at the end!'

Garrett was relieved to read that it was nothing to do with him and mostly about horses. The last lines mentioned the treason of Dr Roderigo Lopez. He had heard about this case at Colonel Stanley's table a couple of months earlier. Lord Essex had uncovered the treasonous plot and Lopez, the chief court physician, had been found guilty of conspiring to poison Her Majesty. Carey wrote that 'the villain' was still in the Tower awaiting execution.

'Is my cousin involved?'

Garrett shook his head and passed the letter back. 'On my very soul, I never heard mention of this Lopez being in your cousin's service.'

Ferdinando drew in a deep breath. 'I am relieved to hear it.'

'But you haven't...?'

The earl snorted. 'Conspired with Lopez? Of course not! He once prescribed me *arceus apozema* for a bellyache — anise and sumac. Can't stand anise now. My breath stank of it for a week. Anyway, that's about the only truck I had with the fellow.

Plenty of lords consulted him. He treated Essex for the Spanish disease and made no secret of it. It was amusing ... at the time.'

Garrett squirmed at the thought of Essex's infected nether parts. 'And yet it is Lord Essex who unearthed this conspiracy?'

'Yes, Towneley. He seeks to convince Her Majesty that he can safeguard her better than the Cecils can and he's encouraging taradiddle that he's Her Majesty's son.' He paused, letting that revelation sink in. 'Now do you grasp where this is leading?'

'*Her son?*' Shocked, Garrett stared at him. 'Can that be true?'

'Hell, no! But you see how I am in his way. My claim to the throne, remember.'

Fear could make a man see devils in every corner, but an ambitious rival was not to be dismissed lightly.

'Her Majesty would never name him as her successor, surely, my lord?'

'*Her Majesty* doted on Dr Lopez until Essex persuaded her otherwise.' He rose and strode to the window, crumpling the letter and tossing it aside. 'If Essex racks my name out of the wretch, I am a dead man. So long as Her Majesty delays in signing the death warrant, I feel vulnerable.'

'Surely you would have been summoned to the Star Chamber by now, my lord. I am positive you have nothing to fear from Lopez.' *But what of Yorke, Williams and O'Collun, if they are ever put to the question?* He shivered.

Across the room, Ferdinando had a jut to his lower lip and a hardening in his eyes. 'I am so out of favour.'

The room was silent until, twisting his hat between his fingers, Garrett stood up. Regardless of danger, his duty was to safeguard this man. 'My lord, your pardon for my bluntness, but wouldn't that be a good reason to call off going to Knowsley.'

'And see Essex become the next king?'

'It may never come to that, my lord.' Yet the queen was old, doting, vulnerable.

'To hear what my cousin offers doesn't mean I'll heed him. It will change nothing.'

'As you say, my lord.'

Or it might change everything.

If the queen assumes that her maid-of-honour's virginity has been lost in Lancashire, she will blame me. Rose's peace of mind felt utterly shipwrecked as she followed Lizbeth back into the Long Gallery. Coming to Lancashire had been a big mistake.

'You both look frozen,' exclaimed Alice, Lady Derby, ushering them towards the nearest fireplace. 'Did you speak with Master Shakespeare?'

While Lizbeth aired her idea for a masque, Rose was silently cursing the Cecils. Pah, making such a fuss of her at Theobalds. She was being used just like her father had been. Report on Ferdy? All that rubbish about birds? No, she was here to be the scapegoat for Lizbeth's immorality. That had to be it. God knows, both Burghley and Sir Robert's minds had more dark alleyways than Southwark. Well, at least there was no babe on the way (they had had to break their journey for several days while Lizbeth had her monthly flow). But which reckless whoreson had deflowered the little wretch? Tight-lipped, she sent a reproving look at her charge but before she could reach out cold palms to the fire, little Bess seized her hand and shook her arm like a skipping rope.

'Huzzah, a masque with fairies! And you've been to meet our tutor. Did he grimace for you? He can pull the most wondrous faces.'

'Oh, can he, indeed?' Then with a view to provoking Lizbeth, she said to the child, 'Did you know he is famous in London?'

'Oh yes, but he has to do what Papa tells him. He taught the Heskeths, you know, before he started writing plays, but now it's our turn.'

'The Heskeths?' Lizbeth met her concerned glance. The hanged man's family?

'The Heskeths of Rufford Hall, our neighbours just up the road,' explained Anne, the oldest daughter. 'Not the ones at Aughton. We don't have truck with Bart's family. Not anymore.'

Not anymore. Bart? Hesketh's brother?

Lizbeth touched her sleeve. Ferdy had come into the gallery with an entourage that included Towneley. At least the agent's gaze found her, Rose noted, even if it slid past indifferently. Why hadn't Wade warned her his intelligencer would be here? Wasn't she supposed to be his safeguard? Of course, maybe, just maybe, Wade didn't know.

'Stop fretting, dear Rose,' whispered Lizbeth, and glided forth to take the earl's arm as he led the company to supper in the Great Hall.

'Shall we, Mistress Byrd?' Golborne held out a neat-cuffed wrist. 'Below the salt, I think.' Another straight-faced jest, for though she was not to be seated on the dais he led her to a place beside Ferdy's daughters. 'You see we are not so formal with rank in Lathom. Enjoy the entertainment.' Well, that was unlooked for, thought Rose, her self-worth mended a little, but she would take care to avoid him even if his observation that she was not cut of the right cloth to manage Lizbeth might be true.

Looking towards the dais, Rose tried to see her charge as others might. With a crimson cap set jauntily over her dark curly hair, Lizbeth was at her prettiest, even though her small bosom was flattened further by the stiff, embroidered stomacher. Ladies Derby and Compton were trying to amuse her, but with no eligible suitors at hand among the invited neighbours, the minx was covertly surveying the men's table. Guiltily, Rose realised her own gaze was also tempted that way, too.

Compared to the women's table, the men's board was crowded and noisy with banter. At the far end, Martin was clinking ale pots with one of the footmen, and wit was evidently flowing at midway where Towneley and Shakespeare were sharing a mess because suddenly a great wave of laughter rocked their shoulders and the captain took his napkin from his shoulder and swiped the playwright with it. Their behaviour was a contrast to the formality above the salt; Ferdy, solemnly chewing, was not engaging with the ladies. Instead, he was looking down the hall as though he longed to join Shakespeare's bench.

'I sometimes think my father would love to be in a play,' murmured Anne.

'I remember seeing him in entertainments at court when I was a child,' Rose told her.

'And don't all courtiers dissemble?' the girl whispered back. Very shrewd.

Frances, the middle sister, cut across their conversation. 'What do you think of our Spanish paps, Mistress Byrd?' the child asked cheekily.

Rose smiled, plunged her spoon into the rosewater blancmange and scooped out the crystallised cherry from its centre. 'Delicious! And speaking of masques, when Lady Vere and I went to speak with Master Shakespeare in the Eagle Tower, we encountered a military captain. Is he a friend of the family, Anne?'

'If you mean Captain Towneley, yes, Papa says they are old friends. The Towneleys are a Lancashire family so I daresay he may be a son or grandson of old Sir John Towneley.' She lowered her voice. 'I'm not sure which side of the blanket the captain was born, you understand, but it was not around here.'

'Surely you mean "under" or "over" the blanket?' corrected Frances, ignoring Anne's hold-your-tongue glare.

'Is Mama going to decide which side when she has the baby?' piped up little Bess.

'Oh, don't ask such stupid questions!'

'I didn't realise your Mama was with child, Anne,' whispered Rose. No wonder Lady Derby had been concerned they had brought no pestilence with them. 'When's the babe due?'

'Towards Michaelmas,' Frances exclaimed. 'Papa is hoping it will be a boy. He's very disappointed that we are all girls. I don't see why I can't become an earl. Maybe I'll be the next queen if Anne doesn't want —'

'Hush, you stupid loosetongue!' snapped her sister.

'Well, one of us should be an earl if the new baby isn't a boy,' retorted Frances, haughtily scraping her biscuit around her bowl. 'Mama doesn't want Uncle Will to inherit, you see.'

Ah yes, Rose recalled a contrary youth refusing to join their games at Theobalds.

'Yes, Papa's brother,' chimed in Bess. 'Uncle Will's been away for years. Grandfather said good riddance and —'

'Bess!'

'Well, actually, that's not a lie, Anne,' corrected Frances.

'But it's a family matter.'

'But Mistress Byrd is to be treated like a cousin. Mama said so.'

'That was very kind of your mother, Frances,' Rose intervened, 'but I think Anne is right. Sometimes there are secrets that other people should not hear. Perhaps your Mama doesn't want the world to know she is carrying a babe yet.'

'Well, she certainly said she doesn't want Uncle Will near him.'

'Bess!' The admonition was worthless.

'Fear not, Anne, I have a short memory,' Rose said quickly, reassuring the girl.

'At last!' exclaimed Frances, bouncing on her seat as the servants moved along the walls, extinguishing all the candles save those at the opposite end of the hall illuminating the huge, wooden screen. Now, its painted stars glinting above the horizon of jagged mountains lent a feeling of suspense as though Misrule was about to turn the ordered world into an anarchy. It was like that feeling Rose always had at the Theatre when the actors stepped out from the wings and all the reality around her vanished. Almost.

Across the hall, Master Golborne shifted round to espy her, his face a glimmer of white as he smirked.

Of course, the wager!

The horns and pipes ceased, a harsh drumming grew in volume, and as the hall hushed, a grotesquely-masked player stepped into their midst. He carried a basket and brandished his long straw tail like a whip.

'That's "Master Tosspot",' Anne informed Rose as the children and guests, familiar with the custom, were harangued to toss painted eggs or coins into the basket. Then as Tosspot withdrew, the din diminished and, one by one, the other players stepped forward.

As in the Christmas mummery, this tale of St George was ludicrous, but the shadows of the actors were eerie in the smoky light, as though they performed a descant drama far more sinister.

Rose found it hard to understand because the dialect was local. Though the players were trying hard, those watching were glib with jests and mockery. Alas, it seemed like Smythe and Golborne would win the wager. Despite the gorbellied 'Doctor' and the black-daubed 'Saracen' making everyone teary-eyed with mirth, the gestures of the muscular weaver playing St George were even bigger than his vanity and he drew the most jeers. His dying spasms brought cries of 'Get on with it!'

The performance ended with him being restored to life by the physician. Invigorated, he approached the high table, presumably with a closing oration to thank his hosts, but before he could take a deep lungful of breath, three men garbed as witches sprang lithely from the darkness, thrusting him aside. The hall gasped, fell silent.

Spindly nails thimbled the witches' fingers, hook-nosed masks hid their upper faces, and hooded, long black tunics disguised their bodies. As they capered, their huge shadows twisted and writhed like tortured souls in Hell.

Then one flung himself on his knees before the dais. 'All Hail, Ferdinando, Earl of Derby and Lord of Man!' he proclaimed, lifting his powerful arms with Hallelujah zeal.

The second witch joined him: 'Hail, Ferdinando, Lord of Cheshire, Lord of Lancashire!'

That brought a rumble of comment, even some unkind chuckles. Those offices traditionally went with the earldom, but Rose knew from Lizbeth that the queen had given them elsewhere. Breath caught, she watched the third witch pirouette gleefully. He made low obeisance, then rising, shouted, 'All Hail, Ferdinando, defender of the faith and king hereafter!'

Ferdinando's jaw dropped but by the time he had sprung to his feet in angry astonishment, the witches were gone, leaving St George gulping like a landed fish and the Mayor of Ormskirk with his face in his hands.

'Lights!' roared Master Farington. 'Light the damn candles, curse it!' For his age and size, he moved fast, grabbing a quaking St George by his tunic. 'Did *you* write that?'

'No, by my very soul, sir. It wasn't in the play. I don't under—'

A turnabout with a flurry of sleeve. Goblets rattled to the floor as a startled Shakespeare was hauled halfway over the board.

'Allow me some common sense, Master Farington!' the playwright gasped, wriggling to avoid the almond cream.

'Don't sit there like dumb beasts, you numbskulls!' Ferdy was yelling with Jove-like fury as the bench of his household officers rekindled to life. 'Find those churls and drag them hither! As for you,' he snarled at the mayor, 'you'd better have an explanation for this outrage.'

This was treason!

'Reckon I'll play magpie and thieve those lines for a tragedy some time,' Shakespeare panted as he loped after Garrett through the kitchen garden; they had been delegated to search for the 'witches' in the orchard. 'Prophecy with that subtle touch of evil.'

Garrett surveyed the rows of budding, ghostly boughs. 'It wasn't subtle.'

He was concerned lest the compass needle of blame should swing again their way. Master Farington, who had organised the entertainment, was clearly avid for a whipping boy and Garrett didn't want the flagellation. Who in hell was behind this mischief? Christ! If news of this reached Cecil or Lord Essex, one of them would be rubbing his soft palms with glee. And news would reach Whitehall. Even if he reported it back to Wade in the driest terms, whoever else the spymaster had planted in the Lathom household would be sending an account.

He would certainly need to bridle Rose Byrd from making her report. Somehow! What did Wade think he was doing sending her up here? Have her wriggle into Ferdinando's four-poster?

'*Ouch!*' He recoiled from the low branch that had just thwacked him.

Shakespeare was still musing. '"*King hereafter!*", eh? What about this for a plot — the witches' prediction plants the possibility in a character's mind so that it becomes a self-fulfilling prophecy and, heigh ho, a great man takes an unwise course towards disaster? I like that. As for the strutting weaver who played St George, for instance, now he —'

'Stow it for the future, ink paws! As for the present, you go that way! No, keep the torch, Will. I'll meet you at the far end.'

Garrett considered drawing his rapier but he was more concerned that instead of catching some fleeing menial, he'd skewer England's leading playwright. When his bootcap disturbed a small fallen bough sufficient for a cudgel, he grabbed it up.

His night vision was good but every few paces, he halted and listened. The wind was rustling the woodland trees beyond the orchard. Then he heard voices, saw Will's torch moving fast along the other side. He started running. It had to be them.

Their quarry had reached the far wall. Garrett managed a massive wallop at one of them before a kick in the chest had him staggering back.

'By Christ! Watch it!' swore Shakespeare, jerking the flame to safety.

Garrett sprang up onto the drystone wall but the three 'witches' were gone into a moonless countryside that was as dark as Hell. 'Devil take their balls!' he growled, slithering back to the ground.

'They certainly had a sense of theatre. Look there!' Shakespeare swung the torch to show three masks and cloaks cleverly hooked upon the tree limbs. 'Like spirits melted into thin air. Probably heading for the mere on their broomsticks.'

'Then I think we'll leave them to it,' muttered Garrett. He didn't like the way things were shaping up. Not one little bit! And he had to silence Rose.

'Night-night, Ferdy's grandfather!'

Lizbeth made a face at the third earl's portrait as they made their way to the White Room — their bedchamber off the Long Gallery. They had not bothered with a page to guide them up, Rose was wishing they had; the deep shadows were troubling.

'Whoo!' giggled Lizbeth. 'Any warlocks hiding along here? Any ghosts? Come out, come out!' Then she grabbed her arm. 'Rosie, don't —' she hiccoughed — 'forget we must collect our wager tomorrow!'

Remembering Ferdy's expression of horror at the witches, Rose could not share her levity. Something sinister was going on at Lathom. Was that why Towneley was here?

Lizbeth sobered somewhat as they reached their door. 'Do you think Ferdinando would like to be king?' she giggled.

'King?' Knowing Lizbeth, the young woman's account of tonight's witches could acquire horns and a tail before it reached the queen. 'No, Lizbeth, no!' she said firmly. 'Why else would he have been so angry? Richard Hesketh's treason has already scorched his reputation.' Putting a finger to her lips, she glanced back along the gallery. 'What happened tonight must not be misconstrued!' she whispered, then softly turned the ring handle to their chamber. With relief, she heard the regular snores from the truckle bed. The night candle showed Amy, Lizbeth's maid, fast asleep.

'Well, he has the birthright, you know,' Lizbeth persisted, unpinning her cap. 'King Ferdinando I!' she giggled, tossing it onto the coverlet cap. 'Lord Essex would hate that. There's not a shred of love between them, you know, and I daresay the other earls would not like it either, they'd be so jealous.' She collapsed on the bed. 'Better to have James of Scotland, see, because he's a king already.' Another hiccough. 'Providing he doesn't turn Papist like his mother.'

'Never know with a Scotsman,' Rose growled. She had accompanied her father on a diplomatic mission to Falkirk and managed to avoid being shackled in marriage to a laird. Frowning at her tipsy ladyship, she wondered if Lizbeth had soaked up her kinsmen's opinions. Were the Cecils laying money on King James as the next king? 'Anyway, let us hope Her Majesty has many more years ahead,' she added tactfully in case they had woken the maidservant.

'Pah, you know the truth as well as I, Rose. The people see nothing but the monstrous dresses, the ropes of pearls, the ubiquitous gems. That's the delusion. She's all wrinkles beneath the paint, and underneath her wig she's —' Laughing at Rose's grimace, she kicked the truckle bed.

'No, Lizbeth,' Rose protested. 'I can help.'

'Too late, it's what the creature's paid for!'

Rose watched in pity as poor Amy scrambled up, beseeching mercy for falling asleep. Everyone was supposed to accept the rank God had given them at birth but the selfishness of the noble-born could still shock lesser mortals. Entitlement bred expectation.

The third witch's voice still echoed in Rose's head.

King hereafter.

Was Ferdinando tempted?

11

The new month gifted Lancashire a shiny, gilded morning with no chill wind whirling the weathercocks. Sharing an early breakfast, Ferdinando declared he would lead a hawking party in New Park, part of his demesne to the north-west of Lathom. His local friends declined, having to leave that morning, and Alice stayed behind to bid them farewell (or perhaps because she feared to dislodge her unborn babe), so it was a small party led by the earl and Lady Compton that collected the birds from the mews. To Rose's surprise, when the grooms led their saddled mounts around to the front of the house, Towneley and Doughtie, the Master of Horse, joined them. Maybe she would be able to snatch a private word with Towneley.

Or maybe not. Save for touching his hat to her and Lizbeth, he took care to ride apart. She tried not to mind, and the mildness of the morning proved her ally.

It was exquisite pleasure to indulge in a lighter mantle and a delight to behold the glory of nature's awakening after the long harsh winter. Following yesterday's rain, the earth smelled sweet and moist. Coppery shoots lent a burnish to the greater trees, fresh fronds of hawthorn and alder mantled the hedgerows and white flowers lit the dark twigs of blackthorn. Colours dappled the banks of the bridlepath; brazen dandelions and aspiring cow parsley upstaged their less showy kindred and behind them in the lush shadows lurked the sinister, hooded lords-and-ladies.

The hawking party was accompanied by two beaters and a cadger, who carried the wooden rack of ladies' birds. Everyone flying the birds wore special gloves and a pouch. The latter had lids of wood, which were covered with silk and simply hinged for scooping out meat morsels for lures. Lizbeth, who adored the sport, was pleased to be flying Lady Derby's merlin but Rose, who had never hawked, planned just to watch. Cloud, her ambler lent from Theobalds, was suffering from a sore fetlock and the substitute mare was proving so skittish that Towneley took pity and reached out a hand for the leading rein.

'I can manage, thank you,' Rose replied coolly.

'Allow him, mistress,' countered the Master of Horse. 'She's a bad-tempered filly. I'll be having words with the head groom. She should not have been saddled for you.'

'Let me be brief, Mistress Byrd,' Towneley whispered, as he lagged back aside her. 'I do not know how you managed to insinuate yourself into Lady Vere's service or whether it was Wade's doing, but leave me to make any reports, do you hear me?'

Insinuate? That was the pot calling the cauldron black. And why be frosty? Had he asked her to work with him, she would have been flattered.

Her response was a shrug — insubordinate and provocative. 'So they fathomed you in Antwerp, Captain?'

'No,' he said through clenched teeth, then turned his head to look at her. 'You're supposed to be languishing for me in St Albans. Why aren't you?'

'I don't know,' she said cheerfully. 'Maybe I failed at languishing.'

'It's not a game,' he said testily.

'Then what is it, Captain, becau—' Ahead of them, the company halted abruptly. Towneley's hand went instantly to his rapier hilt.

'It's only some foolish old woman,' Lizbeth called back to Rose.

Tails wagging, the party's two hunting dogs bounded up to sniff at the creature's skirts; only the humans were baring their teeth at this unexpected obstacle — a quaintly garbed one, for the ancient's brimmed hat, adorned with a daffodilly, sat at a sportive angle over a tangled thicket of greying hair that might have housed a mouse brood. Her age was hard to discern, perhaps some sixty winters since her cradle. Seeing she had successfully blocked the company's progress, the crone's lips puckered in a gleeful smile.

'Move aside, good soul,' cajoled Lady Compton.

'Old grandam, what is it you want?' demanded Doughtie, riding forward.

He was ignored. With a creped, speckled hand, the woman drew a folded paper from her apron band. 'I bring you a petition, Lord Derby,' she declared.

Ferdinando didn't look pleased but nor did he look angry. All in a day's work for an earl, Rose assumed. 'What matter is this?' he inquired, gesturing to one of the beaters to take it from her, but she came right to his steed's head. One of her eyelids was swollen with a stye; her unsullied eye was mischievous, malicious.

'The angels have sent me to stay close to you.'

'Close to me, old woman?' he laughed. 'I am flattered. Do you plan to keep me company o' nights?'

'Aye, if you'd let me.' It sounded like light-heartedness as she handed up the paper. 'It's the only way, *God's way*.'

'And there lies *our* way and you are in it, old woman!' Doughtie tapped his riding crop against his thigh. 'Let's waste no more time on her, my lord.'

Holding the petition in his free hand, Ferdinando perused it. 'I see no reason why I should grant this, old mistress.'

'Then, harken, my lord. The blessed angels told me to warn you. Our Lord God will send you guidance through me but only if you give me a dwelling nearby so I may counsel you.'

The peregrine on the earl's wrist adjusted her wings uneasily. 'I have counsellors.' A glare at Doughtie. 'Is this an April Fools' trick, by any chance?'

'No, my lord.'

The men on foot also shook their heads. 'Wished we'd thought of it, though,' chuckled one.

The hag had the stallion's bridle now. Caressing the beast's cheek, she began to sing beneath her breath.

'Can we ride on?' Lizbeth demanded petulantly and became another victim of the woman's glare. The petitioner cocked her head, as though listening to an inner voice, before she chanted, 'Woman of Man, twice they reject you, twice they reclaim.'

Lizbeth recoiled angrily. 'Oh, very droll. London gossip reaches here, does it?'

'Enough!' Doughtie might have spurred forward and struck the creature, but the earl's gesture forbade him.

'Shall we throw Joan of Arc in the river and see if she floats?' quipped one of the beaters. 'Looks like she needs a scrub.'

'We have more honest sport in hand.' Captain Towneley had at last spoken. 'The birds grow restless.'

'Aye, they do, Garrett.' Ferdinando, with a shrug at Lady Compton, gravely handed back the petition. To give him his due, he had at least read it. 'My regrets, good woman. It would set an unwelcome precedent.'

The crone's good eye grew fierce as she stared up into his face. 'Ferdinando Stanley, be wise, be brave, beware. Keep me by you that I may safeguard you. There is a crossroads in your destiny.'

'Good mistress, there is only God's will.' But his flesh looked paler than it had at breakfast. Rose saw him cross his fingers beneath the reins.

'Then listen to Him, the Almighty!' Her right finger jabbed upwards; her left hand brandished the petition. 'Is *this* too much to ask for your soul's salvation? One little dwelling when you have so much.'

He blew out his cheeks and muttered, 'I am sorry but I cannot grant you what you ask.' Setting his sight forward, he kneed his horse past her.

'Then you are accursed, Lord Earl!' she shrieked, as the grinning beaters edged her back. 'Death is waiting with his sickle. Fare you foul, my noble lord, for thus shall it be.' She spat into the ditch behind her. 'There lies your way.'

Rose met Towneley's glance. Now it was he who shrugged as he handed her back the leading rein. He looked as confounded as everyone else. The old woman was surely demented, wasn't she? But it was uncannily like last night — the unexpectedness. What made matters worse, a lone magpie flew across the earl's path as he started off again and that had the beaters muttering and crossing themselves.

As the company rode on, the resurgence of conversation was forced and awkward. The encounter had scraped the enjoyment from the morning, especially for Ferdinando. He flew his peregrine with little joy, watched stony-faced as it brought down its prey, and the instant he beheld dark clouds brooding from Ormskirk way, he decreed the sport over.

'Do you think Ferdy believes the curse?' Lizbeth whispered in the mews later as Rose untied the dog-skin jesses from the girl's arm.

'I hope not.' Meant in all truth as she remembered Hesketh's words from the scaffold at St Albans: *May the Devil take you to an early grave!*

This was the second time she had seen Ferdinando cursed.

Armed with a wrinkled apple from the earl's cellar and choosing a time after midday dinner when none of the older grooms were around to lecture her on poultices, pustules and the price of oats, Rose called in on her horse's stall to inspect Cloud's rear fetlock, concerned it might be developing mud fever.

Fortunately, the sore was showing no signs of heat, though it might need another day before the ambler could be safely exercised. Just as she set the hoof down, Rose heard the creak of boots. She straightened quietly, but the three men silhouetted in the entrance to the stable did not enter, though one of them was holding his horse's leading rein. She heard a lilt of Irish in the horseman's voice.

Stroking Cloud's nose, she waited, and heard one of the two taller men introduce himself: 'Richard Doughtie, Master of Horse...'

When they began to converse in French, she eavesdropped, just curious at first. She caught mention of Saint-Omer, which she knew to be a Catholic seminary, and one man spoke of a Father Holt. Were all three Papists? No Protestant minister was ever spoken of as 'Father'.

At that instant, Cloud gave a huff and the shortest man turned his head, peering into the darkness of the stable. She held her breath, glad that a mare in the stall near the door shifted her hoofs and snorted. The men recommenced their conversation. Again, she only caught the gist — a hunt at Knowsley to meet Lord Derby — before they shook hands and separated. She heard the jingle of bridle and departing hoofs of just one horse.

Rose believed in common sense. Looking for ill in others had a nasty way of becoming a habit if you let it take over. Maybe she was making too much of this but before she dared move, one of the men returned. Jesu! Through the crack between the boards, she saw his long shadow halt as he stared down the row of stalls, listening.

That vanquished any doubt there was some secret afoot and stoked her fear. With her heart racing, she kept stroking Cloud's cheek to keep the beast from fidgeting.

At last, she saw the man's form relent. Shoulders slackening, he drew a deep breath. With relief, she listened to his footsteps retreat across the cobbles. A more enthusiastic spy might have swiftly reached the stable door and edged round it so she might recognise him, but she did not dare; the man was far too vigilant for her peace of mind, and so she lingered until one of the young stable lads came in. Only then did she leave the stall and wish the whistling youth a good day as she walked past. It was an effort to cross the courtyard with utter nonchalance and although no one challenged her, she had the sense of being watched.

Assuredly, imagining a flea in the lace about your neck could make you scratch, but her instincts were shrieking danger. That had been no accidental meeting. If she had heard what she should not, it was going to be more than a flea biting her. She needed to talk to Martin, ask him how best to deal with this. Now!

Rose had only spoken briefly with Martin since their arrival but it was a relief to know he was here and might advise her. Instead of asking the maid Amy to find him, she went in search herself, glad of the opportunity to understand more of the layout of Lathom House, and she eventually came across him sitting on a bench outside the smithy repairing a tear in his saddlebag. He rose instantly and followed her until they were clear of any eavesdroppers.

'I need to send a letter within the hour.'

'Summat's afoot?'

'Yes, I have just overheard three men saying there's to be a hunt and —'

'Aye,' he interrupted, 'but that's what noble lords do, lass, when the weather's kindly. His lordship likes to hunt at Knowsley, some twenty miles south of here, I'm told.'

Why did men never let women finish their sentences? 'You haven't heard me out. One of them mentioned Saint-Omer and a Father Holt, and something is to happen during a hunt.'

It was satisfying to see his complacency evaporate. 'Did you recognise any of them?'

'Yes, the Master of Horse, Doughtie.'

'Ah, Papist, isn't he?'

'The second man was a stranger but the third, I believe, was Captain Towneley. Did you know he'd be here? Does Master Wade know?'

'I cannot say.' *Cannot or would not?* 'The captain waylaid me yester eve. Swore at me to keep my nose out of his business or I'd pay for it, an' I was to keep you out of mischief.'

The opening of a window above the courtyard stifled her response and prompted him to give a servile bow. 'Go to it, lass.'

'Couldn't you write the report instead, Martin? All these birds I have to mention…'

'An illiterate servant like me? No, you'll manage. I'll see you here at the next hour bell.'

'Wait, Lady Alice says that Lord Derby has regular couriers going south. It might be quicker than you seeking a carrier in Ormskirk.'

'But if the Master of Horse is up to no good, we don't want to alert him, do we?'

'I daresay you are right, though surely an innocent letter addressed to my brother…?'

'But you came here with Lord Burghley's granddaughter, remember. That would light a ruddy bonfire in any Papist rebel's fopdoodle. Off you go an' write about them rooks an' crows!'

'Oh, here you are. You're supposed to mind me, you know.'

'Amuse you, more like, Lizbeth,' Rose corrected affectionately, freeing the written letter from her writing board. 'I went to check on Cloud and then I remembered my family would be waiting to hear from me. Pray, give me a moment.' She warmed the sealing wax in the candleflame, dropped a very large blob onto the letter and pressed in the signet ring that Wade had given her. 'There, done! Now I shall coat myself in sackcloth and ashes and devote the rest of the day to making sure you behave.'

Her charge shrugged. 'Well, it's of no matter, I have been picking bluebells with the children. But guess what is to happen! On Wednesday, there is to be a week's hunt down at Knowsley. The weather promises to be fine and —'

'A week?' Rose's hope of keeping watch on Doughtie and his fellow Papists faded abruptly. Riding all day, then sitting down each night with a gaggle of men stinking of sweat and horses, avid to pick apart the day's hunt and get drunk doing it, was unthinkable.

'Oh there, you are looking sour at me, but wouldn't it be rather —'

'No, Lizbeth, out of the question. Knowsley will be a gentlemen's affair with much carousing each evening. Our presence would put a bridle on their pleasure.'

Seeing Lizbeth's pout of disappointment, she added consolingly, 'Maybe when they return, you could have an afternoon hunt in the Lady Park here.'

With a sniff, Lizbeth plonked herself on the bed and stared sulkily at her embroidered toecaps. 'You haven't finish telling me about Cloud,' she complained as Rose reached the door. 'Ferdy says you can borrow one of their horses again tomorrow if her leg still has those sores.'

'That is kind of him. One more day should suffice. Now, forgive me, Master Lorimer is waiting to carry this to Ormskirk.'

'You took your time,' Martin muttered, straightening up from the mounting block and tapping his pipe out.

'Listen,' she said, handing him the letter, 'it's to be a week's hunt beginning on Wednesday. Make sure you are one of the party if they are seeking servants to go with them.'

He nodded and tucked the letter into his riding gauntlet. 'And you be doubly careful from now on!' He glanced about him. 'There's plenty of the old faith in this house despite Lady Derby being a Calvinist and I've an ill feeling in my gut about being here.'

'And is your gut usually right?' she asked.

'What do you think, lass!'

It had been a mistake for Finian O'Neill to visit Lathom. Garrett had seen Mistress Byrd leaving the stable. How much had she overheard?

Too much!

He knew because he had followed her, seen her speak with her manservant, and there had been ink on her fingers when she and Lady Vere reappeared an hour later in the Long Gallery. When he had made a careful inquiry as to the manservant's whereabouts, he was informed the fellow had gone to Ormskirk.

Thinking like a soldier, he recognised four facts: that he had seen Rose at the Theatre and fancied her; that he had seen her asleep in St Albans and fancied her; and that, yes, he wanted to tumble her in a convenient hayloft; and now she must believe him to be some sort of enemy conspirator.

And her manservant must think so, too.

It was imperative to avoid Captain Towneley, Rose decided, as she accompanied Lizbeth into the Great Hall after supper. The attraction that she had felt must be suppressed. He was a liar, a Papist agent and, as likely, married.

Wade, had he been here to advise her, might have required her to be 'useful' but if he thought she would draw forth confidences after smooches or pillow talk, then he had selected the wrong woman for this endeavour. The temptation to immorality, however, stole up from an unexpected direction.

The hall was once more ablaze with candles. Tonight, the servants' trestles were stacked along the wall and the earl's musicians stood waiting like a musical infantry, with treble viols, viola da gamba, pandors and tabor nakirs. First, however, there were madrigals sung by four boys from the chapel choir. They performed several pieces and then their place was taken by Lady Compton, Anne, Ferdinando and his older half-brother, Edward Halsall (apparently, the old earl, cheerfully separated from his countess, had fathered several children on a local gentlewoman). The quartet sang Thomas Morley's 'April is in My Mistress's Face', William Byrd's 'Though Amaryllis Dance in Green' and ended with a Dowland piece (even though the composer was a Papist in exile).

When the dancing commenced, Ferdinando, resplendent in lion-tawny, led out Lizbeth, while Rose was partnered by the fourth and youngest of the earl's secretaries, Master Smythe. She sensed Towneley watching her even though he was deep in conversation with Richard Doughtie. It would have been satisfying to have enjoyed a private quarrel with him. Ha! She was more likely to inherit the throne than be given that opportunity.

Having done his duty by Lizbeth, Ferdinando joined his daughters in a ring dance and then to Rose's astonishment, he stood before her.

'My dear Elizabeth Davison, at last I have a chance to apologise. Dolt that I am, I did not realise it was you. I just never made the connection with "Mistress Byrd" until Alice put me straight. Even this morning, when we rode out, the stone never hit the bottom. *Mea culpa!*'

She curtseyed modestly. 'You are pardoned, my lord, after all I was just a young girl when we last met.' Dare she be audacious and trade on their childhood acquaintance? 'How old were you when I caught you kissing Lady Burghley's maidservant in the cellar at Theobalds?' she teased.

'Hmm, you were a very discreet — what? — seven-year-old? I've kissed plenty since.'

'You gave me a pet squirrel afterwards for keeping silent.'

'So I did! By the way, wasn't it your brother who presented me with a manuscript at St Albans?'

She bit her lip. 'Yes, my lord, I'm afraid so.'

'Haven't read it yet.'

'Neither have I.'

He laughed as though trying to tamper down the bitter memory of that day and gave a nod to the musicians. 'A galliard, good fellows!' He caught her hand. 'Shall you risk the next dance with me, Elizabeth? Come! And let's have done with ceremony — call me Ferdy, please.'

'I call myself Rose now, my lord.'

'Rose?'

'It was after the queen dismissed my father. It isn't treason not to use her name.'

He gave her a look that said *not here at any rate*. 'Heigh,' he chuckled, halting as they reached the floor of the hall, 'do you remember the time my brother William let loose all those frogs at Theobalds? You were the only girl who helped to catch them.'

'I still like frogs.'

Other pairs were forming a set behind them. Over his shoulder she saw Alice pause in conversation to watch them, and was careful to curtsey reassuringly. Ferdy looked round, too, smiled at his wife then swung his attention back on Rose. 'And now you're a widow, Alice tells me. I'm sorry to hear that. Any children?'

A shake of the head and she spread her skirts to acknowledge his bow as the dance began.

'So how is your father?'

Taking his hand to rise, she said sadly, 'Not well since the Tower. My family have had some support from Mother's cousin and last summer they moved out to Stepney where the air is cleaner.'

'Poor man,' he said, as they paraded forward. 'He deserved better of those he trusted. Are the Cecils feeling guilty now? Is that why they have given you employment?'

'No, it was Lady Vere's suggestion, Ferdy.' They circled each other. 'Believe me, I owe them no allegiance.'

He glanced back down the set. 'So why is the girl here? A royal maid-of-honour in Lancashire! They're usually kept on nursery reins.'

Rose laughed. 'True, my lord, but I thought your wife invited her?'

'No, Robert Cecil suggested it. Alice thinks upon him as a cousin.' He let go her hand so that she may twirl and perform the female footwork. Then it was his turn before their fingers touched again. 'Has Burghley sent her up here because some adventurer has got her with child?'

'I assure you she's not...' Well, enough said.

He thought so too, flinging up a diplomatic free hand. 'Whoa, good! I rejoice for her sake.' Time to twirl again. 'But it still doesn't explain why Her Majesty agreed. Are the Cecils trying to find another match for her? There is no wealthy heir up here unless you count Lord Huntingdon's boy and he is scarcely breeched.' They parted while she led the ladies skipping behind the line of men. 'What about you, Rose?' he asked as they took hands again. With an arm acceptably about her waist, they processioned forward and back. 'Would you be interested in some dalliance later?' His fingers risking a little more altitude.

The olde dance? At least he was being honest.

'I'm flattered, my lord, but I must set a virtuous example to my charge.' It would be a cruel slap in the face for Alice, too, after all her kindness.

'Is that a no, then? Pity.' His downward gaze grew bolder. 'I'll take care with … you know.' Was he implying linen with coloured ribbons, sheaths from intestines, or withdraw-with-a-prayer-and-cross-your-fingers? 'And, Rose, there's a local wisewoman who has made me up some very interesting powders that heighten…' His palm rose, keeping direction with his thoughts.

She smiled and shook her head.

'Ah well.' At least he was too mature to sulk. 'I'd better let you get back to your duty. Lizbeth is safe from me, by the way. As you no doubt realise, I prefer experienced partners.'

They made obeisance to each other as the music ended and he led her back towards the cushioned bench where the ladies were sitting.

'It hasn't been easy for Lady Vere,' Rose reminded him, as they crossed the hall. 'Lord Oxford would not accept her as his child for years and then with Southampton breaking the betrothal…'

Ferdinando halted, his voice low. 'Maybe Southampton did not want a Cecil in his bed. Shall I tell you something, Rose. Robert Cecil and his father may think themselves the greatest power in England yet they are not of noble blood. Sometimes we close ranks. Now, I require you to forget I said that.'

'Said what, my lord?'

'My trustworthy Lady of the Frogs!' he applauded then sighed. 'You always were sensible, but, curse it, tonight I wish you weren't.'

Inside her bedchamber, Rose closed the door and leaned back against it.

'Amy?' she whispered into the darkness, and then louder, 'Amy?' but there was no answer and as Rose's heartbeat quickened, the little candle in her trembling hands shook monstrous shadows across the wall.

Imagination could conjure up devils. Hers told her the very air had been disturbed. And yet the honey-coloured bed curtains were neatly looped to each bedpost, the canopy above would not take a man's weight, nothing sinister crouched behind the bed steps and the ropes holding the mattress were high enough for her to see that only the truckle bed lay beneath.

'Rose!' The door shook against her back. 'You didn't wait for me.'

'I'm sorry, Lizbeth.' She quickly busied herself lighting the bedside candle. 'Why isn't Amy here?'

'Oh, her ague has got worse and she was coughing so loudly that I told her to dispose herself elsewhere.' She fumbled to remove her velvet cap. 'I daresay we shall manage.'

Did Lizbeth not realise that besides contending with a streaming nose, the poor maidservant would have to battle for a corner of the kitchen and fend off the menservants?

She held out her palm for Lizbeth's hairpins. 'Poor Amy.'

'Oh, she will live. Alice says there's a village wisewoman who can give her a posset if she's still sick tomorrow. I shall not bother the earl's physician. What's wrong? Are you in the dumps with me?'

Rose was staring at her writing board upon the bed's counterpane. 'I swear I put that away.'

'Then Amy must have moved it.'

'I don't think so.' This was no tidying by a servant; the board and paper had been removed from their leather pack. Concerned, Rose carried the candle across to the rest of her belongings. Kneeling on the floor, she opened her travelling chest. Her spare ruff was no longer neat and square but toppled to the side and the rest looked thoroughly disturbed. Someone had slid their hands beneath the folds of her clean underlinen. 'Struth, some rascal has searched through my belongings.'

'Maybe Lord Derby's servants don't get paid enough, Rose.'

'And maybe I'm seeing goblins! I am not jesting!' She picked up a piece of crumpled blotting paper from the floor. It mirrored the word 'blackbird'. Damnation!

'Is anything missing?'

'No.' Rose sat back on her heels. It was as though the rifling through was deliberately obvious, done to disconcert her. 'Disappointing for them,' she muttered. 'I've nothing worth taking.'

'But I have!' Lizbeth hurtled across to her travelling chest but its lid held fast. 'False alarm,' she muttered, her breath levelling. 'And thank heaven I was wearing my emerald collar. Goodness, it's knocked the stuffing out of you. I'm sorry.' She came across and set a comforting hand upon her shoulder. 'But you know what, Rose, a lackwit thief is soon caught. We'll ask Amy in the morning whether she saw anyone loitering earlier. Cheer up! I'll go first, shall I?' She disappeared behind the curtain that concealed the close stool.

Wearily, Rose slid the writing board back beside the penner in her satchel. She was about to untie her ruff when Lizbeth shrieked. Grabbing the curtain aside, she found the young woman pointing at the close stool with a shaking hand.

Rose picked up the candle from the washstand. Neither a dazed cockroach nor a leggy spider, caught in mid-stride, lurked upon the velvet lid, but...

'In there!' mouthed Lizbeth.

Expecting a rat, Rose gingerly lifted the lid and hovered the candle. Within the deep bowl lay a mass of soggy white feathers.

A castle dove. Dead. Its neck broken.

'God's mercy! Find me something to wrap it in, dearest.' Action was best. Action kept you from thinking. For now, the poor bird deserved some dignity.

'No! No, just get rid of it!' Lizbeth demanded, her lips tightening as she watched Rose gently scoop up the bird. Opening the window, she grabbed it from Rose and flung it out. 'There!' Shaking, she turned back, frantically scrubbing at her hands. 'I'm not wanted here, I'm aware of that. They probably burn effigies of Grandfather, don't they? Alice warned me all the common people in Lancashire are Papists. We'd be hauled to the stake if they had their way!'

'This is just the work of some misguided soul, Lizbeth.' Rose kept her voice calm. Dear God! Should they make some excuse and leave tomorrow? Closing the window, she added, 'I'll go down and bury it in the morning. Now, let's get to bed.' Playing Lizbeth's tiring woman would help sooth her nerves. First thing tomorrow she'd speak with Martin about this. Martin, bless him, would know what to do.

12

Remembering the poor dove, Rose hastened to the courtyard early but there was no sign of it, not even a feather. Mayhap some mouser had feasted or a servant had cleared it away.

Martin proved hard to find. The three men who shared his mess swore that he had not been at table for supper, breakfast or morning prayers and, in fact, they said Lady Vere's maid Amy had used his pallet overnight. Rose left the kitchen with a peal of alarm bells jangling in her head. When she discovered that the horse that Martin had taken was not back in its stall either, she exchanged her kirtle for a safeguard ridingskirt and hurried back to the stable.

Her request for a Lathom groom to accompany her to Ormskirk was shabbily received.

'Speak wi' Master o' Horse, mistress!' Wainwright, the head groom, told her.

'My servant has gone missing,' she repeated firmly, not wanting any truck with Doughtie.

'Pah, servants go missing a great deal in these parts, especially o'nights. I shouldn't worry if I were you, though he'd better cursed well bring the horse back.'

Ignoring him, she called out to one of the younger grooms. 'You are coming with me!'

'Says who?' argued Wainwright.

'Says Lord Derby!' It was Ferdinando himself, accompanied by Captain Towneley, who came around the side of the building. His endorsement would have been a moment of exquisite feminine triumph for Rose if she had not been so concerned for Martin.

'Saddle a horse for Mistress Byrd,' he ordered and drew her aside with a familiarity that had his companion's eyebrows lifting. 'So, what has upset you, Rose?'

'My manservant is missing, my lord. No one has seen him since yesterday afternoon when he rode to Ormskirk.'

'On what business?' intervened Captain Towneley. His observation of her face had acquired an intensity that made her uneasy.

'Carrying a letter to send on to my brother, sir.'

She was aware of his mouth tightening. Could he have intercepted Martin?

Ferdinando's thoughts were galloping a different way. 'Your servant wasn't ailing, was he?'

She looked at him aghast. 'Plague, my lord? No, not at all, thank God!'

His relief was visible. 'Then I think you should remain here and I will send a couple of my people to inquire for him.' He started towards the stable to countermand his earlier order but Rose hastened after him. 'Permit me to ride out too, my lord. To just wait would be...'

'I'll escort her,' Towneley suggested — an offer that was impossible to refuse in Ferdy's presence.

'Thank you, Captain, but I can manage,' she said, taking the reins of the horse brought out to her, thankfully a calmer beast than yesterday's.

'I'm sure you can,' agreed Towneley, lifting her easily onto the side-saddle without a by-your-leave. Her treacherous body enjoyed that. In St Albans she had imagined just such a circumstance but not anymore, not with her manservant missing. Before either man could argue further, she gave them a nod of thanks and heeled her horse into a fast trot. Surely

Martin could take care of himself, yet she felt a sickening foreboding.

To her dismay, Towneley caught up with her before she passed the outer gatehouse. Any trust had been knifed by his refusal to be honest with her.

'This is not necessary, sir. I am not some green maiden.'

'No, indeed,' he agreed pleasantly, keeping his mount alongside. 'Was it a handsome "sparrowhawk" you were trying to tame last night?' He reached across and set a hand upon the reins, forcing the horse to halt. 'As I warned you before, Mistress Byrd, whatever your instructions were from Wade, I am overriding them.'

She thrust his hand away. 'I'm a companion to Lady Vere, let that suffice!'

'Then why are you so concerned about your letter going astray.'

'I am *concerned* about my servant.'

Her report had been about the three men at the stable and if Towneley was one of them, had he intercepted it? And if he had, why? Because *something* was going to happen during the hunt?

'And I am concerned that you and he disobeyed my —'

His attention had shifted to the road ahead where the driver of a haywain, seeing them approaching, had halted his beasts and was waiting for them to pass. Towneley would have led the way through the narrow gap between ditch and wheel, but the farmer, with a pull of forelock and a flood of speech, begged his help. The broad Lancashire dialect was a challenge to Rose but the man's backward jerk of thumb made her blood run cold. Something lay covered upon the boards and a saddled horse was tethered at the back.

Her knuckles tensed on the reins. Martin? There felt a sinister inevitability about it as she numbly watched Towneley dismount and spring up onto the cart. One knee beside the load, he peered beneath the sacking.

Hardly aware of her fingers crossing her body, her breath catching, she rode alongside. The left half of Martin's head was smashed in and his thick silver hair was matted with blood. Daubs of mud spattered his face but his eyes were clear and open, frozen in pain and surprise.

Fear that she was staring at his murderer gripped her. Yet with surprising gentleness, Towneley closed Martin's eyes and plucked away a leaf that was clinging to his brow. Then he pulled the sack down further. She watched him lift the stiffened right hand and note the grazing on the mired knuckles.

'Where was he found?' he asked the farmer. 'Pray, answer slowly, good fellow. The lady is from the south and the dead man was her servant so she needs to know.'

Rose caught the gist of the answer, tasted the salt of her tears as she fought back her grief, and forced herself to listen.

The story was that on the way to milking the farmer had found a horse cropping the grass by his gate and, recognising the beast's antler mark as belonging to the earl, let it into the field. He had discovered the rider face down in the ditch further along the road. 'Not the first time neither tha' some poor wight, ridin' home wi' a full purse from market has gone to his maker on that self-same spot. The clump o' trees on that bend gives good cover for robbers. Mark my words, tha's what happened an' I looked in his pouch to see if aught was taken or who he might be. God be my witness, there were no coin.'

Towneley slid a hand into the front of Martin's jerkin. 'There's no letter here.' He unbuckled the purse and offered it to Rose. With shaking fingers undid the leather flap and felt inside.

'And?' Towneley was too observant for her to dissemble.

Twinkling upon her palm lay a man's rosary, five decades of small jet beads linked to a silver cross.

'Did you know?' Towneley asked her softly. Cornered, unable to reason, she heard the horses approaching. 'Is there anything else you need to tell me?' he asked quickly.

She shook her head. It wasn't necessary to pretend she was shaken. Her thoughts were like a rudderless caravel on a January sea, swinging this way and that, losing direction.

'Is this Martin found, Captain?' The earl's men caught up with them, their horses frisking at the blocked road and the placid oxen. The exchange was male, concise. Rose backed her mare away as the carter was ordered to convey 'the body' — oh God, she needed to separate her memory of Martin from his battered corpse — under escort to Lathom Chapel.

'This death will be reported to the coroner.' Towneley stood now at her stirrup, a hand stroking the mare's neck. The sympathy in his eyes was almost believable. 'And there will be questions.'

'As there should be,' she agreed softly, knuckling away her tears.

'Perhaps he was not what you supposed? Recusants are encouraged to use rosaries and catechisms as a substitute for being unable to attend Mass.'

She nodded. 'I will think on it, sir, but for the present it is grievous hard to accept that he is no more and ... and I know nothing of his family. How shameful is that?'

He drew breath, another question, and then thought better of it. 'Well,' he said kindly, 'I think it best you return to the house and request a hot, mulled wine or cider. It will help. I'll ride to Ormskirk and see if I can learn more.'

'Thank you.' Then remembering her duty, she shook out some coins from her own purse and passed them to the farmer. 'For your trouble, good fellow.'

As she rode back to Lathom with the earl's men, Guilt rode pillion, blaming her for poor Martin's violent death, and Fear pursued her. Martin, her confidant, was gone and now she must act alone, find a way through this marsh of bewilderment where nothing seemed solid or trustworthy anymore.

Had Martin been a closet Papist? She knew he had infiltrated the community of recusants in St Albans. No, she would have sworn on a stack of bibles that he was Wade's man and if that were so, had he dispatched her letter before he was robbed — if it was opportune robbery? That much she could hope, but instinct told her otherwise.

And now she had Towneley, whom she dared not trust, suspecting she was a Papist, too. Mind, if he continued to believe Martin was not what he had seemed, so much the better. Hopefully, whoever had stolen the letter and read its contents would see it that way as well.

Garrett rode back from Ormskirk feeling out of humour for several reasons. Firstly, none of the town's usual carriers had been visited by Mistress Byrd's manservant, thus confirming his conclusions (from the stiffness of the corpse) that Martin Lorimer had been attacked on his way *to* the town. Secondly, Lorimer's loyalty was clearly questionable. Thirdly, the missing letter to her 'brother' put Mistress Byrd (and possibly himself) at risk. Finally, if the mission of this delectable nuisance of a woman was to warm the earl's fourposter and engage in after-pleasure confidences, he selfishly hoped that Ferdinando would stay clear of temptation. Thank Heaven that the secret conference would be at Knowsley, healthily out of petticoat interference!

Before he could cross to the house to seek out Mistress Byrd, Dick Doughtie yanked him into his office adjoining the stables. Closing the door and keeping his voice low, the young Master of Horse said irritably,' I wished you would keep me informed. A gentleman named Sir Phillip Frayn arrived here after noon and made himself known to me. Says he's to be at the meeting representing the English Papists. Can you vouch for him?'

Garrett frowned. 'Not under that name. I'll have to set eyes on him first. What excuse did he use for coming to Lathom?'

'Claims he has brought a letter from my lord's brother.'

Garrett puffed out his cheeks. 'Well, that was to have been Snow's *raison d'être*, too, but his lordship would not hear of it.'

'Well, this man's a village idiot to come here,' snarled Doughtie. 'Brazenly asking for lodging overnight! Word will get back to Whitehall and they'll get the ruddy wind up.'

'Word from whom?' Ferdinando had spoken of informers.

The Papist glared at him. 'Whichever traitor they are damn well paying to spy for them.'

'Probably have these flies on their payroll, too,' Garrett muttered testily, slapping at one of them on the desk. 'Don't you have any notion? You of all people must see what letters go back and forth.'

'I do not take kindly to your attitude, Towneley,' warned the younger man, with an aggressive lift of chin. 'Plenty of letters go to the court. By the saints! We all have friends — informants if you will — in London.' Then he calmed himself. 'Anyroad,' he added, with a toss of head, 'all correspondence goes through Master Farington's office, and our couriers have been with the family for years.'

'And is Farington loyal to "the family"?'

Doughtie gave a shrug. 'Questionable. His lordship tried to put him out to grass when the old earl died, but no one knows the holdings better. The old cullion wasn't pleased when I was appointed Master of Horse. He wanted the head groom for the post.'

'Because you're a Papist?'

'And "too young". Anyway, what do we do about this Frayn fellow?'

Garrett ran a tired hand across his forehead. 'Keep your distance till I've fathomed him.'

'Very well, but, Towneley... Look, I wish the hunt could be postponed.'

'I don't think so.'

'But it's an ill time with Lady Vere here. You do know she is none other than Burghley's granddaughter? And now, God save us, we have the dead bird business.'

That smashed away Garrett's weariness. '*Byrd*?'

Doughtie waved his hands. 'Dove, pigeon, bloody thing. Thought the whole place knew.'

'I don't. Tell me.'

'Lady Vere found a dead bird rammed into her close stool last night. A marvel she didn't shriek the place down but her companion calmed her. We got a bellyful of it this morning, her young ladyship in a blubbery weep reckoning she was hated and she should leave.'

'Will she? It will be better if she does.'

Doughtie shook his head. 'No luck there. His lordship took the blame saying it was done to embarrass him and she should not take it as an affront. And with that, Lady Derby got all upset and threw a tantrum, his lordship looked like a firecracker had been thrust up his breeches, and now this ruddy Lorimer fellow has been robbed and killed.' His eyes narrowed as though Garrett might be on his list of suspects. 'I hear you got yourself involved with that. Knight-gallantry one of your attributes, then?'

'Opportune, Doughtie. Happened to be in the stables with his lordship when Lady Vere's companion was in a lather. Gave me a chance to stick my nose into that particular pail of worms. From the little I could discover in the town, it looks like the servant was robbed on his way to Ormskirk.'

'Carrying letters, I'm told. You think he was an informer?'

'Possibly,' Garrett replied with a deliberately bleak face and, letting that sink in, he added, 'Has the coroner come yet?'

'With his lordship now. They've inspected the body. His lordship is anxious to hear your report.'

'Hell! Why didn't you say so!'

'Wait!' Doughtie drew close to face him. 'Listen, Towneley, the important thing is the meeting on Thursday at Knowsley, agreed?'

'Agreed.'

'Whatever else is happening must not divert us.'

'Agreed!'

'Then we understand one another. Go to, then, but I warn you my gut is telling me things are getting perilous, and if this Frayn isn't known to you, Towneley, who in hell is he?'

'I was sorry to hear about your servant.' John Golborne came up to Rose as she entered the Long Gallery before supper. 'Have you been at prayer all afternoon? The chapel is not warm, I fear.'

Master Farington and several other men stood conversing at the nearest hearth so he led her to a fireplace further along. 'Mulled perry for Mistress Byrd!' he ordered the page who was serving the others.

'Thank you,' she said, surprised at his unexpected kindness. Tears once more clouded her sight and she blinked them aside. 'Lady Derby tells me there is scant chance of finding the murderer.'

'Alas,' Golborne agreed, 'with the number of ragged beggars on the roads these days…' Intercepting the goblet from the servant, he presented it to her, spoiling his concern by adding, 'I have to say it is unfortunate you did not use one of our regular couriers.'

Rose lifted her chin and met his freckled stare. Was he blaming her? 'Anyway,' he continued, 'I hope Chaplain Leigh has been able to give you spiritual comfort.'

A probe to see if she was of the old faith?

'Yes,' she confirmed, after taking a welcome sip, 'but death is hard to accept.'

'It would have been quick. Be comforted by that.'

'Let's speak no more of it, sir.' Uncomfortable beneath his gaze, she drank again and turned to the fire.

'Your pardon, I forget that you are a widow.'

Go away! She closed her eyes, listening for the stiff fabric mutter of his departure, but he stayed and they stood side by side, like ornaments on a shelf, silent and not touching. Eventually, a burst of young female laughter made Rose look around. Ferdy's daughters raced in with Shakespeare behind them. Armed with a writing board, he waved to Rose, took a seat and the girls clustered around him. Would he know where Towneley was?

'Excuse me, Master Golborne.' As she picked up her skirts, Golborne blocked her way. 'Please, now you are looking more restored, let me introduce you to another visitor to Lathom, Sir Phillip Frayn.'

'I don't...'

'*Please.*' He offered his arm and drew her along to the cluster of men. She recognised Halsall and Smythe. The third man had his back to her and looked to be of higher rank. The quality of his ruff and doublet was impressive; both the starching and biscuit velvet proclaimed affluence.

'Sir Philip,' Golborne interrupted politely, touching the stranger's shoulder. 'Allow me to present Mistress Rose Byrd, Lady Vere's companion.'

The man's back stiffened, but he acquired a smile to greet her. 'A pleasure!' he said, flourishing his Italian hat as he bowed. 'I don't believe we've ever met. At your service, mistress.'

She hid her shock as she curtseyed.

It was the Papist who had visited her in St Albans.

After seeing Ferdinando and the coroner, Garrett scribbled a brief report of Martin's death for Wade, then returned to the town to find a carrier for the morrow. It meant he missed supper at Lathom, so it was not until he had cozened some bread and cheese from the kitchen on his return that he sought Rose out. He was told she and Chaplain Leigh had kept vigil by her servant's body since noon but not finding her by the bier in the chapel, he walked back to the house.

A servant's death was not for general mourning so it was no surprise to find the Great Hall warm with candlelight and half the company dancing. With a great deal of stamping and clapping, too. Lord Oxford's daughter, an excellent dancer, had condescended to partner Shakespeare in La Volta. A pity, Garrett would have enjoyed sitting down with Will over a tankard. Or with Ferdy. However, his perspiring lordship was partnering Lady Compton.

Garrett did spot his real quarry. Sad and wan, though appealing as ever, Mistress Byrd was sitting on cushions on the steps of the dais playing chess with Lady Anne. She noticed him across the hall as though she'd been waiting for him, except when he lifted a questioning eyebrow at her, she immediately turned her attention back to the game. Very well! Let her be huffy-shouldered.

He sat down wearily on a bench and a servant brought him a pot of ale. He drained half, then nursed it, letting his gaze wander over the household people now known to him, wondering which, if any of them, were on Wade's payroll. Hell, he hoped that Ferdy had selected only the most loyal of attendants to accompany him on the hunt. There had still been no news from London and tomorrow they would ride to Knowsley.

Could Ferdinando make a worthy king? There had been serious tomes on government shelved in his lordship's bedchamber. So, was the poetry, hunting and fornicating just a façade? Could there be a true leader hidden above the embroidered codpiece?

And was there a willing queen? Judging by the snatches of text he had heard read out in the gallery over the last few days, Lady Derby was a fast-dyed Protestant and if Ferdinando did decide to play hoopla for the crown and turn Papist, she'd give him a hard time of it. Mind, it was a safe wager she'd come around: what woman would turn down being queen?

The dance set ended. Shakespeare had seen him. Garrett shook his head at Will's questioning tilt of hand. Share an ale? No, he'd changed his mind. Better to get his head down.

'Towneley, is it?'

Chiding himself for not noticing the man approach, Garrett made a swift assessment: well-barbered, shorter in height with quality apparel — large wings at top of sleeves, no fraying edges, pearl earring, jewelled pin in hat brim, good leather shoes. This must be the English Papist claiming to come from Ferdinando's brother.

'Yes,' he replied gruffly 'and you?'

'Sir Phillip Frayn — at the moment.'

'A sudden knighthood! How elevating! Aren't we supposed to have a secret greeting like "I've just seen the first caterpillar of spring" or "The bluebells are looking very blue this year"?'

Frayn ignored his sarcasm. 'So, a week's hunt at Knowsley, Snow tells me.'

'Does he now?'

'Yes, I was at his meeting last week with the English Papists at Lady Vaux's, and I spoke with him again this morning. Doesn't keep you informed, eh? Why would that be?'

'Understand this, Frayn, if you and I are to work together, let's dispense with the insinuations. If you can't trust me, I don't know what in hell you are doing here.'

The man's bearded chin jerked up at the rebuke and Garrett followed that assault with another good military tactic — diversion. A casual check to make sure no one had moved within earshot and he asked: 'Is it too late or is "good news" from London still a possibility? You *understand* me?'

Frayn stared at him. 'Not "good", no.'

'This is Lancashire, Sir Philip, we're not on the banks of the ruddy Thames, so tell me!'

Frayn's face hardened. 'Unfortunately, three men, all suspected of coming from the Spanish Netherlands, have been apprehended. That's all I have heard.'

Pursing his lips, Garrett stared up at the beams. His warning had got through. 'What cursed bad timing for them,' he muttered. 'The discovery of the Lopez Plot must have had every Londoner on the alert.'

'You may think that. I believe they were betrayed.'

As if chewing that over, Garrett fell silent, showing no sign that the accusation troubled him one whit. 'The dilemma with kingmaking,' he declared grimly, 'is that you need plenty of supporters, and that means the danger of too many knowing. In fact, Frayn, I'm surprised you took the risk, given what you've just told me. Assuming they are put to the question — if it is the colonel's fellows who've been taken — they could implicate the earl. The meeting should not go ahead.'

'Mother of God!' Frayn's vehement tone emerged through a faux smile as he waved a page with a flagon away. 'Don't you realise how many blasted months it's taken to bring this about? No, as I said, we go ahead, and you and Doughtie bloody well get his mightiness there on Thursday! Any treachery from you, soldier, and I'll slit someone's pretty throat.'

Garrett followed his stare to the chess players. A trio now. Shakespeare was interfering. Jesu! How in hell did Frayn...?

'I'd never call Master Shakespeare pretty,' he said aloud.

Frayn smiled. 'Captain Towneley, let me be plain. I can describe the interior of Mistress Byrd's house. *Can you?*'

Ah.

For an instant, Garrett pretended to be outwitted and then he joyfully smashed out a swift fist of words: 'There's a painting of Diana and Actaeon in her parlour opposite the hearth, she drinks an infusion of honey before bedtime from a yellow cup with two handles, her penknife has a walnut handle, she keeps her quills in a red-glazed jar with daisies on it, her bed hangings are blue with an ivy leaf pattern and by her pillow she keeps a threadbare lambkin from childhood.' He took a breath. 'You are looking disappointed, Frayn. Well, be hanged to that!'

'You have redeemed yourself. Shall we join her?'

'Of course.'

No help for it now.

Damn, damn, damn.

The two men were coming her way like a pair of hunters. Hawkridge — or Frayn, as he called himself now — was leading with a sinister intensity that made Rose's blood run cold. Towneley's face was as stony as a reluctant bridegroom's. The chess game might be over but she was a pawn in the human one. How should she act? Her bolstered kirtle meant she could not rise swiftly and flee the hall. Earlier, she had been spared any questions from 'Frayn' as to her purpose here; now she must brazen it out.

'I have to apologise, mistress, for not offering my condolences when we were introduced,' said Frayn, with a careful smile. 'I heard that there had been a death but I did not realise it was your manservant's.' She nodded, her sadness genuine, then he added, 'Nor did I realise you were *both* here.'

As if on cue, Towneley offered her his ruined hands. 'How fare you, Nightingale?' he asked softly, blinking down at her like a colossus that had just discovered his inner humanity.

Nightingale?

Before she let him draw her to her feet, she put the last wooden piece, the ebony king, carefully back in the wooden box and slid the lid across. It gave her thinking time. Every instinct told her that whatever she next said was crucial. Why else was the tension from his touch streaming through her? Frayn was expecting them to behave like lovers, watching with more than a matchmaking interest. Her mouth felt dry; it would have helped to know the rules.

'Can you not guess, sirrah?' she answered 'her betrothed' with a defiant shrug and tried to tug her hands away. Towneley kept hold, maybe so she could still sense the resentment in him, like a husband deserving a reprimand and not wanting it, and all the while Frayn waited at his elbow like the Devil. 'I've been anxious to hear how your inquiries went,' she complained, 'but did you come and find me? *Well?*'

Appreciation flared reluctantly in Towneley's hazel eyes. He managed irritated embarrassment: 'You are too ... prickly, Rose.' A hesitant metaphor, so dryly spoken.

'And why not, pray?' she hissed, freeing her hands at last. 'Poor Martin's corpse scarce cold and his murderer still at liberty. It's ... it's...' And then making pretence of remembering Frayn's presence, she shook her head at her lapse in manners. 'I'm sorry, Sir Philip, forgive my womanly weakness...' Distressed, she pressed her hand against her lips and blinked tearfully and accusingly at Towneley.

Her reward was a soldierly, sheepish grin. 'Give us leave, Frayn,' he said curtly, no doubt anticipating she might overdo things. 'Damn it, man, shove off! Avaunt!'

Frayn looked disobliging but he could not object. With a half-bow, he withdrew.

Towneley put a possessive arm about her and steered her away. 'Well done,' he murmured, 'now let us look for cobwebs in that uninhabited corner, shall we?'

She had no intention of standing aside with him. 'Well, you did need me after all,' she muttered, shrugging off his arm.

'It seems so.' A weary rather than contrite admission.

She turned abruptly and found him too close, blocking her face from any observation save his.

'Tell me,' he urged, putting a finger beneath her chin and tilting her face up, 'why St Philip over there thinks he knows you better than I do, Nightingale, and don't take your time about it!'

Peering around his shoulder, she saw that Frayn had accepted two winecups from the page. In an instant, he would rejoin them.

'I already told you in St Albans. He visited me with a priest, checking your story. He called himself Ralph Hawkridge.'

His eyes narrowed. 'Frayn is *Hawkridge*? Hell!' He carried her hand swiftly to his lips. 'Leave the hall! Go! I will meet you outside.'

13

Outside the house, Rose sighed and leaned back against the stone rail of the front steps, relieved to breathe in air that was free of others' breath, others' strategies. She desperately missed Martin.

Music still reached her from the hall. The pavane was a stately counterpoint to the sigh of the trees beyond the outer walls. Across the cobblestones, crosses of light gleamed from the lower slits of the Eagle Tower and although she could hear men's cheerful banter, the timber stairs and platform reminded her of the St Albans scaffold. As if exploiting the ugly memory, the callous breeze flickered chill fingers round her neck and, above the turrets, compelled the ghostly wood smoke from the hall chimneys to twist and spiral.

It was unwise to linger. All her senses alert, she shivered now, aware of the dangerous darkness both in her soul and all around her. Death screeched his presence in a hunting owl and flickered in the lanterns luring the witless moths to his beguiling light. Insects might be pardoned for ignorance; Rose could not. More than once Towneley had warned her to wriggle from Wade's grasp; she should leave Lathom.

The possibility beckoned her through the shadows to the east corner of the house. A thin finger of taper light beneath the stable doors hinted at the play of dice and cards. No chance of stealthily saddling a horse, let alone finding her way to a Mersey crossing before daylight or evading a search party of irritable men, who would prefer to go hunting.

The hunt! Of course! The men would ride out tomorrow. For a week. A wondrous week. The tension fled, her heartbeat took on serenity; reprieved, she turned swiftly, only to find herself against a human wall.

'Whoa, here you are,' exclaimed Towneley. 'Thank you for waiting for me.'

'I was actually thinking about stealing a horse.' Be plainspoken, she told herself, aware that the temptation to carnality needed withstanding.

'In those slippers?'

'Yes, of course,' she said, turning back towards the main steps. 'Horses prefer slippers. And if you don't mind,' she added over her shoulder, 'I have had enough of intelligencers for one night, and tomorrow, heaven be thanked, you'll all be gone, so,' she reached the stone rail and offered a shallow curtsey, 'firstly, goodnight; secondly, God be with you; and, thirdly, I hope all the deer hear you coming a mile off.'

'Weren't such blessings banned under the old king?' Then his tone sharpened, 'Well, too bad, mistress mine, we need to talk tonight and somewhere warmer.'

Before she could argue further, he was guiding her up the wooden steps that led into the Eagle Tower. Just inside the passageway, he kicked open a nail-studded door, surprising a sleepy trio of men who were sitting round the hearth. 'Out!' he ordered. 'Go and relieve yourselves on the cobbles or find some other amusement. The lady and I need to talk.'

'Begging your pardon, sir. This is our guardroom.'

'Indeed, it is, and I am now paying generously for the loan of it!' Taking a large coin from his purse, he flipped it into the air. 'Out!' A jerk of his head underscored his order before he turned to Rose. 'Well, go on, mistress, warm yourself!' His gaze made a slow, assessing climb from her skirt to her lips.

Rose marshalled a fierce scowl and marched across to the fire.

'Before our time runs out,' he announced to her stiff shoulders, 'I need to tell you there is no more information on your man's death. Secondly, I must thank you for your fine acting in the hall — I'd recommend you to Burbage if you weren't a woman — and, thirdly, I warned you not to write to Wade.'

'But I do not answer to you, sir.' A decent lioness would be proud of that snarl (she had at least seen and heard a real lioness at the Tower); inside she was wondering if he was going to attempt seduction and how she might prevent him. They could play chase-me round the trestle table or... She eyed the array of weaponry on the walls, mostly pikes and halberds, but it would need a lightning movement to detach one, let alone wield it, and she would likely get it jammed in the chimney place or caught in the wooden candelabra. The hearth held possibilities. The toasting fork looked too flimsy, a twist of wire rather than a trident of firm metal, so she crouched down and, taking up the iron poker, made a pretence of troubling the fire.

Behind her the room was silent. She prodded the log, and then when the man behind her said nothing and made no move, she further disturbed the embers. And disturbed them some more until it became embarrassing.

It was then he spoke. 'When you've finished playing shrinking Lucrece to my lusty Tarquinius, perhaps you might like to sit down and talk to me like a civilised gentlewoman. You do favour pokers, don't you? Put the plaguey thing down! I could have it off you faster than a harlot could flash her petticoats.'

It was not just the warmth heating her face as she decided to face him. He was waiting, his lazy, amused expression worn like a visor. With a courtier's flourish, he gestured to one of the vacated stools but contrarily she shook her head.

'As you please.' He sat down on the bench, and sprawled back against the trestle table, stretching out his long legs to the fire. 'What, no ladylike curses?'

'Consider them said, Captain Towneley.' Then, because she did not know how long this would take, she relented and chose one of the stools, arranging her skirts because it helped to do something. Then she looked at him and she too waited, hoping her rigid back would keep him assured of her disapproval.

'Well, then.' He leaned forward, resting his elbows on his knees. 'It's time for answers, Mistress Byrd. I need to know exactly what you are doing here and who you really are.'

'I do not follow you, sir.'

He sat back again. 'Come now, Nightingale, you're not that obtuse.' He sucked in his cheeks at her obdurate expression. 'Ah, a guessing game. Let me see. You are sent to charm dear old Ferdy into confidences.'

'Mr Wade calls himself a friend of my father,' she announced quietly, abandoning all her newly minted resolutions, and hoping a brief admission would suffice him. 'I needed work.'

He thought about it and then sighed as though that was the way of the world. 'Aye, that doesn't surprise me. Your late husband spent most of his pay on women and cards.'

That hurt. It wasn't as if she kept Oliver's memory in some sort of Italian shrine all bright and holy, but Towneley was not to know that.

'And who is your father, Mistress Nightingale?'

When she did not answer, he leaned towards her again. 'Oh, come on, I need to know. I'm supposed to be betrothed to you, Rose. Hawkridge has already asked me too many curly ones.'

'Oh, surely child's play for a prince of dissemblers like yourself,' she flared back.

The sarcasm unexpectedly worked. With a puff of breath, Towneley straightened and seemed to reach a decision. 'Very well, we'll play this your way and I'll go first.' He rose to his feet, running a hand across his beard. 'Where to begin, eh? Frayn alias Hawkridge is an apostle of Lady Vaux, a matriarch of English Papists, and he's here — with others — to persuade Ferdinando to find his manhood and have a whack at the crown.'

'God's mercy!' Rose looked in panic towards the door.

'Oh, it's all right,' he said dismissively. 'Will is playing guard dog. The three lads we shifted from yon mat have as much chance of hearing this conversation as growing wings. You and I can speak freely.'

But *had* he? Lies were his coins and craft.

In the grate, the smoke curled hesitantly above the log, as uncertain as she to find a way out. She wanted Towneley to understand that she knew the price of treason. Now was the time to look at him. 'We both saw Richard Hesketh hanged.' Her words, though softly uttered, bruised the quiet.

For an instant, the man's expression sobered. 'Aye,' he muttered, 'and there's a great lump of the poor bastard rattling from a gibbet in Ormskirk, more's the pity.'

'Are you planning to keep him company?' she asked, shaken that his compassion could be daubed with such crude honesty. Did nothing faze him, wobble him on his self-made pedestal?

'No,' he muttered and rose to his feet. 'And I don't want to see a comely woman like you go up in ashes either.'

Ashes? Be burned like a Papist martyr? No, she was an avowed Protestant, Davison's daughter. She was not at risk unless ... unless this man was a double agent, a Papist whetstone, sent to sharpen Ferdinando's ambition.

'Thank you,' she replied coolly, 'I have no intention of becoming the fuel for any man's bonfire.' Towneley could take that any way he chose.

To her relief, he sauntered to the end of the trestle. Plucking a jug from its barricade of surrounding tankards, he sniffed the contents and held it out to her. Seeing she did not want the soldiers' beer; he set it down again. The drink did not interest him either. Folding his arms, he relaxed back against the table edge.

Rose returned stare for stare. Behind the sucked in cheeks, the considering gaze, was he wondering whether he might trust her? Perhaps it was the chapel bell ringing the hour out across the fields that helped him reach a decision.

'Last year I decided to be quit of soldiering. I'd had a bellyful of being told to burn down the Irish peasants' cottages and Her Majesty's government was tardy in giving a pension to worn-out soldiers like me. I decided that maybe I could do my swaggering upon the stage instead and while I was hanging round the Theatre, Wade sniffed me out and sent me to Antwerp. So that's where I've been, as you are aware, in the Low Countries, purring around that arch-traitor Colonel Sir William Stanley's boots like a good, fawning tomcat.'

'But you and Ferdinando —'

'Understand one another, yes. I have been as honest with him as I am now with you.'

Well, that was reassuring, she thought cynically. Providing it was the truth.

'Now it's your turn, songbird. What else do you do for Wade?'

Songbird! Rose's lips tightened. 'Nothing else, I was a hollow tree for your love letters.'

'And what about Martin Lorimer — God keep him — and his mysterious rosary?'

'I've been thinking about that. He would have used it to convince the St Albans Papists. Believe me, he was utterly trustworthy.'

'He was an agent!' Towneley's voice was scathing. 'That makes him the opposite in my opinion.'

'Like you, Captain,' she replied coldly.

'Yes, like me. I'm a juggler, mistress. The truth flashes through my hands so fast you will barely notice it.'

'Did you kill him? I know you are capable.'

He was not amused. His remaining fingers stroked the air as though he caressed her neck. 'Protect this throat of yours, Nightingale. Frayn isn't the only traitor to Gloriana under this roof and you are a long way from London. Her Majesty's enemies up here will break you if you get in their way.' He made a twisting gesture with his hands. 'You've had one warning.'

The dove!

Oh God, she needed time to take in all this. 'They have not broken the earl,' she whispered defiantly.

'No, not yet. They keep what is useful — for a while.'

It was hard to shut out the blazing glare of Towneley's scrutiny. She closed her eyes and took a breath. She had no wish to uncover any sewer of greed and ruthlessness beneath the ground of Lathom, nor smell the foul air behind the lips of courtesy. Ferdinando had already withstood Papist persuasion. He had made Hesketh pay with his life but now, ostracised, would he —

A creak and shift of leather. She snapped her eyes open in panic but there was no threat — *yet*. Although Towneley's boots were only inches from her skirts, he was staring down into the glowing coals, his arms braced against the stone mantel. Subtle and unbidden, the woman's hunger in her stirred — the yearning to be touched, adored — and so for an instant she indulged herself, staring sideways from beneath her lashes.

Towneley needed no padding to look manly. Straining at the seams, the branched velvet of his slate doublet stretched across a back that was muscled by combat, not bowed in worship. Here was no Richard Hesketh driven by religious belief. At least, she did not think so. She did not know what to think.

'*I always evaluate what drives my fellow privy councillors,*' she had heard her gentle father lecture her brothers. '*The greed for riches? For power over others? A thirst for knowledge? Or is it for that jolt of euphoria, that sudden high moment of pleasure like making love to the woman you've always desired or strutting out upon a stage and making your audience weep?*'

So, what was honing Towneley? What whetting knife was sharpening his ambition? The lure of giddy heights? Ennoblement? The chance to become one of 'King Ferdinando's' privy council?

Had Towneley and Doughtie been wearing down the earl, brushing away his protests, shining up the possibilities? And during the hunt there would be more polishing, she guessed. This time Ferdy might listen to the flattering whispers, the promises of Spanish gold, the assurance from His Holiness in Rome of a throne on earth and a pew in Heaven.

Towneley shifted, his body drawing her gaze again as he stretched with a loud sigh. Glib, mercenary bastard! He had admitted precious little save that he was as two-faced as Janus. Well, she would not be inveigled into trusting him.

For seven days, the men would be gone! Seven precious days. She would have time to think, to thresh the truth from the lies before they met again. *If* they met again. God pray that Ferdy would slap this pack of traitors away before they savaged him.

'Nightingale.'

Her body shivered, skin puckering like gooseflesh beneath her partlet. Towneley had moved between her and the embers of the fire — legs akimbo, a gallows of a man.

'I've one final question — for now. I need to know if Garrett Towneley could have met your father, asked him for your hand.'

'No.'

'Pushing up the daffodils in St Albans, is he?'

'No!'

'Let me phrase it another way. Who were you before you were unlucky enough to become Oliver Byrd's widow?'

'My father was secretary to the queen.'

'There has not been anyone since —' The frown between his eyebrows deepened. 'Not since William Davison was sent to the Tower. Is that who you are? Davison's daughter?'

She nodded, surprised.

'Oh, we heard all about it in Ireland,' he muttered. 'Christ!' He scraped a hand across his brow and paced to the table. 'So it seems the agent Garrett Towneley is betrothed to a good dyed-in-the-wool Protestant. That makes no sense. Or...' he swung round. 'Or am I dealing with a cunning traitor? A daughter who hates the queen for the injustice to her father?' He strode towards her and jabbed a finger in the air just short of her nose. 'Ah, that's why Wade chose you for his cipher. People will believe you've been turned.'

Rose was on her feet now, knocking his hand aside. 'No,' she argued hotly. 'That's not so! It was because I needed an income.'

He stood frowning down at her, as though he was trying to create some sense amidst the weft and warp of truth and conjecture. 'And now they've sent you up here to spy on our new earl. See if he's made of loyal gold or gilded counterfeit.'

'No, Captain Towneley,' Rose reiterated firmly. 'It isn't like that. Lady Vere invited me.'

'Cecil's niece,' he sneered.

'Yes, yes, but that's not the reason. They refused to let me accompany her at first, you see, and then, of course, her sister was ill and she could not leave her.'

'What changed their minds? Or yours? Did they trundle you to the palace and give you a dose of the queen and the loyal subject twaddle?' He was watching her face for confirmation. She tried not to flinch. 'Well, they did it to me,' he told her. 'All the taradiddle, the chuffing under the chin, the "my loyal lads" stentorian splutter. Oh, come on, Nightingale, were you taken in? Did Her Majesty apologise for still keeping Daddy in the Tower?'

'He's not in the Tower. He's been home these last two years.'

Towneley, damn his insolence, merely shrugged.

The air between them seethed and then grew quiet. Outside several dogs began to bark until a man's curse quelled them.

'Well, that's scrubbed up a few pieces of dirty washing,' Towneley said amiably.

'Where do we go from here?' she asked, finding the strength to face him again.

'Somewhere cosier?' he suggested roguishly and then shook his head with mock woefulness at her lack of enthusiasm. 'No? That's a shame since Frayn's expecting me to plaster the cracks in your sudden lack of affection.'

She suppressed the urge to seek out Frayn alias Hawkridge and strangle him with his own nightcap.

'I hope Frayn is going hunting, too,' she said with feeling. 'You and he can gull each other to your hearts' content.'

He nodded. 'And no doubt we shall.' He paced across to the fire and turned, his hands clasped behind his back like a commander addressing his captains. 'Two things, Nightingale. Do nothing rash.'

'Pity!' she flared. 'And what's the other thing?'

'The other thing is —' Voices beyond the door made him quickly lift a warning finger to his lips. 'The other thing is something we can discuss another time.' He swiftly beckoned. 'I think you need comforting.'

Rose obeyed. She had to be suffering from lunacy to do so, not to mention the folly of setting her hands fondly either side the buttons on Towneley's doublet just as the door opened and a large man wearing a dressing robe over his nightshirt burst in.

'What is the meaning of this?' spluttered Farington. His candle spluttered too. Three pathetic faces glimmered white behind him. With her own sheltered in Towneley's open doublet. Rose burrowed deeper, staunching her laughter.

'Is there meaning?' demanded Towneley philosophically while his right hand firmed against the back of her head. 'A good man dead. Was God asleep?'

'Don't you spout heresy at me, young man. I ask you again what you are doing here?'

'Comforting me, your honour.' Rose managed to free herself and turned a tearful face upon the receiver-general. 'He was a good soul was Martin Lorimer, served me for over a year. It is too, too cruel.' She stuffed her kerchief swiftly against her mouth, then, managing to regain her voice, she said huskily, 'Captain Towneley was with me when the carter brought in the body. He has been kind enough to make inquiries on my behalf. I did ... do ... not wish my distress to be fodder for common tittle-tattle.'

Farington cleared his throat. 'I see. Well, I suggest you let these poor fellows have their room back now, mistress. Time will heal your sorrow, and as you say, you do not want gossip. This is an upright, virtuous household. None of your London ways here.' Task done, he departed. The three guards sauntered back in.

Taller than any of them, Towneley kept his tone amiable. 'Ratted on us, did you, lads?'

'No, made plenty of noise, we did, an' your watchdog soon legged it.'

Grinning, Towneley set another coin upon the table, which somewhat alleviated the awkwardness. When Rose said a sorrowful, ladylike 'thank you' to them and swept out with dignity, he kept close behind her.

To her consternation, Frayn was waiting, lolled against the arched doorway into the main house. 'That wouldn't have been *my* choice of a courting place, Captain.'

'Courting, Frayn?' A scoff from Towneley. 'Alas, grief prevails and sadly tonight we are like seedlings not quite ready for bedding.'

'Garrett!' Rose chided, smacking his arm.

'*Ouch!*'

Frayn ignored the banter. 'Lady Vere was looking for you, Mistress Byrd. I merely play her messenger — with utter discretion, I assure you.' His fingertips touched his breastbone in a display of deference.

'Nesting box, Nightingale!' Towneley decreed, sliding his hands about Rose's waist from the back and kissing her cheek. 'I'll see you back to Lady Vere. Goodnight, Frayn.'

His hand was welcome between her shoulder blades as he hastened her away. Recklessly, she would have liked so much more. 'You know what, Nightingale,' he whispered, 'if you could joust as well as you can act, you'd win horses and armour all over Christendom.'

'I suppose a breastplate would go well over my stomacher.'

Crossing the small dining hall where the cutler was tidying away the clean knives, they kept silent up the staircase. When the Long Gallery lay in shadows before them, he halted on its threshold. 'No further, eh?'

No time either to question his meaning. It was so tempting to slide her arms about his neck and kiss him but one of the doors to the bedchambers off the gallery was open and, yes, he was keeping a safe distance between them. 'Goodnight, then. Good hunting!'

'You've changed your song. No, wait,' he whispered, taking her arm, 'one last question. Will Lady Vere have blabbed to anyone about your parentage?'

'No, she's aware Father's name lights fuses. Only Ferdy and Alice know.'

'Thank God for that, but you and she must be doubly wary, Rose, for all our sakes.'

'I'm not a fool, Captain.'

'Good, I'll not need to sleep with my boots on!' He raised her fingers to his lips. 'Remember poor Martin in your prayers and write no more letters until I return.'

He was gone into the dark before she could draw breath to answer.

It was not unusual for the earl to stay informally at one of his smaller houses, such as nearby New Park, so happily Garrett heard no one comment that the hunting party was remarkably few as they left Lathom. Apart from himself, the men chosen to accompany Ferdinando were Golborne, Halsall and Doughtie, Giles Clothier, his lordship's body servant, two grooms and two hounds. Had the earl been entertaining a prince or duke, they would have stayed at Knowsley Hall, the royal lodge, which the first Lord Derby had built to entertain King Henry VII. Instead, before his lordship's company reached the environs of the hall, they turned off into deep woodland on a track new to Garrett.

He missed the sun's warmth upon his face as they left the open fields. Ancient smooth-trunked beeches gave way to ash, elm and oak, all still grim and winter-limbed. Spring, however, was busy seducing the woods to readorn; the buds of the hazel and elder saplings had started to unknot and amongst the moss-covered logs, furls of cuckoo pint and spirals of lush green were showing. Within a few days the mesh of dark creepers would be hidden beneath a vast coverlet of bluebells.

His first sight of where they were to stay seemed a cluster of ivy-covered stone ruins that might have lodged King John but further down the glade was a modest, two-storeyed hunting lodge. Brick below and half-timbered above, it looked to be scarce thirty years old and well maintained. Servants from Knowsley Hall had been at work; the upper shutters were thrust open and smoke was doing a twirl from the single chimney.

Inside the lodge's tiny dining hall, the walls were clad in linenfold panels to head height and the whitewash above was decorated with the usual boast of stag heads. However, it was the Cheshire prostitutes awaiting the company in varying degrees of undress in front of the fire that left Garrett unusually speechless. It might be only mid-afternoon but the women were already tippled on the malmsey wine that the earl had generously laid on for them.

Two of them squealed and flung themselves at Ferdinando, leaving Garrett in no doubt they already had a history of intimacy with his lordship. The earl accepted a cup of ale, drew a small packet from his pocket and turned away, leaving Garrett wondering if it contained a French letter or an aphrodisiac.

No one else showed surprise that the women were here. Golborne busied himself with supervising the servants while Doughtie goosed the prettiest leftover, greeted her by name and gave a conspiratorial wink.

'What in hell —' muttered Garrett, grabbing his arm.

'Part of the usual arrangement when my lord comes here.' The young man's quirk of mouth added an unspoken warning: *if we changed the practice, questions might be asked.*

Garrett let go of his sleeve with a scowl. Doughtie should have warned him. This was foolhardy! Whether Ferdy would have a clear head for the meeting next day was anyone's guess. For his part, he was not tempted by these drunken women with their dilated eyes. Offering a maybe-later smile, he fended off an embrace from its over-perfumed owner and, as a counterweight to his anger, slid into his military practice of assessing his surroundings.

The only other room downstairs was Ferdinando's demesne, a bedchamber that was similarly panelled and simply furnished with a bed, one tall candlestick, a flat-lidded storage chest and a row of wall hooks, already occupied with the earl's bow and quiver and other hunting gear. The removables were the bed furnishings, a folded screen, a washbowl on the chest and a small tapestry on the inner wall. A shuttered opening served as the window.

The storey above was accessed by a wooden staircase on the outside of the building. Save for a ladder leading up into the attic and a chamber pot, it was unfurnished. Evidently the stack of thin palliasses in the hall would be shared out and tonight would be cosy if you liked two-backed beasts heaving next to you or sleeping cheek by jowl with snoring drunkards.

Back downstairs, now that the officers had carried in their saddlebags and the servants had unloaded the huge two-handled pannier they had brought from Lathom, there was little space left around the one large table and it was necessary to sidestep the staffs, stakes, bows and other hunting paraphernalia. Ferdy, preoccupied with lechery, had already disappeared into his inner sanctum.

Outside, the smell from the sizzling capons threaded onto the spit was igniting Garrett's appetite. Logs were drawn up for seats around the fire but no one was ready yet so he filled a leather jack from the barrel on the cart that had brought the provisions and, like a good soldier, continued with his surveillance.

His investigation led him past the ruins where the horses were now stabled. There looked to be only one track leading to the lodge but, wandering around, he discovered a well-trodden footpath. It led him down to the brook which provided the lodge's water. Hart's tongue and marsh marigold grew upon the bank and there he stood for a moment, smelling the wood's wild garlic and wondering — wondering whether the man to whom he had sworn loyalty was cunning or downright simple. He did not envy Ferdinando having to make such a momentous decision on the morrow and maybe this whoring was a respite for the man's troubled mind. For an instant, he listened to the Devil's whisper: enjoy a pretty woman and get drunk to your heart's content. No, he needed to stay alert. Let tomorrow be what tomorrow would be; his main task was to safeguard the earl.

Idly, he threw a stick into the stream, watched until it was out of sight and then he picked his way up through a grove of fur-tipped willows and over ancient, moss-covered boughs, skirting the lodge in a wide circle. He did not know if Snow and his fellow delegates were making camp tonight or riding in separately on the morrow, but he suspected they had already scouted the place because there was day-old horse dung among the trees on the far side, where the servants had no reason to venture.

The glade was noisy — a veritable Sherwood Forest — and another firkin, this time a strong, springtime brew, was on offer. It tasted good, good enough to get merry on, except he wasn't there to get tap-shackled.

'Ah, Captain, wondered where you were!' Doughtie refilled a tankard and joined him.

Garrett wasn't just surly with hunger as they sauntered out of earshot. Playing the anxious Papist, he demanded, 'What in God's name is going on, Dick? I don't even know where the ruddy place is we are supposed to meet tomorrow.' A small lie.

'But the earl knows.' *Calm bastard!*

'Sure, if he has his wits back by morning.'

'Do not worry yourself.' Doughtie took a swig. 'He can outdrink the best.'

'Then tell me, is it just you and he going to separate from the others during the hunt?'

'No, it will be my lord, Halsall and we two.'

'Lord's sakes! Is Halsall one of us?'

'No, but he's the earl's half-brother so it's family loyalty, see. If my lord becomes king, Halsall is likely to be his chamberlain.'

Garrett felt some of the tension ebbing. 'Old Master Farington won't like that.'

'Unfortunately, Farington came with the earldom. We would happily be rid of him.'

'And what about Lady Alice?'

'Well, if she doesn't produce a boy this time, he'll have to divorce her.'

Dream on, lad! thought Garrett. As if England would put up with another Henry VIII wife-exchange again. 'And whose idea was it to get these harlots along?' he asked. 'If it was Halsall's then he can go hang as far as I'm concerned, Dick. We want a strong king to uphold the faith, not a self-indulgent —'

'Careful!' growled Doughtie. 'Save your breath to cool tomorrow's pottage.'

'Tomorrow!' muttered Garrett, pretending indignation. 'Friend, it has taken months to get this far. So much hangs upon tomorrow's meeting and if my lord does not have his full wits, it will have been a cursed waste of time, money, and of many a man's hope. If the others knew of this —'

'They don't, so let's keep it that way.'

Fresh voices came from the track. 'Hell take it, how many more clot-heads to conjure with? What time do the heralds and horn-blowers arrive?'

Doughtie gave a finger gesture and returned to the fire. Garrett, deliberately wearing a sour expression, followed.

Two of the earl's local huntsmen had arrived. They had been questing after a very fine buck, glimpsed that morning, and had brought the beast's fewmets for the scent hounds to track next day. They were advising that once the company had sighted the buck, the archers in the party should take up position and those who were riding should attempt to drive the creature towards them to be shot.

And could Ferdinando be driven to treason?

Next day would not be easy. A hunting party was like a dog with its nose to the ground. The lads would rush blindly wherever the scent took them. He just hoped the other party wouldn't come blundering through to find their master listening to the whisper of treason.

Off the conjugal leash that evening, Ferdinando continued to show himself as self-indulgent as any of his peers. He sat down at the supper table with a shapely wench cooing behind each shoulder and it was clear from the fondling and remarks that he had already enjoyed some lusty adventures whilst the other men were outside quaffing.

After grace had been spoken, Halsall acted as the food taster, or to be more precise, passed morsels down the table to the huntsmen to swallow before he served the earl. Dick Doughtie across the table from Garrett cheerfully clashed tankards with him and then the drinking began anew. Used to making pretence of being in his cups while drinking very little, it amazed Garrett that Ferdinando was not managing to do the same, and by the time the noises in the earl's bedchamber ceased and the lodge air vibrated with inebriated snores, Captain Garrett Towneley had resigned his future at King Ferdinando's court. There wouldn't be one.

Jesu! He woke to women's shrieks and something crashing over in the earl's chamber. Golborne, lying closest, scrambled to his feet. Garrett grabbed his rapier and rushed to the inner door. The two women fled out like scalded cats.

Inside the bedchamber, Ferdinando was writhing on the bed, his fingers to his face, utterly distraught. 'Alice, where's Alice?' he shouted, trying to rise. 'She's nigh to death. I must find her. Where is she? Where is she?'

'My lord, we are at Knowsley.' Clothier kept his hands firmly on his master's twitching shoulders. 'In Christ's name, calm yourself!' Desperate, he glanced round at Golborne and Garrett for support.

'Send to Lathom at once!' Ferdinando yelled. 'She's dying, I tell you.'

'No, my lord,' soothed his servant. 'You've just had a nightmare. You were sleepwalking.'

Or was he ape-drunk?

Gradually, the earl's eyes lost their confusion. 'I was looking for her. I thought —'

'It was the potion, my lord. Remember it can be thus.'

As Golborne stepped forward to add more reassurance, Garrett sheathed his rapier and pulled Clothier aside. 'Has he been like this before?'

The man glanced to Golborne as if for permission to answer. 'Yes, if he takes a powder to keep going.' A meaningful pat on codpiece. 'It gives him delusions.'

'*What?*' Hauling Golborne out of the room, he grabbed him by the collar and forced him against the wall. 'Do you encourage him in this?'

'Heigh!' Halsall lumbered across.

'I'm asking you, Golborne! The cursed aphrodisiac or whatever he took, do you en—'

'For God's sake, man,' blustered Halsall.

Golborne calmly removed his assailant's hands from his person with blatant disdain. 'Captain, if you mixed with the nobility more frequently, you would know that those who have everything want even more.'

Believable. It was Garrett who lowered his guard and stepped back. 'Your pardon.'

'It's his refuge,' Halsall muttered. 'You know, when things become too much. I've tried it, too. It's Heaven then it's Hell.'

'Understandable but —' He saw Clothier come out. 'How is my lord?'

The man smiled. 'He's himself again but I am to leave for Knowsley straightway. He wants to be assured my lady is well lest it was some revelation from God.'

Golborne and Halsall exchanged resigned looks. Outside it was light enough to see the road. 'Go quickly then,' Halsall advised, 'but do not alarm her ladyship. Make some excuse. Say to her my lord has forgotten something.'

Yes, he has forgotten, Garrett added silently, glaring at the inner door — *a meeting with men willing to risk their lives to make him king.*

Surely noble lords were supposed to emerge from their bedchambers looking decent, not like the embodiment of debauchment? Whatever apothecary mixture Ferdinando had taken to heighten his arousal had daubed ugly dark crescents beneath his eyes.

His lordship took a mouthful of ale, then knuckled the tankard viciously aside. 'Hardly slept. Had a nightmare about my lady dying,' he informed the assembly and holding out a hand, watched his fingers quiver. 'Oh, blazin' hell, it's never done *this* before. Have the women been paid?'

'Paid, carted and departed.' Behind the earl's back, Halsall plucked a long red hair off his lace collar, making no secret that he had taken his own interest in the arrangement.

'Are we still planning a day's hunting, my lord?' Garrett asked, his tone ironic.

'We are, Towneley,' Ferdinando growled. 'Tell Dick to make ready. It will clear my head.'

At noon, the earl drew rein, loosening his lace collar. 'After my labours last night, I need to take some respite else I'll fall off my horse.'

'I share that feeling,' muttered Halsall.

'We can return to the lodge, my lord,' suggested Doughtie.

'No, too far. Go on, the rest of you.' Ferdinando flicked his fingers in dismissal at the hunting party and dismounted. 'Harbour that fat buck, eh? We will meet you back at the lodge later. Towneley and Halsall, you remain with me!'

'But, my lord —' protested Golborne.

Ferdinando glared at him. 'Go!'

The instant the others were gone, he mounted again. 'Come, let's make haste to the meeting and have this over with.'

Garrett drew a breath and remarked, 'You would make a fine player, my lord.'

'Wouldn't I just.'

Frayn, Snow, O'Neill and Lord Bothwell's ambassador, Andrew Buchanan, were on horseback in a hunched, conspiratorial cluster. Relief lit their faces as the other three rode down the slope. O'Neill was in his fifties, handsome with a saintlike mien — wide gentle eyes and a pad of thick silver hair. Buchanan, on the other hand, had a warrior's frame, and flaunting his nation, displayed a vigorous yellow beard. His bush of hair was tethered at his nape. At least he had a hooded cloak flung back across his shoulders. Here was a stranger any villager would gape at.

And so it began, the arguments clearly rehearsed. Garrett listened with half an ear; his foremost duty was to safeguard the earl, not turn him to treason. While noting their faces, he also eyed the gaps between the old, coppiced oaks, the birches and alders, listening for the sudden cries of startled birds or the betraying rustle beneath feet stealthily placed.

Frayn began: the Catholics needed a leader, a mature English claimant. They felt that Ferdinando fitted their requirements. 'You are fourth in line to the crown, my lord, but if you promise to return England to the true religion, you shall be first.'

Then Snow dangled some financial carrots for the noble donkey: clearance of the £6,000 debt Ferdinando owed to his London tailors (that had his lordship looking rather flushed) and the promise of plentiful Spanish gold to fill his personal coffers. Her Majesty, Frayn reminded him, had kept him short of offices that were rightfully his and thus deprived him of future income and the chance of paying off his debts.

Buchanan spoke next. The funding of a rebel army would be underwritten by the King of Spain and the forces would assemble across the Scots border and march south. They had promises of troops from the rebel lords in Ireland and from Lord Bothwell in Scotland, as well as Colonel Sir William Stanley's army of dissidents and mercenaries. The King of France, too, might be coaxed to lend arms and troops and perhaps Pope Clement VIII would open a few coffers. He then argued that the King of Scots had the best claim to the English throne and if my Lord of Derby refused the opportunity now, he might not get another chance. King James was not reputed to be a strong king, therefore the Cecils might support him so they could manipulate him.

That had Ferdinando nodding, though it was hard to see whether he was being truly swayed by their arguments.

There were successful precedents, Doughtie then pointed out, noble lords who had marched south and made themselves king: Henry Bolingbroke when he deposed Richard II, and Edward IV retaking his throne in 1471. And, most notable of all, Henry Tudor had landed in Wales and seized the crown by right of conquest.

'Speaking of Wales, what about Buckingham's rebellion against Richard III?' Ferdinando countered, taking a swig from his leather flask and passing it round. 'A disaster. Too many factions were involved in the enterprise to keep that secret.' He looked at Garrett for concurrence. 'What say you?'

Garrett wanted to say firstly, that he had heard Lord Bothwell was as manageable as an untethered ship's cannon at the height of a storm; secondly, the Irish had nowhere near the resources and weaponry of the English; and thirdly, a civil war, whether religious or not, provided an excuse for savagery, and with the recent poor harvest and the plague it was the last thing the county needed. Instead, he gave a soldier's answer.

'It would be timing that would bother me. There would be little chance of surprising the queen's forces. The possibility of transporting all these separate armies by ship from the Low Countries or Ireland depends on favourable weather.'

'God will blow the sails,' exclaimed Snow.

No more to be said, then.

'The cause is just. We are promised ships, money, men and weaponry. All it needs is your agreement, my lord,' pleaded O'Neill.

'You know what, though,' put in Halsall, 'the English people won't like the cause being foreign-funded. My lord mustn't be seen to be in bed with Spain.'

'I promise half of England will rally to your standard, my lord,' swore Frayn.

'But which earls?' asked Halsall. 'Burghley and Essex will oppose us. Lord Suffolk may support us, but what about the rest?'

'Remember, Parliament will have to ratify a change of monarch,' insisted Garrett. 'You reckon you may bring the Commons, Frayn, but what about the Lords?'

Hell! He was being drawn into this when he needed to be vigilant, watch the bushes, for if this was reported —

The conversation picked a path through a list of probable supporters and then Snow suggested that Ferdinando might find reasons to set aside his wife and marry Arbella Stuart, thus doubling his claim to the throne.

An interesting argument but misdirected. Ferdinando swiftly pointed out that not only was Arbella plain as a blacksmith's anvil, but there was also no guarantee she was fecund, and in any case his countess was carrying again and it might be a boy-child.

It was then a distant hunting horn had everyone on sudden edge except Halsall. 'Pah, way off, up towards the mosses. Our word for "marshes",' he explained to the outsiders.

Garrett mentally crossed himself in relief but if his nerves were jarred, so were Ferdinando's. The earl took another swig from his leather flask and, finding it empty, accepted Buchanan's.

'As I was saying,' Snow resumed. 'With a Catholic king, England can be at peace again, trade will flourish and —'

'Yes, yes, but what about tolerance, religious freedom?' cut in Ferdinando. 'Can't we just allow people to worship as they please? We don't want to return to the days of Bloody Mary.'

'Agreed, my lord, but we need restoration,' persisted Snow.

'I fear that may mean pulling down a lot of new manor houses, since they were built with the stones of ruined abbeys,' commented Ferdinando dryly. He met Garrett's warning glance. 'Time we dispersed. I will consider your offer.'

Andrew Buchanan was staring at the lengthening shadows. 'Aye, but wi' all respect to your lordship, we canna dilly-dally. We need to carry a definite answer back.'

'I shall be here at least two more days. Towneley here will convey to you my decision.'

'Two days! Forgive my forwardness, Lord Derby, but that gives you plentiful opportunity to hand us over to the sheriff like you did Hesketh,' challenged Snow, shaking off Frayn's restraining hand.

Ferdinando glared at him like a hanging judge. 'Hesketh threatened to kill me. He was out of his mind.' Snow's horse tossed its head at the sudden tug upon its bridle as the earl continued, 'This enterprise may mean many good men's deaths, yet none of you have qualms about that, Master Snow, and don't give me that omelettes and breaking eggs homily, any of you. Those deaths would be upon my soul, my conscience. If this fails, I shall be beheaded, my family disgraced and evicted.' He allowed that to be digested then added, 'And what are we supposed to do with the queen?'

'Imprison her in the Tower!' barked Frayn.

'Behead her like she beheaded Mary Stuart,' snarled Buchanan.

'Assassinate her!' hissed Snow.

Sensing Ferdinando's distaste for such a vile act, Garrett could feel the good will fracturing. 'We should finish this,' he prompted. They had been arguing for an hour. 'There must be no suspicion that you have had this meeting, my lord. We need to return.'

Ferdinando's face was grim on the gallop back to the lodge. They rode out of their way at a hard pace so that the horses would look to have had plenty of exercise. The other party had not yet returned, but the earl's body servant was back with news that her ladyship was in good health. Much relieved, Ferdinando announced he was going to catch up on sleep and withdrew into his bedchamber.

After he had seen to his horse's needs, Garrett sat down on one of the outside logs. His mind was still masticating the afternoon's arguments. He did not envy Ferdinando's dilemma one iota but as an intelligencer he, too, had a decision: how much to report back to Wade. Silence would be unacceptable, but if Ferdinando decided to lead the dissidents, what then? Would he throw in his lot with this possible king? Or hand him over as a traitor? No, the earl might have had the stomach to do that with Hesketh but Garrett flinched at the thought.

The sudden lick on his fingers made him snap his eyes open. The hounds were back, tails wagging, ahead of the triumphant huntsmen bearing a slaughtered hind. Lacking a cheerful demeanour, he left it to Dick to welcome them.

When the hubbub had died down, a toe nudged him. 'What do you reckon he'll decide, then?' asked the Master of Horse, his shadow falling across Garrett's face. There was no one within earshot. Garrett eased himself up. He wasn't up for a wager either way. Although a great lord might profess himself uninterested, greed and the lust for power were like tiny seeds in most men's hearts. A good dousing and they might poke up.

He heard the creak of leather behind them and looked round. 'Ah, Master Golborne, we were talking about tomorrow's hunt,' he said pleasantly. 'You did not catch the buck, I hear.'

'Nor did you. I notice that none of the arrows have been fired. What's going on?'

'What do you plaguey reckon! We sighted no game, Golborne. Ergo, no arrows were fired. Simple as that. His lordship was not in high spirits, either, having slept so ill. He is trying to amend that now.'

'One of the woodsmen told us there were other horsemen in the woods, strangers.'

'What! And you've put two and two together and made six and a half. Well done!'

'Ever since you came to Lathom, Towneley, strange things have been occurring.'

'Leave it, Golborne!' snapped Doughtie.

'Says who, a lawbreaking Papist? Who puts wool in his ears in chapel? Who is not supposed to travel more than five miles from his home? I saw you talking with Hesketh when he first arrived. Brothers under the skin!'

'Whoa, lads!' Garrett rose to his superior height between them. 'Golborne here, bless his Puritan breeches, has a right to be suspicious.' He grabbed the man's black sleeve. 'But not for the common hearing, eh? We don't want it known that the King of Scots' man was holding discussion with his lordship.'

He received two stares. Both of disbelief.

'Why would —'

'Golborne, dear fellow, Lord Bothwell is thought to have trespassed into England. His Scots Majesty wishes the fellow brought to heel. Should he come barking in these parts, his lordship has agreed to collar him and send him leashed to Edinburgh.'

It hit home exquisitely like a well-placed punch. Satisfying. His breath calmer, heartbeat slowing, Garrett stroked the knuckles of his missing fingers. Very satisfying. Even Doughtie was grinning.

For the time being, Secretary Golborne was winded.

14

It was sunset when Golborne went to rouse the earl for supper. Shortly afterwards, Garrett heard the violent retching. With Halsall at his heels, he rushed inside and found Golborne in the bedchamber with his arm about the earl. His lordship was vomiting into his chamber pot. Garrett quickly unlatched the shutters.

'Shut the door!' Ferdinando snarled at Halsall, dragging a hand across his lips.

'He saw a wraith,' exclaimed Golborne.

With his secretary's help, the earl reached the bed and sagged against one of the end posts. 'I saw Hesketh's ghost.'

'The Papist who was hanged at St Albans last November,' Golborne explained.

Even a decent-looking man could look like a gargoyle. Ferdinando did, his lips yanked wide by horror as he relived his terror. 'It was Hesketh. Pale, ghastly, with a livid mark about his throat.'

'You mean of a noose, my lord?'

'Yes, Golborne, that's right. You saw it too.'

'My lord, no, I —'

'The fiend pointed at me.' The earl stretched out a shaking finger. 'Like this. Pointed at me just like Hesketh did from the scaffold when he cursed me.'

'It spoke?' asked Garrett.

'No, but its lips drew back in a curse. Then it turned, cursed me again and vanished into the shadows. Tell me I'm not going insane, Golborne,' he pleaded in anguish. 'Tell them what you saw.'

'My lord, I saw nothing.'

'But you were here beside me.'

'I did not see it.'

'Where exactly did this spirit appear, my lord?' Garrett asked.

'There!' Where the shadows were greatest. Now only a tiny moth sported between the beams and the rushes. Golborne snatched it and wiped the crush of silver from his fingers.

Stanching a withering comment, Garrett checked behind the screen, saw nothing untoward and turned towards the casement. 'The shutters were closed, my lord, so how much light was there? Was the oil lamp lit or a candle burning?'

Ferdinando frowned. 'I think … only what was coming through the cracks.'

Garrett relatched the boards. 'Like this?'

'Yes,' agreed Golborne. 'I came in quietly, closed the door behind me, and sought to wake my lord and it was then that he saw it.'

'But you saw nothing, sensed nothing?'

'The air seemed to chill but that was my own fear, I suspect, because my lord told me what he was seeing.'

Perplexed, Garrett folded back the screen that hid the washstand. Everyone believed in ghosts, though, for his part, he had yet to see or hear the supernatural: no sightings of Our Lady (though being a Protestant, he was probably not high on her list), no voices in the church bells and there had been no wandering dead among the tombstones in Southwark.

Hallucination, he decided. Maybe something still in the earl's belly from last night.

'Have you eaten or drunk anything since your return, my lord?' he asked.

Ferdinando jerked a shaky thumb to a tankard on the wooden chest.

Clothier, the earl's body servant, grabbed it up. 'I tasted it before I served you, my lord.' He took a draught and passed it on to Garrett. 'Believe me, nothing's wrong with it.'

'Give it here, then,' growled Ferdinando. He took a swig to clear the nausea from his mouth, spat on the rushes, drank again and drew his hand across his lips. 'That wraith was the most hideous sight I have ever beheld.'

Shakespeare will be jealous, Garrett thought absurdly, remembering the ghosts and their curses in the last act of *Richard III.*

'But why here, my lord? Why now?' he questioned. 'It's over four months since Hesketh died.'

Was the earl becoming demented? He had seen for himself that Ferdinando's mother could behave wildly. God's mercy! If Ferdinando was so unmanned by this imagining, could he survive the ugliness of leading a rebellion?

Ferdinando was careful at supper to consume nothing that had not been first tasted by Clothier. He ate sparingly but in the middle of the night the men were woken again by his screams. This time Garrett was the first in.

Like a man suffering from a fit, Ferdinando was threshing wildly on the bed and shouting as though he was in a battle. Golborne and Clothier, who had both slept in his chamber, were struggling to wake him.

Garrett grabbed a hunting horn from the wall and blew it. 'Retreat!' he shouted.

Ferdinando's thrashing limbs stilled and he drew deep gulps of air as he opened his eyes and took in the crowd of anxious faces.

'Another bad dream, my lord?' Clothier asked.

'Yes, yes,' muttered his lordship, grimacing. 'An assassin. He stabbed me again and again in the heart and all over.' He blinked down as if expecting to see the wounds. 'I was fighting for my life but… Oh God! The basin, quickly!'

'My lord, we should return to Lathom,' Garrett exclaimed as everyone backed rapidly.

Halsall took charge. 'Enough! Return to your beds, all of you.' He ushered the others out and grabbed Garrett by the shoulder. 'It is not your place to make the decisions; however, I think you are right. Come morning, we will go home.'

Garrett had promised to meet Snow and Frayn at first light by the stream. The two men were clothed in homespun and carried simple handlines so anyone watching would think it a chance meeting.

'You bring an answer?' demanded Frayn.

'In a manner, yes. The earl is ill.' At their recoil, he added quickly, 'There are no buboes, no darkening on his fingers, thank the Lord, but his pallor is like a dead man's. We are taking him back to Lathom. Poison, maybe.' He cocked an eyebrow.

'If you are implying…' began Snow.

'Revenge, yes. Hesketh was your friend.'

'Well, acquit me of that, man. Our cause needs a live leader not a dead one.'

'Is it something rotten that he's eaten?'

'I'm not his ruddy physician, Frayn, but I reckon the nausea is lasting too long and he's hallucinating as well. One of the secretaries has been asking questions about yesterday but we've dealt with that.'

'You killed him?'

Garrett pulled a face. 'Give me some sense, Snow!'

'But you will if you have to?'

'Yes. Now I'd better get back.'

Frayn's snort of despair sounded authentic. 'Wait! Did his lordship reach a decision before he became ill?'

Garrett shrugged. 'Who can say? In his present state though, you'll be whistling in the wind. If you want my advice, gentlemen, disappear! Especially you, Frayn. Hanging around like a bad smell isn't going to help anyone. There is no telling how long this malady will prevail.'

'And when he recovers?' Frayn asked.

'Then Dick Doughtie will send you word.'

Clearly, Snow didn't like being given his marching orders. 'And are you leaving, Towneley?'

'Not yet. If my lord recovers, I'll suggest Her Majesty's government were trying to do away with him. That might win him over for us. Otherwise, I'm not looking forward to reporting to Colonel Stanley. He doesn't like failure.'

A parting thrust from Frayn. 'Do you know much about poisons, Captain?'

'Why,' Garrett answered, with a tepid smile, 'do you?

'An invite to Hell!' Ferdinando spluttered at Halsall's suggestion of a litter slung between two horses. 'I'll not have every jack in this blasted shire seeing me puke! Send for my coach!'

It was tragic, Garrett reflected, that even feeling so wretched, the earl still had to think like a politician. Mind, Ferdinando was talking sense: with no male heir to succeed him save 'his ninny of a brother' (his lordship's words), the news of his illness would unsettle his creditors and everyone who owed their positions to his favour.

Rather like England if the queen fell ill, Garrett thought to himself. *How ironic!*

Subdued, morose, the hunting party waited with their sick lord. It was mid-afternoon when the earl's coach, packed on my lady's orders with pillows, cushions, bowls, chamber pots plus Dr Canon and Mr Bate, Lathom House's resident physician and chirurgeon, reached Knowsley.

The journey back to Lathom was snail-like. It was almost dusk as they reached the inner courtyard and there the whole blessed household was standing ready, frog-eyed in fear and wonderment. Foolish of the countess to permit this, Garrett thought as he wearily dismounted. Whispers of his lordship's indisposition would spread, swift as a summer grassfire.

Flanked by Dr Canon and Edward Halsall, Ferdinando took the steps to the hall with kingly fortitude and all his secretaries closed tightly around him like ants shifting a cake crumb. Once inside, it was another matter. 'Keep 'em out!' he growled at Garrett and doubled over, retching again.

Lady Derby nodded, standing back, her hands aflutter. 'Go, please, Captain Towneley! Do as he says.'

Outside, questions came at Garrett like a storm of arrows.

'Was there an accident?'

'Is he wounded?'

'A boar?'

'Did someone —'

'Whoa!' He raised his hands in the air and the hubbub hushed. 'There has been no accident. Dr Canon says his lordship's malady is due to an excess of physical exertion and surfeit of feasting. He's given him an emetic and advised him to fast until his belly is rested. His lordship requests you return to your duties, all of you!'

As he turned, a nose-out-of-joint Farington drew level with him. 'For a newcomer, you seem to be taking on a great deal of responsibility, Towneley.'

'Maybe newcomer to you, your worship, but I am only carrying out his lordship's orders.'

'Into my office, if you please!'

Garrett shrugged compliance. He might be in for an interrogation, though fortunately it wasn't the Tower of London, and even if Ferdinando was hiccoughing and puking excessively, his lordship still had his wits.

It was hard to decide whether the receiver-general looked like a surly judge or a grumpy chicken as he tossed up his dark gown and seated himself behind his table. Doughtie and Golborne had been summoned as well, and standing before the old curmudgeon, the three of them were being glared at like accused felons. Farington wanted to know everything and it was more than a controlling nature that spurred the questions.

They told him of the nightmares and the hallucinations followed by the sickness that came over the earl early that morning.

'And all of you were with him on the hunt yesterday?'

'Yes, in the morning. He withdrew later.' Golborne looked to the others. 'I wasn't with him after midday but they were.'

Doughtie shrugged. 'He rested. When he felt restored, we began the chase anew but we caught no sign of the buck that everyone was after.'

'But you said —' Golborne, tiresome bastard, swung round accusingly. 'Tell him!'

'Be honest with me, you accursed Papist, Doughtie, or, by Heaven, I'll have you and Towneley in irons for conspiracy.'

'Stow that!' snarled Garrett. His anger was for Golborne. 'You loose-tongued fool! You think his lordship wants you blabbing about his business with the King of Scots?'

Farington took a sharp breath. 'What business?'

'The matter of Lord Bothwell. King James's emissary met with my lord,' Golborne bleated.

Beautiful! Garrett approved, as the secretary continued. Master Smug Inkyfingers had swallowed the bait and was even telling the tale as though he had been part of it.

'What, they met secretly?' Whether Farington was shocked or furious was up for wager.

'Of course, secretly.' Doughtie directed a disgusted look at Golborne before he stared down at their interrogator. 'And you'll not accuse me of being a traitor. I follow orders.'

'Ah, but whose?' Farington rose. 'If it comes to choosing between the Pope and his lordship —' he spread his palms, his expression silky — 'which would you swing for?'

'Why you —'

It was Garrett who grabbed Doughtie back from seizing the old man. It took all his strength until he felt the other's rage abate. Loosed, the Master of Horse straightened his clothing. 'I shall not forget this,' he snarled.

'Of course, we know you are no Hesketh,' Golborne reassured him sweetly. 'But I do hope for your sake that my lord recovers.'

It took effort to manhandle the furious officer away. Had he been made of gunpowder, Dick Doughtie would have exploded before they reached the sanctuary of his office at the stables. Garrett thrust him in and leaned back against the door. 'That was pretty.'

'You see,' hissed Doughtie. 'Bloody-minded Protestants. They'd burn us if they could. What if my lord doesn't recover, Towneley? I'll wager they'll nail me for it and you, too.'

'Sit down and calm yourself. He'll revive. Mayhap one of the capons had sick flesh. Or that filthy stuff he took on the first night was poorly mixed. What was it? Toasted toadstools? Poppy Delight? No? Then maybe Halsall or Dr Canon can enlighten me.'

'Ask the white witch at Aughton and I will not —' Doughtie's mouth snapped shut as the door rattled open and the head groom poked his head in: 'You got any more liniment in here?'

Garrett took his leave. A white witch? By heaven, surely it was too much conspiring not ruddy fairy spells!

'Do *you* believe in ghosts?' Garrett asked Will Shakespeare, as the two men lay on their respective mattresses. The quivering flame of the candle on the upturned firkin next to Shakespeare's mattress was amusing itself sending dark shadows swirling across the bare walls. Garrett's mind was full of shadows too. It had helped to tell Shakespeare what had occurred to the earl at the hunting lodge, but the night-time fears that prick and sting to keep a man wakeful were assembling in a crowd.

'Ghosts? Of course, who doesn't?'

'But do you really think Richard III was plagued by all those murdered souls the night before the battle?'

'What, queuing up outside his tent?'

'Be serious, man.'

'Oh, come on, Garrett, at least half of England believes in fairies and the majority would soon as lie in a gutter than venture into any churchyard at midnight. My ghosts worked exquisitely on stage, but I can tell you there is no mention of them in the annals of Hall or Holinshed. There is a blur betwixt dreaming and waking of what is real and what is not. My murdered souls came to Richard in his dreams not his waking, remember.' Across the chamber, he raised himself on his elbow and blew the candle out. 'All right,' he continued, lying back down, 'what I do believe in is the determination of the mind to distinguish some logical form in shadows and, thus, to strive to make sense of the inexplicable.' Then, he added, 'Could someone — and let's leave God and the Devil out of it — be meddling?'

'I have been going over and over what happened but I can see no way in which that could have been managed, Will. Only Ferdinando saw the ghost, or so Golborne claims.'

'Do you warm to such a magpie fellow, Garrett? I certainly do not, but then I cannot understand why he would lie.'

'It is all very strange and sinister. The witches the other night...'

'Ah yes, the players, but they too were trying to meddle with Ferdinando's mind. He's in some sort of danger, to my humble way of thinking. I know you know more than you can tell me, more than I desire to know.' His long fingers were a glimmer, spread in question.

'Yes, possibly he is.'

'Then, Master Intelligencer, do your best to safeguard him for *all* our sakes.'

Ferdinando had not recovered by next morning and sent for his own physician from Chester (a two-day journey from the other side of the Mersey). Meantime, Lady Alice insisted the men of the household, and especially his 'old friend' Garrett, do their best to distract his lordship. A challenging task since the stratagems of chess and cards were not as engaging for the ill man as everyone hoped.

Despite the expensive bezoar stone swirled in every drink he took, Ferdinando's body continued to void and Garrett found it horrifying to watch a man who had been pulsating with vitality lose both flesh and radiance. What's more, despite his intellect, the earl was becoming vulnerable to all the fears an agile mind could dredge up. A second night passed and as his body weakened, so did his resilience against ignorance. Yet, one thing he remained resolved upon; he would not be bled (a declaration made with the hurl of a goblet against the container of leeches).

By the third morning, Garrett's optimism for Ferdinando's recovery was at low tide. Was all this puking due to some damn aphrodisiac? Perhaps he did need to interrogate the witch that Doughtie had mentioned. And maybe Rose Byrd might accompany him? It would offer him a chance to get to know her better. Yes, a good plan, except...

Except 'women's reasons' had been affecting both her and Lady Vere since his return from Knowsley, so later that morning, he was very pleased when she pushed him into a cupboard. Well, not a cupboard exactly but a recess behind the arras, cosy enough for him to smell the floral perfume that she wore. A further shove and he found himself in some sort of distaff chamber occupied by several spinning wheels and two large baskets of unspun fleece.

'Do I have to spin this into gold?' he asked.

'You'd get calluses. Sit!'

As he was about to ask where, one of the countess's lapdogs appeared from behind his heels. Locking eyes with him, it started to yap.

'Sit, Poppet!' Rose repeated. 'No, don't put it out, Captain! It will bark outside the door. It seems to have taken to me.'

'We all have, including his lordship.' And in the sunlight, she was looking delightful. He'd happily put his arms around that tiny waist. Her hair was prettily puffed up beneath a cap stitched with marguerites and the fine linen scarf between her throat and stomacher offered a tantalising parting over her cleavage. 'You're looking better, Nightingale? Did you miss me?'

'You're large enough not to miss. What happened at Knowsley? I've been out of matters.' She patted her stomach with her free hand. '"The custom of women" as it says in Genesis.'

He looked blank. 'You're offering me an apple?'

Her reply was a growl that the dog matched. 'Don't be annoying! What happened in the woods? Have we seen the last of Frayn?'

He held up his palms in surrender, conceding she deserved some sort of enlightenment. 'I believe so. There was an inconclusive meeting. No plans were made.'

The relief in her eyes mirrored his own. 'Then you are saying he offered no encouragement to whatever was being proposed?'

'Pot firmly lidded, I reckon.'

'And Frayn?'

'Gone to ground, Nightingale.' He hoped his smile reassured her.

'Good.'

'You heard about the nightmares, though? Hesketh's ghost floating in?'

'Yes, Lady Alice told me. Did anyone else see it?'

'That's a good question. No, only Ferdinando saw it and only he is sick. What I don't understand is that, yes, a visitation might make you throw up your supper — if you believe it — but to keep on being ill...' He pulled a wry face. 'His physicians say it must run its course. They think it was too much exertion, *all* sorts of exertion.'

She absorbed that with a lift of eyebrow. 'You mean it wasn't just male company?'

'I'm afraid not, Nightingale. A party of merry harlots was carted in. Apparently, it is a regular practice for his lordship — when he hunts.' He wanted to assure her he had not participated but she was still thinking about Ferdinando.

'It could be the French disease, then?' A worldly lady. 'Would one of his physicians have dosed him with mercury?' At least her attitude argued she had not lain with the earl.

'That occurred to me, too. I asked Dr Canon while we were on the road and he said not to his knowledge and, anyway, that the hallucinations and vomiting do not match. Now tell me, has the coroner or the sheriff sent you any more word about your servant's murderer?'

A shake of head and she gathered up the little dog. 'Assault by person or persons unknown. Poor Martin, we buried him in the villagers' graveyard the day you left.' In sympathy at her sad voice, the little animal licked her under the chin. Lucky creature, being hugged to those breasts. If she'd put the tiresome beast down without it yapping, maybe he could kiss her. No, he'd *think* about kissing her. Would she even let him? Being Secretary Davison's daughter, she'd surely have better taste than getting involved with a man like him.

He cleared his throat. 'And what have you been doing, Nightingale, while you were indisposed? Helping stitch baby clothes for his lordship's heir?'

'No, glittery spangles for Master Shakespeare's fairy play. I think I must play a wall.'

'Pardon?'

'A real wall to keep him and Lady Vere apart. They've become almost too close, Captain.' She looked up, her fingers fondling the animal's head, and there seemed a dab of amazement in her expression that she had uttered that confidence or... He removed the dog from her arms. Yes, he would kiss her. 'We were going to perform the fairy interlude once you had all returned but now...' Glassy-eyed, she cocked her head sorrowfully and turned away, ignoring the struggling dog. Crossing to the window, she stared out at the trees, a green confusion beyond the glass. 'This malady of the earl's, it's not natural.'

'Ferdinando will recover, Rose. Hardly in his dotage!' He set the dog down. It stared at his threatening finger and stood uncertain. Like he did. He was hesitating, wondering whether she would welcome his damaged hands upon her shoulders.

She turned with a frown. 'You seem to be making light of this, Captain. My lady reckons he believes he's been cursed by Hesketh's ghost. God be my witness, what happened at St Albans would have sufficed to shake any feeling man to the marrow! I heard the living man curse him from the scaffold. Didn't you?'

'Yes, but...' Garrett whistled through his teeth. He needed to talk the family out of this nonsense. Such belief could kill a man. He recalled that a soldier in his garrison in Ireland died with not a mark on him believing he was bewitched. 'I hope Lady Alice is not encouraging him in this fallacy.'

'Why would she? No!' She admonished the dog. 'Put your paws down! She is hoping this Dr Case from Chester will make

Ferdy see sense. No! Bad boy! Sit! Apparently, he is quite a renowned Oxford scholar. Have you heard of him?'

He was tempted to say expensive doctors spouted Greek, never handled their patients, and left it to base assistants to administer catheters and suck forth the maladies, but before he drew breath, the latch rattled fiercely and little Bess' voice called out, 'Mistress Rose, are you in there?' With a recognising woof, the dog rushed to the door.

'We shouldn't be found together, sir,' Rose hissed.

'No, wait, I need to —'

But she was gone with a flurry of skirts, leaving him unhugged, unkissed and unable to inform her about the white witch.

Garrett stood, fisting his palm. Yes, he would ask Rose to help him find the woman. If an aphrodisiac was responsible, then it would prove the curses a nonsense. That would give Ferdinando the mental steel to battle his fear that he was damned. Christ willing, if he could find the witch of Aughton, then perhaps he'd find the antidote.

'Ah, there you are, Poppet,' squealed young Lady Bess, as Rose delivered the little dog into her arms. 'Mama wants us all to cheer up Father. Please, will you come? Cousin Lizbeth and the others are waiting.'

There were more questions Rose would have liked to ask Captain Towneley but at least she would see for herself how Ferdy fared this morning as she followed the earl's daughters upstairs.

Since the fire was stoked up, it was like high summer in the candlelit bedchamber — some might say 'like London' since scents and stink were vying fiercely for predominance. Lordly paraphernalia such as weapons and deer heads decorated the walls. However, there was an excellent portrait of Alice and a Flemish tapestry of young David playing to King Saul to add some softness. The furnishings included a virginal painted with caterpillars and moths, several oak cupboards, a prie-dieu, bookcase and an immense four-poster bed, which was hung with cream and green curtains. Rose was charmed to see children's drawings tucked under a mature sketch of Lathom and beside the bedhead, a stumpwork of a podgy golden bee hovering above scarlet flowers.

Happily, the bed was unoccupied. Ferdinando was dressed and sitting at his writing table with Golborne at his side. He did not rise to greet his children. Saggy crescents underscored his eyes and the pallor beneath his otherwise healthy skin was the hue of ashes. Rose noticed he toed the ewer beneath his desk further out of sight as his two older daughters came to stand either side of him. Young Frances wrinkled her nose, bit back whatever she was going to say and stoically stood within reach of having her braids pulled.

'I hear my sweet guests have written an interlude while I've been gone,' Ferdy said, twisting round to smile at Lizbeth and Rose.

'With Master Shakespeare's help,' conceded Lizbeth. Rose could tell she was shocked at how weary he looked.

'It's about fairies, Papa, and magic potions.'

'Ah, magic potions, Anne,' he echoed dryly, giving the child a gentle hug. 'Sometimes they can be good.' He hiccoughed. 'And sometimes ... bad.' Another hiccough.

'Yes, yes,' exclaimed Frances. 'And the fairy king's servant makes a mistake. But we can't tell you any more else it won't be a surprise.'

He nodded but even that demanded effort, as if the floor was invisibly dragging down on his arms and spine.

'We're sorry that you are feeling in the dumps, Ferdy,' Lizbeth said charmingly. 'I can see you have plenty of books to occupy you.'

He shook his head. 'My physicians have advised rest but there are matters to deal with.' A half-written letter with its fine gilt edging lay before him and he grimaced at the pile of documents awaiting his attention. 'Her Majesty wants men mustered and… Oh mercy! I … I think you'd best go. I'm going to be…' The girls sprang back as he clapped a hand abruptly across his mouth. It was Rose who made a swift grab for the ewer and held it for him.

Lizbeth quickly ushered the children out. 'We'll come back later.'

It wasn't the half-digested food and bile that Rose, trying not to grimace, expected, but fouler, fattier, and she was close to retching herself at the smell. Thankfully, Bate took the basin from her.

Straightening, Ferdinando grabbed the napkin that Clothier proffered and wiped his lips. 'Oh God, Rose,' he whispered. 'It doesn't stop. Two days now. My belly is so cursed sore.' He glared across at Dr Canon, who was swiftly writing in a notebook. 'Another scratch for the ledger? A wonder you do not make a wager of it — how many more pukes before noon?'

Canon ignored the outburst and calmly set the book aside. 'My lord, may I suggest a glister before you sleep tonight?'

'Pah!' Despairingly, Ferdinando buried his head in his hands. Rose set a comforting hand upon his shoulder. Across the room, she watched the doctor and chirurgeon exchanging looks as they inspected the vomit and she came to the horrific conclusion that they were out of their depth. Golborne met her gaze and shook his head.

'It will cease, my lord,' she murmured reassuringly, wondering if she should call his daughters back now to distract him. She could hear more voices in the antechamber. 'Ah, it's my lady and Chaplain Leigh,' she exclaimed, diplomatically stepping aside as the door opened. Taking the cue, the chirurgeon swiftly threw a cover over the ewer and scurried through the panelled door. They heard the lid of the close stool.

'Oh, goodness!' Lady Derby raised the pomander chained to her wrist and then as though realising it was not tactful, let it drop. 'Are you still not feeling any better, Ferdy dearest?'

'Doesn't look like it, Alice.' He shakily stood up. 'I—' He glared at the papers on the desk. 'Oh, be damned to it!' he snarled.

The chaplain hastened across to offer a steadying hand. 'You are in all our prayers, my lord.'

'The continual vomiting is exhausting me, Leigh. Jesu! How can aught be left in my belly.' It took a moment of leaning upon the back of the chair before he found the strength to reach his bed. He sat down and collapsed back with a groan.

Alice patted his shoulder. 'Be of cheer, Dr Case left Chester the moment he received your message. He's here already and just changing out of his riding clothes.' A few moments later, Clothier ushered in a tall, robed scholar in his fifties. Like many people of his altitude, Dr Case had a stoop, which might have been due to hours of study or listening to his shorter fellows. Rose decided the latter, for though his prominent cheekbones and neat grey beard added eminence, the newcomer's soulful gaze flitted from face to face with a greeting of benign sweetness until he found his patient, then his smile froze as he took in the earl's appearance.

'John!' Ferdy held out his arms in joy and the two embraced. 'Now I will get better.'

Behind the countess, Canon and Bate exchanged a don't-mind-us look.

'Dr Case taught Ferdy philosophy at Oxford,' Alice whispered. 'St John's College.'

Rose hoped he'd live up to Alice's expectations. Although medicine was part of the course for a doctorate, it did not mean it became a lifetime practice. Frankly, if they had been living in Mary Tudor's reign, she would have mistaken Dr Case for a devoted confessor. Maybe that's why Ferdy had sent for him. He needed brotherly love, for there was clearly a deep trust between the two men.

'Not another Papist,' growled Golborne behind her.

'Let's have a look at you, shall we, my dear friend,' exclaimed Dr Case, but just as he spoke, Ferdy twisted over, retching again, and Clothier came running with a fresh basin.

'Clear the room,' exclaimed the countess. 'Let us leave the good doctor to give his opinion.'

'Mistress Byrd, wait!' Ferdy called out, as Case and Clothier, talking enthusiastically about glisters, settled him against the pillows.

Rose halted on her way out and curtseyed. 'My lord?'

'Find Will Shakespeare and tell him to attend Master Farington, please you! And, Alice, don't look so distraught! John will not let this vanquish me.'

The only trouble being, Rose feared, as she left on her errand, that it was clear not one of them, even Dr Case, knew what 'this' was.

The winding stairs of the Eagle Tower had become no easier through familiarity and Rose was relieved to hear voices beyond the library door as she stopped to recover her breath. Towneley was with Shakespeare and they were discussing the Earl of Southampton. They instantly stopped as she entered.

The captain was seated in the earl's great chair. Shakespeare, to her dismay, looked to be packing for he was carefully arranging several rolled-up scrolls in a leather backpack. Surely, he wasn't leaving? Lizbeth would be devastated.

'Ah, here's sweet Rose, one of my fellow playwrights,' the poet said with a smile.

'Good morrow, sirs,' she gasped and taking up a parchment from the great desk, fanned herself. 'Master Shakespeare, my lord bids you to speak with Master Farington.'

'Hmm, maybe some payment,' muttered Shakespeare.

'Well, Rose, you make a sweeter messenger than Golborne,' remarked Towneley. 'Is his lordship any better?'

'I fear not.' She set the parchment down with a sad face.

Shakespeare exchanged a wry look with Towneley. 'God and his angels heal him! We all revolve around his earth.' He shouldered his satchel. 'And so, farewell to Lathom.'

'You're leaving, sir? But what about the masque?' exclaimed Rose. 'The instant his lordship feels better, we'll be putting it on. Please, stay.'

'Rose,' said Shakespeare, halting to gently clasp her shoulders, 'it is at my lord's command that I'm departing. This morning, he received wonderful news from our friend Burbage. The theatres in London are to open again and I am needed. Honestly, my dear sweet girl, the arrangement here was only until the plague abated.'

'Oh!' Rose bit her lower lip in disappointment and added, 'I suppose the Muse is calling. Has ... has Lady Vere been told?' All very well calling Lizbeth his 'dark lady' and writing her a sonnet then just flitting away without a farewell. If a playwright could look sheepish, Shakespeare certainly did as he took up his saddlebag.

Towneley grabbed the latter from him. 'In other words, no, Nightingale. You're a lily-livered varmint, Will. The young lady will be "dark" indeed when she hears.'

At least the poet looked chastened. 'Be my sad messenger, fair mistress. I'll finish the fairy play in London, tell her.'

'Well, no use drawing this out further like a spinner's yarn, I suppose,' Rose replied stiffly. 'Safe journey, Master Shakespeare.'

He kissed her hand. 'Absolve me, sweetest Rose, I openly confess to bigamy. I've a wife and three children in Stratford but I'm also married to Poetry and she is by far my greatest love. Lady Vere must — *Lady Vere will* — wed some great lord at her grandfather's command.' He paused at the threshold. 'People die, but it's not from love.'

'Yes,' Rose agreed bleakly. 'I do understand what you are saying, Master Shakespeare.' Convincing Lizbeth was another matter.

15

Lizbeth grieved discreetly. Rose offered a shoulder, Lathom's rather weedy knot garden provided the scenery, and a speckled thrush gave song while the young woman's fantasy of being adored was crushed. As with a broken lavender head, such misery would leave a scent — for a while.

God (rather like Her Majesty) played fast and loose with His favours, Rose mused as she soothed Lizbeth; permit you a glimpse of sunlit heaven and then kick you down to earth. It was being valued, she guessed, that Lizbeth would most miss. Whereas the Cecils might see her worth as a bride to link two great houses, and a future husband might view her as a field continually to be ploughed so to bring forth heirs, Will Shakespeare had appreciated a different creativity — a sparkling creativity, denied because of gender. Lizbeth was a wordsmith that the world would never celebrate and Master Shakespeare had opened her eyes to that.

As the private sobs, sniffs, anger and self-denigration abated, the public Lizbeth began to surface. 'At least I am in health,' she said, rubbing a knuckle across her damp upper lip, and casting a guilty look towards the house. 'Ferdy looked dreadful.'

'There's time to go to the chapel before dinner.'

'Yes, let's. If only our poor prayers can help him. Oh lordy, I've made my ruff all floppy, look.'

'This affliction of his lordship ain't serious, is it, my lady?' asked Amy, Lizbeth's maid. They encountered her on their way back from the chapel. She must have come from the laundering shed since her arms were full of their fresh petticoats. 'I mean, should I start packing?'

'No, it's not contagious,' Rose reassured her. 'We shall stay as long as we are welcome.'

Amy, however, was staring at her mistress's ruff. 'Why, look at that,' she squawked loudly. 'That ain't good enough.' In her indignation, she looked fit almost to seize it off Lizbeth and brandish accusingly in the face of Lady Derby's starcher.

'See to it later!' growled her mistress and stormed away.

'Oh lordy, have I —'

'No, Amy, do not go after her. Listen, there is something you may be able to tell me. Is there a regular food taster for the earl? I don't just mean for banquets.'

'Oh yes, mistress, there's no strangers allowed in the kitchens. Only the cook himself must dress my lord's meat and he gives a morsel of anything for his lordship to anyone who's in the kitchen and then again in the dining room before it reaches my lord's table. Happened to me this mornin'. Chicken broth, it were. You think his lordship's being poisoned?'

'No, no,' Rose answered swiftly to stamp out that little fire. 'But sometimes rotten meat can turn the stomach.'

'Or curses can.'

'Curses, Amy?'

'Cursed from the scaffold, weren't he? I'd have thought that carried a bit o' weight, wouldn't you, mistress? And now what wi' his ghost appearing an' all…'

Just then Captain Towneley's shadow fell across them. Bestowing a smile on him and a swish of curtsey to Rose, the maid flounced away without a scolding.

With Lizbeth tapping her foot across the yard, Rose guessed there would be no chance of a private conversation with her fellow agent. Besides, he seemed intent on making his bow to both of them. 'My lady,' he called out, 'I was wondering if you and Mistress Byrd would like to accompany me on a ride this afternoon.'

Lizbeth was too much in grief to flirt. 'Thank you, Captain, I am not in a riding vein today. It is for you to decide, Rose, but you have my leave.' Spoken with a pucker of lip before her ladyship headed for the stairs to change her ruff.

Towneley grinned. 'Heigh, the cage is open, Nightingale. Are you ripe for a flutter around?'

She didn't feel like fluttering. 'Lady Vere —'

'Oh, put Lady Vere in an infant walker and come along. Or pick her some daffodils on the way home. We could amble to New Park, frolic among the old ruins and count the cowslips or preferably ride down to Aughton, it's the other side of Ormskirk.'

'Aughton. How thrilling,' she answered dryly. Was this some errand the earl had given him? 'Why do you need my company to go there?'

'I don't want to terrify a little old woman. If I have you with me, Rose, you can frighten her instead. Or she may frighten both of us since she's a witch.'

'You don't mean the same old crone who cursed Ferdy on All Fools'?'

'No, not the same. The local magistrate has her in custody for questioning.'

'Then who is this Aughton woman?'

'A white witch, supposedly, since she calls herself a healer and supplies potions for rashes, warts, boils and, no doubt, broken fingernails and hearts.'

'Oh, one of the cunning folk.'

'Now will you agree to come along? Surely it would be a good opportunity to continue our exchange of intelligence?'

'I didn't know we had one, Captain.'

'Well, we do, so we shall. Mine about ghosts, yours about fairies.'

Truly hooked now, she took a deep breath, but before she could conjure up a witty retort, the dinner bell rang out.

'Have you sent a report to Wade yet?' she asked as they walked towards the house.

'Yes, Will Shakespeare has taken it.'

'Was that wise?' She was remembering Martin.

'Settle your feathers, my bird. Our playwright can defend himself, I assure you.'

'I think your news will be stale anyway.'

He halted. 'Enlighten me.'

'I know that Master Farington has already sent word to Sir Robert Cecil. The messenger rode out this morning.'

'Has he indeed? And how did you divine that?'

'I had a letter to send to my parents last evening and my lady told me to take it to Farington's office. No one was there but the door wasn't properly locked so I went in and I saw a letter addressed to Sir Robert. Unfortunately, it was already sealed.'

'And you left your letter with his?'

'Of course not. Do you think me stupid, sirrah?'

He looked relieved. 'And no one saw you?'

'No, and when I took my letter to Master Doughtie this morning, he was in an ill-temper and said a messenger had left at daybreak.'

'Ah, so Receiver-General Farington may be serving two masters. I tell you what, Rose, this place is a cursed spider's web. Trust no one.' He patted the back of her farthingale. 'Best you go in alone ahead of me. I'll meet you at the stables at one o'clock.'

'Pretty feather — should impress the most wicked of witches.' Towneley fell into step with Rose across to the stable. She felt her face glow; it wasn't just her high-brimmed hat he was noticing. Mind, if he thought they were going to find a grassy bed on the way back, he was very mistaken. Maybe she had misjudged him; a more serious expression slid across his face as they waited for the horses to be brought out.

'I want you to look at this.' He plucked a letter from beneath his belt. 'Farington's given me a message to deliver to the mayor on our way through Ormskirk. Is this the same writing that you saw on the letter to Cecil?'

'No.' The hand was neat, common, Italianate.

'Hmm,' he stowed it in his purse. 'Well, I saw him write this himself, which means someone else wrote the other one.'

'With Farington's connivance or at least awareness.'

'I fear you are right. Ah, here's your mare.' His hands fastened round her waist and with little effort, lifted her onto the side-saddle.

'I think we should take a groom, Captain.'

'For propriety, Mistress Byrd?' His tone turned frosty. 'Very well, if it pleases you.' He whistled back one of the grooms. 'Hey, Cropper, get yourself a mount and catch up with us! No haste. Tell Master Doughtie it is on my orders.'

She hazarded a smug smile as she rode out of the courtyard and her soul stretched in delight at the cloudless blue sky. It was heady to be out in the sunshine, a respite from the deep sorrow that hung over Lathom.

'Worried I was going to cudgel you into a ditch?' Towneley muttered. He'd spurred up to join her.

'Trust no one, you said.'

'I say a lot of things.'

They rode past the sheep in silence. Rose wondered if he was sulking. 'Could Ferdy be poisoned?' she asked eventually.

Her companion looked at her sharply. 'No, else he'd be with the angels by now — well, to my reckoning, that is.' An admission of doubt or unexpected modesty? 'It's not Colonel Sir William and company behind this if that's what you are wondering. They'd want him intact to pamper.'

'Haven't they done that now?'

'I'm not answering that, Nightingale.' He batted away a fly.

Rose wanted answers before the groom joined them. 'Tell me more about the ghost at Knowsley.'

'Perhaps you should ask John Golborne for his version. He was with the earl but he swears he never saw it.'

'Do *you* think it was the ghost of Hesketh?'

'His lordship thought so. Or he was hallucinating. Half asleep, half-awake — a time for what is real and what is false to be indistinguishable.'

'Those harlots — could one of them have been bribed to poison him?'

Towneley rubbed his chin thoughtfully. 'Possibly, but they were only there the first night.'

'If he takes powders to enhan—' Oh, devil take it, she shouldn't have said that.

His gaze narrowed. 'How do you —'

'Oh, good, here's Cropper,' she said and heeled the mare into a trot. The groom had almost caught up with them.

Towneley rode after her, grabbed the mare's bridle and said softly, 'Wade ordered you to please the earl in any way you can. Did you?'

It would have been brittle to play ignorant, and dishonest to torment him, but she was angry.

'Yes, he did, but I didn't. Satisfied?' If Towneley had laughed, she'd have slapped him, but he took a deep breath, a smile dimpling his cheeks once more, and loosed his hold. 'That's good news, Nightingale. Keep to that. My orders.'

He was impossible. 'You, Captain Towneley, can stuff your orders — with ribbons on!'

'Race you to Ormskirk, Nightingale,' he called out to her rigid back and galloped past.

The hamlet of Aughton lay a quarter of an hour by horseback south from Ormskirk. A small alehouse called The Ring O' Bells presided at a fork in the road, opposite a gentle rise to a windblown church. The sandstone steeple looked rather uncomfortable, a coffin-size piece of canvas was roped over the chancel end of the roof and the grass around the graves needed a hearty scythe.

Towneley flipped a coin to Cropper. 'Mind the horses and buy yourself an ale. Mistress Byrd and I will meet you at the church gate at the next hour bell.'

'Don't tell me we are getting wed,' teased Rose as she followed him into the churchyard.

'Well, we can, but they'll have to read the banns and we may find that my great-aunt who was an abbess and your great-grandsire who was a pardoner met during a pilgrimage together and she had twins and ... ah, vicar, there you are!'

Rose almost squealed as an irritated man with straggly grey hair clambered from one of the graves. He shook his white surplice like a bedsheet before brushing the dirt from his palms.

'Good morrow,' Towneley exclaimed cheerfully. 'Trying to convert Beelzebub? Is it a long way down?'

The man snorted. 'Not that's it your business, sirrah, but the sexton reckoned he heard a bell ringing from the coffin.' Fierce blue eyes assessed them. 'And, aye, I don't marry strangers. I'll expect letters from your parish priests and then you'll need to attend regularly.'

'Reverend…?'

'Nutter.'

Rose pleated her lips and turned to inspect the nearest gravestone.

'We are seeking the village wise woman,' Towneley explained.

The rector's eyes narrowed. 'Daughter of Satan!' he muttered.

'We understand she does some healing.'

'Healing!' the reverend sneered. 'Is that what you call it now in the south, sirrah?' His gaze dropped to Rose's stomach. 'I beg you, mistress, go full term with the babe and I will baptise it for you.'

Rose nodded valiantly. 'I will do so, I swear, but I still would like to visit the healer.'

A bony finger pointed. 'Third cottage down the lane and may God have mercy on your souls.'

'Do you think he will have us arrested as adulterers?' whispered Rose as they left the churchyard.

'Quite likely. Tell me, are we having a boy or a girl?'

'You may jest but they could whip us round the parish. Is he still watching?'

He glanced back. 'Yes, though I'd wager half his congregation are recusants. He's filthy-tempered, his church needs patching, and the parishioners aren't coughing up. Ah, third cottage, this must be it. Faugh!'

Fresh dung peppered a well-tended garden, fenced with brushwood. A rosemary bush by the gate had already recovered from the winter and this year's seedlings were anxiously sticking their heads out of the earth along the path.

'Here's a familiar of the Devil.' As though it heard, a lolling Manx cat raised his head at their coming and idly licked a paw before coming to arch his back against Rose's skirts. Towneley knocked.

'I'm busy! Come back later!'

Unlatching the front door, Towneley led Rose into a room that could have passed for an apothecary's shop with its line of drying herbs hung beneath the beams and the tiers of shelves supporting a regiment of jars. Below these was a sideboard untidy with phials and a higgledy-piggledy collection of rocks and crystals, which included a translucent, smooth-sided quartz as long as a woman's ring finger. The air smelled pleasantly of herbs and the smoked bacon hanging below the chimney. In the heart of the room upon a well-scrubbed table stood a pair of scales with a row of tiny drawstring bags lined up at the side. And behind the table was the mistress of the phials — not the madwoman who had cursed Ferdy, but a woman well into her fifties. A fat braid of hair, the hue of snow, hung over one shoulder, prompting Rose to hope her own hair would acquire such a colour if she lived that long, instead of her mother's dull Spelman grey.

'I said *I'm busy*!' Eyes of a vivid Saxon blue looked up, glared.

'Yes, you did, and good day to you.' Towneley introduced himself with a lift of hat. 'Mistress Jane, is it? Lady Derby spoke well of you.'

Rose gave him a sharp look. Really? However, the insertion of the noble name worked. The woman sighed and set down the pot. 'What does my lady need now, sir? Are them megrims back? I'd dare not give her another dose in her present state.'

Whether a witch or not, this ancient had common sense.

Towneley cleared his throat. 'No, good mother, it's not her ladyship but my humble self who needs your help. May I?' He removed a second cat from a large wooden chest beneath the window and gestured to Rose to sit down. 'This is my betrothed, Mistress Byrd, and we are soon to wed. It's just that I have a problem with my ... my virility,' he added, with a don't-you-dare warning at Rose not to laugh.

'What, a brawny lad like you?'

'To be frank, the problem is keeping my yard up and to the purpose, and this gentlewoman and I should like to have sons.'

'And daughters,' Rose corrected firmly. The cat sprung up onto her lap and circled.

'*Children*,' Towneley conceded. He straightened a jar of dried toadstools and turned, with a sheepish grin. 'So, what can you offer?'

Although the white witch gravely inspected his codpiece, it was his funds Rose suspected she was estimating. 'If you are looking for summat cheap then an infusion of wormwood is your best choice, though beware you do not take it when you are like to be in your cups for the twain don't mix well. Give you bad dreams.'

'Wormwood grows anywhere.' Rose met Towneley's glance. 'As does belladonna,' she added softly.

'What about monkshood?' he exclaimed, lifting down a jar. 'Do you ever give this?'

'Aye, young man, as I might arsenic, it's to kill rats not men. Pray put it back.' Chewing her lip, the she was still estimating his worth. 'Hmm, there's a plant that comes from the east if expense is no problem. Goatsweed, men call it here. I can order it up from London, an' if there be a shipment in, you can have it within a sennight.'

Towneley scratched his head and looked down at Rose. 'Maybe we need to —'

'Ha, knew it!' barked the healer. 'I can tell when I'm being gulled. Come to the nub, the pair o' you! If it is a babe you want to be rid of, mistress, then seek elsewhere! I'm a healer an' though yon priest may call me a witch, I abides the law.'

'Ah,' murmured Towneley, bestowing a wicked grin on Rose. Not for the first time, her heart did a swift little dance.

'I think you'd better leave.' The woman brushed her palms with a loud slap. '*Now!*'

'A wisewoman indeed.' Rose set the purring cat aside and stood to face Jane. 'Enough of this taradiddle,' she declared briskly. 'There's no babe, good soul, but we do need your help. Pray, can you tell us if you have made up any potions of wormwood, this goatsweed or, well, anything else for anyone at Lathom House in the last month or so?'

'Because we've been told you have,' joined in Towneley, 'and the person it was given to is very sick.'

'We are not talking about her ladyship,' Rose added.

'Nor are we here to accuse you,' Towneley confirmed, idly rolling an onyx crystal on his palm. 'But we need to know what was in the potion. What did you give that caused hallucinations and then vomiting?'

'I … I don't remember. My great age, see.'

'Do you not keep a book?' Rose countered, casting around for sight of a ledger.

'Sometimes I do, sometimes I don't. My customers rely on me to keep their confidences.'

'Yes, we can understand that, but it is important, no, *vital*, that you help us.'

'I'm not sure that I can, mistress.' The evasiveness was understandable but annoying. 'Maybe you should talk with Thomas Hesketh up at Rufford, sir. He and my Lord Burghley's gardener correspond about all manner of plants.'

Burghley and a Hesketh? That was interesting.

'I thought the entire Hesketh family were Papists,' Towneley muttered, more to Rose than to the old woman.

'Oh, not the Rufford Heskeths, your worship. They pipe to whatever the tune is playing in Westminster, though it's said they can hide a priest up their chimney. Now be gone with you. Go and get Master Thomas' advice an' not waste time wi' an ignorant old besom like me!'

While the knowledge that Lord Burghley corresponded with Ferdinando's neighbours uncapped all manner of speculation, Rose could see that Jane had cleverly shifted their sights away from her. 'You haven't answered our question, good soul,' she pointed out, sending a look to Towneley that harder persuasion was needed.

'What about witchcraft, Mistress Jane?' he asked, straightening to his full height and ripping aside his mask of courtesy. His menacing tone would have frosted windowpanes. It worked. Rose saw her own astonishment mirrored in the older woman's eyes.

'No, I … I never meddle,' the healer asserted, anxiously looking to Rose for sisterly support. 'Besides, whatever evil goes out comes back twofold.'

Towneley leaned across the table. 'But is it possible for a man to die from curses?'

Jane stuck her chin up, refusing to be cowed. 'Why, yes, sir, if the victim believes himself damned. Curses are like seeds of evil planted in a man's mind, they can grow to destroy all logic, aye, an' stay with a soul beyond the grave through many lifetimes.'

Towneley straightened, swallowing back either argument or shock, and Rose took over. 'Mistress Jane, we need your word that this will not go beyond these walls, but it is Lord Derby we are talking about. He's really been very sick since he took your potion.'

'His lordship? The new earl?' The woman's jaw dropped. 'Be hanged for that!' she exclaimed indignantly. 'Why I'd — I'd give it to a child.'

'I do not follow —'

'See, mistress, I tell him it's for virility, save it's just powdered grass seed. His lordship's a young sprig yet, and he doesn't need my help even if he thinks he does.'

That certainly surprised them. 'What? You mean you charge him for an aphrodisiac but you give him something harmless?' spluttered Towneley.

'Aye, but don't you go tellin' him. I charge him for my time, see. Though I don't like the sound of this. Someone must have interfered with the powder or maybe his fine lordship took summat else instead. An' bear in mind,' she continued, 'that this vomiting of which you speak could be natural, a malady o' his belly or other innards.'

'That's what we are trying to discover,' sighed Rose. 'His physicians reckon excess exertion.'

'Let me get this clear, woman,' growled Towneley. 'You deal directly with the earl?'

'Course not, lad, though I knew him an' all his brothers before any of 'em was even breeched. Taught his mother, Lady Margaret, a thing or two as well.'

Towneley exchanged a glance with Rose. 'Who fetches the potions?'

'Always the same gentleman. Dark-haired, handsome but a mite surly, knows everything about horses. Master D—'

'Doughtie,' Rose and Towneley exclaimed in unison.

'Aye, that's the one,' Jane chortled. 'That's the knave. Dick Doughtie!'

'You cannot have Doughtie arrested, can you?' Rose assumed. Towneley was striding ahead like a grumpy demigod armed with thunderbolts.

'Your pardon?' The icicle tone should have unnerved her but she felt defiant as she joined him at the gate.

'The meeting in the woods.'

'Oh that,' he said coldly.

'Whatever Doughtie planned, you were part of it, too.'

'Rose, this is not a good time… Oh, hell!'

'Wait!' Old Jane caught up with them before they could follow the curl of churchyard wall. 'Master, you should speak to Bartholomew Hesketh about curses. Mayhap his worship put the wind up some o' your fine folk. You'll find him at New Hall, Uplitherland, west o' Ormskirk, but you can ride across the fields towards the Devil's Wall, flat all the way, see.' A bony finger pointed towards an open gate and a track stretching across a cow meadow to a break in the hedgerow. 'Don't tell Master Hesketh I sent you,' she added, turning back homewards. 'I don't like dealing with lawyers, an' watch them big dogs!'

Towneley drew Rose's arm firmly through his. 'Doughtie won't know what hit him when I get back. Let's find Cropper and be on our way.'

'Wait, Garrett,' Rose exclaimed, hanging back. 'Hesketh! Bartholomew Hesketh!'

'It's not an incantation, Nightingale. The district is infested with damn Heskeths. Throw a stick and you'll hit one.'

She tugged free. 'No, listen, we should speak with him.'

'Whatever for? The old woman just wants us off her scent.'

'Please. He's the brother of the man who was hanged. I insist we visit him.'

'You do, do you?'

'Yes, I do.'

'Then I hope you like big dogs.'

English farm gates were rarely in a direct line so it took more than crow logic to negotiate the patchwork of fields, let alone the mud around the gate posts and the variety of latches. Because Cropper had overindulged at the Aughton inn, the chore of opening the various obstacles fell to Towneley. 'You'd be on bread and water for the rest of the week if you were one of my men, lad!' he snarled at the groom. 'It's a blessed wonder you can stay in the saddle.'

Eventually they came out onto a lane and taking the chance of turning westward, found themselves following a high brick wall for some way before they glimpsed the upper storey of a half-timbered mansion.

'This must be the place,' Rose exclaimed. 'Cropper can wait with the horses.'

'If he realises there are horses to wait with. Common sense is telling me this is a mistake, Rose. Look at Hesketh's blessed wall. There's a message here and it isn't friendly. We can't just go bounding in there like cheerful puppies.'

'*I* can,' she said grandly, looking along the laneway to the great wooden gates. 'And shall!'

'What haven't you told me?' he demanded, reluctantly riding after her.

'I think we are equal on that score,' she retorted and set the watchdogs a-barking with a tug of the gate bell.

It wasn't just mastiffs guarding Bartholomew Hesketh; once Towneley had persuaded a surly servant to leash the beasts, and escort them through to the front door, they were confronted by a scold of a wife. The wide black skirts might not have needed much bolstering but the woman's humour did; stony blue eyes glared at them above milky freckled cheeks. The curt rise and fall of a pectoral cross indicated there might be a heart within the black-clad bosom; otherwise, it was hard to tell. Worse still, three broad-chested young men flanked the harridan's elbows. A trio of ginger-haired malevolence.

'I am an acquaintance of your husband,' Rose announced stoutly, trying to ignore the collective loathing. Beside her, Towneley lifted his cap with lukewarm deference.

'A fine day, Mistress Hesketh,' he said, 'and we are not here to steal your silver spoons, although you may search this lady's farthingale on the way out.'

'We have no truck wi' Southerners.' The biggest youth spat to punctuate the sentiment.

'Been damaged, have you, sirrah?' Towneley was observing the large gash that blemished his forehead. 'Recent by the look of it. Did I inflict that?'

The remark banished the leers that had been directed at Rose and four sets of eyes skewed poisonously towards Towneley.

'Bring 'em in, Mither.' Rose recognised Bartholomew Hesketh as he stepped into their midst with the air of a man used to slapping his palm on troubled water. He was much older than his wife and sturdier than Rose remembered, clean shaven this time and understandably healthier of complexion than when they had previously met; a man who could put his hand to a plough as well as an indictment. She introduced herself and Towneley and mentioned St Albans.

'I'm not sure why you are here,' he said frankly, ordering his wife to bring refreshment as he ushered them into his study.

His religious loyalty was defiantly displayed: a silver pyx and a finely wrought crucifix stood atop a carpeted cupboard, the Virgin Mary's statuette beamed open-handed in a wall niche, and a Roman Bible, with margins of Latin instruction, lay open on the bookstand.

Hesketh had been working. A pile of law books flanked a half-written letter on his writing table. Papists were forbidden to venture more than five miles from their dwelling; Rose wondered whether that restricted his legal practice.

'We are guests at Lathom House, Master Hesketh.' She felt he should know.

'I wish you joy.' The sour reply was not encouraging but before she could spur the awkward conversation onto an easier path, Towneley took the reins.

'Who's the knave with the head wound?'

'My son Gabriel. He's broken no law.'

Towneley languidly ran a finger along the cupboard edge. 'He's broken Lord Derby's peace of mind.'

Hesketh shrugged. 'I am glad of it, sir. I owe Ferdinando Stanley no favours.'

'Then you haven't heard the worst, Master Hesketh.' Towneley stopped the pretence of distraction and turned. 'The earl is grievous ill and likely to die. Cursed, I'd say.'

It was as though he had slid an invisible weapon into their host's gut for Hesketh grunted, put a hand to his belt and sat down as though afflicted just as his wife came in with two meagre glasses of sack and a beaker of weak fluid, that Rose guessed was meant for her.

'What in God's name is going on here?' demanded Mistress Hesketh.

'Leave us, Meg!'

'The Lord God strike me dead if I will. I demand to —'

'It's a personal matter, wife. Go!' He winced as the door slammed behind her. 'I'll be paying for that later. Now you'd better tell me about this … illness.'

Rose watched the lawyer's face while Towneley told him of the events of the previous week: the old woman on the road, the players, the hallucinations and the mysterious illness.

'Do you truly believe he will die?' Hesketh asked.

'For sure,' Towneley answered with such conviction that Rose's inner consternation matched their host's expression. For a long moment, the lawyer sat thinking and then he leaned back in his chair. 'You're good at arithmetic, Captain Towneley, except that this time three and three do not make six.'

'Then tell me what does, your honour.'

A silence as they eyed each other. Hesketh took a swallow of sack, grimaced, and set down his glass. 'The players and dove are down to me.'

The dove! Rose gasped.

'I'm sorry, my dear. How could I know it was my good Samaritan from St Alban's who accompanied Burghley's granddaughter to Lathom?' He rose. 'The witch players were my son and nephews. I desired to cause trouble while Lady Vere was staying — yes, to embarrass and discomfort Ferdinando Stanley — but the rest that you speak of, no, that was not my doing.'

'For God's sake!' Rose sprang to her feet. 'My servant was killed, Master Hesketh. Was it on your orders?'

Hesketh looked genuinely confused. 'Do you mean the man who was attacked near Adam Goosebrook's farm last week, he was your servant? No, Mistress Byrd, that's naught to do with me or the lads. As for his lordship's malady, acquit me of that. I swear I have never sought his death, though I shall never forgive him for my brother's.'

Rose sat down again with a grim sigh. Believing in the sincerity of his confession meant Martin's murderer was still at liberty.

'Is there anyone else you can think of who would harm his lordship, Hesketh?' That brought Rose up sharp. Why was Towneley asking when all the evidence was jabbing its finger at Master Doughtie? If Doughtie had tampered with the powder, could he also have murdered Martin?

'Oh, I could list plenty.' Hesketh gave a tight smile. 'The King of Scots? Lord Burghley and that son of his?' Rose was stunned. The suggestions were surely meant as a jest, but Towneley wasn't laughing. *The Cecils?* She blinked. 'Of course, it is my family that carry the greatest grudge. He had my brother hanged and gutted.'

'Captain Towneley was present that day,' Rose offered in a quiet voice.

An angry snort from Towneley. 'And what about Colonel Stanley in the Spanish Netherlands, Hesketh? He sent your brother to his lordship.'

'Ah, yes, a leader who inspires others but takes no risk himself.'

'Could Stanley be seeking revenge, do you reckon? Your brother was his follower.'

'A long shot, Captain.'

'Do *you* follow him?'

'Let me say this. I do not support his ugly threats against the queen and I certainly do not want to see Ferdinando Stanley wear her crown.'

Towneley prowled and turned. 'Are you acquainted with my lord's Master of Horse?'

'The younger Doughtie lad? Aye, we've met once or twice. We attended the same Mass at Easter. He makes no secret of his faith. Nor do I.' He leaned forward. 'Oh, but you suspect him as well, do you? I forget we Papists are to blame for everything, failing crops, cattle murrain, mould on turnips, the French disease!'

Towneley ignored the sarcasm. 'Sir, I merely wish to discover if this malady of his lordship is derived from, well, too much exertion, as his doctors suggest, or from evil.'

'Evil? Now there's a broad term.' Clasping his fingers beneath his chin, the lawyer smiled. 'Now I think on it, Towneley, there have been strangers in town of late. Strangers like yourself. I'll make inquiries, shall I?'

'Aye, if it pleases you,' Towneley replied stiffly. He halted behind Rose's stool and clasped her pouched shoulders in husbandly fashion. 'I need to return this lady back to Lathom,' he said pleasantly. 'Thank you for your frankness, Hesketh.'

As he saw them out through the hall, there was a satisfied tilt to the lawyer's lips as though his case had won a pleasing verdict. He escorted them past the hostile stares of his wife and kinsmen, right to the gate. 'Upon my brother's soul,' he told them as they parted, 'my interference was to create mischief, nothing more.'

'I will accept that,' Towneley answered. 'However, you may have unfortunately started something for which there is no healing.'

Hesketh shook his head. 'I, Captain? If anything started, it was in November in St Albans.'

'Did someone scribble a subtext between the lines of that dialogue?' Rose asked Towneley as they rode east towards the lane that skirted south of Ormskirk. His preoccupation was curious.

'Not to my reckoning, Nightingale.' His horse increased pace.

Evasive wretch! Somehow, she'd winkle the answers from his stubborn shell. Leaving Cropper a couple of horse lengths behind, she kneed Cloud forward to catch up. 'Do you believe Master Hesketh was telling the truth?'

'Yes. For the moment.'

'And what did he mean by "strangers" in town? Was Frayn involved?'

'Peace, Rose, or we'll never get back for supper.'

'Is Master Doughtie behind the rest of the mischief, then?'

'Questions, questions.' With a sigh, he slowed to ride at her stirrup. 'Nightingale, if the powder from Jane was harmless, then the physicians are probably right and Ferdy just needs rest.'

'But you told Hesketh that he'd been poisoned.'

'I exaggerated.' So, he had been playing Hesketh like a fish. And her, too. 'Ferdy will recover, you'll see.'

'You still haven't told me what else happened on the hunt.'

'I thought I had.' His hand reached out to touch her cheek and his face sported a teasing gallantry. 'That was good work today.'

Knave! He was trying to distract her again. Had they been alone, she sensed he would have drawn close and kissed her. What's more, she might have let him, but it was needful to rein aside before she drowned in that intense, amused gaze. Besides, young Cropper was watching them with a lugubrious, happy smile.

'What's wrong?' Towneley asked her.

'Trust might be a good thing,' she muttered.

Nothing made sense. She had no clarity about why Martin had been attacked, and wraiths and visions were all very well, but why wouldn't Towneley explain the conversation in the stable and tell her the identity of the third man. As for Hesketh's allegation that Lord Burghley —

'Spur up!' The jolt shook her as Towneley gave her horse a slap on the rump. 'We're being followed.'

She glanced back. Three horsemen were in sight, their broad-brimmed hats hiding their faces, and something sinister in the way the riders leant forward told her to be very afraid. Perched side-saddle, she had not a hope of outpacing them and as they drew close, she saw they were masked.

'Save yourself,' she pleaded to Towneley, but he drew his rapier and reined his horse round to face their pursuers. 'Flee, Rose! Cropper, take her!' But the wretched groom was too inebriated to swat a fly.

The horsemen divided. Two of them rode at Towneley. The third punched Cropper in the jaw and his panicked pony fled with him slumped askew, his boots snared in the stirrups. When the ruffian came at Rose, she struck out in defence. Poor Cloud reared. With both her heels on one side, unable to grip, Rose was thrown against the prickly blackthorn hedge and tumbled down hard on her left shoulder into the burgeoning nettles. As if the shock was not enough, the attacker was beside her in an instant. His arm trapped her beneath her chin but before he could press a blade to her throat, Rose jabbed her fingers into his eyes. He howled but kept hold and pressed the upper blade of his sword against her throat.

'Dismount or I'll use this!' he bawled at Towneley. 'Dismoun—' His shriek as Rose drove the bodkin into his ribcage gave Towneley the diversion he needed to disarm and wound one of his assailants. It wasn't enough. The pommel of her assailant's blade drove up beneath her jaw, jarring every bone in her head.

Towneley surrendered. They seized his rapier and forced him to dismount. A blow in the guts drove him staggering back, another brought him to his knees, then a punch on the jaw sent him sprawling onto the road.

'You filthy cowards,' Rose yelled, certain it was the Heskeths. 'I'll see you damned.'

'Will you now?' jeered the wounded horseman as he drove his boot into Towneley's curled body. 'Take the woman behind the hedge, shall we?'

'Enough!' The order came from the ruffian who had punched Towneley. He mounted, circled his horse round their prostrate victim and spat. 'Got the message, have you, soldier?'

The lout gripping Rose let her go. 'Next time,' he promised.

As their attackers spurred back towards New Hall, Rose struggled painfully to her feet. The horses had sensibly fled, Cropper had not returned, and there was no other traveller in sight to help them. She stumbled across to Towneley and fell on her knees beside him. Blood was trickling from his cut lip and there were ripening bruises on his cheekbone and jaw. Thank God there were no bleeding wounds.

'Oh, Garrett, I'm so sorry.'

'Sodding, bloody… Did they take my rapier?'

'In the ditch, I think. I can't believe that Hesketh would send—'

'It was the ruddy wife, I'll wager!' He was eyeing the nearby gate as he clambered to his feet. 'Help me over there.'

They staggered across the cow-trampled earth. Grabbing hold of the wooden bar with one arm, Towneley fumbled into his doublet, drew out a flask and unstoppered it with his teeth. 'Your help, please.' With her good hand, she held it to his lips and tipped. 'That's better,' he muttered, straightening. 'Christ! You're as pale as a snowdrop, Nightingale. Take some, too.'

The liquor blasted a warmth through her body, but her shoulder was screaming with every breath. 'Oh, Garrett, we must report them.'

'To what purpose, Nightingale? It will change nothing. At least, thanks to you, two of the mysteries are solved.' Then his expression changed. 'Is your shoulder out, Rose?'

'I ... I don't know.'

'Let me feel.' She gave a hiss as his surviving finger and thumb felt her shoulder bone. 'No, you'll live. Pity, I can't show off my battlefield skills. A chirugeon taught me.' He leaned forward and kissed her. 'Brave lass.'

The effort cost him. His face creased with pain. 'Your pardon. Aftermath of battle.'

She smiled. 'Soldiers kiss?'

'Just the pretty ones.'

The big, bruised puzzle of a man. He had stopped fighting lest she be injured and every place he was aching was because of her and she could see the bruises forming on a face she wanted to frame with her hands and —

'Would you try whistling for the horses.'

He attempted to laugh at her astonished expression; it hurt too much.

'*Whistle?*' Raindrops, she realised, were half-heartedly tilting the nearby leaves.

She moistened her lips but her effort hardly crossed the laneway.

'Lordy, you're hopeless, Rose.' Propping himself against the gate, he put two fingers to his mouth. A fine effort. It not only brought back Cropper's pony and its bleary rider but Towneley's steed with Cloud trotting demurely behind. They all looked rather ashamed and Towneley's black horse began nuzzling an apology. 'You'd be horsemeat in Antwerp, you coward,' he told it affectionately as he stroked its head, then he turned to Rose.

His own injuries compelled him to let Cropper lift her onto his steed and then he used the lad's help to mount behind her. She was sure each jolt was agony. Then, as though the Almighty wished to belabour them further, the rain became earnest.

It could have been an opportunity to enjoy Towneley's arms around her except her shoulders were getting drenched, her side ached, and disillusionment was discomforting her soul. Lathom had become a sinister stage and it was not one of Shakespeare's plays of past kingmaking but real and now.

'Hell!' Towneley finally broke the silence as they sighted Lathom. Plenty of wheels and hoofs had churned the track since they had left that morning.

'Is there ill news?' he demanded bluntly, reining in as the porter touched his cap to them.

'Nay, sir, but word has spread that his lordship has taken to his bed. Owes a lot of money, he does, an' with him being out of favour with Her Majesty an' all, people are wondering if they are going to be paid — and it ain't just merchant folk, neither!'

Fumbling in his pouch, Towneley tossed the man a coin for his honesty. 'Here be the vultures come to peck Ferdinando's liver,' he muttered to Rose as they reached the stable yard.

There were more people than at Easter. The local nobility had come calling, judging by the coaches drawn up and the fine horses being walked. Several merchants were in a cluster on the steps to the house and their tone sounded most aggrieved.

Cropper, soaked and soberer, helped Rose dismount but his offer to Towneley was received with a curse, followed by payment and the strict order to keep a still tongue as the soldier slid from the saddle unaided. 'I'm not reporting the attack, Rose. It was just a warning.' *All in a day's work for Her Majesty's agent?* she wondered. The wretch was grinning at her sodden hair. Her hat was long gone. 'You look like a starling hit by a cartwheel. Get yourself into the warm, hmm?' He wiped a raindrop from her cheek.

Distracting her again? 'But how are you going to explain —'

'Nightingale.' It was a warning to keep quiet.

'Don't you Nightingale me! Oh, Master Wainwright, good morrow.'

The head groom might be checking the healing of Cloud's fetlock, but he was eyeing the soldier's darkening jaw and Rose's muddy apparel.

'Trust me, Rose!' Towneley whispered. 'Now go!'

Pah! She left him to lie about his bruises.

In her dishevelled condition, she avoided the merchants untidying the steps and walked round to the rear courtyard. Going in the servants' entrance would inevitably create speculation, but she hoped the unembroidered truth would suffice: her horse had thrown her.

The scullions, however, had other business, and it was not with the sides of oxen waiting for the cleavers or the fowls lined up for threading onto the spit. Instead, the kitcheners were in a tense huddle outside the Clerk of the Kitchen's office listening to the raised voices within. Rose had almost traversed the kitchen when the door crashed open and a furious man, a farmer by his garb, stormed out, followed by two others. 'You've not heard the last of this,' he bawled back, brandishing a paper. 'We'll speak with my lord not his pet ape.'

'No, no, come back!' shouted Master Johnson, the head cook, hastening out after them. He received an upturned finger and halted on the threshold of his office with a defeated look.

'I haven't been paid for two months either,' exclaimed one of his underlings, stepping forward.

'No, nor I.'

'Nor I,' the rest clamoured, crowding round him.

'You're not starving, are you?' Johnson retorted. 'Take your complaints to the Clerk o' the Kitchen when he next bothers to show his face, an' don't blame me. Have you taken up the platters for my lady's guests? Get on with it!' Then he saw Rose. 'Ah, Mistress Byrd! Her ladyship was asking for you.'

He was using her as an excuse to escape more complaints, she thought at first, but there was genuine concern in his face as he halted, blocking her with his ample girth from the common view. 'Mistress, your arm, your clothing, you haven't been —'

'No,' she declared firmly. 'My horse threw me.'

'Then you'd best see my lord's chirurgeon when he's free.'

'Thank you, I will. Do you know if Lord Derby is any better?' she asked, since he insisted on escorting her.

'Well, I'm told he managed to keep down a broth o' rhubarb and manna this morning, so, God willing, it'll shift whatever mischief's been harming his belly and once that has been voided, he may begin to mend.'

'Amen to that.'

He halted. 'Pray you, mistress, are they saying upstairs that it's my fault?'

'No,' she said kindly. 'Not at all.'

'We have strict rules, mistress. Only I prepare his lordship's meat an' we have no truck with beggars or suchlike coming anywhere the house.'

'Of course, no one is blaming you. Now, forgive me, I am very sore and damp.'

He did not persist. 'Then I hope you have taken no lasting hurt and mistress, may I advise you to take the back stairs an' avoid the gallery. My lady is fending off the fine folk of Lancashire.' Then he added more to himself, 'Now she knows what I have to deal with. Good day to you, Mistress Byrd.'

16

Garrett commanded Cropper to keep a lid on the afternoon's dealings and instinct told him that Rose would keep a still tongue. She'd be thinking about her sore shoulder and a sleeve that needed repairs. If not, well, that was a bridge he'd cross if need be. Meantime, a certain Papist needed to be cornered. He hobbled across to Dick Doughtie's office but the Master of Horse was absent. If he had not felt so sore, he would have looked through the man's papers. Grimacing with discomfort, he grabbed a jar of horse liniment from the shelf and rubbed it over his chest and belly. Feeling more comfortable, if pungent, he finally ran his quarry to earth in the sleeping quarters that Doughtie shared with Secretary Smythe.

The Master of Horse was on his knees beside his mattress and it was evident from the scatter of coins on the blanket that he was not praying. A small strongbox stood open beside him, a yawning saddlebag neighboured his other thigh, and his forehead, normally pale, was sweating as if it was midsummer.

'God's wounds, Towneley!' Irritable at the intrusion, Doughtie's eyes widened at his visitor's bruises. 'You choose your friends well.'

'I've just come back from Aughton,' Garrett announced coldly. 'You could have saved me that trouble, Dick.'

'Aughton?'

Ignoring the pretence of puzzled brow, Garrett closed the door. His stare took in the monastic bareness above the bed. There was no crucifix on the whitewashed wall; a lonely hook and a vertical smudge of cobweb hinted there had been. 'Packing, are you?'

'No,' Doughtie climbed to his feet, brushing his palms upon his slops. 'Looking for something, that's all.'

Garrett waited for the silence between them to do its work.

Edgy already, Doughtie's jaw eventually clenched. 'Questioned the old witch, did you? I suppose she blamed me.'

'It's looking that way.'

'You know that's ludicrous.' Somehow, the defensive snort fell short.

'Ludicrous but not impossible, Dick, so convince me that you can shine up pure and sparkly because Mother Jane says she didn't give you an aphrodisiac for the earl. She never has.'

'Why, the lying cow! She —'

'She says his lordship has no need of any potions and what she's been selling you wouldn't serve a lusty flea. You might as well have been buying dust. I think the process is called "fleecing" or maybe there's a local word.'

'You mean...' Open-mouthed and turning redder than a cockerel's wattle, Doughtie managed outrage. 'Holy Mother of God!' he exclaimed, as Garrett's stern face unsettled him further. 'No, wait, the old bitch is just trying to shift the blame. You surely don't believe her?'

'Yes, Dick, I do. So, what *did* you give his lordship?'

'Damn you, you bastard!'

But before Doughtie could spring at him, Garrett's rapier point was hovering at his breast. 'My lord's far from dying, God be praised, so let's keep cool heads, shall we, Dick. I asked a question which you have yet to answer.'

'What, confess I poisoned him? Is that what you are after? Whose side are you on?' Spittle flew from his angry words.

'*Did you?*'

'By the living God, no! Why would I?'

'True.' A half-hearted concession. Garrett's bruises were aching but sitting down on the bed would lose him the advantage. Sheathing his blade and with a sigh to calm the younger man, he proceeded with a quiet voice, 'Have you seen my lord today? Is he any better?'

Doughtie's ruffled feathers were yet to settle. 'About time you asked!'

'And?'

'Still heaving up. Worse since noon. The doctor from Chester gave him an infusion, but it's only increased the pain.'

'And what about the glister last night?'

'It helped. A little.'

Garrett took a deep breath. 'He should be getting better by now.' He rubbed a hand across his upper lip, thinking hard. 'Look, for hypothesis, let's suppose a substance was given to my lord at the hunting lodge either deliberately or by error.' His swift rise of hand stifled interruption. 'Let me finish! If the powder from the healer was harmless and you are still bleating innocent, what else could be affecting him?'

The younger man kicked at the saddlepack. 'If I'm so ruddy gormless, ask Master Sawbones and Doctor Glister.'

The knock at the door hushed them. Doughtie strode across. 'Can you come back later?' he muttered at someone.

'This won't keep, young'un.' Master Johnson, the head cook, stuck his large foot across the threshold. He pushed past, looking quite distraught for a man of his breadth, only to find he had a witness. 'Oh, Captain Towneley! Perhaps, I should —'

'You're in now,' growled Doughtie. 'So, what's the matter?'

Dragging his gaze from Garrett's bruised chin, Johnson recalled his errand. 'I need you to send word to your brother in Leverpole seein' he's Clerk of the Kitchen. With his lordship ill, I'm being plagued for payment as though it's my fault, and not just by the townsmen, neither; none of us downstairs have been paid this last quarter. We want our wages.'

'My brother paid you at Yuletide out of his own coffers.'

'Aye, I know, Dick, but we're now past Lady Day. What if God takes his lordship from us, where are we then?'

'Do not even think it!' Doughtie crossed himself. 'Listen, I'll send to my brother first thing tomorrow, though how much good it will do since his lordship is already fathoms deep in debt to Michael already. You must realise I haven't been paid either.'

Johnson threw up his hands in despair and turned to Garrett. 'I'm sorry you should hear this, your worship, you bein' his lordship's friend. I'd best get back to work.'

Garrett straightened. 'No, wait, good master. I'd appreciate your opinion. We were discussing whether his lordship's malady could be down to some human error.'

'Not mine!' asserted Johnson, hackles rising. 'I alone prepare his lordship's platters, same as I did for his father before him, an' there's always a food taster.'

'Did you prepare any of the victuals for the hunt?'

'Only his lordship was affected and remember the meat was cooked on the fire before our eyes,' snapped Doughtie.

'But is there anything that could have got mixed in by mistake, Master Johnson?' Garrett persisted. 'Seeing as it's April, I assume we can discount toadstools.'

The head cook snorted. 'Savin' your pardon, your worship, but you're talkin' like a city lad. What about death cap?'

'Death cap!' Doughtie rolled his gaze heavenwards. 'Who'd make that mistake?'

'Aye, Dick,' agreed Johnson, 'most folk in these parts know the difference. What I'm saying, though, Captain, is that while we might gather it in the autumn, death cap retains its poison even when it's been boiled or roasted, dried and mortared, an' it makes your liver and kidneys slowly decompose so you take a week or more to die.'

Garrett whistled in surprise. 'But wouldn't the powder have a bitter taste?'

'Folk say the contrary.'

'And you are sure it could not be gathered in error?'

'No, no, Captain, it's greenish and white-gilled.' Master Johnson held up a finger. 'Has a skirt on the stem, here, an' grows from a sort of collar. See, we know our business so don't you go blamin' me or any of my people because his lordship's sick, God help him! Anyroad, can't waste more time blatherin'. Dick, you write to your brother. As for you, Captain, I'd be considering arsenic. Plenty in the stables.'

'And what do you say to that, Dick?' Garrett swung round on Doughtie as the door closed behind Johnson. Arsenic was on his list of possibilities and, yes, accessible, since it was commonly used before horse sales to enhance a beast's colour and lustre.

'I say damn you!' snarled the Master of Horse, further incensed. 'Anyone could give it in small doses over weeks or days without raising suspicion. Go question the laundry women. They use it for stains on velvet and suchlike. Christ! You can point the finger at anyone in the whole ruddy household.'

'I know.' Wincing at the tenderness of his bruises, Garrett sat down wearily on Smythe's bed. Eventually he said, 'Help me get to the bottom of this. What if someone *tried* to poison his lordship and botched it — didn't give him enough?'

'I don't know. Maybe.' Doughtie sank down opposite and tugged out the *agnus dei* from within his shirt.

In the silence that followed, Garrett decided to acquit him because the 'why' seemed to be lacking. If someone wanted Ferdinando dead, the 'why' was everything.

Doughtie eventually raised his head. 'What about the servants who came with Lady Vere? The man who was killed? Maybe he meddled. Yes, and you know what, Amy, Lady Vere's maidservant, slept in the kitchens for a couple of nights. Think what mischief she may have done. She's come from Lord Burghley's household, so the Cecils could be behind this, and we know nothing of the companion, Mistress Byrd, save she is an old acquaintance of his lordship.'

'But the women weren't at the lodge,' Garrett pointed out, defending Rose.

'One of them could have poisoned the hampers here, and you've forgotten the harlots.'

Garrett fisted Smythe's bolster. Today had not brought the answers he had hoped for. Had the earl really been poisoned? He needed to see Ferdinando again, make his own judgement. 'Look,' he added, dragging a hand across his forehead, 'No more wild guesses. Let's admit our plans for the succession are at a standstill unless his lordship recovers.'

'You care, don't you?' observed Doughtie.

'Yes, I care. Ferdy's a good man and, future king or not, we need to keep him alive.' Garrett's body ached. He needed rest, but he'd promised to report on his visit to Aughton. 'Give me time to clean myself up and then let's see how he is for ourselves. Shall you come with me?'

'Yes, I will, but, Garrett, must you tell him what Old Jane said?'

Garrett sighed as he rose to his feet. His answer was stern: 'No, Dick, I think *you* must.'

*

Ferdinando's pallor had yellowed since yesterday. Gone was the vigorous lord of the hunt and in his place lay a shadow. Hour upon hour of retching and voiding — what mortal man could withstand that?

A poultice pancaked the earl's chest, and waiting on the bed steps was a stoppered glass jar of leeches — blood-hungry if their attempts to escape were any indication. Garrett moved the vessel aside and sat down, wishing he could give Ferdy some answers. He knew from his military service that an ounce of hope might turn the tide, help a sick man resist and fight the infection.

Standing beside him, Doughtie fidgeted uneasily because they had too great an audience: not just the three medical practitioners either. Giles Clothier was hovering, fussily tidying the bedclothes, while Farington and Golborne were murmuring over some ledger at his lordship's writing table. Garrett could almost smell the hostility from the Lathom men — the religious superiority directed at Doughtie. Maybe he should ask the earl for a private hearing except Ferdinando's energy was on ration and no doubt nosy old Farington would argue to stay.

'I'm still not letting them bleed me,' Ferdinando muttered. 'Letting out evil humours, pah! Well? What have you to tell me, the pair of you?'

'My lord, I've been speaking with the wisewoman at Aughton.'

'Have you indeed, Garrett! She treated you well, I see.' At least the earl's humour was healthy.

'I still have teeth.' His attempt to grin fell short as he ran fingertips across his sore jaw.

'And what did she have to say, my friend?'

Might as well include the whole room since they were listening anyway, he decided. 'Ferdy, I've heard that a man may suddenly develop an aversion to a substance even if he's been taking it for a while without harm.' Over by the fire, Dr Case nodded. 'That's why I went down to Aughton to see this woman, because I wanted to find out what was in the aphrodisiac she sold you. If it was different this time or whether the effect could be cumulative.'

'Wise thinking.' The sick man's tone grew hopeful. 'Was it?'

'No, my lord, but more about that in a moment. What I did discover today was that the dove in Lady Vere's close stool and the incident with the players were acts of mischief by the same man.' That had everyone's full attention. 'However, he swears that was all. Nothing else.'

'Who was the scoundrel?' barked old Farington, coming over to the bedside.

'Bart,' whispered Ferdinando. 'I wager it was Bart.'

'Was it?' the receiver-general demanded. 'Or that foul wife of his? Let's bring 'em in.'

'Wait!' gasped Ferdinando. 'You said there was more, Garrett. What of the potion?'

Garrett turned to Doughtie. 'Your cue.'

A drag of breath from his companion, then the stillness — the moment a storyteller knows he has his listeners in his palm.

'Apparently,' Doughtie cleared his throat. 'Apparently, I have been her gull.'

'That can't have been hard.' Contempt lit Farington's eyes.

'According to Towneley, the woman has confessed to selling us — *me* — nothing but ground-up grass seed. Oh, my lord...' He carried the earl's hand to his lips. 'I earnestly beg your pardon. I will pay the full cost, I swear.'

Ferdinando tried to laugh but his sides were too sore. 'Why, the cunning old besom,' he muttered, 'charging me a blessed fortune.' Then his gaze fastened sadly onto his Master of Horse. 'Is it you to blame, then? Did you tamper with it, Dick?'

That was unexpected. Garrett caught his breath.

'*No*, my lord, no!' Despite indignation weighting each word, the balance tipped against Doughtie. The chamber had become a courtroom and the jury had passed verdict.

Clothier sniffed; Golborne came to the foot of the bed exchanging a smug smile with Farington; and the doctors, gathered like crones around a cauldron, straightened at the hearth. The unspoken hiss of 'Papist' stank the air.

'*I did not tamper!*' Doughtie asserted forcefully. As he glared across the bed, his fingers sought his beads, hovered, did not touch, and if he was praying for absolution, it didn't come. Instead, Ferdinando began to retch. Bate rushed over with a basin. Canon and Case followed.

The agonizing spasms passed. Ferdinando fell back exhausted. 'Should have brought your pomander, Garrett,' he jested weakly.

The basin was removed, the noble lips dabbed. Flecks of blood from his sores dotted the cloth. With a curl of lip, the surgeon glanced speculatively at the leeches but it was not the time. The room was silent again; only the fire spoke as it savoured the logs.

At last, the earl's eyes flickered open and fresh suspicion trembled his lower lip. Perhaps he felt like a half-dead rabbit on the roadside with the crows about to peck. As another spasm threatened, his stare stumbled from face to face as though seeking a scapegoat. Doughtie's was the last he fixed upon. 'Get out, Dick!' he snarled, writhing in pain. '*Get out!*'

'My lord, I swear —'

Garrett rose swiftly, touched the shocked man's sleeve. 'Later,' he advised gently, urging him from the chamber.

Farington followed, filling the doorway with his broad, furred bulk. 'Later?' he sneered. 'There is no "later", Captain Towneley. As I see it, that was a dismissal. My lord no longer requires this knave's service.'

'That's how I saw it, too.' Golborne peered over the receiver-general's shoulder.

Garrett gave them both a scoffing look. 'Nonsense, that was the pain talking.'

The old man looked past him, his wrath was for Doughtie. 'Consider yourself dismissed, Master of Horse. Good day to you!' Farington elbowed Golborne back into the bedchamber and slammed the door in Doughtie's face.

'Jesu!' The Master of Horse would have pounded the boards if Garrett hadn't pulled him away. 'And what are you staring at?' the wretched man snarled at a page, cross-legged in the anteroom. The child's eyes were round as shillings; the news could spread as soon as a blink.

Opening his purse, Garrett said quickly, 'Breathe not a word and I'll double this tomorrow.' The child caught the penny and nodded.

Getting the furious young man down to his office was another labour entirely.

'See, see, I'm the whipping boy,' roared Doughtie. 'I knew it would be so. Because I'm a Papist.' Then he swallowed hard. 'Mercy, Jesu! What if he dies?'

'Hush, man. Keep moving!' But even Garrett was admitting that possibility at long last.

Befriending Doughtie had been necessary but risky. Now Garrett's priority was to protect Ferdinando's honour and stamp out any fires of suspicion. Meantime, he had one very panicky Papist to deal with.

'Oh God, oh God!' The Master of Horse was fumbling with a flint. 'Don't stand there catching flies. Help me light the blessed candle!'

'All right, give it here. What in hell...?' In astonishment, Garrett watched Doughtie clamber onto a stool and reach for a strongbox on the highest shelf.

'I need to burn these. Everything!' Unlocking the box, he shook the papery contents out onto the desk. Garrett caught a letter before it escaped to the floor.

'This is from your mother.'

'No matter.' Doughtie grabbed it from him and held it in the candle flame.

'Calm down!' Garrett gripped his wrist. 'Answer me! Are any of these from the Low Countries?'

'You think I'm a fool? Don't you understand those bastards upstairs will read treason in a bill for oats?'

Probably true.

'Then I'll fetch a sand pail before you burn the whole bloody place.'

Black flakes were piling up round the candlestick base when he returned with the pail. Doughtie, his face bitter, dropped a burning letter onto the sand and seized up another. 'My lord said he didn't care about my faith so long as I was loyal. And I am, Towneley, I am. Golborne was at the hunting lodge same as I, but, of course, he's a blessed Protestant.'

Protestant, maybe, but Golborne didn't fetch potions from witches. Garrett picked up an old monthly roll for the stables. His eyes might have been scanning the figure but he was thinking fast. If word leached out about the meeting in the woods... He reached a decision and restored the parchment to its curly state.

'Two things,' he said gravely. 'Firstly, you are right, Dick. If the earl dies, blame will fall on you. Secondly, I think he could die. By the look of him, his liver is failing. So, what are you going to do?'

The words hit home. 'By the Blessed Virgin!' wailed the Master of Horse. 'What if they send me to the Tower?' Doughtie pressed his fingers to his temples. 'I am going to have to leave. I won't let them blame me and stain my family's honour.'

'If you leave, it will look like guilt, but I think you should go, Dick. Now, while you still can.'

'Oh, Holy Mother of God, before dusk? Where?' Doughtie shook his head hopelessly. 'London, I suppose. Lose myself there until I can get ship to Flanders.'

'Let them think that,' Garrett muttered. It wasn't the first time he had thought through an escape from Lathom if matters became tricky. 'Listen, what you must do is flee to Ireland. Ride to the river mouth and find a fishing vessel to take you.'

'But they'll search the coast, surely?'

'Not if you were seen heading south to Warrington.'

'Sure, if I can split myself in two.'

'We just need to confuse them somehow. After all, it's still raining, an evening when a rider pulls his hat low and his cloak tight.'

'So?'

'It was my task as a child to get our chickens back in at night, but the rooster was the very devil. The only way to catch the blessed creature was to confuse it, grab from left, grab from right until it didn't know which way to run and then at last, I'd snare it. Let's treat the porter that way.' He flung an arm round Doughtie's shoulders. 'The plan is this. I am now going to ride on several errands in and out of the gate. The third time I will ride out in your gear east towards the Warrington road. You will follow in my hat and cloak and on the road we will exchange clothes and horses. Then I will ride back in your hat and cape before curfew. The porter will be so confused, he'll not know which of us is you.'

The distraught man pulled away. 'But what if Farington puts me under lock or tells the gate I may not pass?'

'Then we must make haste.'

'I can't just... I need to make things right with my brother.'

'I'll do that. In Leverpole, isn't he? Listen, my ribs ache and the last thing I need is to get back in the saddle, so let's ruddy well get on with it, shall we! I'll finish here. Go and bring only what you need. Ride light or the porter will notice.'

Doughtie's lost-boy look was suddenly replaced by suspicion. With a swift grab, he seized up his saddle knife. 'How come you can think all this up in an instant? I was blind not to realise. You're the poisoner!'

'I shall ignore that,' muttered Garrett, unbuckling his purse and taking a risk that he might get stabbed. 'If you'd fought the Irish, you'd be full of stratagems, too. Have you sufficient coin to see you right?' He was aware of the knife slowly lowered as he set several gold angels upon the table. 'Take this as a gift from the colonel.' And although the blade tip was still pointing his way, he picked up the pail and began to brush the burnt flakes into it. If Doughtie lunged, he'd use it as a weapon.

'Did you poison Ferdy?'

'No, Dick,' he said, busy with his task. 'As God is my witness, I'm going to try and save him!'

'Towneley.' Such despair was in that breath. Looking up, Garrett recognised the familiar flame of zealotry. Despite ugly betrayal by the man Doughtie wanted to be king, the temptation to martyrdom was gathering heat.

'Shouldn't I have the courage, the faith, to stand up to their accusations?'

'That's up to you, Dick. It also takes courage to leave, and faith to fight another day.'

Don't be a fool!

With relief, he watched the younger man's jaw slowly unclench, the decision made.

'The die is cast. I saw what he let them do to Richard Hesketh. You are right, it's time to leave.'

'It has been a horrid day. Master Shakespeare leaving without a farewell, Cloud throwing you and me having my hand kissed *ad nauseam*,' grumbled Lizbeth as she rubbed ointment into Rose's bruised shoulder at bedtime. 'All the local gentry were fawning and Alice was behaving like an empress. Pah, you should have heard her: "Oh, Mistress Pudding, do meet Lord Burghley's granddaughter, Lady Vere", and "Oh, Sir Bombast Ormskirk, here is Her Majesty's favourite maid-of-honour, Lord Oxford's daughter". I tell you, my dearest, Ferdy wasn't the only one in this house who felt sick. There, that should ease you!'

'Ah, much better,' Rose drew up the shoulder of her chemise. 'Do you suppose some of those people were the earl's creditors?'

Lizbeth shrugged. 'Very likely. That's why they were being feted with expensive sweetmeats and the best Rhenish — to allay their fears and staunch their whining. But two of them seemed genuine. Do you remember the friends of Ferdy's that were at the Easter dinner, Edward Scarisbrick and Humphrey Davenport? Mind, perhaps they are owed money as well.'

Rose thought back over the fine repasts of the last week. Nothing had been stinted and yet... 'Some of the servants here haven't received any wages for months.'

Lizbeth gave a snort. 'Sounds like my father's household. Believe me, if you're a lord, you're always in debt! The money's spent on court clothes and, well, God forbid if Her Majesty deigns to visit! Ferdy and Alice are fortunate that hasn't happened. Then, of course, there's inherited debt. Lady Compton reckons that Ferdy's hardly finished paying for his grandfather's costly funeral.'

'Oh dear, no wonder Ferdy needs the offices that the queen is withholding.'

'She knows blessed well he needs the money,' muttered Lizbeth. 'And, mark you, these were the offices he held when he was Lord Strange so she's being utterly vindictive.'

There could be other repercussions, Rose thought. If Ferdy was months behind with his servants' wages, it could become a real test of their loyalty to him. Huge debts would also leave him open to all sorts of offers. She thought back to the meeting in the stable.

'Rose?' Lizbeth waved a hand in front of her. 'You'd better lace back up. Alice did tell me she wants to speak with you. Go and see if she's still up.'

'Now, Lizbeth? Why didn't you say earlier?'

'Forgot. Don't keep her up too long. She was very testy after supper.'

Gritting her teeth, Rose slid her stomacher back on. If Lady Derby was feeling "testy", could it be her fault? The unpleasant thought that she might be berated for accompanying Towneley and asked to leave Lathom was a possibility, or perhaps

Doughtie had been locked up and she was about to be questioned about the white witch's testimony.

Lady Derby dismissed her maidservant to the outer chamber and received Rose in her bedchamber wearing a simple, fur-trimmed wrap. Her head was uncovered and her waist-length dark hair not yet plaited for the night. Without her ruff and broad, puffed sleeves, she sat at her writing table looking as round-shouldered and tired eyed as any weary copyist. Turning to Rose, she directed her to pour them both some strong canary and, propping her feet on a footstool, leaned back with a sigh.

'Master Towneley has spoken with my lord about your visit to Aughton,' she murmured, savouring a sip from the delicate crystal goblet. 'I am sorry to hear your horse threw you, Rose. I gather vagrants were responsible. Another matter for me to deal with.'

Vagrants! Was that Towneley's story? Rose did not argue.

'And the queen wants another muster for the army,' sighed Lady Derby, bringing a ringed hand down on the pile of documents. 'Oh, I am so weary of it all. Too many visitors and hangers-on today. To be expected, I suppose.' She sipped again and acknowledged Rose's nod of sympathy. 'Ah, I know this sounds heartless but Ferdy should have showed more sense. Letting himself get ill like this! He should have heeded what he was taking and not exerted himself so recklessly. Dr Case tells me this evening that his spleen is swollen and hard to the touch. Indeed, I am quite beside myself with what the future may hold for me and my girls if he succumbs to this wretched sickness. And Captain Towneley — why exactly he graces us with his presence, I am not sure, but Ferdy seems to want him here — anyway, he tells me that Mother Jane is unable to throw light on this malady. I should have thought she could since the physicians are so useless. What is your opinion?'

Prompted, Rose finally managed to slide a word in. 'The woman does not deny she has made potions for his lordship as she has for your ladyship, but she swears they were harmless unless someone tampered with them. She did suggest it could be witchcraft or some natural affliction.'

'How unhelpful. Well, I shall order the creature here to see for herself. I just cannot have Ferdy ailing like this. It is too tiresome.'

This was a side to the countess that Rose had not glimpsed before.

'There has been gossip, though, my lady,' she added, not mentioning Hesketh. 'People are saying that the dead dove and the witch-players were mischief commissioned to embarrass my lord in front of Lady Vere because she is Lord Burghley's granddaughter.'

Lady Derby gave it a moment's consideration. 'Oh, more than likely,' she snorted, forgetting what a fuss she had made. 'Such is Lancashire. Wait for the rumours and the dirt will float to the surface. Some Papist meddler, no doubt. And the lot of them are steeped in witchcraft like the hag who accosted my lord last week, but at least that is dealt with now. I received word from our magistrate, Sir Edward, who has her in custody. He questioned her this morning and while the creature could not fully repeat the Lord's Prayer, he says the rest of her answers were so demented and witless that he deems her curses are of little value.'

'That must be a relief to my lord.'

'It helps.' The countess rose, swept to the nearest window and stood for a moment watching the plump raindrops racing down the diamond panes. 'But evil is like mercury, it slithers and changes its shape when you try to catch it.'

Rose shivered. The bedchamber fire was throwing out scant heat and her shoulder was aching. She was about to murmur she should take her leave when the countess turned and began to pace.

'It is being treated with such ingratitude by the queen that tears at me so, just like it must have aggrieved your poor parents, Rose. But it's my lord's own fault, I told him he was being a fool to still be protecting that traitor Stanley's father and sons when Lord Burghley has several times requested they should be sent south for questioning. You can see how my lord's refusal could be misconstrued.' She refilled her goblet. 'I am opening my heart up to you, Rose, because your family has endured misery too, and I know you understand. Oh, if only a letter were to come from the queen restoring her favour, it might turn the tide.'

The tide of Ferdy's health or the tide of debtors? Rose pondered.

A deep sigh, then Alice lowered her voice to a bitter whisper. 'Her Majesty's suspicion is unjustified. Age must be addling her wits or else that serpent Essex is filling her ears with lies. As if Ferdy would ever rebel against the Crown. But, of course, his wretched mother is forever ranting that she is the rightful queen.' She halted, realising perhaps she had spoken rashly. 'There, I have unburdened myself and I hope you will not betray my confidence.'

'No, madam, I am honoured by your trust.' Was that why she had been summoned tonight, to listen and absolve? Or was there more?

Alice finally came to the point. 'I hope Lizbeth will write to her uncle and grandfather that there is no treason here.' A definite hint that Rose should use her influence.

'I'm sure she will, my lady.'

The countess nodded. They understood each other and for a moment silence was enough.

With her aching shoulder urging her to bed, Rose wearily hoped the audience was over but the countess seemed reluctant to dismiss her. Smoothing the silken folds upon her lap as though such touching might transfer the tension from her overwrought mind, Alice murmured, 'In the meantime, for the sake of his family, Ferdinando must get better.'

Rose could excuse such tepid compassion because Alice was under such stress, yet it made her wonder whether there was much affection left in the marriage.

'Madam, I pray that all your worst fears may seem like nothing in a few days' time and that God will restore his lordship's health.'

'Thank you, you are a dear girl, Rose, and I realise I have kept you from your slumber. I hope you have taken no perpetual hurt from your day's adventure.' The countess escorted her to the door and then with a clap of hands to her temples exclaimed, 'Your pardon! Wait! I have this for you.' Hastening back to the writing table, she picked up a letter.

For an unpleasant moment, Rose thought it might be the one she had given Martin, but a swift glance showed it was in her brother's hand and still firmly sealed. Thank God for that! Advice from Wade or news from her family? Either would please her.

'From my brother, madam.' Happier and much relieved, she left Lady Alice's apartment, only to give a gasp of shock as Golborne materialised from the shadows.

'Master Farington desires a word, if you please, Mistress Byrd.'

'Then he's out of fortune,' she exclaimed, wondering how long he had been lurking outside the countess's antechamber.

'Now, Mistress Byrd!' He set a compelling hand upon her elbow.

'This is untoward, Master Golborne.' She pointedly glanced back at the countess's door as she unfastened his fingers.

'The matter is important. I would not trouble you otherwise.' He *was* troubling her. In the light of the candleholder in his other hand, his chill blue eyes told her there was no refusal. 'I insist, Mistress Byrd.' His hand was on her shoulder now. It was his power that she felt — that she sensed he wanted her to feel — and it had a sinister quality, so different to Towneley's.

At least he was urging her towards the dining hall and she knew the receiver-general's office lay just beyond. With relief, Rose saw Farington's stout wife standing ahead in an arc of light from her husband's office, but there was no courteous greeting and when Golborne ushered her inside, Master Farington did not rise from his chair and Rose found herself standing before his desk like a wayward daughter. No, worse than that, Rose felt outnumbered, on trial.

The receiver-general deliberately carried on writing without looking up. 'Where were you this afternoon, Mistress Byrd?'

Showing her displeasure, Rose glared disdainfully at all of them. 'I have been to Aughton. Captain Towneley wished to inquire into the potion that was given to my lord. He felt the wisewoman would be more comfortable with his questioning if a gentlewoman was present and he asked Lady Vere and I to accompany him.'

'And was it, mistress?'

'Was what, Master Farington?'

'Was your presence enough to encourage an admission?'

'I think you should ask him. Now, if you are done —' But her way was blocked by his wife.

'I am not done, Mistress Byrd,' the receiver-general stated coldly. 'You will seek permission in future.'

Permission! There was an ugliness in this. They wanted her afraid. 'And why should I do that?' she asked, haughty serenity providing her armour.

He set his quill back in its pot and leaned back. 'My wife and I are at pains to support her ladyship when the burdens on her may blind her to others' self-interest. To come to the point, young woman, it may be advisable for you to make some excuse to leave Lathom.'

'Are you ordering me to leave, sir?'

Farington's small eyes fixed on her like a frog relishing a mealtime fly. 'We realise this incident of your servant's death has been distressing for you but we are informed he was a Papist. Papists are not allowed to leave their parish. You broke the law by bringing him here, putting Lady Vere at risk. Moreover, you neglected to inform us of the fellow's leaning. You are aware, of course, that last year a Papist traitor threatened to kill my lord.'

The pompous upstart! This was unbelievable.

'What faith do you follow, Mistress Byrd?' asked Golborne.

'You have seen me attend chapel.'

'*Attend* can mean presence without commitment,' uttered Farington. 'We have to ensure the welfare of Lord Burghley's granddaughter.'

'Then pray ask Lady Vere if she trusts me.' She directed a cold look at Golborne. 'So, you think I am a recusant?'

'Indeed, we do,' Farington replied. 'Especially as his lordship is now possessed with an inexplicable malady. And there is this.' He took a paper from beneath a book on the table. Dear God! It was her letter to Wade, unsealed now, the one Martin had carried.

'Where did you come by that?' she demanded. 'Have you found Martin's killer?'

His ringed hand tapped the letter. 'Explain it!'

'No, sir! No, I shall not.' Oh, dear God, these fools thought she was a Papist agent. 'It is none of your business.'

'Whatever touches Lord Derby is our business and it is obvious that you have been reporting on him.'

'Your pardon, but I take it you have never gone birdnesting, Master Farington.' Before he could splutter a reply, she added, 'Birds fascinate my brother, you see. He wanted me to observe which are most common in Lancashire and whether there are any unfamiliar to him. The hooded crow is supposed to be in greater numbers but I haven't seen any. They have pale grey bellies and rump but are mostly black.' She frowned. 'Aren't you interested?'

Golborne gave her a slow, sceptical handclap. 'The lady tries hard, Master Farington.'

Oh yes, and she could try further, but that would mean admitting she was Wade's intelligencer. 'I could tell you a great deal more about dark plumage,' she said sweetly.

'Enough of that.' Old Farington steepled his fingers. 'Lady Vere tells us that you were living at St Albans last winter.'

'Yes and so were all my neighbours. It doesn't make us Papists.'

He brought his palms down flat upon the table. 'We are not getting answers, Mistress Byrd.'

'Nor am I! How did you get possession of that letter, Master Farington?' An ugly rear of logic. 'By heaven, did *you* order my man to be waylaid?'

He nodded. 'Unfortunately, your servant resisted the command to empty his pockets.'

Rose was speechless. Farington was responsible? 'And, of course, you told the truth to the coroner?' she said with poisonous sweetness.

'He didn't ask, Mistress Byrd. In fact, he declared it was one less traitor in the kingdom. And speaking of treason...' Her letter was pushed towards her. 'Who were you reporting to? Is this Francis Davison a Jesuit?'

They wanted to see her shake like a fearful penitent but they didn't know her, didn't know who she really was, and the irony of his question would have been amusing if it had not been ripping open old wounds: the memory of her father exhausted after facing another day at the Star Chamber, forced to endure the accusations and interrogations when the verdict was already decided.

'We are waiting, Mistress Byrd.'

'Be hanged to you, you murderers! It is none of your blessed business!' She swung round to leave. 'Get out of my way, woman!'

'Not before you answer us,' asserted Mistress Farington, too vast to push past.

Rose turned back to face the men. She didn't want to play her ace except these people might go to any lengths. 'You have no idea, have you, of who you are dealing with?' she taunted, with every inch of pride she could muster. 'I am the daughter of William Davison, the queen's secretary, the man who obtained her signature on Mary Stuart's death warrant! Is that Protestant enough for you?' The astonishment in their faces appeased her beyond measure. 'So how dare you have the temerity to —'

'And where is he now?' That was from Golborne.

She stared at him perplexed. 'At home.'

'No longer trusted. No longer Her Majesty's secretary.' A masculine fold of arms to disconcert her further.

'He is not well.'

'Nor like to work again, I assume. Your father was sent to the Tower. Maybe you resent his unfair punishment. Maybe you have been turned.'

'And maybe your mother cuckolded your father to conceive you, Master Golborne!' Rose countered. It was degrading to speak ungraciously but she was furious.

Goading further, her accusers looked down their noses at her lapse of manners. 'You may go,' Farington decreed, taking up his quill once more, 'but we shall be watching you. This illness of his lordship has only manifested since you arrived in Lathom.'

'That's not true,' she exclaimed defiantly. 'He was in good spirits until three days ago and he and I are old friends.'

'*Old friends.*' Mistress Farington made it a calumny. 'Lady Derby will be delighted to hear that. Is that why you came here, to slither yourself back into his trust?'

Rose looked at her appalled. Everything was being twisted, wrung, to yield ill-meaning. 'I see now that you are all so fixed in your opinions that nothing I say is given credence. I came at Lady Vere's invitation and with the permission of Sir Robert Cecil. Write and ask him.'

'Oh, be sure we shall, Mistress Byrd,' Farington told her. 'In the meantime, if his lordship's health fails to improve, we shall seek out those responsible.'

'After all,' Golborne murmured, 'poison can be administered by a woman's hand.'

Rose slammed her fists against her skirt. 'Or anyone's, John Golborne. Even yours! Maybe the ghost was not a ghost!'

Hatred like she had never seen gleamed fiercely in his cold blue eyes as Mistress Farington grabbed her arm and pulled her out.

'You look like Her Majesty in a bad mood, about to let fly at someone.' Lizbeth's voice was muffled by the bed sheets. The candles, left burning either side the bed, were almost stubs.

'Yes.' Rose realised her fists were still clenched.

'Tears?' Her friend sat up. 'And you look frozen. I thought you would have been back an age ago. Is there some dispute between you and Alice?'

'Not with her, no.' Rose muttered, hastily wiping away angry tears and stepping out of her skirt and petticoats. She checked Amy was fast asleep on the truckle bed before she added in an angry whisper, 'I've just been accused of trying to poison Ferdy.'

'What!' Lizbeth sat up, all levity gone, and there was almost a hint of her stately grandfather in her expression. 'You of all people? Whoever said that? Not Cousin Alice?'

Pulling angrily at the laces of her bodice Rose sat down on the bed and exclaimed, 'No, thank God. It was both the Faringtons and Golborne. Just now. They told me they had my man Martin waylaid and when he resisted being searched, he was "unfortunately" killed.'

Lizbeth cursed like a stable boy. 'They should be made to account for it.'

'Some chance, with Ferdy so ill. What's more, they think I'm a Papist agent.'

'You?' Lizbeth clapped a hand to her mouth.

'It's not amusing. I suppose they are looking for someone to blame because they failed to protect their master.'

Her friend's face sobered. 'Presumptuous upstarts. I hope you told them so.'

'I told them who my father was. You know what, they sneered at me. Sneered!' She wriggled down between the sheets.

'Pah, as if you would harm a fly. You were not even at Knowsley.' Lizbeth toed the hot brick to her and they lay for a few minutes in silence before Rose fisted the coverlet.

'Get some sleep,' chided Lizbeth. 'You're only worsening matters by seething.'

Despite the warmth oozing slowly into her soles and hearing her friend's breath grow even, fury proved a restive bedfellow. Lordy! She'd forgotten Wade's letter. The flame on her side of the bed was close to sputtering as she retrieved the paper from the tangle of her clothes. Maybe this could give her the direction she so needed.

The script was entirely in Francis's hand and while the first part contained cheerful news of her family, Wade must have dictated the final more sinister paragraph:

Your betrothed has not been in communication with our family of late and we are wondering if he has met with an unfortunate fate or broken off the engagement, so consider yourself forewarned, dear sister, if our next letter brings news of his demise.

Surely Towneley had been reporting? But then the Devil made her start to question her faith in him. Could he have been turned? After all, he had admitted working for the Papists in Antwerp and she had witnessed his acting ability. Of those that had attended the earl on the hunt, he was the only stranger.

What if he was the poisoner? It made dreadful sense.

17

'Wake up, sleepy head!'

Lizbeth's voice was too insistent and the wretch was dinging a beaker with a spoon. Rose opened one eye. Her friend was already ruffed and farthingaled. The air smelt of honey possets; Amy had been down to the kitchens.

'There's news!' Lizbeth handed Rose her drink and mouthed, 'You are off the hook.'

'Hook?' Rose echoed sluggishly, then the unpleasantness of last evening flooded back.

'Amy says they've found out that Dick Doughtie poisoned Lord Derby.' Behind her, the maidservant nodded. Rose cupped her hands around the beaker, feeling an immense sense of relief. Had Towneley denounced him? But then she recalled the horror, the hanging at St Alban's; Richard Hesketh's bitter face still haunted her. 'Is he in custody, then?' She set the cup aside and swung her feet onto the bed steps.

'Lord, no, that's the whole point, addlepate. He's fled so it just confirms his guilt, doesn't it? Did you know he's an ardent Papist though the rest of his family are Protestant? Grandfather says you can never trust anyone who has been turned.'

'He made no secret of his faith.' Rose picked up her wrap and raised her eyes to Lizbeth's disparaging face.

'It's a shame. The young man was —' Noting Rose's raised eyebrow, she added sheepishly, 'rather comely, but not as much as Sha...' She trailed off and flounced away from the bed.

Rose looked round at Amy. 'When did Master Doughtie leave?'

'No one quite knows, Mistress Byrd, but his horse was missin' this morning. Master Wainwright reported it an' that Master Scarisbrick, what stayed overnight, has sent word to the sheriff and offered a reward, see, so every able jack o' the menfolk has gone riding off like a pack o' bounty hunters. Only Master Farington is left on account of 'is gout and he's complainin' like a cow wi it's calf taken.'

'Sounds like life in the kitchens will be rather a challenge,' murmured Lizbeth, her composure regained.

Rose did not answer. Had Towneley gone on the manhunt, or had he also fled?

Presented by a trickle of pages and the two grumpy women who had been pilfered from the laundry, breakfast was cold, late and lumpy, conjecture was rife, no one wanted to eat in case more food had been poisoned and the dining hall looked as though plague had ravaged Lathom and taken all the men. All except Farington, who heaved himself in and with his usual pomposity announced that Doughtie would soon be taken; lookouts were being posted at the major bridges, as well as proclamations pasted on church doors and guild halls.

Rose could hear the distant bells. From Formby to Leverpole, Preston to Warrington, the whole shire was being alerted: horns blown, alarm bells rung. By late morning, the household heard that the Sheriff of Lancashire had ordered a search of the houses of leading recusants. Trapdoors to attics and cellars would be flung open and all known hiding holes exposed.

Rose, her feelings still raw from the previous evening, felt vulnerable with Towneley gone, vulnerable to accusations of collaboration. Any desire she had acquired for him needed to be locked into a casket, and the latter must be jettisoned along with the key.

At least Farington had not accused her of working with Doughtie, but — her hand froze as she raised her cup of morning ale — he still might.

While Garrett had been away on the manhunt, someone had gone through his belongings in the Eagle Tower. The thread he had wound about the buckle tongue of his satchel had been disturbed. Well, a pox on whoever it was! He owned nothing that betrayed any allegiance. Anyway, after two uncomfortable days in the saddle, poking his nose into the hovels along the coast and plaguing the fishermen of Leverpole, he was too cursed weary to think. He tugged off his boots and threw himself down fully clothed on his mattress. The main thing was that Dick Doughtie had escaped, a trimmed explanation had been given privily to the Protestant older brother and Ferdy was still alive. He'd see him in the morning.

Before he fell asleep, he wondered if Mistress Byrd had missed him and then he was aware of nothing else past midnight until someone slapped his face. It wasn't a woman. The lantern showed Giles Clothier.

'What in hell?'

'We've found a wax image under his lordship's bed. Master Halsall thought you —'

'Pissin' hell!'

His language provoked a sheepish correction. 'Well, *I* thought that you…'

'All right, the answer's yes, friend. I'll be there.' He joined Clothier on the landing and hastened down to the passageway that linked the keep with its later relatives.

Ferdinando's bedchamber looked more like an angry council assembly than a sickroom. A pale-faced Lady Derby was sitting on the bed holding her husband's hand; Farington, in a dressing wrap and wearing something that might have been sent from Persia on his head, stood behind her; the doctors were in a row like the three wise monkeys; the secretaries were in nightcaps and shirts, and Chaplain Leigh was wearing the expression of a flagellant who hadn't drawn enough blood.

'What's *he* doing here?' snarled Farington.

Garrett ignored the insult and hastened to the bed. 'My lord?'

Ferdinando was wide awake, his blue eyes stark against skin that was yellower and more blotched than two days earlier.

'It's happening again,' he said through cracked lips, and Lady Derby gave a sob.

'All right.' Garrett swung around and marched into the circle of arguing men, using his bulk as a stifler between them. 'Where's this wax thingamy then?'

Golborne, his fair hair ruffled for a change, jerked his chin at Halsall. 'Ask him! Though why it is any of your business —'

'The ruddy fool threw it on the fire,' complained Smythe.

Garrett rolled his eyes in disbelief. 'Why?'

Halsall, lurking red-faced by the wall, looked about to wet himself. 'I thought, well, that burning the abomination would destroy the cursed witch who made it.'

'Dolt!' hissed Farington. 'I cannot believe how stupid —'

'You found it where?' Garrett asked Halsall.

'No, he did.'

Garrett's gaze moved to pinion Smythe.

'It was under the bed, Towneley. I was holding up the coverlet as Bate put back the chamber pot. That's when I saw it.'

'How big?' A few inches separated Garrett's palms.

'No, bigger, now less, yes, about so. There were hairs resembling my lord's pressed into the belly above the genitals and the belly was spotted with pits, dirt ground into them.'

'How very pleasant.' He deliberately let his gaze examine their faces. Was the maker of the monstrosity in the room? 'Anything else?'

'Isn't that enough?' Farington snapped and received a reproving look from Lady Derby.

'The thing wasn't there at suppertime.' Clothier looked round condemningly. 'Any of you could have done this.' That provoked a hubbub worthy of a Tyburn crowd greeting the condemned man's cart.

Had the Hesketh family been meddling again? Garrett cast a pitying glance at the frail man on the bed. 'His lordship was getting better two days ago. Planting this image is like mining beneath the walls of his morale but it's not going to work, is it, my lord?'

'By the Blessed Christ! How can you say that?' demanded Golborne in a fierce whisper. 'Halsall, the bloody numbskull, *burned* it.'

'That doesn't matter, Master Golborne. See, whoever created the thing is playing with here.' He tapped his temple. 'It only causes havoc if you let it. Isn't that right, my lord?'

'Yes,' gasped the earl, his fingers tightening round his lady's hand.

Disbelief simmered in the others but Garrett persisted. It was like addressing men before a battle. You needed to convince them they'd live to see the sun come up tomorrow. Ferdinando had to believe the image had no power.

'Now how about you all go and start creating snores, gentlemen? Let's see — you, you and you can stay.' That included Clothier, Dr Case and Chaplain Leigh. 'With my lady's permission, of course,' he added, facing off Farington.

'With mine,' asserted the earl, trying to sit up with a burst of authority. 'I'm appointing you the new Master of Horse.' He sank back exhausted.

Garrett drew a breath. That was a surprise.

'But —' spluttered Farington, only to be silenced by the adamant finger lift on the coverlet. 'Well, I have to say your father, the late earl, had far more sense,' he snarled and left.

'Well, well, Captain, *veni, vidi, vici*,' quoted Golborne sweetly and with a bow to the earl and countess, he followed the receiver-general out.

As the room emptied, Garrett drew Dr Case and Chaplain Leigh aside. 'Once my lord's asleep, I think you should do that bell-rattling and candle stuff.'

'*An exorcism*?' Leigh's thumbs patted against his surplice.

'Yes, Chaplain, just to be sure. Tell his lordship afterwards. Let him believe it worked.'

'It might help.' Case's agreement, however, was at odds with the sad gaze he directed towards his emaciated patient. 'I think we need the Lord Christ himself to rebuff the evil lurking in this place.'

Garrett crossed himself. 'Unless we can find it first.'

'Blow my stocks off with a cannon, if it isn't a nightingale fluttering in to visit a poor sparrow.' A quick glance outside to make sure snarly old Wainwright was not watching, then Garrett closed the door. 'Well, behold my new kingdom as Master of Horse!' he invited, dusting off his seat for her. 'And what can I provide for you, my sweet lady, besides bone-setting and saddles?'

'The truth.' If she was trying to look growly, it wasn't working for him.

'Ah, official, is it? And I was hoping you had come to see if my bruises had faded.'

She picked up the jar of liniment. 'This works with horses.'

'So do spurs, but I've always found a friendly pat gets a better result.' He saw her swallow back a crabby answer and glance away at the floor. Did she see the tiny black flakes that had evaded the broom? 'No pats then?' he asked quickly.

'I thought you had fled with Doughtie.'

'There's trust for you. Well, now we have that out of the way perhaps we can reassemble what facts there are. I suppose you have heard there's been more witchcraft?'

'Of course. The household is buzzing like an overturned hive,' she conceded and at last sat down. 'Lady Derby has sent to Aughton for Jane. It's a pity the image was destroyed because she might have been able to discern whether it was a real witch that sent it or just someone adding to Ferdy's woes.'

'Ha! The dark craftwork of Lancashire!'

'Or is it the Heskeths meddling again?'

'That's possible.' He noted she was giving the open ledger, which he'd salvaged from Doughtie's bonfire, a covert perusal. He'd better not underestimate her. 'What is curious with this latest mischief, Rose, is why?' He began to circle the office, tapping his fingers one by one. 'The poison seems to work, someone else gets the blame, all is going to plan but then the sick man starts to recover and...'

She turned, following his progress. 'But he's already been cursed so this is a cruel reminder —'

'Calculated to terrify him to death,' he finished for her.

'Well, there are plenty of rivals who want him dead, Captain. Maybe there is a second murderer in the shadows' — spoken with irony — 'and a wax image is easily made.'

By anyone. Rose was also Wade's agent. He mustn't forget that.

'Well, God give Dr Case and his fellow leeches enlightenment!' he exclaimed. 'Now, tell me, how fares your shoulder?' He watched her slide her hand across her breast and turn her head. So simple a gesture but so seductive.

It was a long time since he had plucked off a sweet little ruff and kissed a woman's perfumed neck. Not that he would dare to attempt it now but Rose Byrd was making a delicious assault on his senses. Rein in, lad!

'The bruises have gone, thank you. Listen, there's something else.'

'What, life here is not all basins and bedpans, then?'

Receiving her sharp-edged glare, he added sheepishly, 'Your pardon. Is there anything else I can do to bring about your relief?'

'You can sit down, be serious and hear me out!'

He obeyed, his thoughts about her attractions set aside as she began to describe the harassment by Golborne and Farington and what she had been told about Martin.

'Jesu, Rose!' he muttered. This would need some chewing over.

She was looking less tense. Perhaps the Papist practice of confession had merit, he decided. In the old days, absolution offered reconciliation with God and enabled self-forgiveness (at least so he gathered). People wanted reassurance, safety. Rose wanted it now.

'Garrett, what shall I do? When people are afraid for their own skin, they believe false witnesses and lies. I could be boiled to death in a Lancaster cauldron if Ferdy dies.'

'I can see you're tempted to come clean to Farington about being Wade's agent, eh? Not wise, my bird. He'll go straight to Lady Derby with that morsel.'

'I suppose so, and I'd not blame Alice if she accused me of poisoning Ferdy on the Wade's orders.' The tears came at last. 'Dear God, how did I let myself become entangled so?'

He instinctively drew her to her feet and, holding her against his chest, let her sob. 'Persuade Lady Vere that you should both leave Lathom,' he suggested. Holding her by the forearms, he took a step back. 'Doughtie deemed it best though he claimed he wasn't guilty.'

He watched her eyes widen. 'You helped him,' she accused.

'Yes,' he admitted. 'I seem to be the cauldron of advice.' She had lips that needed kissing. It was wise to let go of her. 'I observe you wear no jesses, Nightingale, so make some good excuse to Lady Derby and fly south while you can.'

'And if I don't?' Was she testing whether he would — or could — safeguard her?

'Ah.' That opened Pandora's ruddy box. If his standing at Lathom was only dependent on Ferdinando's survival, they might both be vulnerable. Of course, Rose might be a she-wolf disguised as a tangled ewe. If he were accused, would she give testimony against him?

'A lot of thinking is going on in that head of yours, Nightingale. Are you going to share it?'

'I was wondering if the other man has fled?' she asked.

'Pardon?'

'The man you and Dick Doughtie met with in the stable. Did it happen — whatever it was that you had planned?'

He rubbed a hand slowly across his chin. 'Nothing is the sum of it. I mean it, Rose. That's all you need to know. *Nothing.*'

'Is that what you will report to Wade?' she snapped, and before he could parry that attack, she charged in with: 'But what about Frayn or whatever his name is?'

'Gone back to his Papist coven. At least, I damned well hope so. Forget! That's an order.'

'If I'm supposed to assist you…'

'Enough, sweetheart.' God's death, he sounded patronising. Hearing the anger as she drew breath, he quickly said, 'I'm thinking there's a pattern in all this.'

'What do you mean?'

He prowled again, and halted, swinging round to her. 'I was missing something just now. You and I have agreed it's remarkable that the instant Ferdy's health and morale begin to improve, someone kicks him in the ba— belly again. Someone in the household.' Encouraged by her nod, he continued. 'See, Rose, as we both realise, it doesn't have to be a witch who made that image but perhaps just an ill-wisher, a bystander. You'd call the earl intelligent, even cynical, and I reckon the same could be said of you, Rose, but when the candles are out…'

'Yes,' she agreed, remembering Lady Derby standing at her window, 'we believe our greatest fears. So you think someone is fuelling Ferdy's belief that he is cursed, that he cannot recover?'

'Exactly. Someone who doesn't want him to claim the crown if the queen dies.'

Rose was looking up at him. 'I think I know who it is.'

'Wait!' He checked outside the door and then turned. 'Tell me.'

'Garrett, when I lost my temper with Golborne and implied that the apparition at Knowsley had been a nonsense, he looked daggers at me. Do you think that Golborne could have...'

They smiled at one another.

Bullseye!

At least he had a plan now. If he could prove that Hesketh's ghost had been some trickery by Golborne, maybe the earl would start to mend again. Somehow, he had to counter Ferdy's terror. Knowsley Woods might provide the answer. It would mean a fast gallop if he set off within the hour, except it would be impossible to return before nightfall, and time was not on the earl's side.

'I need to search that lodge before dark,' he told her, grabbing his saddlebag from the wall hook. Mind, he might find nothing at Knowsley.

'Ask my lady for leave, first,' Rose warned. 'One Master of Horse has fled already, presumed guilty. They may think the same of you.'

'True, but I don't want Golborne alerted.'

'Then tell Alice you are going to look for evidence of poison to convict Doughtie.'

Wise counsel.

He smiled. 'Flit quickly to her, clever Nightingale, and ask if she will see me.'

The antechamber to Ferdinando's rooms was like ruddy Cheapside, too blessed public for Garrett's peace of mind, but Lady Derby had summoned him to attend her here. Pacing to and fro, he could see the candle wicks burning lower along the windowless passageway. How much longer? He was on the point of leaving without permission when her ladyship finally emerged from the bedchamber with, curse it, Golborne at her heels. Good that she cut to the core but concerning that she spoke so loudly.

'Mistress Byrd has informed me of your suspicions, Captain. I have mentioned your intention to my lord and it has cheered him. You have permission. Here!'

He accepted the short letter of authority, his thanks a polite murmur and his thoughts a shrill descant of misgivings. Now the whole household would hear of his purpose, and if it was Golborne stoking Ferdinando's fear of bewitchment, the fellow must be ruddy angry at this interference.

It was gratifying to find Rose waiting for him in the courtyard. One of the palace dogs was bringing something for her to throw.

'Lady Derby has agreed, then?'

'Yes, Nightingale.' He ignored the stick, shiny with saliva, that had been dropped before his boot. His fellow intelligencer looked like she might be coming down with a head cold. Her nose was pink (mind, that could be the chill wind) and the rims of her eyes matched. Maybe someone had said something to upset her but he did not have time to ask. His main concern was would she be safe?

'Keep your head down, Nightingale. I'll send word when I'm back.' He reached out but she flinched. It wasn't that he had been going to embrace her without her leave, more like a grateful clasp. 'Farewell then.'

Despite the urgency, some instinct, guilt probably, made him stop off at Lathom Chapel. He was not of strong faith yet he bowed his knee at the back of the nave — just a one-line prayer since daylight made no concessions to the devout —

before he resumed his journey.

Doubt rode pillion with him. Was this journey a wasted effort? A courtier like Ferdinando could have rotted his innards with plentiful carousing, and a diseased liver could lead to both a swollen spleen and my lord's noble kidneys waving a white flag over the battlements.

If the malady was God's decision, he shouldn't need to feel so plaguey guilty about not safeguarding Ferdy, so why was he trying to pit his wits against Heaven? Most of the men in his regiment had believed that nothing happened by chance. If you were a soldier hit by a musket ball or a merchant collapsing with chest pain, it wasn't bad luck or incompetence, it was all down to the Almighty trying to teach you a lesson or deciding your time was up. Not that that made much sense. Did the Lord God notify Master Death that at noon an aged trader in Ormskirk must die of apoplexy or arrange that a bloody cannonball must hit you when you were next in a battle?

A murrain on that! Over the years, what Garrett had learned — if anything — was that the world was full of greedy, conniving bastards who didn't share any plans with the Almighty. Ergo, conspiracy existed! Plenty of people from Holyrood to Greenwich wanted Ferdinando removed from the succession. Which made finding the truth vital. Even though he might never get paid for finding the answer, he spurred his horse to a gallop.

South of Aughton, a party of soldiers heading north in a blessed hurry forced him to rein into a ditch. Apart from that inconvenience, avoiding an overturned wagon that had lost its wheel and then a half dozen ragged vagrants, he made good speed to Knowsley.

Built as a royal lodge to entertain King Henry VII, Knowsley Hall boasted a more concise grandeur then Lathom but Garrett wasn't there to admire the masonry. The steward in charge proved a miserable stiffneck who only changed his whistle when he read Lady Derby's instructions to provide lodging and all assistance. Generous of her, Garrett conceded gratefully, as he set off with the key for the hunting lodge.

Approaching the latter from the Knowsley hamlet proved easier than going through the woods from the north and provided him with an hour before dusk to sniff around. Plentiful hoofprints, wheel marks and dung from the week before still showed upon the track but some were more recent. He must ask the steward how often the lodging was checked.

Sensing he could be dealing with two separate evildoers, Garrett decided to search for evidence of poison first. The Knowsley servants had been diligent after the earl's departure; the grate in the outer room had been reset with twigs and small logs. This time he noticed the basket of dried toadstools for kindling. He carried it into the daylight for inspection and shook the shrivelled contents out onto the ground. Cropped six months earlier, the fungi were so emaciated that identifying a death cap or its ilk was a challenge.

With a sigh, he returned the basket to the hearth and unlocked the aumory. All the ordinary tankards had been washed and put back, anything valuable must have been carted to Knowsley, and there were no traces of any powder on the unhooked board.

Outside, he found the midden where the scraps had been tipped. Droppings indicated that wild dogs or foxes had been around. The servants had shovelled earth across the waste, but he noticed a narrow piece of quality cloth sticking out. A tooth cloth? Could poison have been put on that? He yanked it out with distaste. It smelled of earth but if poison had been administered, he could not detect it. Had the dose been small and thus insufficient? He probed further, wondering if any tooth sticks had been used.

Finding nothing else and conscious that it was the same time of day that Ferdinando had seen the ghost, Garrett went back inside. Opening the shutters showed him only the bare bones of the inner chamber: all the bed hangings and tapestries had been removed, the rushes were gone and the boards had been scrubbed. The scoured pot beneath the bed contained a dead spider.

Heaving aside the wooden chest, he observed no obvious trapdoor to any cellar and, apart from a few sprigs of herbs, the chest was empty. Garrett stepped into it. Taking care not to shut himself in, he lowered himself down. Yes, a child might hide here, but a man? Without making a noise? Surely impossible?

Trying to recreate the scene, he fastened the shutters and stood by the bed, looking to where the earl had alleged the apparition had appeared. He remembered the screen in front of the narrow washstand and that he had checked behind it. What had he missed? Where could the 'spectre' have hidden after everyone rushed in?

Letting daylight intrude again, he turned his attention once more to the walls. The linenfold panels had been hidden beneath wall hangings and he could see why. The paintwork of a hunt was faded and ill done. No Hampton Court artist here, more like some local man who hadn't cleansed his brushes well. Garrett touched a streak of white and it came away on his finger. He remembered the youth in the Theatre's tiring room smothering it on to play Lady Anne's ghost.

Ha! To play the ghost!

He studied the wall again. There looked to be no catches, nothing remarkable. Excited, determined, he ran his fingertips over the panelling once more, wondering how a grown man might slide out of sight. No, each panel was too small, unless...

It was then he heard the creak of leather in the outer room.

'Jesu, Buchanan! Why the devil are you hanging around here? I'd have thought you'd have buggered off a week ago.'

The Scot filled the doorway of the bedchamber. Something in the fellow's manner lit a ruddy great warning beacon. Garrett's mouth went dry. 'Have you heard Lord Derby is like to die?'

'Aye, an' takin a cursed long while o' it. What are ye doin' back here, Towneley?'

Garrett made pretence of relaxing a little. Legs akimbo, he stared at the panels. 'Trying to find out if there's a priest hole.'

The Scot came to stand at his elbow. 'Why? Are ye lookin' for Doughtie?'

'No, he's well away.'

'Then it's for you, is it?'

'Maybe.'

'Try feeling along that lower rib, man.' Garrett crouched. The wood was a bit splintery underneath. 'Push up now.' It was on the third try that he heard a release click. The long panel above swung open. He ducked his head and peered inside. A brick-backed space scarce bigger than a large broom cupboard adjoined a pit down below the hearth. 'Well, I'll be! Thank you, Buchanan.' But before he could swivel and ask how the Scot had known, the knave seized his right arm and wrenched it back. His rapier was seized and flung aside.

'What the —' Garrett gasped, half-choking. His dagger followed with a clatter.

'Bloody fool, pokin' your nose in.'

A damaged hand was useless at trying to locate his assailant's eyes so he slammed his sole back into the Scotsman's shin. 'You hairy Scottish numbskull, I'm here trying to find out who's killing the earl.'

'Well, seein' as I'm about to cut your throat, I'll tell ye.'

'You're as ignorant as I am, you dog,' he hissed, despite the discomfort. 'Admit it! And can't we talk about it like gentlemen?'

'Nay, laddie, I wouldna trust you an inch.' A tightening of grip. 'Bothwell an' the Cecils want our wee Scots lad to be the next King o' England. An' right now, our bonnie Bothwell is seizin' control of young Jamie an' Scotland.'

'Now? What have you got, second sight? *Ouch!*'

'My orders were to remove your earl before the bloody Papists could make use of him.' Punctuated with another vicious jerk on Garrett's tethered arm! Above the pain, Garrett's mind was doing sums.

Bothwell plus Lord Burghley and son minus Lord Derby equalled King James.

How in hell had he missed this?

'Are you saying you poisoned Ferdy, Buchanan? Christ, you're cursed hurting —'

'Let's say I tried. I dinna know the brew was not quite strong enough an' he's puttin' up a fight, but it shouldn't be long now since his liver's shot.' For a moment, Buchanan paused as though distracted but he did not loosen his hold. 'An' I've had help from the Cecils' agent. Make a man think he's bewitched an' his mind will do the rest.'

Help from whom? Golborne?

'Oh Lordy! Then we're all on the same side, you bloody Scots idiot. Loose me!'

An exaggeration that seemed to work. The intense pain ceased but before Garrett could haul his arm free, Buchanan's great bulk slumped beside him with a grunt. 'What in —' Jerking his head round, he swore in horror. Just inches away, blood was bubbling down the Scotsman's beard, the man's eyes were wide in anguish and the haft of someone's dagger was sticking out of his back.

'Christ!' Gasping, he heaved Buchanan aside and stared up in shock at his rescuers: Jacques de Francesci, Snow and Gabriel Hesketh, who was beaming like a basilisk and holding a cudgel.

The deputy commander of the Flanders troop put his foot on Buchanan, freed his blade, and smeared the blood off on the dead man's doublet. 'What, no gratitude?'

'I'd dip you in gold if I were royalty.' Garrett clambered warily to his feet. De Francesci in England? The vision of an assassinated queen threatened to flood his thinking. 'Is Her Majesty —'

'No.' De Francesci's eyes were cold. 'Our fellows arrested in London an' now this. I'd hoped you'd have good news for me, Captain — the Earl of Derby nicely turned against the Tudor harlot.'

'Well —'

'Let me finish! But instead, you've helped the bloody Protestants to poison him.'

Garrett did not have to feign astonishment. 'No, you've misunderstood. I've been trying to save him. The earl's a good man.' He stared helplessly at the dead one. 'That's Buchanan, Bothwell's agent.' He clawed a hand through his hair. Of course, he remembered now — the Scot passing his drinking flask around and only Ferdinando taking a swig. Jesu, they could all have been dying in agony, him and Snow and Halsall — a pestilence come to Knowsley.

Clever. But he must get back without delay, tell the doctors.

'The earl is still alive, thank Heaven, but he believes he's been bewitched. His secretary staged a ghost using that,' he pointed to the hiding hole. 'I came for proof, see.' A show of white on his fingertip. Why were they looking at him like that? 'I need to return, tell him, so he'll live.' Then de Francesci's words hit him at last. They knew.

'The others arrested?' he muttered. 'Are you certain?'

'Taken before they got anywhere near the queen. Two of our best. The soldiers were waiting.'

'By Our Lady!' Garrett crossed himself. He needed to contain this. 'Listen,' he said quickly, 'Buchanan said that Lord Bothwell is in league with the Cecils, but we need proof.' He knelt and searched the dead man's pouch. 'There's a passport here, look, signed by Bothwell. Could be useful.' He handed the paper up to Snow. 'Come on, man,' he muttered, pushing over the corpse to get to the doublet. 'Give me something to bring Robert Cecil to trial. If we could prove... Bugger! Nothing!' With a bitter shake of head, he was about to turn and rise when he felt the prick of rapier on his neck. He lifted his hands, trying to staunch the panic. *Think like a soldier.* 'If you want your future king to live, I have to get back to Lathom.'

Snow's tone was bitter. 'The king we planned for is almost coffined, the Tudor she-devil would give her crown jewels for our heads, and you expect us to let a stinking cur like you walk free?'

A distant horn sounded. The sheriff's soldiers with any luck. Half a mile away? Had Farington set the hounds on him? He hoped so.

He pulled out the rosary he carried inside his doublet, clenched it in his maimed hand. 'By the Blessed Christ, if you lads want to pick on someone, piss on Buchanan. I set up the meeting with the earl, did my best.'

De Francesci turned to Hesketh. 'Get some cord from my saddle, Gabriel. He's one of Wade's dogs.'

'No,' Garrett corrected calmly. 'I am the earl's man.'

'Ah, a confession at last.'

'I'm trying to save him, you ruddy fools, can't you grasp that? He's our future.'

'Reckon this is strong enough to cut his head off, Jacques?' Snow swung his rapier.

'It isn't,' Garrett intervened. 'Anyway, it's only for nobles. Try a lunge through the ribs. It worked for him.' He was looking at Buchanan's body when a great kick in the back flung him forward. He felt his hair grabbed and his head lifted. 'Because of treacherous bastards like you,' snarled de Francesci, as Gabriel Hesketh bound Garrett's arms behind his back, 'every blessed day, good, honest Englishmen and women are being martyred.'

This was it, then, his life's ending. If only he hadn't admitted to Buchanan he was on the same side. Thank God he hadn't brought Rose with him. He hoped she wouldn't see his corpse. Not fair on a woman.

'He's too heavy to hang. We could bury him alive or tether him at a stake. There's plenty of firewood.'

Christ receive his soul!

Then something hit his skull. The world became stars of light as his eyesight failed and he knew no more.

18

'*Leave*? Dawn tomorrow?' spluttered Lady Derby, confronting the unexpected soldiers in the audience chamber. Her daughters, her sister Lady Compton, Lizbeth and Rose flanked her. Farington and Hugh Ellis, Lathom's steward, stood to one side.

'Orders of Her Majesty, madam.' The leader, a man in his forties, all spurs and creaking leather, presented a letter. 'Now that the pestilence is past, Lady Vere is to be escorted back to court to resume her duties as maid-of-honour. Her Majesty desires that Lady Compton return as well.'

It was not appropriate for the queen's subjects to display outrage. In the stunned and rather stony silence, the officer drew a second missive from his belt. 'And this is for Mistress Byrd from Sir Robert Cecil.'

'For me?' Rose stepped forward, surprised. Knowing it was not from 'her brother', she broke the seal. The message was brief. 'Your uncle says I am to remain here,' she exclaimed, passing it in puzzlement to Lizbeth. Why were they being separated? Was she still supposed to play the intelligencer? She did not like this one bit.

Even though Lizbeth had been wanting to leave, the young woman resented the interference. Catching Rose's hand, she played her haughty card. 'What misunderstanding is this? While I would welcome Lady Compton's company, I am certainly not returning without Mistress Byrd.'

The soldier's moustache twitched. 'It is Her Majesty's wishes, Lady Vere. We depart tomorrow morning.'

'As though I am a box of herring to be delivered,' Lizbeth muttered to Rose. 'Oh, Cousin Alice, I am so sorry!' she turned to Lady Derby.

'And so am I!' fumed Lady Compton.

'I don't want them to go, Mama,' Anne Stanley protested to her stunned mother. 'Nor I,' chorused Frances and Bess.

'Lady Derby,' the soldier cut through the wailing, 'I realise your household have already supped, but my men require victuals and lodging. If you would kindly give the orders.'

'I'll see to that, my lady.' The steward stepped forward. 'Come with me, sirrahs!'

'Wait, sir.' Lady Derby's tone reminded the captain she had not given him leave. She might have no power to countermand his orders, yet she still outranked him.

'Madam.' He turned with a curt bow.

'I shall be sending a letter to my cousin, Sir Robert Cecil. I trust you will be able to deliver it direct to him.'

'Of course, I am happy to carry any letters.' His glance flicked to each of their faces.

'I also require you to witness how ill my lord husband is at present,' Lady Derby added icily. 'You will be able to provide the details to Sir Robert and he will inform Her Majesty.'

Uncertainty, reluctance perhaps, tainted his bow. 'As you will, Lady Derby.'

'Excuse me, my lady,' Farington stepped forward. 'Considering his lordship's grievous condition, may I suggest you send an urgent letter to summon his brother and heir.'

'Is my lord so lacking in his wits that you must act for him, Master Farington?' Lady Derby demanded.

'No, madam.'

'And since I am with child, most likely a son, your suggestion is irrelevant.'

Disbelief glimmered. 'If you will not send for him, my lady, then that shall be my duty. I shall seek him out myself.' He bowed and with a haughty swirl of cloak marched out.

The instant all the men had left the chamber, Lizbeth tugged at Rose's arm. 'I don't have to go if I tell them I have my monthly flux.'

'Then they'd ask why you aren't quietly sewing somewhere.'

'Bother! If I were a man, they'd not —'

'Yes, they would. England is terrified of disobeying Her Majesty.'

Lady Compton put a motherly arm about Lizbeth. 'I shall tell my maidservant to pack while there is still daylight left. It might be best if you do so, too, my dear. They will leave us no time in the morning.'

'That's good advice,' Rose agreed, countering Lizeth's long expression, and although she wished to assist her, she felt sorry for the poor defeated countess. 'Shall I keep you company, madam?'

Lady Derby's face showed gratitude as she turned from comforting her daughters. 'Will you be my amanuensis, dearest girl? My feelings are so distraught that I cannot trust my hand to be legible. Let us do it now.'

'Of course, my lady.'

It was not until they were in her bedchamber that Lady Derby showed anger. 'Oh, if only I might counter the queen's orders,' she exclaimed bitterly. 'She needs to know how we suffer here.'

Misapprehension for her own safety filled Rose as she sat down at the countess's writing desk. Lizbeth's departure would leave her vulnerable. What if Farington's wife and Golborne should turn Lady Derby against her? However, her fears were nothing compared to poor Alice's situation. The distraught countess stood for a moment, fingers to her lips, then she clasped them to her heart as if in prayer. 'Begin with: "Bear with me." God give me words to make the Queen of England weep.'

Bear with me to use a secretary, for my senses are overcome with sorrow. It hath pleased God to visit my lord with sickness, that there is little hope of recovery except in His mercy, and —

'God have mercy!' She collapsed onto the window seat, clapping her hands to her head as though it might burst asunder with her anguish.

Rose waited, goose quill poised, biting back her own tears. Lady Derby's maid brought her mistress a glass of wine. The countess drank a little and put shaky fingers to her brow. 'Your pardon, where was I?'

'Except in His mercy, and...'

And therefore must entreat your favour and assistance, both of yourself and to my lord your father, on behalf of me and my poor children, and that as you were dear unto my lord in love and friendship, so you would be pleased to continue it for the furtherance of me and mine in the justice of our causes. Lathom, 11 April 1594.

Dashing away the tears, Alice took the quill and signed *A Derby* and waited while Rose blew the ink dry and softened the wax stick in the candleflame. When the impression was done and the sad message sealed, Rose put her arms about the distressed woman. 'He's still alive, Alice. Have faith!'

'It need not have happened. Oh God, what did we do to deserve this!' The tears were bitter; the resentment unrestrained. Eventually she drew away from Rose's damp shoulder, and once more took up her glass and gestured to her maidservant to refill it. 'Did you rail against Heaven when the news was brought of your young husband's death?'

No, Rose realised. 'It was more the suddenness, the shock. This is worse.'

'Does it sound blasphemous to say I wish God would make his mind up?'

Rose smiled with compassion and shook her head.

The countess reached out a hand to hers. 'This visit has brought you little happiness. I am sorry that I upset you earlier by telling you of Captain Towneley's mistress and child in Manchester but I thought you should know the truth. Did you have words with him?'

'No, my lady, there was no time.' Her heart was heavy. She should have known this would all end badly.

'Pray use my desk to write to your family, Rose. I, alas, must tell my poor husband that Lizbeth and my sister are leaving, then I shall write to my brother. My family are not as powerful as Her Majesty's favourites but we are loyal to one another.'

His mind struggled to the surface. For an instant he believed himself in some Papist cupboard then he realised, his mind screaming with anger. The bastards had shoved him into the pit below the bloody panelling. Not alone either. Christ! His bound wrists brushed against the ghastly stickiness on a man's wiry beard. Buchanan's corpse.

He wriggled away as far as he could, cursing that the dead man was still within a finger's reach, and attempted to assess his plight. While his head still throbbed from the cudgel blow, any bleeding had dried; there was feeling in his limbs though his ankles and wrists were tied (the latter inconveniently behind his back); his movement was restricted to kneeling or sitting with bent knees — that was not good — nor was having a rag stuffed in his mouth like a boar's head roast.

He needed a blade. Something sharp. Christ! Even his spurs had been taken. Maybe they hadn't searched Buchanan? He struggled to turn, to feel over the dead man's clothing, kick the boots for a telltale jingle. Nothing!

Would they come back, haul him out to be hanged, or was this it? A slow, cramped death? In panic he thrashed against the boards and then, bruised and defeated, knew despair.

It was sensible to return to her own bedchamber to compose her letter. While Lizbeth fumed and supervised Amy, Rose tried not to think about Towneley. She slung the writing board about her neck, abandoned the nonsense about birds and related what any other guest at Lathom might have put, telling 'her brother' of her servant's death, the earl's sudden and mysterious sickness, the manhunt for Doughtie and the wax image discovered under the bed. 'I am but a witness to these events,' she added before signing and then added as a postscript:

My betrothed is here. I do not know if I am foremost in his affection but I trust to God that all will be resolved.

After it was securely sealed, she handed it to Lizbeth. 'Would you give it direct to your uncle, pray you? He promised to forward my letters.'

'My meddling uncle! Honestly, Rose, I feel like spitting. You may be sure he and Grandfather are behind the queen's command, dragging me away when Alice and Ferdy need me! And ordering you to stay behind, I cannot believe it.'

Rose hugged her. 'Lizbeth, we wanted to leave, remember. Now you have your wish.'

'But abandoning you here and knowing those accusations have been made against you…'

'They were made only to me, Lizbeth. I withstood them once and I can do so again.'

'You ever have a friend in me. Remember that.'

A knock at the door prevented further conversation. 'The captain wishes to speak with you, Mistress Byrd,' squeaked a young page, bowing to Rose.

Towneley was back as promised. Well, that was something. They would discuss ghosts — and then she would tell him she knew about the woman in Manchester!

Oh! It was not Captain Towneley but the Cecils' officer, who stood waiting before the hearth in the shadows of the audience chamber, hands behind his back. He was alone.

'Come in, Mistress Byrd.' He gestured to her to join him 'I've spoken with Lord Derby. He's as ill a man as ever I saw.' His expression added: *not long for this world*. He waited until she was beside him before he asked softly, 'Have you a letter for Master Wade?'

'Lady Vere will carry it.'

For a moment he looked thwarted. 'Well, I daresay that should be acceptable to his worship.' She would have nodded and left but then he added, 'It's been suggested to me that you're a Papist who may have poisoned the earl.'

Was she about to be arrested? *Try not to show any panic!*

'Really,' she replied witheringly. 'Some people believe the moon is made of cheese.'

To her relief, the soldier smiled. 'Indeed. I really must congratulate you on keeping your powder dry. Lord Burghley's man here is convinced you're one of Lady Vaux's agents.'

'Lady who?'

'You haven't heard of her? The woman's a meddling Papist scold. But to come to a more important matter, Mistress Byrd, where's Captain Towneley? His report is overdue.'

'He told me he has sent it with a trusted friend. Maybe the fellow has been delayed.' She hoped Shakespeare hadn't met Martin's fate.

'So Towneley *is* here?'

'Not exactly. He rode to Knowsley yesterday. It's where Lord Derby took ill so he is trying to find out if my lord has been poisoned.'

A sour grin. 'Well, he'd be the one to know.' He paced, pensively patted his fist against his palm. 'Disappeared, has he? And the other fellow Doughtie, too?'

She tried to keep her feelings out of it. Was he implying Towneley was a murderer? 'I'm not sure where any of this is leading,' she said carefully.

'Don't worry your pretty head. Someone does.'

'Wait! The agent already here, who is he and why was he not told you who I am? I do not intend to be the whipping boy for your masters, stow that, sir!'

He took a step closer and without permission ran a lascivious finger along the top of her breasts. 'The less you know, the more innocent you can sound.'

Rose smiled sweetly. 'Do you have your face regularly slapped?'

'No,' he laughed.

'Pity! Touch me again and you shall! Goodnight to you.'

Wallop! It helped to smash out anger and suspicion next morning as Rose played *tenez* with the children after Lizbeth's tearful departure. Captain Towneley a — *whack* — murderer? A — *whack* — liar and Papist? If he were not back — *whack* —

by supper at the latest — *WHACK!* Then she took the girls riding to New Park to distract them. The deer park contained a small hunting lodge, probably like the one at Knowsley, which made her fret all the more as to why Towneley had not returned.

Hers wasn't the only mind speculating on the captain's loyalty that day. Like yeast in warm dough, estimates of his guilt doubled; the earl's officers and visiting neighbours were adding the known facts together — a sum that could end in a hanging. Proclamations and a manhunt were being suggested but Ferdy, still in his right mind, refused to consent.

Rose felt the despair that hung over Lathom that night as the sky darkened. Wan-eyed from bedside vigils, the doctors were losing the battle; Chaplain Leigh, when he was not taking divine service in the chapel, had become almost as fixed as the wall sconces in the sick chamber, spending hours in prayer as he pleaded for Ferdinando's life. Downstairs, the household was as irritable as a hungry, chained mastiff, even the repasts had grown lacklustre with the head cook grieving for his dying master, while in the great chamber, the earl's friends and lawyers met with Lady Derby, and an hour later, pale but pragmatic, she led them upstairs to witness her husband's will.

But next morning, things changed.

Like an angel of hope to the shepherds at Bethlehem, the wisewoman of Aughton asked to be received into the presence of Lady Derby and could Mistress Byrd please escort her?

Garrett heard a horse. With all his strength, he slammed his heels against the panel then listened, praying.

A mindless rattle of the outside latch. The steward at Knowsley sending a menial to make sure he'd locked up yesterday 'and why wasn't the key returned?' Again, Garrett kicked. Was the numbskull deaf?

In hope, he heard the crunch of footsteps around the outside, the shutters being tested. Once more, he slammed the wall, screaming against the gag. A dog barked. Then a man's swearing, a whistle and nothing more.

Garrett's tears of fury and self-pity ran into the cloth that suppressed his tongue like a scold's bridle He was going to die here, slowly, famished, parched until God in his mercy severed his soul from his body and Death kicked him down to Hell.

Hell? Why bother? He was already there.

Rose was not grateful that the white witch was led directly to her but one glance at Jane's face changed her mind. The laden basket told her how tired the poor woman was. Seating her before one of the fires in the Long Gallery, Rose sent a servant to inform Lady Derby and a page to bring ale and food.

Mother Jane had taken care with her appearance. The apron over the Sunday grey kirtle was spotless and the exuberant snowy hair had been tamed beneath a proper cap and veil. Her garments smelled of herbs — sage perhaps — and she sat straight and proud with the basket of phials at her feet. Only the mud daubing the edge of her boot soles and the dirtied skirt hem betrayed that she had walked to Lathom.

Lady Alice swept into the hall with her daughters at her heels. 'Where have you been, old mother?' she chided, albeit she graciously clasped the woman's hands as the healer bobbed a curtsey. 'I sent for you days ago.'

'My lady, it were useless me coming sooner. The moon needed to be in the last quarter, the time of cleansing and unbinding.'

'Come along, then, now you *are* here!'

'But surely...' protested Rose. The page had brought refreshment.

'Later, boy.' Lady Alice gestured him away. 'Let no more time be wasted.'

'Can we come?' asked young Frances, daringly approaching the white witch.

Jane nodded. 'Aye, the sweet smell of youth can do no harm. But no questions nor chatter when I'm about my business, eh?'

Alice took little Bess's hand and led the way. Following the healer with Frances, Anne lifted hopeful crossed fingers at Rose. The family's desperation was almost tangible, but would the woman's alternative lore do any better than the physicians' skills?

The great bedchamber stank of incense, woodsmoke and bodily discharge. Steaming over the fire, a pannikin, tended by Dr Canon, at least added a more acceptable aroma.

The sight of the white witch beside Lady Derby was received with as much enthusiasm as the Saxons facing the Norman invasion. Bate hastily threw a cloth over the chamber pot he was about to decant and set it behind a screen; Secretary Smythe crossed himself; and Chaplain Leigh halted in reading aloud from his prayerbook. He and Canon rose and bowed, each narrowing their eyes in disapproval. Only Dr Case appeared interested. He got up from his stool on the other side of the bed.

Looking shrunken in the immense bed, Ferdy had his eyes closed. Rose could hardly bear to see how changed he was. No wonder the children hung back. His cheeks were convex hollows as though the continual voiding had sucked away the flesh beneath his skin.

Jane's lips parted in shock and it was clear she was swiftly reassessing her involvement. Then with an expression of resolve, she walked briskly round the bed like any regular physician and lifted the earl's right wrist. 'Good, his pulse is strong.' She shifted her hand to his forehead, noting the bleeding around his dried lips, then she folded back the brocade coverlet. 'If I touch here and here,' she asked, feeling the earl's belly through the sheet, 'do you feel any pain, my lord?'

'Ouch! Jesus yes!'

The chaplain strode forward. 'Lady Derby, I must protest.'

'And so must I!' Dr Canon lumbered across to join Chaplain Leigh at the foot of the bed. Like men-at-arms, they stood shoulder to shoulder. Dr Case stayed silent, like a hovering archangel in a discarded altarpiece.

'I understand your feelings, Doctor,' declared Lady Derby, 'but so far you have achieved nothing. My lord's illness has not abated.'

'My lady, he has refused to eat the vomit to scour out the bile. It's also possible that the feathers in his bedding are preventing his recovery.'

'And he still refuses to be bled,' lamented Bate. 'We need to make him sweat out the vileness.'

'A murrain on that!' Ferdinando hiccoughed and opened his eyes at Jane. 'What are you going to charge me for this, you old besom?'

'Good morrow to you, too, my lord. I'll heal you if I can an' you will give me leave.'

He nodded agreement to his countess, but his attempt to smile at Jane proved more a grimace. 'Get on with it then, spellbinder. You two skedaddle,' he growled at Canon and Bate. 'Get some sleep. You, too, Chaplain! Case?'

'I'll stay, my lord.'

With the other men's departure, the tension eased.

Jane picked up the bowl by his bed. 'What's this, your worship?'

'A compound. Diascordium with lemon syrup and an infusion of Devil's Bit,' answered Dr Case. 'He managed to keep most of it down yesterday but today…' He spread his hands. 'And as to passing water, well, there has to be a blockage. But for that, we'd be able to cleanse out his belly.'

For a moment, Ferdinando rallied. 'Up my backside, down my gullet, poultices, potions!'

Heartened by this paternal outburst, young Anne threw off her mother's consoling arm, scurried round the bed, and pulled at Jane's sleeve. When the old woman nodded at the girl's whisper, Anne took Ferdinando's hand. 'We've been practising a song for you, Father. Would you like to hear it?'

'For you, sweet love, anything.' With assistance, he struggled to prop himself higher against the pillows.

It was pitiful to see the sadness in his face as he watched the girls take their places. Behind them, Jane moved the physicians' pans out of the way and hung her own tiny cauldron of water above the fire and, chanting, shook in a mixture of dried herbs as the children sang:

Soon comes the month of May
When all the world rejoices.
And Love will have its day
And maids will make their choices.
Sing dilly, dilly, dally-o,
And maids will make their choices.

Farewell Winter's frosty hand,
And welcome Lady Spring
Amyntas, rise at her command
And with Amaryllis sing

Sing dilly, dilly, dally-o,
And with Amaryllis sing.

'Lizbeth wrote the lines, Mama, and Mistress Rose gave us the melody,' explained Frances. 'Mother and Father were Amyntas and Amaryllis,' she explained to Jane.

'The poet Edmund Spenser called us that. Our halcyon days.' Lady Derby wiped the moisture from her eyes and looked down at Ferdinando, but his eyes had closed as though listening had drained him.

'Little ones, could you sing something gentle like a lullaby?' Jane requested and Ferdy, hearing, nodded. 'Aye, girls, the one by William Byrd.'

Anne sang the first note.

My sweet little Baby, what meanest Thou to cry?
Be still, my blessed Babe, though cause Thou hast to mourn,
Whose blood most innocent to shed the cruel king has sworn;
And lo, alas! behold what slaughter he doth make,
Shedding the blood of infants all, sweet Saviour, for Thy sake.
A King, a King is born, they say, which King this king would kill.

O woe and woeful heavy day when wretches have their will!
Lulla, la-lulla, lulla, lullaby.

'Enough, sweethearts, the words offer no comfort though you sing like angels!' Tears flooded his eyes. He fisted the bed and turned his face, his body racked with sobs. '"*This king would kill.*"'

'Ferdy, hush dear one.' His wife sat down on the bed and gathered him into her arms.

'To not see them grow —'

'It's not over, Ferdy. Don't surrender.'

Across the room, Rose put her arms around the distressed children. 'Trust,' she whispered, wondering if God was even listening.

The aroma of the herbal infusion began to scent the air as the countess settled the earl once more on his back. At the hearth, Jane lit sprigs of white sage, then she circled the bedchamber waving the smouldering fronds and shaking a bell. 'To cleanse the air of evil,' she explained, over her shoulder. When that ritual was done, she shook some green and black stones from a small leather bag onto the bed coverlet.

'What are they for?' asked Frances.

'Green calcite to heal and cleanse.' She placed a shiny pebble over on the earl's heart and then a darker green stone on his lower belly: 'Jade to safeguard, and to soothe the kidneys.' The third green stone, which she set between the other two, was the hue of moss with a surface like pitted glass. 'Moldavite to heal the spirit.' Then she drew from her pocket the wondrous pure crystal of quartz that Rose had seen in her cottage and placed it on the pillow above the earl's head.

Could stones truly heal? Rose wondered. Certainly, Dr Case was not protesting. He seemed equally fascinated as they watched Jane unwrap a piece of translucent amber which she set upon the earl's belly. Finally, it was the turn of the black stones. 'Smoky quartz and black onyx to deflect evil and possession because there is need here to heal and safeguard. Lastly, obsidian.' Jane arranged the dark stone a span away from Ferdy's soles. 'So very potent, for it will clear away blockages and confusion and secure the spirit within the body.'

Fetching out little earthenware bowls, she emptied a phial of water into one, tipped earth into another, and lit a candle in a third. The four elements, Rose guessed, as Jane positioned them at each corner of the bed.

'Fall back now, my dears.'

After pouring a second phial of water into a beaker, the woman shook in white crystals. 'From a holy spring,' she told the countess as she held it to the earl's lips. He gulped down half; the rest soaked the sheets. 'Now, my lord, I pray you to will your body to be at ease. Close your eyes and be at peace. Give me your trust. I'm going to transfer the evil from you to myself.'

His eyes flickered open for an instant. Whether scepticism or hope flared in his soul, Rose could not tell, but Lady Derby fell to her knees, tears running down her cheeks, her fingers fastening tightly upon her cross, her lips moving in prayer. Hesitantly, her daughters knelt beside her.

Walking around the three sides of the bed, Jane began to shake the bell and chant:

Earth, Air, Fire, Water and Spirit,
Angels of Light and Ministers of Grace,
I ask you to cleanse this man's body of all evil,
In the name of Divine Light, Divine Love, Divine Healing.
Amen, amen, amen.
Blessed be.

As the voice cascaded to a murmur like the humming of bees, Rose knelt and held her breath, wishing that the magic might work, her own prayer intense. There was no harm in the ritual but could there be effect? Slowly she breathed in the aroma of the herbs and heard Dr Case's garments rustle as he sat back down. The fire interrupted the growing peace with a shift of log and then it too settled.

How long she knelt, Rose was not sure, but when she opened her eyes it was almost evening and a soft and gentle quiet embraced the room. The stones and pots were gone from the bed, the infusion from the hearth had been drunk and

Ferdinando lay at peace. For a moment, she thought his soul had departed because it was as though a Divine hand had soothed his forehead and drawn the tension from his flesh.

Dr Case raised his head and faced Jane and Lady Derby across the bed, but there was no hostility in his demeanour, more like wonder, and as though she read the scholar's thoughts, Jane nodded. 'Yes, let him sleep, good doctor. It will help heal him.' Then she began to sway. Her features slurred into a mask of anguish, her mouth a hollow of pain.

'Jane!' Rose rushed forwards. The countess shooed the children out.

Unable to speak, the woman caught at the bedpost, bent double and clutching her belly. 'It's working, my lady,' she croaked. 'God willing, the evil will dissipate through me and he'll be troubled no more. Oh mercy!'

It was Dr Case who brought the basin and when Jane could straighten, he and Rose assisted her away from the bed. The woman's eyes were streaming from the nausea. She wiped a hand across her lips and took the ale that Rose offered her. Then her gaze found Lady Derby. 'Get some rest ... my lady.'

'You'll stay with her?' the countess asked Case and he nodded.

'It's too strong,' the healer muttered. 'There's such evil here. The man that was hanged is relishing his pain. Aargh! The Devil's work!' She began to retch again.

'*Come*!' Lady Derby took Rose's arm. She threw a last look at her peaceful husband as they left. Outside, they embraced in celebration of life and hope.

Like ripples, the tidings that the earl lay in peaceful slumber spread throughout the household. The servants smiled as they brought in the supper platters and the children chattered and ate with revived appetites. But there was no cheerful Towneley at the board.

The Devil paraded his past sins through Garrett's mind like a York pageant. He sobbed and kicked again, out of frustration and fury and regret — poxy, cursed regret. If only he had neither listened to Wade nor taken employment with the earl.

Was God on the Papists' side?

Yet Our Saviour had compassion, wasn't that what the Gospel writers taught? Christ cared for everybody.

Merciful Lord, I beseech you help me find a way out of here.

For the umpteenth time he manoeuvred, bound fingers scrabbling to find the catch that might free him.

Out in the peaceful garden, the chill wind was at rest and a blackbird was carolling an evensong as Rose drew in a deep breath of air, so sweet and wholesome after the heavy aromas of Ferdinando's bedchamber. Trailing fingers down a forlorn stem, she begged Christ to bring healing to the earl and ensure Towneley's safe return. That alone would prove he was not the poisoner.

Loneliness shadowed her as she strolled. Still asleep, the roses, honeysuckle and eglantine, planted to adorn the trellised paths, were dull stems, yet there were flowers to cheer her heart. Pretty usurpers from the wild: rosettes of primroses and clusters of cowslips brightened the borderland between the garden beds and the bonfire pile. Beyond the knot garden, below a modest medlar, she sought a bench in the hedged alley that separated the garden from the courtyard and listened for a horseman returning.

She was eager to tell Townley about Mother Jane. Would he believe that white witch could achieve a miracle or would he scoff and say it was coincidence? Surely he must return soon? Alas, as the light faded so did her hopes. Only a robin in the high hedgerow kept vigil with her, calling as the other birds fell silent.

Gathering her mantle about her, she stood and looked towards the house, watched the inner lights blossom behind the upper windowpanes as the twilight candles were lit, and sighing, knew it was her curfew to return inside. Then she heard weighty footsteps. For a moment, she thought it was Towneley, but the massive fur collar proclaimed the receiver-general's arrival.

'Mistress Byrd.'

'What do you want, Master Farington? I thought you had quit Lathom.'

'Your pardon if I frightened you. I need to speak with you.'

Perhaps he was seeing her as a duct to Lady Derby since my lady was no longer on good terms with him. He was alone, but still she felt vulnerable. He was old but strong.

'More accusations, sir?' she asked defiantly, lifting the violets to her nose. 'I told you before, I am no Papist.'

He drew a ragged breath. 'Mistress Byrd, because my lady will not send for my lord's brother, I am leaving to bring him home. I know you are at Lathom for a purpose other than friendship and I wish to clear some misconceptions that may have arisen.'

She let her silence unsettle him. Over near the main gate a dog barked, but there was no thud of hooves.

'Misconceptions, sir? I think you made your opinion of me very clear.'

'Please hear me out, Mistress Byrd. It is important.'

'So, is this tête-à-tête supposed to be in the shadows or do we return to the candlelight?'

'Here will do,' spoken reluctantly. Clearly, he resented the scales of power dipping in her favour. 'Young woman, I'd have you understand that I was steward here for many years under the present earl's grandsire. Earl Henry elevated me to receiver-general as reward for my service. However, five years ago, I and my family were accused of being Papists.' A pause as he let her interest quicken. 'Lord Burghley himself wrote to me and said that if I continued in the old faith, he would request Earl Henry to dismiss me. I beg you to tell Lord Burghley and Sir Robert Cecil that I have done nothing to support the Papist cause, that I had no hand in bringing Richard Hesketh to see his lordship last year, and that I am a loyal servant of Her Majesty.'

'You ask this favour after your treatment of me last night?'

Like a dog sniffing for danger, he looked about warily before he answered softly, 'Mistress, I can explain. Golborne is Lord Burghley's agent here. He reports regularly to Sir Robert Cecil. He demanded that I question you, perhaps to test both you and me.'

Golborne again. Stroke the needle with a lodestar and it always swung to Golborne.

'He is a great hater of Popery,' continued Farington. 'A very Janus, Mistress. All deference and charm to the earl and men of influence, but a scourge to the rest of us.'

'And you believe I am an intelligencer too.'

'Your possessions were searched and we reached that conclusion. I am truly sorry about your servant, Martin. He should not have resisted but Golborne's man was overzealous.'

'Is that what passes for murder in Lancashire?'

'I understand how bitter you must feel but I crave your forgiveness, Mistress Byrd, and ask again that you assure Lord Burghley of my loyalty.'

She could tell that the grovelling pained him more than his gout.

'Master Farington, in truth I do not know what I could say to Lord Burghley about what is going on here. There's too much duplicity and utter evil!'

'Yes, yes, too many curses … poor Lord Derby.' He waved his hands sadly and she sensed genuine helplessness. Then he added, 'You know the proverb that it takes one last straw to break a camel's back, mistress?'

Rose broke off a sprig from a nearby quince. 'You mean a *noble* camel?'

'Yes, I see you understand me. If Lord Derby were not already in disgrace, his body might not be so susceptible. As for the witchcraft —'

'I don't think I believe in curses anymore, Master Farington. I believe his lordship was poisoned and it happened at Knowsley before he saw the so-called ghost. Come, sir, share your suspicions.' Hooking out the cross about her neck, she held it up. 'As the Lord Jesus is my witness, I will not report your opinion.'

Another deep breath. 'Then I suspect it was Lady Vere's maid, mistress. I am told she would often flirt in the kitchen with my lord's food-taster.'

Amy? God in heaven! Amy, who was safely on the road, accompanying her mistress back to London? *Amy, Lord Burghley's agent?*

'Not Master Doughtie then, sir?'

Farington wearily shook his head. 'No, we, I mean they — his cousin Sir William and his allies — need the earl alive to become the next king, though, to be frank, I do not believe my lord has the religious zeal to fulfil their purpose, or the mettle that martyrs are made of.'

'Agreed, Master Farington, but he appears to be in somebody's way. I can think of several other somebodies — Lord Essex, King James, Arbella Stuart's supporters or others with a grudge, like Hesketh's family.' The hour bell sounded.

'Or the Cecils. It's getting too cold for speculation, young woman.' Beneath his great collar, he shuddered. 'And I have a long journey ahead of me tomorrow.'

Her hand touched the bulk of his sleeve. 'Before we go in, sir, answer me why the earl's brother has stayed away so long? I understand he did not even attend his father's funeral.'

'Only because he was unable to return in time. It's not common knowledge but he was sent away by Earl Henry because he was found in … well … in shameful circumstances with another youth, a Ganymede who fled before anyone could see his face. The matter was hushed up, as you can imagine.' He paused as though expecting Rose to comment, but as a woman of the world, she uttered no judgement, and with a nod, he added, 'Whatever his inclination, he is, nevertheless, my lord's heir unless my lady bears a living son, and it is his right to hear what has happened and make his peace with the family.'

'By your voice, you wish him well.'

'I do, Mistress Byrd. It is time he came home.'

At the gate to the courtyard, he offered advice. 'I warn you, lass, when I am gone, stay clear of Golborne.'

'Thank you, I intend to. One last question, though. If Lady Derby's baby is a girl, then Ferdinando's brother has a right to become the next king. Is he likely to retain Master Golborne in his service?'

'Yes.' Firmly, concisely, insufficiently answered as he bowed. 'We shall go our separate ways now. God keep you safe.'

'And you, sir.'

Safe? No, she did not feel safe and she wondered how many more surprises the Almighty was keeping hidden.

Hours! And the hunger. No, the thirst was worse. Garrett's throat felt sand-scoured. A few moments of sleep came now and then, but the nightmare was never over. He must keep moving his legs against the cold. Next to him, Buchanan was stinking and the flies were coming in from somewhere. Black blowfly undertakers.

Terror crawled over Garrett like a thousand maggots, worming into his mind, gnawing at his sanity. *Nightingale, can you hear me? Believe me a traitor! Send a search! Send the whole blessed shire! O Sweet Christ, make her hear me!*

19

'Good morrow, Mistress Byrd.' Heedless that it was the women's table, Dr Case slid onto the bench opposite Rose at the breakfast board.

'Good day, sir.' She passed across the mess of bread and a dish of damson marmalade. 'Did Lord Derby have a peaceful night?'

To her dismay, he shook his head. 'No, not at all. I thought maybe...' He sighed. 'The healer is still up there fussing with her potions, but my lord has stopped passing water.'

That was ill news. Rose pushed her unfinished bowl of spiced pottage aside.

'We are trying everything we can, of course,' he continued. 'Bate is administering another catheter. Can you inform my lady when she —'

Angry shouts penetrated the dining room, and with a unison scrape of benches, everyone, barbed by curiosity, tore outside. Close at his heels, Rose followed the physician through the throng of servants and beheld John Golborne standing astride at the house's great door, fists on his waist. Beside him stood Chaplain Leigh, while below on the outside steps Jane of Aughton lay sprawled upon her back, her basket on its side with all the stones and phials scattered.

'A pox on you, John Golborne!' she yelled, struggling to her feet.

Scoffing, he held up his first and last finger against the evil eye. 'Be on your way, you old hag, or I'll have the magistrate try you for witchcraft.'

Jane spat. 'You won't stop me trying to help him, you snivelling arsewiper! He's been cursed and you are part of it.'

'Enough!' exclaimed the chaplain. 'Back to your duties, all of you!'

'You threw her out?' Ripe with indignation, Dr Case confronted Golborne. With a self-congratulating smile, the latter brushed his palms. 'Yes, Doctor. Useless, mumbling crone. Lord Derby cannot even piss now, thanks to her. I cannot imagine why you let her near him.'

'It wasn't your decision to make, sirrah,' Rose exclaimed, aware that the earl's children had witnessed the confrontation. She began to gather up the scattered stones hoping the lingering servants might help, but they hung back fearfully. Only Dr Case helped pick up the shards.

'You did your best,' Rose whispered to the distraught woman as she dropped the healing stones back into the basket.

'He'll die for sure.' Jane stared up at Lathom's walls as though the great house itself was doomed. 'I wasn't strong enough to break the curse. Tell your soldier that I tried.'

'Can a curse kill?' Rose asked Dr Case as they returned inside.

'I don't know, Mistress Byrd, but I once witnessed a fellow student die from being bewitched. The hanging in St Albans has played heavily on his lordship's conscience and made him vulnerable, and, consequently, whatever poison the Master of Horse gave him to clog his belly has encountered little resistance.'

'Yet he was in such good health when he rode to Knowsley.'

'So everyone says. His lordship tells me that his friend Captain Towneley has gone down there looking for the ghost. Do you know if he has returned yet?'

'Not that I know of.' Her brief answer hid the bitter betrayal she felt. No, Towneley had not returned. It looked like now that he never would.

'Mistress Byrd, Lady Derby and the children will need all your support in the tribulation to come. You will need to be strong for them. In fact, I think you are needed this very instant.' Following his glance, Rose saw the countess's page waiting at her elbow.

'My lady wishes to see you in her bedchamber before she holds council, mistress,' he said with a bow.

'Thank you for your advice,' she told Dr Case, as she swiftly gathered up her skirts to go with the boy.

'I'm told you've been finding occupation for the children,' he called after her. 'Keep doing so. They need you.'

Alice was dictating a letter to Secretary Halsall as Rose entered the chamber. The countess had abandoned her black kirtle for an expecting gown of cream farthingale embroidered with yellow wheatears. Her strategy must be to manifest optimism and authority at the council board. Though she might be deeply in debt, the adornment of diamond eardrops and jewelled collar was to convince otherwise.

'That will be all, Ned. Get that sent and then await me in the council chamber.'

When the man had left, she hastened across to Rose and took her hands.

'My dear, I want you to go to the munitions room in the Eagle Tower. Ellis and Smythe are already there with the keys. I need the estate rolls and anything else that pertains to my daughters' and future son's inheritance to be locked up here from now on.' She indicated an ironbound chest that must have been newly brought in. 'The men will do the carrying but maybe you and the children can help to pack the papers into carry boxes and satchels. I can see you wonder at this action, and it's because I do not trust my brother-in-law, especially when Farington and Golborne are likely to take his side.'

Alice was bracing herself for Ferdy's death, Rose thought sadly, as she collected the children. It was a sad little group that climbed the twisting stairway of the keep.

'Is Father going to die? Is the Lord God punishing him for being a sinner?' Little Bess asked tearfully as they reached the munitions rooms.

What answer could she give the child? *Darling, whatever Divine Hand or earthly agent is killing your papa, it is being done with slow, vindictive cruelty.*

The frustration and powerlessness that she had experienced when the queen imprisoned her father was with her again in full measure. Lord Burghley had stood by while her father carried the blame for Mary Stuart's death. Were he, his son and Wade involved now? If Golborne was their agent, had he administered the poison and put the wax image beneath the bed? Or could it have been Towneley?

'Oh, goodness!' That was Anne exclaiming. Rose followed her through the heavy wooden door and gazed in dismay at the number of chests and coffers with their lids thrust back.

Smythe nodded at Rose. 'Mistress Byrd, Ellis and I have already begun, and that pile yonder can be taken.'

Rose's task was mostly to keep the children busy and although she knew some Latin, assessing which documents needed to be carried down required a great deal more experience. Ellis and Smythe proved efficient in deciphering agrarian terms and making decisions, but the unfolding or unrolling was tedious, dusty work. Soon, little flakes of ancient vellum from the brittle edges scattered the floor.

'Are you missing Cousin Lizbeth and Master Shakespeare?' young Frances asked, holding out her apron to carry a packet across to the carrying chest.

'Yes, very much. These letters can stay.' Rose set a ribboned bundle to one side.

'I expect they are missing each other. Do you think they will meet in London and fall in love?'

'Don't distract Rose, Frances!' scolded Anne. 'I need you here!'

'My apron's not full. And what about Captain Towneley?' Frances prompted, mischief lighting her brown eyes.

Rose sat back on her heels. 'Now why should I miss him, Frances? In any case, he's left.'

'Oh, he'll definitely be back,' Anne declared.

Rose did not answer but a few moments later, she drew the girl aside. 'How do you know that Captain Towneley will be returning?'

'Because all his belongings are down below, Rose. I looked in quickly on my way up. I know I shouldn't have stuck my nose in but he seemed kind and Father said he was here to protect him so I hoped that he would be coming back, and I think you hope so, too, don't you?'

'You,' whispered Rose, planting a kiss on top of the girl's pinned braids, 'are a very intelligent, observant poppet.'

'Well, Father said that at court it was important to watch people's faces when they weren't speaking because it often told him so much more than when they were, and he —' Her stoicism shattered. 'Poor Papa. Oh, Rose, I've prayed so hard.' Her lips trembled. 'I-I can't be brave anymore,' and she burst into tears. Then Frances and Bess were sobbing too and wrapping their arms around Rose's skirts.

Soothing the distraught children, she scolded herself for not checking Towneley's possessions. True, a man might flee with nothing, but what if he was in trouble? She must, she *would*, go to Knowsley because she cared. She had been an absolute fool to tarry so long.

'I do not think highly of you for this request, Rose. Abandoning me, when I am in such need, to go chasing after a ne'er do well.' Although the meeting had ended, Alice's mouth was a thin line of displeasure as she received Rose in the council chamber. Like a queen, she sat back in the great carved chair at the end of the table, with Humphrey Davenport, her lawyer, on her right, Golborne on her left and Ferdy's will and testament in front of her.

'Please, madam,' Rose pleaded, like a desperate petitioner. 'I sense Captain Towneley has met some disaster, and Master Wainwright has refused to let me have a horse and escort.'

Golborne leaned forward. 'That is quite correct, my lady. I gave those orders. The horses are reserved for ... for far more important matters.' A wave of elegant hand that implied *news of my lord's death*. 'Certainly not for a *whim* of Mistress Byrd's.' A pitying smile. 'On the other hand, my lady, may I suggest you should inform the sheriff of Towneley's flight, since the captain and Dick Doughtie were thick as thieves. To speak candidly, I suspect they are both agents of Colonel Stanley.' Now came the stab of accusation. 'As perhaps you are, too, Mistress Byrd, a dyed-in-the wool Papist despite your famous father.'

Rose had expected this and she knew she could not assert she was Wade's agent if she wanted to stay on the happy side of Lady Derby's ledger.

'Captain Towneley went to Knowsley, Master Golborne, because he believed that you also saw the "ghost" and that it was you who put the wax image beneath my lord's bed.'

That had Davenport lift his head and inspect their faces like a prosecutor.

A gasp from Lady Derby. 'We are all on tenterhooks and I do not need this ... this nonsense from either of you.'

'Madam,' said Rose, 'Towneley has sworn to me that his loyalty is to Ferdinando. That is why he was so ashamed at failing to protect him. He is trying to find out the truth.'

'Then why hasn't he returned?' sneered Golborne. 'If I had a gold piece for every time a woman has swallowed a man's lies, I'd be a very wealthy man.'

Lady Derby gave him a quelling look and turned to Davenport. 'What do you advise, sir?'

The lawyer stroked his beard. 'Permit the young woman an escort to Knowsley but if she has not returned by tomorrow, ask the sheriff to proclaim a search — *for both of them.*'

Master Wainwright, with his apparent disdain for women, frustrated Rose by arguing that she could only have a sidesaddle and then, having lost that battle, he singled out young Cropper to accompany her and ignored her argument for a brawnier escort. Well, she'd not let the youth within sniffing distance of an alehouse, and while the lad seemed determined to redeem himself, his bombastic assertion that he had a mind like a map was not reassuring.

Rose had rarely used a man's saddle and the seams of her riding skirt were not happy with the arrangement but at least she would be able to ride fast and, Fortune willing, reach the hunting lodge before nightfall. It was in their favour that the road had been hardened by the cold wind over the previous two days, though it was concerning that there were so many vagabonds watching like hungry kites and when one pack tried to block her way, she had no choice but to ride straight at them. They scattered but it left her fearful that it could happen again, especially when Cropper declared they must quit the highway and turn off onto a narrower bridlepath.

The latter soon forked. Cropper wanted to take her direct to the Royal Lodge where they could ask if there were any tidings of Towneley and request a bed. Rose refused, wary that Golborne might have an accomplice there and, besides, the remaining daylight was precious. The more southerly track took them within sight of a miserable camp of ragged vagrants on the edge of the forest. Cropper increased the pace lest the outcasts follow, and Rose had to duck and weave through the hazardous branches to keep up with him. While the bluebells might look like a wondrous lake of flowerheads, the last things she needed was another fall.

Reaching the silent, padlocked lodge further dismayed her. What had she hoped for? Towneley whistling in front of a campfire roasting a rabbit?

Shivering, she dismounted and while Cropper tethered the horses, she walked briskly round the brick base of the building. Had Towneley come here? Heart beating wildly, she looked about lest there was a coffin-shaped disturbance of ground and, seeing none, breathed again.

Cropper met her at the foot of the outside stairs. He'd found the door above also locked. Then, surprising her with an unexpected dash of resourcefulness, he drew his knife, manipulated the blade to open the downstair shutters on the other side of the building and helped her over the rough sill into some sort of sleeping chamber. Stark without hangings and mattress, the bare frame and ropes of a fourposter bed stood along one wall. The only other furnishing was a large chest. This had to be Ferdy's room where he saw the ghost, she realised with a shudder. Going through into the adjoining chamber, she could see no one had been here because the board was bare, the grate clean of ash and the air cold, lonely, damp.

'Mistress!' She turned at the groom's whisper. He signed her to listen and drew his knife again. Now she heard it too. Hooves, fast then slowing, circling.

Stealing swiftly into the bedchamber, they flattened themselves against the wall either side the open window and held their breath as the rider approached. A huge fierce black head with angry eyes thrust in.

Rose shrieked and Cropper swore. 'Strewth, that be the captain's steed. Here, boy.'

With an ill-tempered snort at such a welcome, the beast backed. Cropper sprang after him and Rose heard him whistle and speak softly. 'It ha' been badly used,' he muttered, returning. 'Likely it'll stay but there's no saddle nor bridle. It's gotten away from someone.'

'Maybe those beggars found it.'

'No, mistress, it's travelled far, fit to drop, I'd say.'

If Towneley had escaped to the coast, maybe he driven it hard and then set it loose. Or could he have been set upon?

'Can it be seeking its master here?' Rose shivered as she stared around and tried to think sensibly. Could Golborne have talked Ferdy into seeing a ghost and used an accomplice? But how?

'We haven't looked in that chest,' she muttered and, bracing herself for a bloody corpse, she took a deep breath and flung back the lid. 'Oh!'

Empty save for fragments of rosemary leaves! With both hands she lowered it again and then she heard a noise. A moan.

'I think we'd better go, mistress. It's blessed freezin'.'

'A little longer,' she bade the groom and, cupping her lips, called out, 'Garrett, can you hear me?'

'I think this place be truly haunted,' muttered Cropper, crossing himself. 'I don't want no ghost cursin' us. We'd best get to Knowsley afore nightfall. There's no moon tonight.'

'Hush! *There*! I thought I heard something.'

Anxiously, Cropper unslung the little wooden cross from about his neck and held it out like a torch. 'Christ save us. It sounded like a hanged man, mistress.'

'No, if it's Hesketh's ghost, Cropper, it's a long way from where he died and why would he haunt here?'

'M-maybe they buried that bit o' him that was on the Ormskirk gallows here.'

'I very much doubt it.' Mind, the hairs on the nape of her neck seemed not to share that logic. 'Is there anybody there?' she called out.

Then they heard a thud.

Terrified, Cropper looked desperately towards the window space.

'Help me move that chest,' Rose ordered, but the lad seemed frozen. She shook her head at him and tried to move it by herself. 'Cropper, please! Help me!'

Mustering his courage, he took a tentative step, swallowed, and in a quavering voice cried out, 'If you are not a ghost, give two knocks.'

A heartbeat and then they heard two muffled thuds behind the chest.

'It could be the ghost trying to fool us!'

'Well, we'd better find out,' Rose exclaimed, heaving at the chest again. This time Cropper helped her shove it aside. 'Garrett?' she called out and set her ear against the timber. Another thud. 'Dear God, there *is* someone behind there, Cropper!' Her hands frantically explored the panelling. '*Cropper*?' Turning, she glimpsed his terrified face before he crumpled against her, tumbling them both. No wonder! Grinning at the window was a ragged man with unkempt hair and beard. She could be scared or —

'Don't just stand there, friend,' she exclaimed in her best Lancashire dialect, scrambling to her feet. 'I need your help. Come in!'

To her amazement, the ploy worked. 'What's to do then, mistress?' the beggar demanded, setting a filthy leg over the sill.

Hiding her fear, she pointed at the wall. 'Please, there's a man trapped behind there and I need an axe.'

'Mistress, I ain't even got a pan.'

The moan came again. 'That's him!' she insisted. 'I beg you, help me get him out.' Crouching beside Cropper, she gently patted his face until he groaned and a healthy pallor returned.

The vagabond stared at the painted panels and then, hefting his staff, he drove the butt against the boards until the wood began to splinter. With blow after blow, he demolished the rest of the panel. 'Urgh!' he exclaimed. 'Smells worse than I do.'

'Dear God,' Rose whispered. Death stank like that.

Her unexpected helpmate was already inside. 'There be a dead man and a live one, mistress,' he hollered. 'Which do you want first?'

'O Christ be merciful,' she exclaimed, kneeling to peer in. 'The *living* one!' *Let it be Towneley!*

Cursing and muttering, the stranger was dragging and hauling a body upwards.

'Mistress!' Cropper crawled across on his hands and knees to help. Rose reached into the hole, her hands brushed matted hair as she searched for clothing to grab and together they hauled. A man's head and shoulders emerged into the fading light. Hardly recognisable, Towneley had his eyes closed. His mouth was gagged, his skin had lost all lustre, and his hands were bound behind his back.

'Far gone with cold,' the beggar muttered, scooping back one of his eyelids. 'Must ha' taken his last strength to make you hear.'

Lying Towneley on his side, Cropper undid his wrists while Rose's nails tore at the knot behind his head and wrenched the rag away. His lips were cracked and dry. She didn't have a flask so she improvised and kissed him.

Across from her, the ragged Good Samaritan smiled, showing broken teeth. 'The right one, then, lass?'

'Yes,' she said through her tears. 'Yes, it is.'

'Breathe warmth into his mouth. You need to keep his soul in.'

Taking a deep breath, she obeyed. Beneath her fingertips, the pulse in his neck was barely there. Inches from her face, the beggar began to rub Towneley's chest through his clothing and Cropper was cupping his large hands around his wrists. 'My mother always wears bands about her wrists o' winter,' he muttered.

With Death louring upon them, Rose knew despair.

'Longer,' urged the beggar. 'He's a strong man not a babe.'

And at last she felt a strengthening beneath the skin and then a shift beneath her lips.

'I came to see if you lacked anything, Garrett.' Rose, his wonderful saviour, closed the door and came across to his bedside. 'I'll have the steward's wife bring you something to eat now you're awake. You must be ravenous.'

Words that might thank, appreciate and load Rose Byrd with garlands of praise were preparing in his heart, yet for now he smiled and reached out his hand to her across the coverlet. Shadows of weariness lay beneath her eyes and tendrils of hair strayed across her cheeks. Had she kept vigil lest Death come for him?

He could not remember last night but this morning he had woken to find himself cocooned like a caterpillar in a fourposter bed with heated bricks against him. Later, a cheerful Cropper had helped him into a bathtub, which the servants at Knowsley Hall had set before the hearth, and after a long soaking, the youth had treated him like a ruddy horse, vigorously rubbing a salve that the steward's wife had provided into his limbs. Cleansed and clothed in a borrowed shirt, he had been settled back into the depths of the feather bed and must have slept again because now the southern sun of noon was sparkling the lozenged panes.

'Is there any news from Lathom?' he asked sadly, his thumb stroking her palm. He had tried to safeguard Ferdy and failed.

'None good. How do you feel?'

'Weak.' He was lucky to have survived. In Ireland, he had seen comrades with sodden clothes lose body heat in the wind's chill and die swiftly. 'My head aches.' His speech was cumbersome, breathless, but she seemed not to mind.

'You haven't drunk much,' she added, inspecting the tankard on the bed steps.

'I have been sipping the ale very slowly. Learned that from an army physician. You sick it all up otherwise. Why are you looking so concerned? Is there something else?'

'I was so ignorant in trying to revive you, Garrett. If we hadn't had help…' She bit her lip, sadly shaking her head.

'A beggar, Cropper said.'

Rose nodded. 'Bless the man. Of all the people in the world, he had no cause to help us. I badgered the steward here to send out food and ale to his camp in recompense this morning. Took some insistence, but I won. And I've sent Cropper back to Lathom with the news that you are safely found. Golborne was threatening to send the sheriff after you — us.'

He nodded, his mind weary, unwilling to mount that saddle again.

As though she read his thoughts, she smiled. 'Your horse came back to the lodge, scared the life out of us. That's when we knew you had to be there somewhere.'

'Clever Byrd,' he murmured drowsily, drowning in the sweetness of that gaze.

'You're looking dozy again.' She began to slide her fingers away. 'Rest.'

He carried her hand to his lips. It was the most he could manage — for now.

Shortly after, probably at Rose's bidding, the steward's wife brought him in some pottage and although he craved sustenance, he forced himself to eat slowly. He'd partaken only a little at breakfast because the different parts of his body were not mustering together yet. Like a mill pond after a dry summer, he thought wryly, with the wheel not scooping up enough water to move the grindstones.

During the afternoon, he walked about the bedchamber, flexed his limbs and his mind, attempting to make sense of what had happened. It was tempting to plan revenge, save that de Francesci and Snow would be long gone, probably hiding in a priest's hole by now he thought happily, and hoped they would be stuck there for days. As for Gabriel Hesketh, Garrett was sure he was one of the three villains who'd attacked Rose and himself on the road. The bastard should be outlawed but he doubted a local court would find him guilty.

By early evening, he felt restored enough to be sitting by the hearth. Hopeful of Rose's promised company, he was delighted when she came in with a supper tray, which she set on a small table at his elbow in wifely fashion. Seeing her warmed his soul, inspired dreams of a future though, alas, why would the queen's secretary's daughter be interested in sharing it (even if her father was in disgrace)? The lady's thoughts were clearly on the present.

'Don't let it cool,' she warned, and he reluctantly dragged his gaze away from her and obediently took up his spoon.

The stew was rich in flavour, generous with meat, but he must not gorge himself. 'Have you eaten? Can you finish the rest?' he asked, holding it out to her. She shook her head and set the bowl away. After arranging another log on the fire so it did not diminish the heat, she knelt, her skirts settling to petal her on the fur rug.

'You look like a flower,' he murmured.

'A flower with questions. Do you feel well enough to explain what happened to you?'

'I remember that you kissed me.'

'Really?' she disputed, looking up at him with laugher in her eyes, and he marvelled this woman who was the friend of earls was here alone with him, her hair uncovered. He could reach out and stroke the lovelock that lay across her lovely shoulder. She was beautiful. Did she know that?

'Cropper told me how you saved my life.'

Now she did blush. 'It was the vagabond's suggestion. He told me afterwards that his cat keeps him alive. Every night it sits on his chest and he reckons its warm breath helps him survive the winter.'

'Well,' Garrett whistled, blessing the cat and its owner.

'So, tell me what happened, Garrett. The body that they pulled out with you, was he the one who played the ghost and got shut in there?'

'No, see, before everything went berserk, I found traces of white face paint on the panelling, so I think our conjecture was right and someone did play the ghost. The dead man you found me with was a Scot, Sir Andrew Buchanan, a follower of Lord Bothwell and one of the delegates who met with Ferdy during the hunt, trying to persuade him to lead a rebellion.'

'Buchanan?' Rose frowned. 'That wasn't Sir Andrew.'

'What?'

'I was at the Scottish court with my father when he was the queen's ambassador, Garrett. I met Sir Andrew — he has a large strawberry mark above his left eyebrow. It may have been getting dark when the dead man was hauled out, but I saw his face clearly and it wasn't Sir Andrew.'

He stared at her, both awed by her past and confounded by her testimony. 'Well, there must be quite a few Buchanans called Andrew,' he blustered.

'No, the man I knew was definitely a friend of Bothwell's.'

Garrett raised a hand to his brow, too exhausted to chase the truth. 'Your pardon, I cannot think straight tonight. Can we save this until tomorrow?'

She wasn't pleased. 'Will the truth gain interest like a Lombard loan?'

'No,' he corrected, insulted by her cynicism, 'hindsight.' Then knowing she meant well and deserved more, he added, 'I will be open with it, I promise.' When he had time to work things out himself.

'Well, you'd better. My patience is like the olive tree that the Blessed Christ cursed — withering fast.' For a while they stayed in an amiable silence, while the flames licked back and forth. 'I received a letter from London, by the way. Wade is not sure where you are.'

'Good,' he said happily.

'They'll be thinking you've been turned.'

'To them, we agents are like chickens on a spit, revolving all the time.'

'This is like a spider's web, too many threads, and I have yet to determine the spider. Is it the colonel?'

'Yes and no. Tomorrow, my dear girl, you may interrogate me like the Spanish Inquisition. Is there more ale, pray you?'

The diversion worked — to a point. She refilled their ale cups and resumed her position before the fire. 'I could have died,' he said at last. 'What may I do to repay you?'

She looked at him. 'I do have an answer, though you may not care for it.'

'Try me.'

'Give up being an intelligencer. Go and settle down with your woman in Manchester and be a decent father.'

'*What?*' It was the wrong response, and in an instant the contrary wench scrambled to her feet, shaking her skirts at him like a Fury. 'Oh, pah, you are just like all the rest. A night of love and then leave her with the consequences. No, you had rather go swashbuckling and —' The rest went unsaid as he stood and grabbed her to his chest.

'We are supposed to be betrothed, Rose,' he said, staring down into her eyes.

'Yes,' she squeaked, looking away.

He kissed her forehead. 'Is it possible that for just one night we can behave as though we are?'

'You're a sick man, an adulterer, a bigamist and a father! *Go to them!*'

'No,' he murmured, tightening his grip. 'I'm feeling better and there is no woman in Manchester. Well, there is — no, don't kick me! — but she's Ferdinando's and the child is his as well. Just as you were my history in St Albans, remember? Sending dolls to his little girl was my means of communicating with Ferdy.'

'No woman in Manchester?' Behind those wide eyes, she was evaluating her sources of information.

'Nor in Tyrone or London or Antwerp, not that I remember, and I don't remember being kissed by you either but now I should welcome the experience.'

'I…' Her sweet mouth lifted to his and at last he was able to kiss her lips as lovingly and thoroughly as he had always longed to.

'Could you bear for me to make love to you?' he asked eventually.

'Why should you ask?' she replied dreamily.

'Because…' Stepping back, he lifted his ruined hands.

'Is that what's been preventing you?' Incredulity mingled with compassion.

Preventing him? Well, yes, apart from the fact that adultery at Lathom would have been like the performance of a secret Papist Mass at Her Majesty's court — illegal, hasty and life-threatening.

'Ah,' she said, 'you mean undoing my laces! Between us, we'll manage. Now please stop looking like a bat in daylight.'

'It's … it's my dazed look.' He wanted — needed — to make love to her.

'There's something else.' Pulled from the nest of her cleavage, and dangly with a tiny ribbon drawstring. 'I raided the cupboard in Ferdy's bedchamber. I thought you might refuse otherwise.'

'*Refuse?*' While he was flattered that she thought him honourable, didn't she realise he wanted her more than life itself? 'And you thought all this through despite me having a woman in Manchester?' he challenged gravely.

Her fingers fastened round his shoulders. 'Garrett, all right, for a moment I was in error. Yes, I admit to planning this, though not if you are not feeling up to it. You see, I did not have a happy marriage and I would like to be held and ... loved ... even if it is just for one night.'

He smiled, his heart rejoicing, and then had the mischief to look innocent. 'You mean you would consider doing this more than once?'

She ran her fingertips wickedly across his lips. 'That depends, but I will make allowances. After all, you have been shut in a cupboard.'

He did not argue. Kissing her mouth, he fumbled with the laces down her back and as her hands rose to help him, they moved with one accord towards the bed, and then he was feasting upon the sight of her beautiful breasts, scarce hidden by her chemise, then adoring her and caressing her in every way he knew.

20

Covert adultery, unlawful, sinful, pleasurable, shared, perfected, was a tempting reason to delay a return to Lathom. Unfortunately, because the Knowsley steward and his wife leaned towards Puritanism and were becoming inquisitive, and because Garrett felt a duty to tell Ferdinando what had happened, they travelled back in the afternoon.

'Look, the horses are still being exercised,' exclaimed Rose, pointing to a long line of beasts being led through the meadows. 'That's a hopeful sign.'

'Nightingale, he is too ill to live.' Arsenic, or whatever was in Buchanan's lethal concoction, had poisoned Ferdy's body; the second murderer had poisoned his mind. 'I'll see justice served,' he muttered.

His horse started at the sudden tug of bridle.

'Garrett, be wary. Whoever was behind this slow assassination is very powerful. Make accusations that a future king has been removed and you will be hauled before the Star Chamber and found guilty of treason.'

'The Privy Council know very well that I am working for them. I'm a soldier, Rose. You think I haven't the courage to stand up and tell the truth as I see it?' He had set out on this course to restore his honour; to stand by, condone by silence, would go against his conscience.

'Prove you haven't been turned, Garrett!' Before he could rebuff such nonsense, she rode her horse across his path. 'Listen, I know you are feeling guilty that you haven't safeguarded Ferdy, but he tinkered with treason, did he not? An inquiry could dishonour him in death.'

'Not if handled carefully, Nightingale. We're wasting time.' He rode round her.

'Don't be patronising!' She edged up to his stirrup to argue further. 'It's so clear to me now.'

'What is?' She might be right about speaking out, but he wasn't going to surrender yet.

'Lord Burghley let my father take the blame for Mary Stuart's death because he wanted him removed so Robert could take over as the queen's secretary. The Cecils are terrified of the Papists coming to power again. Do you not see they want Ferdy dead because he'd be too tolerant a king?'

Garrett knew where this was leading. If the Papists regained supremacy, Burghley and son would be ashes.

'Where's *your* proof it's them, Rose?' he countered. 'Why not Essex or the King of Scots?'

'Essex was ever my father's friend. I grant you he is ambitious, but it will be the King of Scots who will make Robert Cecil chief minister in gratitude.' Guessing he was still being stubborn, she burst out, 'You don't understand how the court works.'

Her attitude made him angry. 'Closing ranks?' he accused. 'I never could fathom you, Rose, so at ease with the high and mighty.'

'And what is that supposed to mean?'

'I'm not sure.' Spoken with the breath of winter. His heart breaking. There was no future with Rose, he could see that now. She was one of *them* — whether complicit or not.

Like a general losing a campaign against a brutal enemy, Dr Case met him in Ferdinando's antechamber with a worn expression which told Garrett more than words. Sending the page for small ale, Case collapsed on the bench where the boy had been sitting and bowed his head for a moment before looking up despairingly. 'Even if you brought an antidote, Captain, it's too late now. His lordship is in immense pain, cruel to behold. I held him in my arms just now and he begged me to hasten the end.'

'May we see him?' Rose had come up the stairs.

Case clapped his hands to his knees and rose. 'Why not, Mistress Byrd? Anything, anyone, that can distract him for a few moments is welcome.'

Ferdinando, yellow as vellum against the snow of his pillow, lay short of breath. A flicker of life rekindled in his eyes as he recognised them and as Garrett stooped to speak with him, the earl's fingers curled like talons around his arm. 'Did you find out who did this to me?' he gasped.

'Buchanan confessed he gave you poison from his flask, my lord. Who he really was, I do not know.' Aware of Golborne watching him tight-jawed on the other side of the bed, like Vengeance given human form, he glared back.

A fragile stir of air as Ferdinando laboured to swallow. 'Incompetent whoever he was! The poison … was not enough to kill, damn it.' His other hand tightened round the cross that barely rose and fell upon his breast. 'I was cursed. It was Hesketh…'

'No, my good lord.' Garrett covered the hand with his own, wishing for all the world that he could send healing through his fingertips into the thin valleys of flesh between the bones. 'There was no ghost, my lord. I found —'

'Enough, you tire him,' Golborne intervened smoothly. 'This talk of Papist curses does you no good, my lord. I pray you trust in Christ's mercy.'

'I-I … do.'

'Golborne is right.' Garrett straightened. 'Curses are just arrows of air and nothing more, tricks to subdue your thinking, make you fearful.'

'No, the evil is done.' Ferdinando's bleak gaze fixed upon the bed hanging, his fingers left the cross and fluttered towards the woven eagle. 'John, John.'

John Case reached out. 'Here, my lord.'

'I would take these eagle wings, so might I fly swiftly into the bosom of Christ, my only Saviour.' Turning his head to Garrett, he whispered hoarsely, 'It's too late, friend. My enemies have won.'

In a rustle of skirts Rose stepped forward and kissed his forehead. 'Christ be with you, Ferdy.'

He touched her hand. 'Fetch Alice, sweetheart. Go, the rest of you. Garrett, stay.'

Alone with the dying man, Garrett could have wept. 'Forgive me, my lord. I should have protected you better.'

'No, *mea culpa*,' the earl muttered through cracked lips. 'I was tempted, Garrett. Ah, we could have had good sport at Westminster, you and I.'

'Yes, indeed, my good lord.'

'Help me!' Ferdinando nodded to the infusion that stood upon the bed steps, and when Garrett held it to his lips, he took a mouthful. 'Now ... tell ... me.'

'Buchanan followed me to the lodge and, to my shame, overpowered me. Your cousin Stanley's men came back, slew him, called me traitor, then immured us both, myself tethered like a capon.'

'Immured?'

'Aye, there was a hiding hole behind the panel. That's where your ghost came from.'

In despair, he saw the struggle to understand in the dying man's eyes. 'If Mistress Byrd had not discovered me...' Then he tried again, 'But what's to the point, my lord, is that there have been two different attempts upon your life. One with poison and the other to make you believe you are bewitched.'

Enlightenment widened Ferdinando's gaze, swiftly replaced by desolation. 'Too late,' he gasped. 'Christ's forgiveness is my only hope.' Frail fingers plucked his sleeve. 'Go to Carey in London. Leave ... first light ... tell him of my death and to care for my girls. And bid our glorious Will to keep writing. He is for all time. He and Kit Marlowe... At least I —'

'My lord!' In panic, Garrett felt the earl's pulse. The regular quiver of blood was there, though barely discernible. He hastened to the door. 'Dr Case!'

The earl's physician and friend came calmly in. 'Exhausted himself? That's good, Captain. I gave him valerian just before you came. I pray God takes him soon and ends his suffering.'

Rose had neither expected Golborne to follow nor to grip her shoulder halfway down the stairs. 'Where did you find Towneley?'

She refused to turn around. 'Half-dead in the cellar you hid the ghost in, Master Golborne,' she told him over her shoulder.

'Hid a ghost!' he exclaimed, still following. 'For an educated woman, you are coming out with ridiculous babblings. Listen, it's clear that Towneley is a Papist agent.'

Rose could have told him that Towneley was an intelligencer in the queen's service but instinct bade her hold her tongue; better to argue matters out on even ground since she did not want a fall to break her neck. In the lower passageway within sight of the servants in the dining chamber, she swung round to face him.

'Are you on good terms with the future earl, Master Golborne?'

His face hardened further. 'Yes.'

'Hmm.'

'And what is that supposed to mean?'

'Just hmm. I should not go hurling accusations at Towneley if I were you. Remember what the Lord Jesus said to those who wanted to stone a sinner to death. The First Stone?' Angry blood flamed his cheeks as she stared up at him. 'I think we understand each other at last. I must inquire where I can find her ladyship. Good day to you.'

As she walked away, she was trembling. It had been a mad guess that Golborne could have been the mysterious Ganymede who had been found with the earl's brother, yet somehow it made sense. Perhaps she had been reckless, but with Towneley back at Lathom, she felt protected.

Garrett found Rose in the Long Gallery with Ferdinando's daughters. She must have been telling of his adventures because three young faces brightened at his approach and he was pelted with questions. Rose's face lit up with cautious welcome, too, until he drew her aside and told her he must leave.

'Ferdy has ordered me to carry news of his death to Carey, his brother-in-law, in London. I'll be leaving at first light.'

'But he's not dead yet,' she protested in dismay.

'Rose...'

'I know, I know,' she sighed. 'Only a miracle could heal him now. I am concerned for you, though. Are you well enough to make the journey?'

'I've been worse. Look at it this way, it will also give me a chance to inform William Wade what has been happening before all manner of mischief gets spread. If you are questioned, keep only to what happened here. I still owe it to Ferdy to protect his honour. And, please, if you are asked who attacked me at Knowsley, I pray you say that the blow on the head disturbed my wits and I could tell you nothing.'

'But shall you not make accusation of Gabriel Hesketh?'

'Pah, he'll have witnesses who'll assert he was with them at the time. It will be creating another martyr if he is taken. I just want to be quit of this whole cursed business.' He toed the hearth. Would this be the last time they would meet?

'I wish I could come with you.'

'No, you cannot desert Lady Alice. Nor, I might add, accompany a dissolute soldier down to London without your honour getting as mucky as a stable boy's apron.' Aware that they were being watched by an over-attentive young audience, he turned so his face could not be seen and ran a gloved finger idly along the stone mantle. 'Imagine yourself kissed at this very moment,' he murmured, glancing sideways at her. 'Is there a chance of tonight together?'

Her cheeks were the hue of rose quartz as she shook her head sadly. 'The Bishop of Chester has my room and I'm in Lady Compton's chamber with Davenport's wife and two other ladies.' Biting her lower lip, she added, 'Garrett, be careful. Golborne still thinks you are a Papist. He may try and accuse you of poisoning Ferdy. What's more, I may have accused him of wanting Ferdy dead.'

'Did you now? Not very wise, my sweet. Mind, since you're in with a pack of hens tonight, and he and Chaplain Leigh are under orders to bear the news to Her Majesty the instant poor

Ferdy draws his last breath, you should be safe enough. I'm here until dawn.'

It was so tempting to find a way of being alone with her. 'By the way,' he said, needing to divert his thoughts from such intimate imaginings, 'I heard one of the footmen muttering that it's my lady who has poisoned Ferdy.'

Rose's eyes widened. 'On what logic?'

'That the babe isn't his and that the remedy she sought from Mother Jane the week before Easter was to poison his lordship.'

'How dare anyone say such a thing! That is so cruel.'

Carefully, he added, 'I take it there is a babe, Rose?'

'I'm not her laundry woman, Garrett.' For an instant, she stood frowning and then she exclaimed, 'No, wait, Lady Anne told me of the babe when I first arrived here and that was before Ferdy fell ill. Besides, Alice doesn't trust Ferdy's brother one jot, so why would she kill her husband and jeopardise her daughters' inheritance?'

'Aye, true.' Then, 'When will you return south?'

'As soon as I may,' she said despairingly. 'Leave word with Will Shakespeare where I may find you.'

That at least was heartening. He hoped it wouldn't be on a mortuary slab.

By the time his soul finally slipped its leash in the presence of my lord Bishop of Chester, Ferdinando Stanley, Fifth Earl of Derby, was no longer aware of his kneeling wife and daughters or the officers and friends who had kept solemn vigil during those dark, final hours. Given the bishop's blessing and dismissal, everyone rose stiffly to their feet with a creak and rustle of bone and leather, velvet and taffeta. For some, both hearts and feet were numb; for his kinswomen, more tears came.

Rose was grateful that Ferdy was past all pain. Watching a healthy man slowly and cruelly destroyed when he could have had so many years ahead of him challenged her understanding of God's involvement. Of Golborne's subtle role, she was more confident, though she could not see how that could be proved either.

It was almost noon as the sad company trailed from the bedchamber, past the basins of rosewater, wine and vinegar, the bags of dried rosemary and lavender, the unguents and Cyprus cloth that would enable the physicians to perform their final duty. Reassembling in the Long Gallery, there was much shaking of heads and hands, and exchanging of conjecture in muted, polite tones.

Rose saw to the children. Little Beth and Frances were somewhat distracted by the sweetmeats progressing through the company and it was mainly Anne who needed comforting. Sitting with her, Rose watched with relief as John Golborne and Chaplain Leigh, already spurred and cloaked, formally took leave of Alice. Though both men had been at the deathbed all night, it had already been agreed they would carry the news of the earl's death to the Privy Council. Rose crossed her fingers in the folds of her skirts. God willing, Garrett Towneley could stay ahead of them on the road south.

Ferdy was hastily coffined (understandably, to contain the miasmas), and the funeral procession that accompanied his bier to Ormskirk Church next day would no doubt have appalled his ostentatious grandfather with both its lack of professional mourners and Puritan simplicity. The common people, who witnessed the procession from the roadside, appeared to do so with bewilderment rather than awe or sorrow, and the unison verdict of 'cursed' seemed to be in everyone's minds, even if it was not actually mentioned during the valedictory sermon. Rose wished Will Shakespeare and Ferdy's troupe of players could have been there; maybe they would hold their own farewell in London. As for the household, while they were not speaking ill of their dead lord, there was muttering about whether the countess would honour his debts.

'Mistress Byrd.' Dr Case broke into her thoughts as the company rode back to Lathom. 'My dear, I need to thank you for sending up that platter to us just after his lordship's death. That was a very kind thought. We were so wearied.'

While the black robe and physician's cap emphasised the strain he had been under, she was pleased to note colour once more in his complexion after the confinement of the last week. 'You all tried so hard to save him,' she said sadly.

He sighed and, as if requiring further reassurance, added, 'I have to say it was like no other case I have ever attended, Mistress Byrd. I am still mystified. However, if there is an inquiry, Dr Canon and I can show records of every treatment that we gave him as well as every void he made. I noted down the healer's part as well. No blame will attach to her on my authority.'

'That is kind of you, Dr Case, and if anyone asks, I, also, am willing to speak for her.'

The man's eyes misted and fumbling in his sleeve, he drew out a handkerchief and blew his nose. 'Ferdinando was a good friend, generous, noble,' he declared huskily. 'Taken too soon, Mistress Byrd, much too soon.'

Sir George Carey, Mary Boleyn's grandson, proved charitable, providing food and ale, as aching and gritty-eyed from hard riding, Garrett delivered the sad news. Beginning with the mad woman's curse, he described events from his perspective. It was necessary to mention Buchanan, but in such a way that Ferdy's meeting with him might be interpreted as a reluctant encounter.

Overnight at Carey's, he slept with a borrowed blanket in a passageway and then was asked to repeat his account once more before his lordship was satisfied and he was permitted to leave. Taking a circuitous route, he made his way to the Compter. Wade was absent but had left instructions that Garrett present a written report for the Privy Council, so armed with paper, ink and sufficient coin for lodgings — enough to acquire an unshared room at an inn in Bishopsgate — Garrett knuckled down to the task.

Because of the sensitive circumstances, it was out of the question to employ a scrivener, and it took him almost a day to compose and make a decent copy. He was tempted to seek out Will and Burbage at the Theatre that evening but until he had surrendered the report next morning, it was safer to remain at the inn and avoid the streets.

A few days later, he was instructed to present himself at Whitehall Palace. He knew the routine: leave his rapier and dagger at the inner gate and head for the well-guarded cipher department. Before the second body search, he was hailed by Wade.

'Ah, Captain, good morning! Come, we are expected.' He gestured Garrett to fall in beside him. 'You are recovered from your adventures? Good, good! Lord Burghley is well pleased with your report.'

Before Garrett could comment, Wade spurred on again: 'Of course, since your true colours are now known to Colonel Stanley, we shall not be requiring you to return to the Spanish Netherlands, but I presume you did not expect otherwise. You will receive full payment for your service to Her Majesty. We expect you to be discreet in this matter.'

Following him up a fine staircase, Garrett smiled. 'You mean I am not to voice the hypothesis that Her Majesty's cousin was murdered, Master Wade?'

'So were the Princes in the Tower, Towneley, probably by Her Majesty's ancestors.' The spymaster halted and looked round at him. 'I assume that was a jest on your part. Just be aware, my boy, that Topcliffe could rack your name out of Yorke or O'Collun this very night. Could you truly prove you haven't been turned while overseas? Think about that, eh? Ah, here we are.' He stopped at one of several doors off the passageway. 'Do go in.'

Garrett obeyed, his anger controlled behind a mask of politeness as he recognised the people at the long table: Sir Robert Cecil and Sir George Carey, and, looking surprised to see him, Chaplain Leigh and John Golborne. He bowed to Cecil and Carey, unpleasant possibilities barking at his mind; then straightened, aware of a gentlewoman's skirts behind him. Rose? No. He breathed in a different perfume as he turned and in shock recognised Amy, Lady Vere's servant, no longer aproned nor simply coifed, but in a damask kirtle, her hair handsomely curled and hatted. She held out a gloved hand as Rose might, well pleased with his astonishment.

'Good,' exclaimed Wade, 'we are all here and seated. Sir Robert, I will hand our meeting over to you.'

Sir Robert Cecil nodded. 'We are gathered in sadness at the passing of Lord Derby, taken from us in the prime of his life. Chaplain, would you, please?'

What does one call a collection of alabaster-smooth hypocrites? Garrett wondered testily, as Leigh prayed aloud for Ferdy's soul.

A unison 'Amen'. Bowed heads lifted. Sir Robert again took charge. 'Her Majesty thanks you all for your service to her most noble cousin, the late Lord Derby, whose death she mourns, and she has seen fit to accept that the reason for his lordship's early death was witchcraft.

'Sir George, as a representative of Lady Derby and the family, are you willing to accept this verdict?'

'Yes, I have perused the doctors' ledgers that have been presented to me, and that seems to be their conclusion unless you can lay hands on this Doughtie knave and he confesses.'

Wade cleared his throat. 'The proclamation for his arrest is still in force, my lord.'

Sir George sniffed. 'At the present moment, then, in view of the strange circumstances surrounding Ferdinando's death and the testimonies of those here, who were at his deathbed and heard him confess that he felt himself cursed, I agree with Sir Robert, that "witchcraft by person or persons unknown" is the only possible verdict. There will be conjecture, of course, people will blame the Papists.'

'Or the King of Scots,' Garrett suggested, directing an innocuous smile at Sir Robert.

'Indeed,' the queen's secretary glibly conceded. 'We must, however, be aware Her Majesty's health is not what it was, and if she should name the King of Scots as her successor, it would be better that our new king doesn't begin his reign with the label of "murderer" fluttering above his head.' He sat back. 'Are we in agreement? Perhaps then we can put the lid, and that is not meant in jest, on this unfortunate event. I shall inform Her Majesty.'

'Just a moment,' Sir George interjected before they could rise. 'Master Golborne and Revered Leigh, I am sure you understand there are various officers of Her Majesty's government who will wish to speak with you touching the matter of Lord Derby's estate, especially any moneys that may be owed to the Crown. I should like you to attend me at the chamber of the Master of the Rolls at Lincoln's Inn tomorrow. Early days, but we shall be appointing commissioners in due course.'

'Yes,' agreed Sir Robert. 'We already have a list of five names.'

Garrett bit back his sarcasm. Of course, money was everything. An inquiry into Ferdy's holdings was more important than an investigation of a great lord's unnatural death.

So, this was it, the epitaph? The patron of England's greatest writers, the noble lord whose ancestor put the Tudors on the throne, who could have been a king, was now a mere entombment in Ormskirk Church and dismissed from history?

Across the table, Amy smiled at him beneath her lashes as she nonchalantly shook out her skirts. 'Maybe our paths will cross again, Captain Towneley. Thank you for being civil to a hard-worked maidservant.'

'You were very convincing,' he said huskily. He did not flatter by asking her true name; behaving with courtesy needed effort. Could he have been wrong in blaming Golborne for the wax image? Poor Ferdinando!

Left alone, he sat down and buried his face in his hands, conscious of failure, guilt and every other fault his inner prosecutor could hurl at him.

Wade came back in for his hat and gloves. 'Oh, for Christ's sake, Towneley!'

'"*By persons unknown*"! Won't people ask?'

'Aye,' replied the spymaster, drawing on his gloves, 'they will over a tankard or two and then it will be all forgotten. If you want to stir up the mud, the dirt of treason will stick, his lordship's estate will be taken from the family, his honour besmirched.'

Garrett rose and strode to the window. 'What if the truth trickles out from Lancashire?' he asked over his shoulder, sure that someone like Lord Essex might rub his hands at the chance to bring the Cecils down.

'What is the *truth*?' Wade challenged. 'I'll be damned if I know.' Seeing Garrett's sullen shrug, he added, 'Be warned, my young friend, you and Mistress Byrd are just small grains in the great mill wheels of government.'

'And easily crushed? Is that what you mean?' He swung round to observe Wade. 'Shall you be employing her again?'

'Mistress Byrd's future is to be decided on her return to London — you have developed a fondness for her, I believe — so you would agree it would be kind of Her Majesty, given the young woman's impoverished circumstances and as a reward for her service, to find her a wealthy dotard, who enjoys a quiet country life, far from London?'

'I doubt you could make Mistress Byrd agree,' Garrett replied calmly, keeping his temper sheathed with immense effort, and trying not to show that he cared. 'Besides, she has Lady Vere's protection and a position in her household.'

'Alas, that arrow falls short already. It was agreed yesterday that Lady Vere is to marry Ferdinando's brother William, the new Lord Derby. I have been told the young lady is not happy about it, and that her father is already asking what jointure she shall receive, however, Lord Burghley and Sir Robert Cecil could not be more delighted. In fact, were Her Majesty prepared to recognise the bridegroom's royal blood and appoint him her successor, Lady Vere may become the next Queen of England.'

Slack-jawed, Garrett gazed at Wade. So that was what this was all about. And if that did not happen, the Cecil family still had King James in their debt for disposing of a fellow claimant.

'Poor Lady Vere,' he said dryly. 'And shall the queen be murdered for her sake?'

Raising an amused eyebrow, Wade smiled. 'Captain, that is a question I hope I shall never have to answer.'

21

It was late April as Rose began the tedious journey south in Lady Alice's second best two-horse carriage, a wood and leather affair with roll-down shutters. As far as Warrington, she shared the escort of the bishop's entourage and after that it required endurance — fortified by the fact that each post inn and change of carriage horses brought her closer to London. With so many hours alone while her bones were being jolted by every rut, the sensible side of her reasoning was quite vanquished, especially as the highway took her past occupied gallows. Local felons' fates enforced the sad fact that it was hard to prove innocence, especially if the witnesses were bribed or bullied. She just prayed that this had not been some huge chess game and neither she nor Garrett were to be 'removed' from the board. If God did enable her to survive, she vowed she would somehow extract not only herself but her brother from Wade's service.

Her fear of being used and accused came true during the change of horses at The Mitre in Barnet, and she was marched to a smaller conveyance by a small group of soldiers wearing no badges of allegiance on their shoulders. Appealing for rescue to the numb faces of the travellers across the yard was as useless as expecting the innkeeper's chickens to intervene. She had seen Papists hauled away in such conveyances with the door and shutters locked from the outside, like this one was.

Her feet were numb with cold when the coach door bolt was finally slid open hours later. There was still an afterthought of light left in the sky, enough to see they were drawn up beside the outer wall of a substantial building. Down the laneway she could see the Thames. Would the last part of this journey be by boat? No, it was not to be Traitors' Gate or Bridewell. Not yet. The leader of the escort knocked on the gate in the wall and with admission granted, Rose was led through a knot garden into the house, then up servants' stairs to a small, panelled room where a fire was lit. It was empty save for two small settles facing the hearth; a platter of food was set out on one.

Despite being hungry, Rose inspected the wooden walls for spyholes. Behind the room's only tapestry, she discovered a door into a chamber of ease where she availed herself of the close stool. Returning, she picked up the flagon. While its contents did not smell unwholesome, how could she be sure? Whose house was this? She could hear conversation and music from the floor below, although putting her ear to the boards brought no enlightenment. For an hour, judging by the melt of the sole candle, she was left alone, then, at last, the ring handle turned.

Framed in the open doorway stood a small figure. A lady in sombre clothes wearing a simple bongrace over her hair. With the blaze of candles held by the man standing behind her it was hard to see the woman's face. Perhaps this was Ferdinando's mother, Margaret, the queen's outspoken cousin. It would be natural for her to want an account of her son's death. Ferdy had told plenty of stories about his crazed alchemist of a mother and how she was becoming deaf from her experiments to create gold.

'Your servant, my lady.' Rose politely stood and gave a small curtsey. 'Your servant,' she repeated louder.

It evoked a deep snort from the woman as she stepped further into the room. 'That will do, George,' she said softly, and the man obediently closed the door, leaving Rose alone with her. 'Suspicious, aren't you?' the lady accused, reaching out long fingers to pluck a dried fruit from the untouched platter. 'Sit down before you fall down!'

Astounded, open-mouthed, Rose almost collapsed. Without the huge skirts, the altitude of lace against her ageing neck and the cascades of gems, this tiny lady was the Queen of England.

'Pour us both a cup of ale, Elizabeth,' said Her Majesty, using Rose's baptismal name. 'I hope it's a good brew. You look far too pale.'

This had to be some bizarre game. *Elizabeth Tudor.* She was being lulled into the old familiarity that once had been between them. Nervously, she obeyed and was glad of the clink of cups so she might drink at last. 'To Your Majesty's health,' she whispered.

'And God pardon you for shouting at me.' The queen seated herself, turning the toes of her embroidered slippers towards the warmth of the fire. 'I want you to tell me how Ferdy died,' she said, her mouth full of sugared almond. 'I want the truth, my girl. Without tailoring for the Privy Council — no snips here or embroidering there, no tiny mirrors stitched on to reflect yourself in perfect light.'

A log adjusted itself in the fire's hot embers as Rose, wondering what might have already been related by Golborne, Garrett and Lizbeth, searched for a place to start, but before she could draw breath, the queen held up a staying hand. 'They asked me to sign my physician's execution order today. It reminded me of the hurt done to your poor father. I'm sorry.'

Elizabeth Tudor was *sorry*?

Was this to mellow her, to soften the wax of suspicion into trust? What use unleashing the bitter anger that had bubbled and simmered since her father had been committed to the Tower? A good man's life destroyed, his honour ruined, his health his self-esteem gone. Instead, she found other words.

'Is Dr Lopez guilty of treason?' She remembered him once giving her a throat lozenge.

'I don't know.' A royal sigh.

'Then...'

'I shall delay as long as possible.'

'Must you sign, madam?'

'Oh, yes, child, I must. I cannot be above the law. Lord Essex provided sufficient evidence and the court gave its verdict. Now they are all baying for blood. Poor Lopez hasn't been able to prove his innocence — that's so much harder, especially as he's a foreigner and a convert. Of course, I shall safeguard Roderigo's family, that much I can do for him.'

It was so sadly spoken that Rose felt the urge to bestow forgiveness and throw her arms about this woman, who had once been such a kindly godmother, except... Except the queen was like a spinning bauble, capable of showing different facets, and she had made Rose's father take public blame for her signature to behead the Queen of Scots. If she had not executed Mary, might Ferdy still be alive, and might Rose's father still be royal secretary instead of Sir Robert Cecil?

'Ferdinando is — was — forty years younger than Dr Lopez,' the queen reflected, and turned her sharp gaze on Rose. 'What was this so-called witchcraft?'

Without embroidery, Rose narrated her view of events.

'You think he was poisoned?' Her Majesty asked when she had finished.

'I think the currents that swirl about Your Majesty's feet at court ripple far into your kingdom.'

'Ha, you're a diplomat like your father and that Captain Towneley.' Rose drew a breath. That she could argue with. However, the queen continued, 'I'm thinking of using him that way. Maybe your father could teach him a thing or two *in the fullness of time.*' Before Rose could even digest the enormity of what had just been suggested, Her Majesty caught her further unawares. Rising and stretching her back, she said, 'They want me afraid, Elizabeth.'

'Madam?'

'Essex, Burghley and the imp, they all want me to sleep with a sword beneath my bed, and to please them, so I do. Oh, they wag their tails and bring me sticks. They growl at strangers, pretend to keep me safe but, like real dogs, they are jealous of each other. "Keep off, she's mine!" Oh, I'm old, Elizabeth. They will maul me if I live too long. Please accept that if young Ferdy's murder was conceived at court, it was not for my sake but theirs.'

'Madam, is there to be no inquiry? Surely —'

'Oh, there has already been one of sorts. Cousin Carey has heard several witnesses, there's a warrant for the arrest of the Master of Horse, a Papist fellow, and a list of suspects which includes you and Captain Towneley.'

'I?'

'Oh, don't go all vapourish on me, girl. I sent you up there, didn't I?'

'Yes, madam.' She was able to smile, the fear of being brought before the Star Chamber that had haunted her this last week finally dispelled. Emboldened, she decided to ask a favour. While she dared not ask that her father's honour be restored — she guessed the queen would never grant that — a modest request might wriggle through the royal portcullis.

'May I ask for your counsel, please, Your Majesty?'

To her relief, the royal brows rose in curiosity. 'Well?'

'I don't want to work for Master Wade anymore and I don't want my brother to, either.'

'Hardly a Kit Marlowe, is he?' Oh, she was perceptive, this queen. Understanding flickered in the shrewd Tudor eyes and the sails of the royal mind turned swiftly. 'What I can suggest is we let the lad go abroad to study. I believe a visit to Italy might be of benefit. Mind, we don't want him being turned so a suitable tutor must be found to accompany him. Yes, I like the notion. One of my gentlemen can be persuaded to *fund* him, I'm sure.'

'That would be excellent, Your Majesty.'

'And what about you, you minx? You are not well-born enough to be a lady at court and you're a widow so you cannot be a maid-of-honour.'

Rose knew sufficient of the queen's character not to suggest marriage. Elizabeth Tudor did not trust love any more than she trusted anyone.

'If Lady Vere can find a place for me, I would be most content.'

'I'll shall inform Lord Burghley.' Long fingers touched Rose's cheek. 'Time to go, I think. Thank you for what you have told me. It is a sad, strange business, but for the sake of the public good I shall not argue with the conclusions that my councillors have reached. I have learned through experience that suspicion is like a secret lover, best not mentioned to anyone.'

She rose and held out her hand and this time a grateful Rose had no qualms in falling to her knees and kissing the pale creped skin. She was still on her knees when Her Majesty, halfway to the door, expressed an afterthought. 'The trouble is, my dear, if you get rid of the dogs that protect you, you have to find others and they have to be trained.' She rapped upon the door. 'George, I am done here. Send for my carriage!'

'Forgive my presumption, Your Majesty,' Rose begged, risking the displeasure, 'but would you have named Ferdinando as your successor?'

For an instant, the royal eyes narrowed fiercely, and then forgiveness blossomed and ripe laughter burst. 'Heavens, no, it would give my cousin Margaret far too much satisfaction. Ah there you are, George. Here is Davison's daughter. Spoil her a little — for her father's sake.'

22

January 1595

Garrett was glad to build some warmth into his body as he helped Shakespeare, Burbage and the other players unload their musical instruments and properties onto the wooden jetty outside the redbrick gatehouse of Greenwich Palace. It had been a cold voyage down the Thames — words turning into vapour, eyes watering in the unkind air — yet they would create magic here. Despite the dismal dull of England's winter, Her Majesty's court would be transported to the sunshine of a Greek midsummer wedding feast.

Under the supervision of Edmund Tilney, Master of Revels, panniers of false bosoms, furry breeches and spangled bodices, a signpost, two thrones, and a chest containing pots of face paint, glue and several pairs of eyebrows, were carried along from the jetty opposite the treadmill crane and into the trade entrance, past the kitchen and buttery into the Great Hall.

'Take care! One of the rubies is loose!' Shakespeare exclaimed, as he threaded two diadems onto Garrett's arm before burdening him with a high bundle of fairy wings that had already speckled a trail of silver across the flagstones. 'Do you reckon your Rose will be here?'

Garrett pulled a face. Maybe. This was probably his last chance. God knows what her feelings were now. Absence was not supportive of newly kindled love. Nor had Fortune been compassionate. The day after the Whitehall meeting on Ferdinando's demise, Wade had sent him to Scotland. It was not a mission he dared refuse. Her Majesty wished him to deliver a large, ornate cupboard as a gift for King James' newborn heir. A Christening mug might have been more welcome.

'You can, of course, inquire into the identity of the now deceased Buchanan while you are up there,' Wade had suggested with a straight face.

'And not inquire here?' *I am being sent away so I cannot ask questions?*

'Exactly, Towneley. We understand each other. Be grateful.'

By the time Garrett had returned to England (none the wiser, of course), everyone had conveniently forgotten Ferdinando's sad end. Unfortunately, Rose seemed to have been snipped off, too. Her one, rather weathered, letter awaiting him on Burbage's desk had been written on her return from Lathom telling him that Lady Vere was permitted to keep her in attendance. Where was she now?

By cultivating one of the servants at Lord Burghley's Holborn house over a few ale tankards, Garrett learned that both young women were at Theobalds and that the pair were being closely kept. So, before he undertook another mission, he journeyed up to Hertfordshire. He asked to speak with Rose, only to be told the earl's daughter and her companion were now at Lord Oxford's. That meant a turnaround and when he arrived at Castle Hedingham, the earl's seat in Essex, he was unable to get his foot past the gatehouse.

Of course, he could have tried a disguise or ventured over the wall like a thief in the night but maybe Rose wanted no more truck with him. A lover's spirit was easily bruised.

Lady Vere's wedding seemed his next best chance, then that had been delayed until it was certain Lady Derby had not given birth to a male child. Now, with the marriage festivities tacked on to Yuletide like a gaudy streamer, *A Midsummer Night's Dream* was giving him what Shakespeare referred to dryly as 'a Rubicon moment without the elephants'.

Conducted into the palace's Great Hall, which smelled of woodsmoke, meadowsweet and musk, as well as the chypre of the Master of Revels' over-perfumed gloves, the players strategically arranged all bits and pieces behind the permanent oak screen. The latter offered entrances to their performance area from the sides and middle just as the London theatres did, and it also hid the palace buttery, where they could change into their costumes.

Beneath the great cartwheels of flickering candles, all was set ready for their audience: a carved seat draped in miniver had been set on a wooden dais for Her Majesty; upholstered chairs awaited the bridal pair and their noble kinsmen; and skirting these, like scattered lilies on the woven rushes, were crimson cushions for Her Majesty's ladies and maids-of-honour. The rest of the court would make do with trestles.

Ignoring the aumbries and stacked tables of the tiring room, the tightly packed players were as tense as newly broken colts. The lads playing the young women, Hermia and Helena, stood apart in the only alcove. Burbage, wearing stag's antlers and baldricked with flowers as Oberon, the King of the Fairies, traded a jest with Master Kempe about asses and then annoyed Titania by saying his bosom bags needed pressing.

Garrett's chief concern, apart from greying his hair and beard with ashes as Hermia's father and remembering to stoop when he walked, was to discover if Rose would be attending Lady Vere. His feelings lurched like a drunkard's gait towards hope. However, compassion for Will Shakespeare was also within his gift, not only because *A Midsummer Night's Dream* was being performed for the first time but also because its writer was wearing a paper-thin, flesh-coloured tunic and his uncovered forearms resembled plucked goose skin. Tight-lipped, with a pair of medium-size horns glued to his domed head, the latter circumnavigated by a laurel wreath, and his arms folded against cold and failure, Will had his eyes on the far door, where trumpeters stood ready to fanfare the queen when she made her entrance.

'Do you imagine the new countess will not be pleased?' chided Garrett, gently elbowing his friend. 'She wanted fairies up at Lathom and this play is better than any masque.'

Music drowned out Shakespeare's answer. Her Majesty, floating at the heart of a vast amber kirtle embroidered with golden eyes, and flanked by Lords Essex and Oxford, led in the bridal procession. Beholding Ferdinando's brother, whose dark curls were so like Ferdy's, Garrett felt sorrow anew. There was not a day when he did not say a prayer for the dead earl's soul.

'Poor Lizbeth, I reckon she painted her public face on with her cheek colour,' muttered Shakespeare, as they sighted Lady Vere. 'See how she comes with drooping head — like Tragedy in petticoats, born to calve. From an impoverished father to a penniless husband, an earl with no estates and empty pockets.'

'You'll not be seeking his patronage, then?'

'We'll see, but —' he suddenly pointed. 'There's your Rose, all finely petalled.'

Past the glittering queen, past the rouged bride and her tall, gilded-satin bridegroom, past magpie Golborne attending his lord, and the several noble virgins carrying the bride's train, Garrett's famished gaze found his love at last. Her fine neck ruffed, her sweet body embraced by a cherry kirtle, and her hair neatly parted beneath a French hood, arched with pearls.

Had she been wed as well? Was there a new ring beneath her gloves?

He wanted to go to her, pierce through the shining bubble of courtiers like an insolent dart, but embarrassment was not to be offered between friends. Besides, his tongue felt hobbled.

'*Benediximus*, friends!' muttered Shakespeare as the fanfares ceased, and putting panpipes to his lips, he led the company out — fairies, lords and lovers — into the opening dance.

Rose would have to come to him and to Garrett's joy she did, stepping across the divide of rank that separated audience and performers. Between acts, between the Athenian court and the forest of the fairies, she sidestepped the ass's head that would adorn the clamorous, spellbound weaver, and the grassy bank on wheels, her bright face manifesting the same joy he felt as he'd welcomed her into his arms at Knowsley. The trouble was he had an audience of grinning actors. Obligingly, Shakespeare shooed some of them into the coop of the tiring room, but the rest hung around like chickens waiting for a hurl of scraps.

'You've aged,' she remarked. A puff of grey powder burst into the air as she poked one of his locks. 'And you're sticky — ' a swift frown at the smear on her glove — 'but you are looking well.'

He nodded, smiled, basked in her gaze. 'I have been trying to see you all this year.'

'It's been difficult,' she agreed. 'A few of your letters winged through. Lizbeth threatened to have an affair with Lord Essex to spite her grandfather, you see, and both of us ended up being kept close. I was told you had gone to Scotland at Her Majesty's request. Twice she ordered you forth, I believe. She doesn't like anyone falling in love.' *Falling in love?* Was he hearing this right? 'I hear it involved a cupboard,' she added.

Feasting on her face, he said ruefully, 'Yes, the perfect christening present. It took over the entire nursery.' He so wanted to tell her how much he'd missed her, how much he'd thought about her.

'By ship or packhorse?'

'Both. We almost got shipwrecked and could have rowed ashore in it. Oh, Rose —' Jesu, did he have to have an audience of grinning loons for his wooing?

'Ignore them and listen,' she said, pulling off her glove and running a manicured nail across the St Albans ring. 'I have swept whole queues of suitors — princes, emperors, an occasional bishop — from the door because of this. Are we still betrothed or not?'

His lower lip quivered. 'If I said not, would you be disappointed?'

'If I said not, would you?'

'Yes.'

'Yes.' Beyond the carved oak barrier, the audience was settling once again.

Rose turned and, tucking her arm in his like a bride, she bestowed a gracious nod on the congregation of players. 'You do know I love you,' she said through her smile.

'Beyond measure, beyond the outer ring of all the universe —'

'No, a forest outside Athens.' Burbage came down on them like a storm torrent, swept an arm around round Rose's waist and scooped her to the side. 'Back to your cushion, sweetheart!'

'Speak to my father, Garrett,' she called. 'Stepney, Friday morning.'

'Wait!' Garrett shoved Burbage aside. 'Can we not meet after the play or tomorrow?'

'No, Thursday is the wedding and I have to be here to put the bride to bed.' A blown kiss and she returned to her place and a pebble shower of comments.

'Ooh, can we not meet?' mimicked Burbage, then wagged a finger. 'Friend, I think you're already putting your bride to bed.'

God willing!

As the great bell of Stepney tolled ten, Rose and Garrett strolled hand in hand (or rather glove in glove because of the January cold) in the garden of her parents' rented house. An entourage of bored chickens accompanied them.

'And what did my father say?' Rose prompted, halting in the sunniest spot, where the frost had melted from the path and her mother could not see them from the upstairs chambers.

'He gave me a lecture on diplomacy.'

'Really? You are not doing a very good task of it now.'

Apology clouded his face. 'But you told me to hang on his every word.' Then the mischievous dimples crept back into his cheeks. 'He said you'd told him I had a lot to learn.'

She poked between the buttons of his mulberry doublet. 'Stop hedging.'

He grinned down at her. 'He said that although it was entirely your decision, he agrees to us marrying.' Then he added, with a stern folding of his arms. 'I'm not sure that *I* do. I could be away on this next mission to Scotland for several months. I have some savings but I am not sure I can promise you anything like this, rented or otherwise.' His sudden gesture to the modest black and white gables startled their feathered attendants. 'And you could be foregoing your chance of being in the next queen's household. But what I can promise you,' he murmured as he gathered her into his arms, 'is love, Rose, with all my heart.'

She remembered again the marital loneliness and the angry demands of an inebriated Oliver Byrd. Yes, the scales of marriage could tip to misery, but she had already weighed Garrett Towneley in the balance. With this husband, there would be kindness and laughter.

'I'm coming with you to Scotland,' she said. 'Her Majesty's suggestion.' A massive exaggeration but no matter. 'You either agree, sir, or get put in a small cupboard in the Tower.'

Sucking in his cheeks, her betrothed gravely ran a surviving fingertip along the white fur that collared her mantle. 'That's a hard decision.'

'Yes,' she agreed happily. 'And I'll become Mistress Rose Towneley. You see, I rather like that. No more jests about birds.'

'If that's your only reason for marrying me then I am all concurrence,' said Captain Garrett Towneley. 'Although you know what, my dearest darling? I rather like the sound of it, too.'

GLOSSARY

ALARUM — alarm

AMANUENSIS — scribe

AVAUNT — go away!

BOARD — dining table

CANION — band of fabric

CATHETER — the metal tube was inserted into the patient and the surgeon or physician's assistant started the process by sucking

CHIRUGEON — surgeon

CLODIE — light grey

CLOSE STOOL — Tudor toilet

CROCKET — stone carving of leaves or flowers

CROSS THE TIBER — convert to Roman Catholicism

DEVIL'S BIT — scabious (*Succisa pratensis*)

DIASCORDIUM — a herbal medicine that included germander

DOUAI, SAINT-OMER and **VALLADOLID** — places with religious colleges

FRENCH HOOD — typical Tudor headwear of cap with veil hanging down the back

GLISTER — enema

JACKSTRAW — nobody

JENEVER USEQUEBAUGH — gin

JESUITS — member of the Society of Jesus, an order of Roman Catholic priests founded in 1530s for missionary work

KASSEISTAMPERS — nickname for the watch and inhabitants of Aarschot; means 'cobble stompers'

KERNE — Irish Gaelic for soldiers

MANNA — derived from flowering ash, used as a laxative

NOLI ME TANGERE — touch me not!

MESS — people you sit with at the table; setting for several people

MONSTRANCE — ornate Roman Catholic cross containing a lunette holding consecrated bread Roman Catholic Mass

PALLIASSE — thin mattress

PANDORS — musical instruments like tambourines

PAPIST — Roman Catholic

PARTLET — covering between the bodice neckline and the throat

PAVANE — slow stately dance

PENNER — pouch containing quills and inks

POIGNARD — dagger

PYX — receptacle used for Roman Catholic Mass

RUBBING CLOTH — the Tudors believed that clean underlinen and a good rub down with a cloth could keep you sweet-smelling. Historian Ruth Goodman put it to the test and found it worked

SAINT-OMER — seminary (French style spelling)

SPARROW FART — early morning

ST ALBANS — (English style spelling)

STUMPWORK — a special kind of embroidery with raised features

TRUCKLE BED — also trundle bed

TUCKES — rapiers

A NOTE TO THE READER

So what happened to the historic people in the story? Rose's disgraced father, William Davison, was never reinstated as Her Majesty's secretary. He died in Stepney in 1608. His will mentions his two daughters but not their baptismal names (I'm guessing one was named Elizabeth after the queen and the other, Catherine, after her mother) and Davison refers to his son-in-law only as Towneley. That is about the only record of my two main characters, so I have taken a great deal of liberty in weaving them into the espionage of the time. It is known, however, that Rose's brother, Francis, received a grant to tour Europe with his tutor but never really became famous as a poet.

Sir Robert Cecil was the great survivor. Lord Essex foolishly led a rebellion against the Crown and was beheaded in the Tower so with him out of the way, nothing stopped Sir Robert Cecil ensuring the crown went to King James of Scotland when Elizabeth I died, and he continued happily as the king's chief minister. Did he have Ferdinando murdered? The jury is still out, but more on that in a moment.

O'Collun, Williams and Yorke were executed in 1595. In 1605 Colonel Stanley sent over Guy Fawkes to blow up the king and parliament. After a tip-off, William Wade was able to arrest the conspirators. Stanley was somehow exonerated and died in Ghent in 1630. Wade enjoyed a long career. He was knighted in 1603, retired in 1613 and died in 1623. Gabriel Hesketh was eventually outlawed.

There were four medical men in attendance on Ferdinando but I have omitted Dr Joyner. John Case, Ferdinando's friend and physician, was well compensated and in his will, he begs his wife never to sell the ewer, great goblet or chain of gold given to him by the dying earl.

If Alice was carrying a baby after Ferdinando's death, it did not survive and she fought hard to make sure her brother-in-law got nothing more than a title as his inheritance. Michael Doughtie MP and Hugh Ellis escorted the sealed-up estate papers to London as evidence during the drawn-out legal dispute. In 1600 Alice married the Attorney-General, Lord Egerton, and gave him a tough time by all accounts. Her three daughters, staunch Protestants, all married. Not one of them claimed the throne.

There is no historical evidence that Lady Vere visited Lancashire in April 1594 but nine months later she was married off to William, Ferdinando's brother. Had he been named successor to the crown, she would have been his queen consort. *A Midsummer Night's Dream* is said to have been performed at their wedding in Greenwich on 26 January 1595.

Ferdinando's brother and Lady Vere had a difficult marriage. In the first few years, the new countess had some notorious affairs, however, the couple did end up having five children. They eventually separated and the earl left court for a quiet life in Cheshire. Although the prophecy about Lizbeth by the mad woman in this novel is fictional, Lizbeth did become ruler of the Isle of Man in 1612. Whether William was gay is not known. He is reputed to have had exciting overseas adventures during several gap years before he inherited the title.

Farington's name appears on Lord Burghley's *Lancashire Map of Recusants* so he was definitely suspected of being a Papist. I admit to taking liberties with the character of Golborne because he was the only person with Ferdinando when the earl saw Hesketh's ghost and someone must have put the wax image under the bed. Many of the Stanley archives were destroyed in the Civil War so I was unable to find out whether he continued in service with the new earl.

Public conjecture as to whether the earl was poisoned was eclipsed by the Roderigo Lopez case. The Cecil Papers do mention Golborne and Leigh arriving in London to report the death to the Privy Council and an order was issued to arrest Richard Doughtie, who was never heard of again.

I have some very kind people to thank: actor and director John Bell for the initial inspiration for this novel; Nicholas Evans for his account of toadstool poisoning; wisewoman and healer Sophia Lytton; toxicologist Robert Forrest and Dr Peter Stride for their opinions on Ferdinando's illness; Dr Stephen Lloyd, Curator of the Derby Collection, Knowsley Hall; Richard Cullinan of Stoccata School of Defence, Drummoyne, NSW; Joan Satchwell, descendant of the Heskeths; and John Martyn for Ferdinando's family tree.

Guinea pig readers are wonderful: I am grateful to former publisher and much missed friend, Bert Hingley; Susan Shaw, Jenny Savage, Babs Creamer, Margaret Phillips and Angela Iliff; and fellow novelists, Cheryl Hingley, Felicity Pulman and my writers' group who have all provided helpful comments on the various drafts.

Sometimes sheer good luck can kickstart the research when you're in a new location. Thank you to the young man at the hotel reception in Ormskirk who directed us to the location of the lost palace of Lathom and provided literature on the Historic Lathom Project and Medieval Deer Park Survey.

I'm very appreciative of the UK's National Archives for the wonderful treasure trove of documents that are now online. As well as the Calendar Papers, the most useful primary sources were the Cecil Papers, a collection which throws light on the shadowy world of Elizabethan espionage, gives evidence that Ferdinando was under surveillance and contains the testimonies of Papist prisoners including Richard Hesketh. John Stow's *Annals of England* provides not only the mention of the old mad crone and the wise woman healer but also gives vivid details of Ferdinando's slow death and it is likely that Stow actually interviewed one of the earl's physicians. Discussions of the earl's illness are in Dr William Jeffcoate's article 'Why did the 5th Earl of Derby die?' *The Lancet*, 2001; 357: 1876–1879 (available online) and Professor Adrian Reuben's 'The Last Gasp or Caveat Cenans!' *Hepatology*, Vol. 38, No. 1, July 2003. The official Post Mortem Inquisition was disappointing because it was only focused on Ferdinando's estates and what he might have owed the Crown.

For details of Ferdinando's houschold, both his last will and William Ffarington's *The Derby Household Books* (The Chetham Society, 1853), a diary written in the time of Ferdinando's father, gave plenty of insight. Judging by the surnames of the Lathom servants, many of their descendants still live in the district. Lathom House was destroyed in the Civil War but accounts of the siege offer some idea of what it looked like in Ferdinando's time.

The Arte of Warre by William Garrard (1591) is an excellent handbook on running an army in Tudor times, though I'm sure Colonel Stanley's force never lived up to such high standards.

For insight into Ferdinando's family, I delved into Vanessa Jean Wilkie's PhD thesis: '"Such Daughters and such a Mother": the Countess of Derby and her three daughters, 1560–1647,' University of California, Riverside, 2009; and Barry Coward's *The Stanleys, Lords Stanley, and Earls of Derby, 1385–1672*, The Chetham Society, 1983.

There are many books on Ferdinando's protégées, Shakespeare, Marlowe and the theatre companies. Whether young Shakespeare did have an earlier connection with Lancashire is still open to conjecture. It is plausible that Ferdinando, as his patron, may have given him refuge from plague-ridden London in the 1590s.

The most elusive part of all the sleuthing was Ferdinando himself. In true sensational fashion, more is written about his death than his life, so it is hard to ascertain whether England lost a worthy king and harder still to get to the truth about what killed him. Chronicler John Stow comments on page 767 of the *Annals of England*, 'The manner of his death was wondrous strange, whereof I hatte been often required to set it downe plainly, but I could never get the particulars Authentiquely.'

Let's just say that Ferdinando believing on his deathbed that he was bewitched suited a lot of people.

If you enjoyed this novel, it would be lovely if you can give it a thumbs up on **Amazon** and **Goodreads** and word of mouth is terrific too. I hope you will try some of my other novels too, and I'm grateful to Sapere Books for bringing them out again for a new generation of readers. Finally, a big thank you to illustrator Louise Hogan for the Tudor gentleman on the cover and to Amy Durant and the publishing team at Sapere Books for being so lovely to work with.

Isolde Martyn

www.isoldemartyn.com

Sapere Books is an exciting new publisher of brilliant fiction and popular history.

To find out more about our latest releases and our monthly bargain books visit our website: **saperebooks.com**